Resounding praise for
JAMES REESE
and

THE BOOK OF SPIRITS

"James Reese's startling second novel is filled with magic and heartbreak, eerie, unforgettable characters and the heady atmosphere of a bygone era brought deftly to life. It is a sumptuous feast for the senses."
New York Times bestselling author Eric Van Lustbader

"Fascinating . . . Like Anne Rice, Reese loves the tangled plot strands and lovely period details of historical fiction . . . *The Book of Spirits* is as lush and engaging as its predecessor . . . A little witchcraft is just the thing to while away the hours."
New Orleans Times-Picayune

"An involving, richly detailed chronicle of witchcraft . . . Reese's extensive research is apparent in his weaving of real historical characters into the story . . . [who] come to life in stunning detail. No less vivid are the characters Reese creates himself . . . Part historical fiction, part supernatural tale, this is difficult to put down and will surely delight fans of Reese's first novel as well as convert new readers to his fascinating style."
Booklist (★Starred Review★)

"A series of highly unusual adventures, any one of which would make a mighty fine novel . . . Herculine invades our consciousness, a sympathetic character from another dimension."
Tampa Tribune

"A novelist of immense talent and promise."
New York Times bestselling author Caleb Carr

Books by James Reese

THE BOOK OF SPIRITS
THE BOOK OF SHADOWS

Forthcoming in hardcover

THE WITCHERY

JAMES REESE

The Book of Spirits

AVON BOOKS
An Imprint of HarperCollins*Publishers*

This book is a work of fiction. The characters, incidents, and dialogue are drawn from the author's imagination and are not to be construed as real. Any resemblance to actual events or persons, living or dead, is entirely coincidental.

AVON BOOKS
An Imprint of HarperCollins*Publishers*
10 East 53rd Street
New York, New York 10022-5299

ISBN-13: 978-0-06-056107-9
ISBN-10: 0-06-056107-6
www.avonbooks.com

First Avon Books paperback printing: September 2006
First William Morrow hardcover printing: August 2005

Printed in the U.S.A.

10 9 8 7 6 5 4 3 2 1

To JER, MMR, PL, MR, AJL, and MCF
With love and gratitude

". . . death is but to cease
to be the same."

—Ovid, *Metamorphoses,*
Book XV

The Book of Spirits

Prologue

WE are becalmed, rolling on blue-green seas. The moon hangs as a well-honed blade in a blackening sky. I've gone topside to see it, and now I am returning to my cabin, wondering will I take again to the *Malleus Maleficarum* or will I cut fresh pens and write away the night.

Headed astern, down the dark corridor that separates our two cabins, I hear her singing o'er the sounds of the ship, and vying with the song of the sea.

Over my head, I hear music in the air.
There must be a God, somewhere.

I stop. I pleasure in the song.

I near their cabin door. It is latched by its hook-and-eye, but the sea swings it open, just so.

Lanterns light the scene; suspended from a beam, they sway in sea time. Light like ink washes o'er what little I see. Till there, *there:* a gilded, mirrored square, fixed low to the wall, shows me more. I see them. She singing, he standing before her, openhanded. Into his she places her hands: blackbirds atremble in an ivoried nest. She sublime. He well made. Naught but a few years stand between them.

She sings on, slowly, the two lines only. With whispers he asks her to stop. She sings on, defiantly, the two lines only; and limns them for a strength he does not hear. Deaf with lust, he is, as he lowers his lips to her neck. Now I see only her back, clad in yellow gingham: a sheet of molten gold. I take it for a kiss; till the inconstant light catches the bony glare of his teeth. Biting her. Somehow he smiles all the while.

Roughly he spins her. The two face me in the mirrored dark. I fall back from the door. Knowing I ought not to spy, knowing I ought to go. Wanting to watch. Having to.

Hand on the jamb, I steady myself. I sink to a crouch.

From between the teeth it comes poking, prodding like the red member of a randy cur: his tongue. The light shows the sticky trail of his licking kiss. His arms enwrap her. His hands rise to her throat. Her head tumbles back to the crook of his neck. She is shadow. With fish-belly fingers he frees her breasts. I hear fabric tear.

I draw from the dark breath enough to live. The sea cannot toss me from this door. My tingling body tells me, *Stay*.

On she sings. Till he takes from his waistcoat pocket a child's toy. A slingshot, it is. No: strapping suited to falconry. No. . . . I do not know the thing for what it is until he fits it to her face: a ball of bunched fabric within her mouth, and two leather straps he ties off behind her head.

She stands naked to the waist. Enshadowed though she is, I see her skin is light, showing but slightly her African blood. Her head is back, her eyes clenched tightly as fists. It is pleasure she takes from his touch. This I tell myself; for I know no other way to tally the sum of flesh-on-flesh.

He cups her full breasts, pulls them forward by their blackest tips. She shudders. Her shoulders hunch. With her bound mouth she can neither smile nor scream. His hands roam: up from low on her belly to her hips, and higher. They settle—fingertips first, then the whole fan of his hand—on the curves of flesh beneath her breasts. Sweat shimmers. His fingers rise to his own lips for licking.

With a hand that is and is not my own, I seek my correspondent parts. Beneath this swaddling, beneath this costume . . . : will I find some odd, unknown locus of delight?

From within the cabin, a command: to hold her own breasts high.

The two lovers—so I deem them, still—shift, slightly, toward the mirror and thus toward me. Stillness. My blood courses too quickly. I hear it. *Now* is when I will pull away. . . . *Now* is when I wait, and watch; as:

From off the galley table he takes a glove. Fits it to his right hand. To the side of the table he slides . . . what? Some instrument of iron. A tiny stove, it seems, more tall than wide. I see its shimmering heat: a furnace. From it there extend several . . . no. *No.* (I taste blood upon my bitten tongue.) He takes from the forge the first of the finger-length rods. Its sculpted tip shows an orange glow. Closing behind her, he begins to buck, slowly. We share the mirror: he and I watch his careful work. Dumb I am to the risk of discovery. Dumb, stunned by all and everything.

Only when he takes her left breast in his ungloved hand, only when he lowers the brand to her skin with his right, only then do I fall from the door. Only then do I flee. But not before I hear the searing hiss, *feel* it, and see her neck snap rigid and her eyes go wide. And not before I see her fired eyes in the mirror, finding mine.

In my cabin I vomit. Not from the toss of the sea.

* * *

No less freighted was the stare with which she seized me a second time, when finally we made landfall. At Rockett's Landing: Richmond: state of Virginia.

1826, that was; late in the month of September.

Part One

1

The Interior Port

As I watched from the wharf, my stomach went sour; for here she came, down the bouncing gangway, in a collar and chains.

They were five in the debarking party: Celia, in a violet dress, with her matching eyes of amethyst; her wrangler; and two other men who'd come aboard to carry the stretcher bearing Celia's shivering, stammering master. He called himself Hunt: a name to shield him from scandal. Tolliver Bedloe, he was; possessed of plantations on the western shore of the Chesapeake, properties in Baltimore, Annapolis, and Richmond, stock certificates in banks and incorporated companies all down the seaboard, the lot of it inherited along with herds of livestock and some two hundred slaves. Of which Celia was one.

They made their way down a steeply set plank at the bow

of the boat. The stern was already aswarm with stevedores and the like, the boat's holds thrown open, pulleys and slings and ropes swung into place. The gangway was set with strips of timber, meant for footholds; but they were placed to align with a man's stride, and so it was I watched Celia stumble. Her step was stunted. She showed none of her grace. But it was the odd sway of her full skirt that told it: she was shackled at the ankle as well as the wrist.

What had she done? Yes: I'd witnessed certain acts in the cabin across from mine, but of late I'd heard not the least discord. With Bedloe growing ever sicker—a touch of *le mal de mer,* I thought—all had been quiet.

Yet here she came, enchained. The collar—more like a yoke—around her long, lissome neck was of canvas, stretched drum-tight upon a wooden frame; through it poked iron prongs, upraised like beckoning fingers. The manacles were of rusted iron, and glinted red in the late-day light.

Midway to the wharf, Celia raised her head slowly. Her jeweled eyes shone o'er the scene: Richmonders abuzz; bees in the hive of commerce. No one seemed to notice her. No one but me.

I stood staring, benumbed, fifty paces distant. I was all but a statue when her eyes found mine. My heart rattled the cage of my chest. My eyes fell low from habit—the habits of shyness and shame and secret-keeping. Too, she simply overwhelmed me with her beauty.

I fought to raise my gaze to her; but my hand rose quickly, of its own accord, and I waved down the length of the wharf. Hello? A sort of salute? I'll say only that it was an inappropriate gesture—one she did not, could not, return; but I'll excuse myself by asking: What gesture is appropriately made to one so debased? Still, I'd recognized her: she had her witness; and this seemed to content her: only then did she turn away. Once she'd descended to the wharf, I lost her, could not see her through the crowd. All was confusion; without and within.

* * *

We'd shared hardly a word, though we were twenty-nine days sailing from my homeland; from the port of Marseilles, in particular. If Celia knew me by name, it was not my true name, which is Herculine. This I'd shared with no one.

No, we'd not spoken freely, despite the fact that life at sea, in close quarters, will breed a certain . . . familiarity.

There were only two cabins on the *Ceremaju* outfitted for comfort. These sat astern and were not intended for paying passengers, as the *Ceremaju* was a merchant brig. Bedloe and I had let these cabins, for reasons all our own. Our doors stood ten paces apart. Between them ran that ever dark and ill-used passageway. As I say, the doors of the cabins did not close well from within: the hardware was insufficient; and even when fastened the sea would cause the doors to clap. When first we were seaborne, often my shipmates propped their door open. This I did not do; rather, I settled some square-bottomed, blunt object at my door's base, to hold it fast. . . . What I mean to establish, simply, is this: I was not in a permanent crouch in the shadowed corridor, peering into a quite private space not my own. It was not like that; leastways not all the time, and not at first.

(O, there's shame in this, yes. But shame is a suit I've worn before. I'll don it again, here, in service of the truth.)

Returning to my cabin, I'd pass the pair in theirs. At first, I would but nod if noticed. I said nothing, and invited no friendship. Instead, I would return to my table, piled high with books on the Dark Arts, my manuscripts and magical paraphernalia, the lot of which I'd gathered as I'd traveled down the length of France, from the Breton shore onto the plains of Provence.

In my cabin, I read and wrote through the night, lowering my lamp as the sun rose. At dawn I'd retire to sleep away the day. I'd rise at noon or just after to take a meal—seagoing fare: salt beef, or Bologna sausages and biscuits, and tea.

Perhaps I'd venture topside to sample the sea air. At sunset I'd return to my cabin and arrange the night's study: ready my pens, pour my ink, refill the lamp with that malodorous whale oil; having chosen my books, I'd cut the pages of those that were unread, and arrange the lot of them. When I was not reading, I wrote. I'd set myself a mission: I'd write the story of my life, even though I was—by as close a calculation as can be made—not yet into my twentieth year; or so. I'd cull sense from recent, strange events; and in so doing I'd discover—so I hoped—who and what I was.

For I'd recently been told I was . . . singular. I'd been told I had talents.

You are a man. You are a woman. You are a witch.

Oddly, I was not long overwhelmed at discovering myself a witch. . . . Witchery: it was a tradition I'd tackle o'er time.

Neither was I overtaken by the truths I'd learned, truths that would set the popes spinning in their sepulchers. These truths were somehow beyond me; . . . *of* me, yes, and of interest, but beyond me.

Of far greater interest to me, then, was my *sur-sexuelle* state. This I had to explore; it was a physical imperative. My mind was sufficiently limber from years of hard study, and was fast growing accustomed to the mental acrobatics requisite to the study of the Craft, et cetera. But my body? All my life I'd lived . . . *entombed* in strangeness. And though now my strangeness had a name, it is one I disdain.

I'll say only that I was, *am* a child of Hermes and Aphrodite. It was this physical truth I sought to understand. To do so, I turned to Celia.

Indeed, I made of her a mirror; for what had any *true* mirror ever shown me but shame? My self reflected was a thing I was loath to see: an odd confluence of the common sexes. A duality, indeed; for in me, you see, the two sexes are entwined. Neither this nor that, I am both. I am . . . a third sex, with a body, a being, a self that had only recently been disclosed to me. *You are a man. You are a woman. You are a witch.*

Yes, it seems to me quite logical that I sought to define myself in terms of opposition, and so turned to Celia.

She was dark. I was light.

She was petite. I saw myself as tall, ungainly, and graceless. True, the men's dress I wore concealed and excused some of my traits: large hands and feet, and my height; but it set others in relief: my smooth skin, overly fine features, and a throat that showed no manly apple. Still, it had been wise to travel as a man, to leave behind the fripperies of female dress (for a while, at least).

Celia wore her hair tight to her head: a bun of woven braid. My blond plaits had recently been cut to further my manly guise.

Celia's figure was deliciously full. My much smaller breasts I wrapped in a length of white muslin; and lest my silhouette betray me, I favored shirts as blousy as fashion would allow.

In short, Celia was beautiful; and I longed to both *be* and *possess* her, never once considering the fate to which her beauty had doomed her.

As I knew it must, the offer of conversation had come our second night at sea.

As I passed my neighbors' cabin, eager for my own twilit room and a night's work, the offer came: Would I step in and take a pipe? I demurred. Tolliver Bedloe looked at me askance. I lowered my voice, and furthered my excuse: I said I was ill. O, but one needs a sounder excuse than that if one is to deny a Virginian's offer of tobacco; and so I came to find myself within both Bedloe's cabin and his conversation, each of which were deeply shadowed; and from neither could I extricate myself.

Bedloe stood as tall as I; gesturing to the cabin's low, timbered ceiling, he joked that it would be safer for us to sit. This we did, in matching armchairs covered in green baize. Between us stood a table, its top a painted game board. Celia sat as far from us as the cabin allowed, reading by the light of a single candle. This, then, seemed to me not the least bit odd. I wondered not *how* she was reading, nor what kindly criminal had taught her. I wondered only *what* she was reading.

"Chess?" offered Bedloe, when quickly our conversation flagged; for I barely had the confidence to meet his gaze, let alone converse in an untried tongue.

I declined, said again that I was ill, and attributed my discomfort to the sea.

"Sherry?" he tried; appending, "Some sherry will set you right, sir."

"Please, yes." To decline yet again would have been rude, conspicuously so.

Celia was summoned from her corner. As she bent to place the silver tray—regrettably set with two, not three tiny flutes of crystal—upon the checkered table, I saw her eyes, shimmering in defiance of the dark. I smile to wonder what I might have done had she trained them on me fully.

Before we'd raised sail, I'd seen her, yes—her skin, her hair, her hips so much broader than mine—but here she stood in glorious detail. . . . The fruited scent of her skin. The tight curl of her lashes. The dark stream of her neck, flowing down unto an ample bosom. The tiniest booted foot peaking out from under the bell of her skirt. (She wore the dress of yellow gingham that first night, its bodice low-laced and its hem *parsemé* with cherry blossoms.) I wanted to speak to her. Perhaps would have tried to speak to her, had not Bedloe sent her back to the corner from whence she'd come. "You'll sup, I trust?"

Again, I declined his offer, saying I'd already dined and had a quantity of work awaiting me.

"And what *is* your work?" asked Bedloe, turning in his chair to face me.

He was handsome in his way, I suppose. His brownish, longish hair was threaded through with blond, and worn tied back into a pig's tail. His face was angular; and though it seemed well suited to severity, he was not severe now, seated in the relaxed confines of his cabin, in the company of a woman he owned and a man he did not know. *O, pray let him see me as such!* thought I; as a man, merely.

He trained his colorless eyes on me and asked after my work:

"The captain and I have wondered about our busy shipmate. What is it you're working on with such diligence, if I may be so bold as to enquire?"

I did not respond. I was distracted by Celia, busy in that galley crowded with apparatuses seemingly better suited to the scientific than the culinary arts. Too, an English response (and a lie at that) stalled in my mind.

"Pardon my conjecturing," said Bedloe, "but in my mind I've formed the facts of our fellows: the captain, certain distinctive crewmen . . . yourself, certainly. A biographical game, if you will; harmless, I should think. . . . One has so much time on a voyage such as this, you understand. And so little company." At these last words, I turned toward Celia, verily begging an introduction.

"Ah, yes . . ." said Bedloe.

Melody, he called her; and he spoke of her as one would any prized possession. She bent at the waist, said something salutatory. I said nothing in response; and was glad to have shown as much sense as that; for my tongue was all atwist.

Bedloe swirled his sherry in the lanterns' light, coating the crystal to its rim. He breathed the aroma in, deeply, and said, "Of you, sir—again, take no offense—my *facts* are these: you are sailing to Norfolk, perhaps on to Richmond, from whence you will proceed overland to teach your native tongue at Mr. Jefferson's . . . at the *late* Mr. Jefferson's university?" He sat forward, eagerly: a gamesman. "Tell me: do I have any of that right?" His smile was more sly than full. His jaw: squared and stubbled. I remarked the broad plane of his chest; and the hairs—like shaven gold—which overflowed the lacings of his shirt.

"You, sir," said I, "are quite astute. Indeed, I do hope to teach." Of course, I had no such intention; but as plans went, it seemed as sound as any other. In truth, I'd not yet considered how I was to earn my keep in Norfolk, Richmond, Charlottesville, or elsewhere. Happenstance had landed me in this state named for Elizabeth I, the virgin queen. Happenstance, too, had us sailing on a river named for her kinsman, James; and I remember marveling that I might well have been upon the Nile, the Tiber, the Thames, or any lesser river of the world. See, some weeks prior, I'd found myself in Marseilles, desperate to do what my discoverer, my Soror Mystica—Sebastiana d'Azur—had told me to do: put out to sea. And the first captain who'd have me had set sail for Virginia. "*Oui*," said I, "*c'est ça:* teaching."

"Ah, you see, my darling Melody, I am right! He has plans to teach, our Monsieur—" Bedloe stopped midsentence. I was silent.

Despairing of ever having my name—I'd not yet chosen the first of my many American names—still Bedloe spoke on. His words were a quite generous offer intended both to show his stature in the commonwealth and secure my shipboard company, such as it was. "If it's a recommendation you need, sir, you must simply ask. Mine is a name well known at

Monticello." He mused further: "Shameful, don't you find it, that so great a man should die indebted?"

"Surely your countrymen will remember him for more than his monies owed," I suggested. But this the planter could not grasp; to him, success accrued as coinage.

"Rather a lawless place, the university," said Bedloe, twisting the issue of Jefferson's legacy. "No doubt more so now that the great man is gone. It's not a half year past, I should think, that a professor found himself at the working end of a student's pistolet."

"I shall take great care," said I.

In point of fact, all I took—then and there—was a green-eyed inventory of the room in which I sat. I didn't envy Bedloe his surroundings as much as I was angry at having been deceived by our captain, who'd said mine was the premier cabin. O, but where were my crystal glasses, my silver flatware, my mole-hair divan and gilded mirrors?

I stood. I'd excuse myself, steal a glance at Celia, and go.

Instead I found myself taking from off the table a fistful of objects. I'd mistaken them for game pieces. What sort of game? I wondered; for these were heavy in the hand: thin rods of iron, no longer than a finger, at the tip of which were tiny, well-wrought figures. Letters? Pictographs? Their handles were wrapped in black wicker. The dark denied me a closer inspection. So, too, did Bedloe, who rose to snatch the rods from my hand. His eyes narrowed, and sapped the flame from a nearby candle. Meaning only to be polite, to compliment something before taking my leave, I'd misstepped. But how?

Bedloe cast his fiery glance toward the cabin door. I left.

I'd see Tolliver Bedloe again; would watch him, even; but those were not occasions for speech. And soon he fell sick; and sickened the more as we neared shore.

When first I'd espied them, we were still some weeks from the American seaboard. I'd watched them once, twice, perhaps three times more. Always unseen. Or so I thought. And what I saw distracted me terribly: wanting to read or write, I'd sit instead in my cabin passing my fingertips o'er candle flame. What was it I'd seen? What was it within me had stirred at the sight?

I did not witness any scene too shockingly similar to the first; but I saw enough to confuse me further. I saw them in various states of undress. I heard her reading him to sleep. I saw her asleep, too, curled on the floor at the foot of his sickbed. I saw her on a bedside stool, tending him as he worsened. Rarely did I hear them converse. Oddly, the mirror was often down from the wall. Only once more did I scent . . . well, I thought I caught the scent of seared flesh.

Eventually, the threat of conversation passed; for Tolliver Bedloe, midway from Marseilles, had begun to grow ill. The two of them withdrew. By the grace of that same movable mirror, I saw the prone Bedloe but once more. He lay asweat and shivering beneath too many blankets. His hair appeared plated to his head. His eyes bore a glaze. Candlelight trembled in the sweat pooled at the hollow of a neck which had appeared to me so strong when first we'd met, but now was sallow. Through cracked lips he moaned, nay keened: a sound that bespoke death, and soon replaced Celia's sorrow song.

One evening, near the crossing's end, as I came from topside—where the sun had just set in kaleidoscopic display—I stopped, listening in the dark corridor. No song. I moved nearer their cabin door. It was unlatched, half open; from within there issued a sickly smell the like of which. . . . Well, I supposed it was the scent of sickness: a sweating off of fever; but later I'd learn this had been compounded by the specific stench of Bedloe's sickness: suppurating gums had rendered his breath rank as steam seeping from some infernal fissure.

I looked first to the mirror, but found only the bare wall.

What possessed me I cannot say, but I did not proceed to my own door, nor did I knock on theirs. No: I simply pushed their cabin door wider, wider; till there she sat, at the table, head bent o'er that mirrored square which I knew by its gilded frame. Was she writing on its back? In her hand was a stylus, or a palette knife, or something similar. On the table before her stood the small iron stove, a circle of grillwork affixed to its top. A browned apple sat before her. On the scale of ripeness, it measured far nearer Marseilles than Richmond.

She did not start when finally she saw me. Neither did she speak.

Already she'd risen and stepped to a bushel, from which she drew another apple. Said she, "Master wants his roasted apple when he wakes. Always." And she nodded behind me: *Go*.

Thereafter, for what sea hours remained to us, Celia kept their cabin door closed.

I returned to the tasks I'd set myself. I kept Celia from my wakeful mind as best I could. Hour upon hour I wrote. I hardly slept; but when I did, Celia reigned o'er my dreams.

When next I saw her, she had come home. Chattel. In chains.

I pushed nearer the bow of the *Ceremaju.* There were barrels to step around, bladed things to skirt, people pushing. . . . When finally I achieved the gangway: nothing. I thought I saw them: *there,* disappearing behind a tallish building of brick. I thought, nay would have *sworn* I saw a swish of violet and. . . . No: doubtless it was a shadow I'd seen. Celia? She was gone.

I stood near the river's edge, my legs jellied, my knees and heart knocking. Through the warped boards of the wharf I saw the silty, butter-colored churn of the James. All around me the song of this new city played on—the mercantile buzz and hum, the grind of the rapids upriver, the shouting in a language not my own. . . . I dared not look up; for I knew I'd not see her, and she was all I sought. Moreover: if the breeze from off the river caught my tears, well . . . tears would belie my pose; which was this: *here stands a man, newly come to a new land.*

As I stood stifling, swallowing those salt tears, there came a tapping upon my shoulder.

I turned fast; but found no one there.

2

Rockett's Landing

SIR? 'Scuse me, sir?"

The word came I know not how many times; when finally I heard it plain, I heard, too, the impatience of the speaker. *"Sir,"* said he; polite, yet persistent.

Turning, I had to lower my gaze to see the speaker: a boy from the *Ceremaju* whose name I did not know. I'd seen him monkey-high in the rigging. Here he stood barefoot on the boardwalk. His trousers of brown broadcloth were cut off inexpertly at the knee, and his blouse of yellowing silk, patched like a sail, was far too large to be his own.

"Oui," said I.

"Say again, sir?" said he, having no French.

"Yes? What is it?"

"I'm sent to ask, sir, do we have an address? Here, in

Richmond town?" English, he was; not American. By *we* he meant me; that much I knew.

"We do not, in fact."

"Thought so," said the boy. "Leastways, the cap'n did. He says to me that so fine a gentleman as you, sir, without a roof in this town, would take to Mrs. Manning's. Like a duck to water, said the cap'n. He told you as much, sir, did he?"

Indeed he had; that and naught else.

I'd debarked a quarter hour earlier than Celia and company, coming down that same gangway beside the captain. He'd been quite solicitous at the French port, where—with money, and what I hoped was a suitably masculine show—I'd persuaded him to take me on board the brigantine. He'd voiced myriad reasons why he could not accommodate me; but I overcame each, finally securing for myself the ship's finest quarters (or so he'd said). Upon our arrival in Richmond, I'd been surprised to find the captain grown cold. It was as though I were little better than the casks and crates being off-loaded. Indeed, at the approach of a man asking after the ship's manifest—doubtless he'd come from the customs house, and represented that corps of weighers and gaugers—the captain turned from me, squarely, with finality, though I'd been asking, in halting English, where I ought to go.

Understand: I knew no one in Richmond, and had come to the city rather by accident. Norfolk, miles nearer the sea, had been the ship's original destination. (Not that I knew anyone in Norfolk, mind.) But as we'd neared Norfolk, it had somehow been conveyed to the captain that the city sat under seal: quarantine, owing to the threat of fever. Its port was closed to all but the requisite craft: mail and packet boats and the like. No foreign vessel would be welcome, its belly breeding who knew what pox. Neither did we skirt this quarantine, as we had the one at Marseilles. (I'd been smuggled onto the *Cere-*

maju, more or less; and the ship had slipped from the harbor at Dieudonné under cover of night. . . . And this occurs to me now: they'd snuck Bedloe off the *Ceremaju* similarly, lest his sickness lead to talk of fever, quarantine, and crash, which three come in quick succession.) Instead, we simply sailed further up the James, on to the interior port of Richmond.

From the captain I'd gotten only a name: Eloise Manning. She, said he, kept a home "suitable for a gentleman." His words buoyed me, quite; for still I worried that my manly guise was thin, and easily seen through.

I of course recalled the captain's hasty recommendation. "But," said I to the boy before me, stating what was all too plain, "I know no Mrs. Manning."

"You will, sir, I s'pose," said he, smiling now; and with that he raised a chapped hand to point vaguely *up,* a reference to a scrub-covered hill that rose none too distant. He proceeded to say that the captain had ordered him to deliver my trunk to said Mrs. Manning's—"and a murtherin' heavy box, it is, sir, if I may say as much"—and then to find me to report the success of his mission. This he did. With relish: whilst crooking his arm to show a bleeding elbow, the boy began to rub at his neck and shoulder, saying, sotto voce, "Liked to *kill* me, that box did." I drew forth a coin and offered it as recompense. But there he remained, staring at the single coin in a great sarcastic show. "All right, then," said I, drawing forth another.

Coins in hand, the boy spun on a callused heel and made off; leaving me to shout after him, as one would a thief:

"Arrête!" People turned from their business to stare. "Stop, boy," I said, rather less bold with the English imperative. "This Mrs. Manning, where might I find her?"

He shouted back the simplest of directions, words which faded on the air.

Already I was berating myself: how could I have forgotten the *nécessaire*? I'd debarked with not a thought for that box which held what little I had in this world, including my *Book of Shadows,* in which I'd written all I'd learned of the world. Indeed, that Book bore the narrative of my life to date; for on the Atlantic passage I'd suffered the *fervor scribendi,* writing, writing, writing of all the strangeness I'd recently seen. I'd written of witchery, yes, and all I'd learned since Sebastiana and her otherworldly associates had saved me from a red fate at the hands of the miracle mongers of C——, that convent school to which I'd been consigned upon my mother's death. So impious, so impure those girls and nuns were, the lot of them equally devout and deadly. Too, I'd copied into my Book from Sebastiana's own, tales of her novitiate 'neath the Venetian sister Téotocchi; and how that had ended with Sebastiana receding into the shadows as old France fell—a fate, a fact for which she blamed herself. Preposterous? Perhaps; but in the shadows the light knows little of the dark, and when a witch whispers, her words may echo all through history. This I have learned.

That particular *nécessaire* was a bulky affair of tulipwood, with brass fittings and canvas strapping, and inlays of mother-of-pearl and ivory. I'd rendered it a veritable *cabinet de curiosités,* the contents of which would have perplexed anyone daring to shimmy its several locks. . . . Bundles of herbs, harvested near Nantes; a deer's bladder packed with powdered bone; a brass-capped horn full of dried rowan berries; vials of half accomplished potions, et cetera. A queer shopping list, indeed, the one I'd compiled from what books I had, all of them packed with recipes, rituals, and rites. . . . And from it all I'd simply walked away.

Finally, naught remained but to set the *Ceremaju* at my back. Thousands of newcomers there have been down through the years, surely; but I'll wager few ever set foot onto Rockett's Landing with measures of fear and confusion equal to mine.

* * *

Tripping along the wharf, I saw a vast and varied array of goods, some of which had sailed to market in the belly of the *Ceremaju,* shifting beneath me as I'd written my *Book of Shadows.*

I wandered among the coarse: kettles hammered of copper, stills and corn crushers headed to the country; and the fine, destined for city use: India dimity, Brussels carpets, paste buckles for shoes and knee breeches, hoops and stays from France, worked and spotted muslin, cassimeres and buttons covered in silk.

What a clutter it all was: wares piled pell-mell, set wharfside. What a mass the people were, hurrying among the varied goods, eager to conclude their business before the sky split and loosed its weight of rain. Spottily the sun showed itself, shining strongly enough to render the port city stiflingly hot and humid. Sweat-drenched, I was, in my too-fancy attire; attire which caught the eye of more than one merchant, each of whom assumed I'd money aplenty and did not hesitate to approach me.

As I stood among the massed wares—there in the open air for sorting, for fast inspection and purchase—a woman came at me, as brusque, as bold as the blue, bedotted skirt she raised to step o'er the handles of a plow. She smiled. Of teeth, she seemed to me deficient. She spoke in the most urgent tones, but her meaning eluded me completely. It seemed she sought . . . something. Finally, she shoved past me and continued picking like a magpie among the miscellany. I watched her; and when she found the object of her search—a cast-iron skillet, of all things—she glanced back at me, brandishing it. A most inauspicious start, this.

It was some time before I realized that Richmond, like every port, was a polyglot place. Down at the wharves I heard the clippety-clop accent of the Scots. Indeed, they were manifold; and the burr of their tongues stuck in many an ear besides mine. Add to this corrupted English—corrupted if one's sole exposure to English has been bookish and written, Shakespeare and such—the greater cacophony of trade: the bosuns' whistles; the stevedores' songs; laborers—black and white, bonded and free—going about their business; the sons of planters larking about, armed with letters of credit; children scattering like shot; women young and old, of indeterminate class, moving among the merchandise. Too, there were manufactories in action, mills achurn.

Did I tremble from the port's activity, or from that watery disconnect that marks a body too long at sea? More likely, my slight swaying, my timorous step and on-rolling innards were owing to my fear—of newness, of discovery, of the storied wilds of America with its savages and furred beasts standing twice the height of a horse. O, the walloping solitude that struck me as I stood amidst that scuttling crowd, knowing no one—scarcely could I count as an acquaintance the taciturn slave, who now was gone—and having nowhere to go but to an unknown hostelry. Mrs. Manning: I had a name and nothing more.

Still, I set off: upward; and into the city proper.

As we'd ascended the James, there hung overhead a low sky, greenish gray, as if beaten, bruised by the fists of Providence. Rain stalled in the sky.

Topside, the deck grew ever busier with the approach to port. I'd already packed my belongings into the *nécessaire,* and had naught to do but sit tucked near the bow, out of harm's way, awaiting sight of my first American city.

On we sailed. Under the mossy sky, all was off to the eye: the black water mirrored the bankside poplars in blue, as if spills of ink had taken tree-shape. The clipped lawns of plantations rolled up from the river, anchored by homes of ivory; at their fore pillars bulged, as fat men will after too fine a meal. Boats put in here and there, offering the planters first choice of their merchandise; elsewhere, tobacco was being loaded onto barges that would be poled upriver to port. Nearer Richmond, the river was busy with ships of every description—schooners and barks and brigs, flatboats and packet ships. . . . The port: it must come into sight soon. I'd hoped to see Celia before it did; but no.

Finally—*there*—high above the river, on its several hills, sat Richmond.

It was the capitol I saw as we approached the city, gleaming and Grecian, high on its central hill. From the capitol, the city declined to the river's stony banks, where washerwomen worked the rocks and shoeless boys fished, heedless of the troubled heavens. On either side of the capitol rose two more hills, beset by buildings of marble and timber and bounding the city to the west and east, upriver and down: Gamble's to the west, Church Hill to the east.

As we neared the city proper, I heard a sound that defied identification. Rather, I identified it: a hard-falling, oddly churning rain; but the sky above, though leaden and low, still held its rain. This riddle was not solved till hours later, when finally I discovered the rapids sitting upriver, west of the city's core.

Unable at first to account for the watery sound of the city, I turned instead to its scent: the treacly-sweet tobacco rising from the warehouses, imbuing the port and its surrounds. Too, the tang of sawn timber rose from a riverside mill. In addition to the sound of the rapids and the strong leaf and lumber scents, a mantle had slipped o'er the shoulders of the city: coal dust blew from the pits across the river and from points west, coming in quantity enough to burn the lungs and aggravate sight.

What a fight the lowering sun had that September afternoon, battling both the storm-bedimmed sky and the warm wind, which whipped the coal dust around and darkened the aspect. Of course, I knew as little of the city's pits as I did its rapids; so what did I assume but that the whole hopping place must be burning? That, yes, as Fortune would have it, I'd arrived to find the city asmolder. And this beneath a skyful of rain refusing to fall. But I took my cue from those already on the wharves; and as we neared I saw that though they danced hither and thither, they did so to the tune of commerce, nothing more. Whatever its cause, they were accustomed to this ashen air and worked on, sore-eyed and coughing, consoling themselves with coin.

From off the quayside I wandered, watching for Celia, seeking some show of violet within the colorless city.

More practically, I began to link in my mind those words with which—if ever I could forge them into a sensible chain—I'd ask directions to Mrs. Manning's. But I could not draw up from the well of English the word for "boarding-house," and I was fearful of sounding foolish if I substituted "hotel," or "house." (I had no recourse to my dictionaries; for they—deep in my trunk—had already found their way to the good lady's establishment.) I worried myself to no end, and o'er what? A single word of English. O, what a pitiable thing I was then, scared as a hare and dumb as a doe. *La pauvre!*

Wanting to be clear of the milling crowd, I wandered on, away from Rockett's. Still the sky was a sickly green. Still the rain held off. Occasionally the sun deigned to shine, setting the dew-slick cobbles to steaming.

I came to stand downwind of a tobacco factory; turning, I followed that scent to its source. As I neared, I discerned the voice of men, raised in song weighted with psalmody. A lush and languid chorus. By the dim light of late day, I saw the place: SEABROOK'S, read the sign.

Standing behind a column of stacked leaves, colored to match the stormy sky, I listened to the fifty-odd men at work that late Friday afternoon, their voices raised in song. The building was but a roof, open on all sides; outward wafted that narcotic which teased a cough to my throat, soothed only by the licorice with which they treated the leaf. Center all stood hogsheads of tobacco, stripped of their staves. Each man had his task: stripping, sorting, sprinkling the leaves. . . . Their song, lighter than the air, ended with neither flourish nor applause; and another was taken up.

I fell in behind two mules trailing a hogshead that rose to my height and clattered hollowly down the cobbled street. Slipping on a splat of you-know-what, I cursed myself—having (silently) cursed blue the blameless beasts—for who but I would be so foolish as to trail mules through the streets?

Still, the beasts led me nearer to the center of town. And nearer, I hoped, to Mrs. Manning's.

In the hopes of same, I read every sign I saw.

I walked uphill and down, o'er stones that nipped at the soft soles of my boots and down avenues and alleys of packed and pocked dirt. I learned fast to keep an eye trained on the city terrain; for the streets were a course of dung heaps and puddles, rocks and refuse. Coaches, traps, and carryalls shared the way; constant was the threat of being overrun by some nag at full trot. I was only slightly more at ease on the sidewalks of the city—platforms of raised wood menaced not by horse-drawn things but by boys playing at bandy, swinging sticks and batting balls this way and that in a game the object of which was, surely, the breaking of windows and the blinding of passersby.

But the worst of all obstacles was that steady stream of spittle put forth by the populace. To expectorate seemed as worthy an act as any other. For a short while I thought it a form of greeting—truly, I did—and despaired of having to master such tact.

On the streets I saw many women—their skin a hundred shades of brown, their dresses a hundred shades of blue—but none were she.

By evenfall, it seemed I'd covered the city entire. I happened not upon Mrs. Manning's, but I discovered much else; and I began to fancy that place which I thought I might call home. After some weeks at sea, I had no interest in traveling on, not straightaway. Richmond it would be, for a while at least.

. . . But O, the vanity of plan making.

As dusk settled o'er the city, something discovered in the streets reminded me of that place from whence I'd come, and the company I'd kept there. I could not shake the sensation, nay the conviction that I was being followed. Yes: I had again that sense of a *presence,* unseen but near.

Such presentiment was nothing new, indeed; for:

Into the odd lot of my saviors there'd been introduced two. . . . But what to call them? Medievalists would deem them incubus and succubus. The Church, of course, would condemn, deny, and dismiss them. I came to know them by name: Father Louis and Madeleine de la Mettrie.

Of their genesis I remain less certain. Elementals, they were; that is, they siphoned their sustenance from the sea, and had at their command—to varying degrees—fire, earth, and air as well. Transmutable—now a chilling mist, now all too mortal seeming—they could shape-shift at will, and hold to any form that served them in their sex-haunting. Of course, they'd lived and died as mortals do. In the first quarter of the seventeenth century. They'd been but priest and parishioner, man and girl; and for their love they'd been first punished in life, and later in death, fated by the rites of the Church to wander the world unmoored, and immortal.

When first they came to me—me: imprisoned, accused of Dark Congress—the elementals had made themselves known similarly: as a simple, strange, and undeniable *presence.*

They'd circled nearer, nearer, leaving their distinctive, cold trail—a literal down-dropping of the temperature—

before they showed themselves. They'd haunted me, till finally, in the most unique of shows, they came from the shadows to edify and educate. To use me. To scare and save me.

You are a man. You are a woman. You are a witch.

Had these beings returned to trail me through the streets of Richmond? I was glad of it, if they had; for such was my solitude that I'd have welcomed company no matter its nature. But even as I whispered their names, even as I convinced myself that they had come, I knew they had not. I stood staring deeply into a storefront's plate glass window, wondering could I catch some sign of them in the reflected play of shadow and light. Nothing. Did they move among the Richmonders, in common, corporeal shape? No.

Of course they had not come. Hadn't Madeleine's end been absolute? Hadn't I read the rite of her dissolution myself, at the crossroads near Les Baux? Hadn't I sifted with my own fingers the ash and bone that we—Father Louis and I—had rendered from her? As for the priest, his farewell had been only slightly less definite.

Finally, I knew it to be true: neither of my surreal companions had come. This *presence* was merely mortal; concluding thusly, my fright redoubled.

I turned quickly, once, twice, trying to catch out my pursuer; but no one amidst the throngs took notice of me, and I found myself alone in every alley I tried.

I renewed my efforts to find Mrs. Manning, herself a phantom of hospitality; for what if someone should open the *nécessaire* and from its contents conclude that I was Hades-sent? Emboldened by this thought and the late hour—not to mention my sea-struck legs and empty stomach; and that fear born of being followed—I opened the heavy door of a commission merchant on Cary Street. Within the store I found two clerks—rather, they found me; and fast. I made enquiry: did they know where I might find Mrs. Manning? In the end, never having struck upon the suitable word, I resorted to my

French. *"La pension de Madame Manning,"* said I, without result. I proceeded to describe the redoubtable Mrs. Manning as *"mon hôtelière."* Neither did this second shot meet its mark. Instead, the two men sought to impress upon me an assortment of ready-made goods. I desisted, declined their every offer; more easily when they resorted to touting the virtues of a thresher which, apparently, sat discounted in a back room of their shop. "I have no need of a thresher," said I, backpedaling toward the door.

Down Cary Street toward Rockett's I hurried, lest the salesmen pursue me with their more portable wares. Rattled as I was, I ended up taking a less than direct route. I became lost, to put it plainly. My only guide was the sounds of the rapids, which I strove to keep on my right side; which tactic, I reasoned, would keep me on a course headed back toward Rockett's. I confess: I considered asking the captain of the *Ceremaju* if I might not reoccupy my cabin for the night. But I could not, would not, retreat from the streets of Richmond so spectacular a failure, and so afraid.

Before a set of double doors at Cary and Nineteenth, I steeled myself. It was the Virginia Agricultural Machine Shop, I recall. In I would go, and I'd ask of the proprietor—Jabez Parker: still I see the golden letters on the silvered glass—did *he* know where the elusive Mrs. Manning was resident. This I did; but it was Mrs. Parker who knew Mrs. Manning by name; and thusly did that good lady spare me a second attempt at describing her whom I sought, setting forth the reasons I sought her, et cetera. I liked Mrs. Parker even more when she bade me a simple adieu, and did not seek to impress upon me the virtues of this or that plow, the rakes and tines and blades of which were pendant from the ceiling in a Damoclean display.

Mrs. Parker's directions were explicit. They would (said

she) lead me back to the market at Main and Seventeenth. From there the way would be easy.

Back on the darkening street I saw a shadow slip too quickly from sight. I hastened in the other direction—the wrong direction, evidently; for I saw a gesticulating Mrs. Parker hurrying to the fore of her shop. I took several corners quickly; and in time, and with luck, I came upon Seventeenth Street.

There sat the market, its stalls and carts and stores shuttering up. Rattled, I tried to recall the words of Mrs. Parker: now that I'd gained the market, what was I to do? As I wondered which way to turn, I leaned against the building beside me.

Its roughened boards were warped and nailed together artlessly. Iron strappings here and there seemed its only security. This one-room tinderbox, its roof rudely thatched, sat at the market's end. Was it a smokehouse? No: it was not sufficiently sealed; and showed an unsafe roof of reeds. What then? Too odd a location for a domicile of any kind. And its aspect certainly would not lure any shopper. All this I observed as I walked alongside the structure, to its front, across which I found an oaken door inset with a tiny window crosshatched by iron bars. I listened for the rooting, rustling sounds of livestock. Nothing; and so I leaned nearer to peer into the dim interior. Within I descried a rude bench, running the length of the back wall. Upon the bench, I saw a shock of violet cloth—its shades deeper, richer than the shadowed dark—and the still, outstaring, and collared form of Celia.

3

News of the World

CELIA would not speak. I peered in at her, making no concession to politeness: my wonder was greedy. I asked was she all right. As my eyes adjusted, I took in the fine leather of her button boots, the full violet spray of her dress, and that hideous collar. I asked again: Was she all right? Nothing.

I am embarrassed to record that I asked Celia what it was she'd done; for it was unthinkable to me that she, if innocent, would have been so debased. Understand: I knew more of Roman slavery than American. And still I trusted in justice—man's, if not God's. My righteous heart was hard. I was primarily . . . curious; for never did I doubt that a just explanation of Celia's confinement was to be had. I would simply wait to learn the reason why the bondwoman sat locked away, and on public display.

When finally it was clear that Celia would not speak, and

with darkness coming on fully and the rain renewing its threats, and with me still lost and in search of Mrs. Manning's, I . . . I turned and walked from the pen. Despite her silence and cold stare, I turned back to Celia at the last and vowed to return on the morrow.

I made my way from the market square. I knew myself to be unsteady—from fatigue, hunger, and the lingering sea-sway, not to mention the sudden sight of Celia; for, when there appeared before me yet another public house—Bowler's Tavern, it was—my step grew suddenly *too* steady; and toward that place I betook myself in search of . . . what? A stiff drink, perhaps (if I could summon the nerve to order one). A room to let, and Mrs. Manning be damned? But there remained the unlocated *nécessaire,* and . . .

And scaring me witless there came up beside me a girl.

"Mrs. Manning has no room, not this night nor the morrow's." There she stood, having made this odd pronouncement. I did not wonder, at first, how she knew the object of my searching; for so odd was the girl herself:

Teenaged, yet tall; shorter than myself, yes, but still quite tall for a girl of fifteen or sixteen. Lanky, slack-limbed. From her head there depended two long black braids, somewhat frayed—like rat-chewed ropes—and hanging in lifeless imitation of her arms; arms which seemed to hold no bend at the elbow. Beneath a pale brow were two black, beetling eyes which bored into mine. Her nose was overlong. Her lips were colorless and thin. The whole of her face held steady—a floe of ice, it seemed—as her voice came cracking forth to repeat, "Mrs. Manning is full up."

"Who . . . how do you know it is Mrs. Manning I seek?"

"Mammy Venus told me. She saw it."

"Who is . . . She *saw* it, did she? Well then," and I made to walk away from this singular and too solicitous creature; but, with the ungainly grace of a heron rising from reeds, she took two strides and was beside me again.

"I am to tell you that your trunk is secure."

At this I stopped. I turned to face the girl. I might have cut into her with razoring questions; for I was at my wit's end, and dreadfully tired, quite off keel; but I saw something . . . something not right about the girl's eyes. Was she daft? But soon my sympathy was overwhelmed and I demanded the stranger speak her mind, and spill what it was she knew of me, my aims, and my misplaced possessions.

"Bowler's," said the girl, jerking her head toward the door of said establishment, not twenty paces distant, "they've a room for you. It's not nearly as fine a place as Mrs. Manning's, no, but within you'll find no dying . . ." Her words trailed away; and behind the splay of her tendrilous fingers she hid an idiot's grin.

"No dying what? What are you talking about? And who is this Mammy Venus of whom you speak?"

That same grin, nay smile, redeemed her aspect somewhat as she said, "Tell them it was a Mackenzie sent you. . . . Rosalie Mackenzie." Her right arm swung forward. She touched a finger to her chest. "Rosalie, *c'est moi*." Whereupon she bowed, quickly, showing a suppleness, a severity akin to that of a cracking whip.

I turned to look at Bowler's. Its door was dark and windowless; but a dim light shone onto its brick footway through grimy windows of mullioned glass. Fine enough. Mackenzie, had she said? But when I turned back to the girl for confirmation, already she'd disappeared.

So stealthily she'd quit me; . . . but it would be a while longer before I understood that it was she—Rosalie—who'd trailed me all through the streets.

That first night on land I had a hard time sleeping; if I closed my eyes the world swayed in time with some illusory sea;

and if I kept my eyes open, and through the moonlit dark fixed my gaze on a framed engraving of General Lafayette affixed to the far wall, well . . . wide-open eyes would perforce keep sleep at bay. Either way, eyes closed or open, I could not help but see Celia, penned down in the marketplace. Indeed, this seemed a sort of haunting; and I thought of returning to her that night. Instead, I lay on my side in an upstairs room of Bowler's Tavern, staring out into the night through a begrimed window, open six inches or so and paneled in curtains of bone white muslin. When finally the rain fell, later that night, I'd watch droplets break upon the sill. The rainfall overrode the groan of the river, for which I was glad; too, it would tamp down the coal dust, rendering Richmond a cleaner-seeming town.

Bowler's was but a grog house, with three or four rooms abovestairs, let to traveling merchants and tradesmen. I'd gone in earlier, Rosalie having flown off to Mrs. Manning's, where she'd arrange to have my trunk brought to me; or so I assumed. Inside the tavern, I'd found the publican. I stated my aim: the securing of a meal and a room, for one night at least. I laid down the name Mackenzie; but the man rejoined with, "We've rooms for the first that claim them, is all I know."

The windows of my room gave onto the street, for which I was glad. And it was sufficiently clean; this I remarked when the serving girl who'd led me thither bent to light a lamp. She stared at me, satisfying herself that I had no complaint. Neither did I have any luggage, of course; and when I told her this she merely arched an eyebrow, as if to say, *So be it,* and proceeded to ready my bed. Having dragged the sagging mattress onto the bare wood floor—exposing the web of rope which supported it—she drew from the folds of her skirt a peg of sorts, fastened to her waist by a length of braided twine. Twisting the peg through loops at the bed's end, she proceeded to tighten the ropey web. This done, she plopped the mattress into place. "Sleep tight, then," said she, taking her leave.

By lamplight I saw a smallish hearth of brick and slate across the room; beside it, in an ironware basket, were piled logs. I'd light no fire. Rather, I opened the window to free from the room a certain bodily musk, a fuller description of which I will not essay. The room's sole adornment was the aforementioned, framed Lafayette, so beloved by America for his selfless role in her Revolution.

Securing the room, I'd also arranged for a meal; and now I returned to the tavern's common area, where I procured an ample portion of hard venison set in peach sauce. This I washed down with the proffered grog: rum, cut with what my tongue suggested might be river water. Having eaten, I remained in the common room a while longer, in anticipation of my trunk's arrival, but when a mantel-top clock struck a late hour, I climbed again to my room. I lay down, fully clothed, deeming my mind too active for sleep. It was then I watched the breaking rain.

. . . I woke to a chirping sort of whistle.

Morning had come, the sun rising in a cloudless sky. The night's rain had pooled on the sill, spilled onto the floor before the window; where now I stood in sopping stockings.

Of course the whistler was she: Rosalie.

She had no message; neither did she answer any of the questions I all but shouted down at her with ever lessening patience. Chiefly: *Where was my trunk?* She merely stood there staring up at me, shifting her weight from foot to foot. Her hands were raised to shield her eyes from the high sun; once or twice she broke this pose to wave up at me as though she were much more distant and not, in fact, close enough to converse. I shut the window (slammed it, perhaps) and watched the girl perch beside the door of Bowler's, atop a barrel painted cherry red.

Rosalie's whistle had woken me, but I was not at all rested. Nor was I fresh, finding the washbasin and ewer empty and having nothing to wear but those same clothes in which I'd traveled, tramped, and slept. And so I pulled my boots o'er sodden socks and descended. I'd eat, and wring answers from the eerie sentinel at the door.

I found the tavern half full of men busy not at their breakfasts but at lunch. I had slept through till noon. How long had Rosalie been whistling to wake me?

At the open door of Bowler's, Rosalie refused to quit her barrel. With gestures she made it known: she would wait for me without.

Fine. In a quarter hour—after a fast meal—I'd have my answers. She'd lead me to Mrs. Manning and my possessions. Understand: I assumed Rosalie was somehow in league with the captain of the *Ceremaju.* Never did I think that there might be a secondary source by which she'd learned my plight.

A luncheon of hare stew, potato pie, and rye coffee was readily had (if less readily delected); and with coin I confirmed that my room be held for one night more. I ate in the low-ceilinged, heavily timbered tavern, the whole of which seemed hollowed from a single tree. Tables and chairs sat crookedly upon the stony floor. Red drapes of baize were drawn aside, but still the sunlight was hard-pressed to force its way through the windows. Pots of stalky geraniums were set about, scarcely redeeming the place, which stank of the gamy stew, a cauldron of which sat abubble somewhere.

I'd found a seat at a small, round table far from the window and too near the fireplace, from which there spilled a mound of cold ash. Time and again I saw a pale flash: Rosalie peeking in at me. The more anxious she appeared, the longer I lingered. Cruel of me, yes; but I knew the girl would wait, anxious as a hound before the hunt. It puzzles me now to know that I—who'd recently witnessed such strangeness *d'outre mer,* who'd seen the inexplicable—so readily divested Rosalie of all mystery: she was but a girl. . . . Still, I would not have left her quite so long had it not been for the newspapers.

Midway through my meal I noticed them.

At the convent school we'd had scant news of the world. The few *journaux* that arrived from Paris and elsewhere were weeks, sometimes months old; and, like as not, they came clothing a fish. Whole papers—quite rare, and deemed to be of no interest to a virtuous girl—had to be purloined, pored o'er in private. And privacy being rather scarce, I'd learned little by such means. In America, that would change. Or so I determined the instant I saw those newspapers so carelessly strewn atop a table, and seeming common property.

I'd need a watch, yes, and a clothier or tailor, and shelter of a more permanent sort. These things I'd find through the newspapers. What's more: I simply wanted them. Wanted *it:* News of the World.

Their banners showed they were current and of a wide variety: it was a collection assembled by hazard: the *Charleston Mercury,* the *Smithland Times,* the *New Orleans Bee,* the *Cincinnati Western Spy,* the *North Carolina Minerva* . . . (Reading, I'd see Rosalie popping up puppet-like between the parted curtains.) Of the newspapers themselves, well . . . I find that I cannot recall a single headline. O, but too well do I recall the adverts for absconders; which "news" put my stomach in a state of upset; for those ads were such as these, which are current and come too readily to this copyist's hand:

> Delphin shows all the Baseness of an ingrate Negro, and has neither honr or Gratitude. The sole cause of his absconding is Your Petitioner's failure to treat him as an equal, which gives the negro offense. He is a skilled cartmaker and has saws, the better to impose himself upon the Community. . . . His high notions of liberty

have already prompted him to make repeated attempts to go to the State of Ohio, in which he expects to find an unmolested enjoyment of freedom. He still has about a hundred buckshot in him from last time he absconded and was caught. . . . Charts of his geneology are available to those who will search. He is worth $300 but your Petitioner will sell him as he runs, for $150.

Zeno . . . is ungovernable and refractory. He made off with a green silk purse containing $180 in gold, principally half-eagles, and $65 in silver, principally dollars and half-dollars. . . . On the dandy order, he eloped wearing a black hat, gray wool pants, a striped gingham jacket and a black bombazette frock coat. . . . Known for rascality, he stands accused of committing a Ravishment upon the Body of a white woman. . . . believed to be following a mustee named Jupiter who has run from Kentucky into Tennessee and is supposed to be in the nation of the Creek Indians.

A notorious Runner, 14 yr. old Mary is a very bright Yellow girl who shows a large bump protuberant from her neck. . . . trim made, walks very proper. Sulks when spoken to by Whites. Though no eye servant she is Very smart & Capable, smarter than most of her age and culer. . . . Might dress herself in boys clothes, and has her hair cut short for the purpose of passing as a boy. Has two marks on her cheek deeply cut with the cowhide. Bears the R brand on her neck for Runaway. . . . carries forged papers. Thought to be lurking about the wharves of Charleston, seeking sail to a foreign port.

Lymus is pumpkin colored and has rather a sugar-loaf sort of a head. By the lines about his eyes I suspect him to be in his 40th year. He is certified against leprosy, in-

> sanity, consumption and ill-health. He ran before last harvest season, was caught and so bears the brand of your Oratrix, PB, as well as O for Orleans on his lower back. . . . absconded with a pocketbook belonging to your petitioner and containing $1,700, including $400 in city money and the rest in Mississippi paper on the Brandon Bank, which he will doubtless seek to convert into specie. A reward for his capture stands at $200, with $25 offered for proof of his being harbored by a white person, and $150 for proof of his being taken out of the state by any persons white or free.

O, yes, I read those newspapers. And fell ill; was sickly, with my soul in retreat. How, how could a world so iniquitous end in aught but bloodshed or ice? I thought again of Celia; but from my shame I was summoned: someone had come to stand too near.

Daylight seeped from behind him: a silhouette: not Rosalie, but a boy not much younger than myself. I shifted to see more clearly his hard eyes: eyes the milky gray of moonstone. From out behind him there poked Rosalie, shaking her head, desperate to convey some great negation. Tears streaked her cheeks, yet still her features were firmly set. When finally the boy spoke it was to ask what business I had with his sister.

Doubtless I would have told the truth, had I known it.

4

The Helluo Librorum

HE had about him that same coiled, muscular menace seen in breeds of terrier: a belligerent mien accented by a darksome gaze and a toothy sneer. A forelock of ebon hair fell o'er his pale and prominent brow, beneath which burned those eyes hard and gray and protuberant (if less so than his sister's). His clothes were sad-colored and showed a want of taste, if not tailoring; for, though the cloth was rich, the style—even to my eye, innocent of all fashion—bespoke a season well past.

I was unused to such bald confrontation. I half expected the next sentence spoken to feature the word *duel*. At first, I fell back where I sat; and perhaps instinct led me to show one or two defensive gestures more common to the fairer sex. Eyes may have welled. Hands may have trembled. But finally, in support of my manly apparel, I managed to stand. I knew decorum dictated the offering of hands, the trading of names; but I feared that if I extended my hand I'd find his shaped into a fist, and my newly adopted name escaped me. More: he cared little for decorum. Standing, I discovered myself taller than my foe, a fact in which I took scant comfort. Now he closed upon me, coming so near I had to lean back to see him; the slightest shove and I'd have overbalanced.

All present sat staring. The forks and fingers of those who'd been at their luncheon fell still. The only sound to be heard was a sort of flutter—an exhalation: half whistle, half sigh—issuing from Rosalie.

Bade by her brother to take a seat, Rosalie did so. Still she shook her head. What was it she did not wish me to say?

Again came the enquiry: what business did I have with this gent's sister?

I cannot here record my response; for I don't know what it was I said. But, unnerved as I was, I came to my own defense in French.

Next I knew the boy had backed down. A smile overtook his sneer as he sat beside his sister. *"Asseyez-vous, monsieur,"* said he; but to report that I retook my seat, as he too politely commanded, would be inaccurate. *To collapse* would be the better verb. Or: *to crumple.* Yes, I crumpled; and only by luck did I end up seated across the table from the becalmed brother and sister.

The boy called out for two tankards of peach-and-honey. Rosalie, whose relief was second only to mine, sidled nearer her brother and laced her arm through his. With a sigh, she laid her head on his square and sturdy shoulder. It was a stance better suited to a slattern, or a child. Perhaps the publican agreed; for, when he brought the two drafts, he nodded Rosalie toward the door. Her brother—Eddie, she called him, when begging to be let to stay—told her to retake her perch.

This she did, obediently; and it was from there she'd stare at us through what business ensued.

The boy busied himself with downing his peach-and-honey. This he did athletically, almost maniacally. I felt my brief reprieve would be at risk if I did not follow suit; so down it went, that too sweet, fermented stuff.

He turned to regard his sister; and turning back to me, he implied his question a third time.

"Elle est," said I, for it was evidently the music of my French that had soothed this savage beast, *". . . elle est remarkable, votre soeur. Mais, monsieur, je vous assure—"*

He laughed. *"Mon ami,* you'll not flatter me on that front; for a pumpkin has more angles than our dear Rosalie and is altogether a cleverer thing. She is *'remarkable,'* as you say, at one point only—that of being remarkable for nothing." Thusly having dismissed his sister, he spoke on in an animated French, asking from whence I hailed.

Having tuned my ear to the Babel that was Marseilles, and having already heard the varied accents down at Rockett's Landing, I did not give this linguist his due. Rather, relieved to retake my own tongue, I told my sudden friend a story. It was a story sparse on detail, and less than half its details were true. (A lie, some might say.) Hoping to distract him, I then complimented his French and asked where it was he'd learned it.

Most recently, said he, he'd been enrolled in the Schools of Ancient and Modern Languages in Charlottesville, by which he meant the University of Virginia; or, as he put it, "old Tom's place." His French was second to his Italian; and this he proved by launching into some lines of Torquato Tasso. Further proofs were offered to establish his proficiency in Greek and Latin. From the pockets of his linen roundabout he pulled two small volumes for which he, or someone else, had sewn tiny canvas covers. Cicero's *Epistles* was one, Milton the other.

For too long he said nothing. Suddenly, excitedly, he thumbed his Milton. *"Monsieur,"* said he, with an appraising eye, "I take you for a helluo *librorum.* A devourer of the word. Am I right? Do you *prowl* the stacks of every bookshop you find?" He gestured to the spread of newspapers, through which I'd ripped. "I am certain you do. I see it in your eyes."

I made no answer. None was wanted. When he found the passage in Milton for which he'd been searching, he called again for more of the hideous spirits. Leaning nearer me—as a gossip would—he said, "He's got it wrong. He does! *Écoutez:*

" 'May thy brimmed waves for this
Their full tribute never miss—
May thy billows roll ashore
The beryl and the golden ore!' "

He sat back, satisfied, as if his point had been plainly made. The publican poured and the boy threw back his portion, exhaling steamily as that toxic blend burned its way home. He then explained in a rush: "You see, the great force derivable from repetition of particular vowel sounds in verse is little understood, and too often overlooked, even by those versifiers who dwell most upon what is commonly called alliteration. Now, Milton's lines—from *Comus,* of course—are richly melodious. Don't you find them so?" He spoke on before I could answer. This was fortunate; for I hadn't an answer. "Well," said he, "it seems to me especially singular that, with the full and noble volume of the long *O* resounding in his ears, Milton should have written, in the last line, 'beryl.'"

He paused. *"Beryl!"* he repeated, with an emphasis intended to clarify all.

I feigned a sudden longing for the peach-and-honey, and

busied myself with my mug, nearly spitting the sweetness forth as my companion brought his fist down upon the table and shouted, "*Onyx!* Surely he ought to have written *onyx,* and not *beryl*!"

What could I do but agree?

I saw then that this poetic outburst, with its punctuating fist, had occasioned some liquor to spill from my skittering tankard: the middle pages of the *Richmond Commercial Compiler* were stained, certain lines of the Congressional Record, and some stanzas of Moore's *Lalla Rookh* rendered illegible. This I openly regretted. Seeing my concern for the papers, my companion said, with a contemptuous wave meant to dismiss the whole of the journalistic trade, "Slang mongers they are, nothing more."

"Well," said I, "though I've not yet mastered the language proper, someday I may have need of its slang; and so, I'll save these, if you please." He helped me tidy them, till they sat tucked beneath my elbow.

Seeing I'd nothing to add on the topic of Milton's shabby alliteration, my friend turned his talk to politics, as Americans always will; but whereas most Americans speak only of their own politics, eager to argue same, this fellow spoke of French politics. Worse: the bloody politics of years past: our Revolution.

"Do you not think," he asked, caring not a whit for what I thought, "that the goddess Laverna—who is, you'll recall, a head without a body—could not do better than to befriend *la jeune France;* which, for some years to come, must otherwise remain a body without a head?" The horsey and prolonged laugh that followed scared a patron from his stew. Not noticing this, the wit drew a stubby pencil from behind his ear and wrote the line in the margins of his Milton, so as not to have wasted it on me.

My hand reached out in search of drink. A fair desperate

grasp, it was. I'd barely drawn a sip when there came more of my compeer's show: a range of commentary on all things *françaises:* Napoleon, Louis-Philipe, Rousseau, et cetera. Shouting for more liquor, the boy was refused. Our host said nothing but remained immobile behind his counter. In his hand was a note. Immediately I took it for a bill, some reckoning of long standing. So, too, did my companion; for his talk crept nearer the subject of debt.

He'd been going on about his university days, choosing as his tense the *passé simple.* He told of the professor who'd horsewhipped his wife in the street. He spoke of student duels. He spoke of how, on the occasional Sunday, he'd been invited to dine at Monticello; and had gone but once before Jefferson's death. "And at term's end," said he, "I sat a lengthy exam administered by not one but two of our Elites. For two hours I was before Monroe, who is rector now, what with Jefferson gone. And Madison, he had me sit well nigh *three* hours! But from each I earned the highest honors, of course."

"Of course," said I.

"Mais hélas," said he, "I found myself unable to pay a hundred and fifty dollars' worth of dues with a hundred and ten. And"—here he rubbed at his eyes with his fists—"I descended into debt; till now I find I have involved myself irretrievably. I am indebted to several sons of Abraham in Charlottesville. And further to several fellows at school, to whom I lost two hundred and forty dollars at a single session of loo. Sharpers, they were!" He raised his stony eyes to mine, imploringly. "But my sole intent at cardplaying was to win money enough to meet the debt, and remain at university, *je vous assure*!"

I said he'd no need to assure me of anything. Still, he spoke on; and at times I wondered if he even saw me sitting across from him, so occlusive was his anger. Just outside the door, Rosalie grew agitated, hearing her brother's voice running red, seeing his gestures growing ever more broad.

Finally, the boy spoke himself out, finishing with, "And so I am defeated, and left to tutor myself. A slave of commerce, I am. Visit me, won't you, in my penitentiary? It is Ellis and Allan, by name; and sits at Thirteenth and Main." He stood. "Certainly a newly arrived gentleman will find himself in states of want and need." Leaning toward me, he added, "I will steal for you all I can."

I said I'd money enough to buy all I might need or want. (Did I? I didn't know.)

"That, *mon ami,* is not the point."

He asked was I intending to stay long in Richmond. Though he showed scant interest in my plans, still I replied that yes, I thought I might stay in the city a while; at which news he all but barked: disapproval, I presumed.

Perhaps it was the sheer oddity of this encounter, perhaps it was the thrown-back tankards of peach-and-honey . . . regardless, my head was light, my sight a bit starry, when he asked again, by way of adieu, just what business I had with Rosalie. Perfunctory, this; for he seemed no longer to care.

"Your sister was kind enough to show me to this place. And, if you'll allow her, Rosalie will, I hope, show me to Mrs. Manning's." He nodded his indifference; and readied to rise, and leave.

O, how I'd rue adding the following, just when all seemed settled: "There's a certain someone—a Mammy Venus, is it?—whom Rosalie says has—"

At this, Eddie—had not Rosalie referred to him thusly?—threw down his fist yet again and spat the name back. "Mammy Venus, is it? I see." He proceeded to storm the open door. Nose to nose they were, brother and sister. He was incensed; she, to my surprise, stood fast. She shook her head back and forth—*No, no, no!*—such that her long braids swung in a widening arc.

The publican braved this communion, to force upon the boy his bill. This he snatched at and stuffed into a pocket. And then he left. To my great relief.

There sat Rosalie, atop the red barrel. Saddened, silent; and suddenly smiling.

When she leapt down upon the footpath, I understood that I was to follow.

Wordlessly, I left Bowler's and fell into step beside her. Rather, I tried to; but her stride was extreme, and she kept well ahead of me. So: I simply followed her, assuming she'd lead me to Mrs. Manning's; where I'd be done with her and her brother both. Once settled, I'd make my way to the market; and to Celia.

But Rosalie led me not to Mrs. Manning's.

And as for Celia, well . . . .

5

The House on Shockoe Hill

THE rainstorm of the previous night had indeed washed the city down; but as I trailed Rosalie—who loped with intent—I'd puddles to skirt where the paved *trottoir* ceded to the street. The sky was bright, and the high sun was fast burning the gleam of rain off all surfaces: the silvered cobblestones, the shimmering windows of storefronts. I saw a fine woman in a pumpkin-colored dress step down with a footman's help from her coach; and I thought it quite queer when she popped open a frilled umbrella, for there were no clouds about and the air was not rain-heavy, as it had been all the day before. Staring, I realized the lady sought shelter from the sun. When later I'd learn the word *parasol,* I would remember that woman, and the day my American fortunes were put in play.

We set out o'er the city's grid. As we neared the market, the streets grew more crowded with carryalls, basket-bearing women, and boys at their Saturday play. Quickly I learned to keep watch for the swine: packs of pigs—no tender in sight—roamed streets down the middle of which refuse had been piled for their perusal.

At the market proper, I saw the commoner purpose to which a pig might be put: ham, that is. Hocks hung from iron hooks at several of the stalls. Beneath these sat the porcine heads, on wooden salvers slick with congealed blood, and busy with buzzing flies. Too, there was beef as well as mutton, veal, and full-size fowl selling table ready at twelve cents, less if bought alive. Never had I seen such array; for the common table of my youth had featured what little the nuns and externs had been able to grow or grub, all of it grayish green or greenish gray: occasional slabs of meat suitable only for stew, or fish of sickly hue. Here the fish lay glistening on beds of sawdust and ice. Finned, shelled, and shucked, they sold by the pound, bushel, and basket.

At stalls rather more savory than those of the butcher and fishmonger, I found mounded fruits and vegetables. The late-season watermelons struck me particularly. Rather more familiar were apples of every red, green, and golden shade, strawberries—which I heard an Englishwoman dismiss as "small"—currants, cherries, and pears. There were beans of sundry shape. And of course corn, sold in its various states: whole, crushed, pickled, or ground for flour.

Beyond the miller's cart—some sixty, seventy paces distant—there sat the jail.

I saw that the thatch of its roof was black from age, stained by rain and sitting snow. Beside it (and unseen the night prior) there stood a whipping post, o'er the cross arm of which hung a red-stained length of cowhide. Slack-jawed, I stared at the barbarous thing, the simplicity of which spoke too eloquently of its horrors.

When Rosalie knocked an elbow into my ribs, I followed her line of sight. . . . Celia! Being led not from, but *to,* the pen. She was collared, and the iron prongs appeared even more loathsome than previously they had. The uniformed man at her side had not connected any sort of lead to the collar, sparing Celia that greater indignity. She walked without her habitual grace, manacles and ankle chains in place.

My spirits buoyed to think perhaps she'd not passed the night penned; and to see she'd had a change of clothes; but just as quickly they sank: I saw that confinement—and the public show thereof—was to be her fate for a second day.

Might I have approached the pen? Perhaps; save for Rosalie's urging—as the oaken door was shut and its lock snapped into place—"Come! Hurry on, hurry on!"

She had me by the hand, did Rosalie. I found myself running through the streets at her side. Seemingly, she had no need of breath; but I did. Having trotted a quarter hour or more, I insisted we stop. We'd run uphill from the market in Shockoe Bottom. We'd attained a height—Court Hill, it must have been; or perhaps Shockoe Hill proper—from which, down and off to the left, the river was visible.

Quite near us, a clock tower dropped two chimes. I stood breathing deeply, despite the gritty burn of coal dust blowing in from the western pits. Rosalie stood at idle beside me. Of her I asked, "Why must we run? It's a boardinghouse we're after, not a stage set to depart." I'd not gotten the question out in full before Rosalie, with an acrobatic leap-skip, set off again. I followed, resolving to rid myself of my guide before that same clock sounded thrice.

We were near the capitol. The Court Road was untrafficked, save for the occasional dray. Thereabouts, there stood the finer homes of Shockoe Hill. I took it as a triumph that the captain of the *Ceremaju* had deemed me gentleman enough to take rooms in so grand a district. Of course, I'd have been as content—or nearly so—to have found Mrs. Manning's in less posh surrounds.

Among the homes of Shockoe Hill I saw signs of residential life. Children played with their hoops and sticks on green lawns, their black stewards watching from deep within the blue shade of porticos. An old white woman rocked on a side porch, eyes closed, listening to the tinkle and trill of a piano being practiced upon in the parlor. Boys teased catbirds from the low branches of a live oak. One scoundrel wore trunks that still dripped from a swim, no doubt in Shockoe Creek. Another hobbled about with a kerchief tied around his foot. Near a kitchen outbuilding—from the open doors of which heat radiated—two black men played at mumblety-peg, tossing their rusted jackknives at a circle traced in the dirt.

Rosalie stopped at a fence behind which a wall of privet loomed. Untrained by any shears, woody tendrils of hackberry threaded through the privet and the pickets. As I readied to ask if finally we'd arrived at the Manning property, Rosalie took my hand and together we slipped through a scratching slit in the hedge. At that moment, truly, I'd had quite enough of the girl; and resolved to tell her so.

O, but on the far side of that bordering hedge, there sat the strangest of properties:

Lawn spread spottily from one street to the next; an entire block was occupied. Outbuildings were scattered about. And at the far corner of the yard there sat a house three stories high, regally square in the Federalist fashion and showing its back to the river. Its white facade was smooth, a marriage of wood and plaster. Its windows were tall on the first story, shorter on the second and third; none gave onto porch or gallery.

Taking steps toward the house, after Rosalie, I was arrested by the swoop and scurry of several black hens. Each was dark as pitch; the odd rooster was about, too, its blood-colored comb and pale claws no less menacing. One hen pecked at the soft leather of my boots; several of her sisters launched themselves gracelessly, and one struck my hip. A giggling Rosalie returned to rescue me. She ran at the hens, her own arms aflutter. She succeeded in her charade: the hens scattered. And I stayed at her side thereafter.

We walked along a gravel path planted with fruit trees. Their branches were bare, but amidst their exposed roots I saw mounded, desiccated pits. Innumerable trees stood elsewhere, their shade murderous to what once had grown beneath them, in beds bordered by boxwood. These trees clung to their summer dress, though already they showed scraps of autumnal cloth. Leaves of seasons past had blown to the corners of the yard, sat massed and matted against what obstacles they'd encountered: the fence, the hedge, the brick foundations of the outbuildings. . . .

Near the main house there sat a three-door necessary; and beyond that—still safely distant from the main house—I identified a kitchen. From this kitchen no heat radiated. Indeed—uncommon for a boardinghouse, I thought—there were no signs of life anywhere, if one discounted the patrolling poultry.

Now we were closer, the house showed itself in need of plaster and paint. Windows were cracked; and several panes were papered o'er. The bricks of the back stoop had fallen away at the corners, and the wood of the banister was vacant as the shed skin of a snake. A tap of the finger produced a reed-like *plonk,* and the banister betrayed itself: it was hollow with rot.

If this was the finest *pension* on offer in the city of Richmond, I reasoned tacitly, huffily, well then, I would simply have to . . .

But in we went. From the silence and the weight of the air within—redolent of fruit left to rot; musty and still—I knew the place to be untenanted. Or rather, I assumed as much.

"This isn't Mrs. Manning's, is it?" I asked of Rosalie; who, despite my tapping intently at her bony shoulder, would not turn to face me. Instead, those shoulders—and it was as though she'd left the hanger in her blouse of summer cotton—rose and fell in a fit of ill-suppressed giggles.

Before I could ask, or demand of the girl what she was about, I'd trailed her down a darkly paneled hallway, its walls unadorned, to the grand foyer, where gray-veined marble spoke beneath my heels. There, a winding stair of exquisite workmanship rose up and up, and seemed suspended in midair. Sunlight entered the house through the transom above the door—across which an iron bar lay—to tangle in tears of crystal, pendant from a great chandelier. In that shaft of sunlight I saw a slow flow of dust.

Silence, all around. Oppressive silence.

I followed my guide into a formal dining room, the walls of which were cornflower blue and adorned with Grecian motifs. Down its length ran a table of dark poplar, flanked by eighteen chairs covered in sapphirine silk. A black crepe runner spoiled the delicacy of the dining set, and drained the luster from the silver candelabra at its center. Rosalie, giggling still, pulled the servants' rope and set into play a summoning chime. Of course, no servants came.

I was impatient with Rosalie, yes; but also I was intrigued by these *de luxe* yet oddly shabby rooms. In the parlor—or might it have been the music room?—the girl finally deigned to speak:

"This is all the doing of that relation of hers," said she, "for the wife is dead, dead, *dead*!"

With a withering look, I made it known to Miss Mackenzie that my patience had been exhausted, and she had best speak plainly.

She came to stand before me (rather too close, thought I). She spoke as though her every word were a secret. Rosalie said that when first she'd seen the parlor it had been resplendent in salmon damask—upholstery and draperies both—

and finely turned, delicate, dark wood furniture had been set about. "It was that dread relation came and redid it to suit a widower." I supposed Rosalie referred to the straight-backed mahogany furniture, with cushions of horsehair covered in unpatterned, chestnut-colored linsey-wool. "When I was a babe, I would tap at a piano that sat just there"—she pointed to a discolored space on the wall—"and *that* was played as well." This last reference was to a harp, which now sat draped in black cloth, quiet as a night-covered canary.

"Of course, the missus was already dead then, but that other—a sister of hers, she is—hadn't yet come up from the country to make the place so . . . so plain!"

"I take it," said I, "that neither of the missuses to whom you refer—be they dead or alive—is Mrs. Manning?"

"What? Who? . . . Oh no, no, no. I don't know the living missus; for she doesn't come round anymore. And the dead one is Mrs. Van Eyn, silly," and she rolled her eyes toward the mantel, also draped in black crepe, as was the ovoid portrait hung above it: that of a delicately featured woman of advancing age.

"Of course," said I. "Silly indeed." Turning to walk from the house, and from Rosalie, I stopped when she explained:

"This is the home of old Jacob Van Eyn," said she, "but he doesn't come here either. Not since . . ."

"Since what?" But my enquiry was ignored. Instead, Rosalie babbled on about Van Eyn, and from her words I gleaned a history of sorts:

I was in the home of a Dutchman whose fortune had been inherited from the generations of traders and planters who'd preceded him in the New World. This Van Eyn had lost his wife; and when she died he'd retired to a tiny cottage on the banks of the Chesapeake, where he lived free of all society. And not even his decorating sister-in-law visited nowadays; for she, said Rosalie, deemed the house haunted. Still, by caveat of old man Van Eyn, the house was not to be sold. Moreover: he directed that funds be applied to its maintenance for as long as its last tenant lived.

"And who, pray tell, might that be?" As I asked the question, I heard the distant carillon strike three, reminding me that I'd not yet recovered the *nécessaire,* nor had I rid myself of Rosalie. Worse: there I stood in the dim and deathful parlor of a house alleged to be haunted. And so, as Rosalie refused to answer my very direct question—on whose property were we trespassing?—I considered favoring her with all I'd recently learned of hauntings. I smiled at imagining her hands atremble, her bloodless lips aquiver, and her popeyes popping further from their sockets as I let fly with what tales I could tell. . . . But no.

Instead, I fell in behind the girl and followed her to a narrow door—disguised by wainscoting and wallpaper—in the shadows beneath that grand swirl of staircase. She caused the door to open by pushing on it; its spring sang a slow, creaking song.

Darkness. I hesitated, but down I went behind Rosalie, who proceeded without fear.

It was ten steps down to the cellar; and well I recall every rasp and crack of our descent. At the base of the stairs a lamp was lit. This Rosalie took up. The walls of the cellar were whitewashed; in the flickering light they seemed to glow, as if from within. The beamed ceiling was low, and I took care to stoop as I crept behind Rosalie.

Windows were cut high in the cellar walls, but each had a black shade drawn down to its sill; from behind these shades, daylight insinuated itself. Room to room we went, through the chilled and airless warren. Here and there I discerned the simplest of furnishings, bedsteads and such.

My shoulder met one unsmooth wall, and the resulting clatter and clink caused me to step back; for my too active mind heard . . . the rattling of chains. Rosalie turned, and shone the lamp on hundreds of dusty wine bottles set on their sides: the true cellar.

The dampness and dark were relieved, if slightly, by a fireplace. Toward this we went. I heard its crackling before I saw the golden shadows it threw.

In the firelit room of the cellar, I discovered the *néces-saire*. It lay like a gutted fish: open, its contents spilled out before it. It had not been ransacked, but each object had been handled.

I wheeled on Rosalie; for I saw that she was not surprised to find the trunk in its present state. Had she rifled it herself? This I would have asked, assuredly, had she not stood staring, as if transfixed, into a dark corner of the room. *There.* Where the shadows bore a peculiar, watery weight, and showed a dark cast different from elsewhere.

By the flickering flames I saw it. Rather: her. In the cor-ner. And when she spoke, her breath and the one word that came—“Welcome”—caused her dark veil to quiver.

6

Mother-of-Venus

THE timbre, the pitch of that perverse voice, identified the speaker as female; and, I thought, older. She spoke with an odd constraint; as if she hadn't mouth enough to speak, as a lame man hasn't legs enough to leap.

As I stood in that benighted cellar—dank, and redolent of decay—this black-clad creature rose where she sat. Clues came: she was stout, and far shorter than myself, shorter, too, than Rosalie; and her stoop, as well as the shuffling steps she took toward the fire, did indeed seem testament to her advanced age. As she neared the firelight, I saw that her veil—a sort of mantilla—fell from her crown to meld with a shroud-like dress of blackest silk.

As she bent to tend the fire, I could see but the vaguest of profiles behind the layered lace of the veil. From a small barrel beside the hearth she took a fistful of . . . something. By their clickety-clack in her fist, I deemed them to be stones, or (improbably) dice. These she dropped into a basket of sorts—a midsize turtle's shell, half its bowl plated with copper—attached to a long handle of wrought iron wrapped in dark, or charred cloth.

These were bones, the tiniest of bones; as though from a bird, or human hand. Armomancy, this: in the fire-caused cracks of the shell and bones she'd read the future. I was unfamiliar with the method, then; but already I knew of the art: divination.

Still she was heating the scapulae—for the shoulder bones of birds are preferred—when finally she spoke:

"Girl," said she to Rosalie, "raise high a blind."

Rosalie set to work on a black shade, and raised it by its simple pulley. By the added light I saw again the spilled contents of the *nécessaire*.

There lay the dried herbs I'd so carefully collected, their stalks and stems tied with black ribbon: hellebore, belladonna, vervain, cloves of garlic gone woody and bitter, thyme, et cetera; all rather easily acquired. Others of my witchly wares had been harder to find: hog lard, robin's eggs (pinpricked and hollowed), cat's urine; but I'd read they were requisite. Too, there on the packed dirt of the cellar floor, were my vials and bowls, my sieves and filters; among this paraphernalia were the mortar and pestle of ebony which I'd found in Montélimar, and with which I'd concocted that heinous eye-paste that had both marked and marred my own first attempt at divination. A dream had been induced, yes; but it had been devoid of sense; worse: the paste had stung, blindingly so.

The old woman now rigged her basket to a crane which held the copper-bottomed shell above the flames. This done, she retreated to the shadows; whereupon Rosalie said, "Herculine, meet Mammy Venus."

"How do you know my name?"

"I seen it." It was the crone who spoke. "I seen it in the bones." Slowly, so very slowly, she neared, her hand extended. "Mother-of-Venus, be the name in full. My Rose, and most others, they calls me Mammy Venus. Or worse, betimes."

Her ashen skin felt like the mourning crepe abovestairs; yet her hand had the density, the weight, of a waterlogged thing. The fingers were short, stunted. . . . It was instinctive: my withdrawing my hand from hers when I looked down to see her dark fingers conjoined by a pinkish caul of skin; and each finger (save the thumbs) was tipless. None were topped by a nail. Rather, each ended knot-like, with a burl of brownish bone.

I fell back from this Mammy Venus. I stood ready to run, should Rosalie show herself similarly inclined. She did not; instead:

"Mammy Venus saw you coming," said she, "from as far away as France!"

"In a dream, do you mean?" I questioned the woman, who now retook her stool in the chimney corner, so slowly I wondered if her feet weren't as misshapen as her hands.

Neither the girl nor woman answered; and so I spoke on, giving voice—however tentatively—to the question whose answer I knew; or so I thought. "Are you . . . are you a witch?"

Rosalie fell into hysterics. "A *witch*? How absurd! Mammy, do you hear? She wonders are you a witch!"

"Girl," said Mammy Venus, raising an arm and pointing with a ruined finger behind us, "go on and feed them hens, hear? Do me the favor." Was I to stay? Alone? Suddenly I did not want to be rid of Rosalie. "Come find yo' new friend later, Ro. Me and . . . me and her, we needs to sit a spell."

Her. She'd said it pointedly, a pause preceding the word.

Rosalie quit the cellar with neither query nor complaint. She fairly skipped off, in fact; and before leaving the house, again she set the servants' bell to ringing. In the cellar, high in a cobwebbed corner, I saw a silver wire vibrate. This I followed to where—just above Mammy Venus's head—a brass bell rang out rustily. "Mercy," said she with a sigh that ruffled her veil, "that girl. She live in a world of wonder, she do." While speaking, she gestured to the fireside stool I was to take.

I followed the turn of the veil toward the spill of my things, there on the ground. "Sorry for that," said she. "I curious."

I surveyed the lot of my things, none too happily. I asked again, "Are you a witch?"

Silence.

"Is you?"

"I am, yes." So very strange to say it aloud.

In the bowl—its belly licked by flame—the small bones began to spit and pop and jack about.

"A witch? Hmm. I s'pose maybe I is. . . . Alls I know fo' true is I can conjure."

"Conjure? Spells and such, do you mean?"

"No'm. I can *see.* I can read these here hen bones and I can see." She nodded toward the fireside barrel, and told me to lift its lid. I dared not refuse. Within I found a corps of scuttling beetles—their shells shining black and jade—eating the hen bones clean. I let the lid fall back into place. There followed laughter; which came not from me.

"Visions?" I asked, once I'd recomposed myself.

"Chile, I'm sayin' it simple-like: I can see. Don't go buyin' words with what coin you got. . . . Now bring 'em here." She made a cup of her ruined hands, and I understood I was to drop into them the heated bones. I hesitated. "Bring 'em. Ain't no harm in it."

I took the basket from its cradle and dumped the hot bones into the hands of Mammy Venus.

She did not flinch, but merely sifted the bones from hand

to hand, shook them, and set to humming and swaying. In her hands the bones popped on, and what must have been marrow skittered across her scarred palms.

A string of affirmations followed. "Yes, yes. Lord alive, yes!" And then she said, "I seen you was comin'. I did. And I heard a pretty white woman all in blue speak yo' name. And say you be comin' by sea. And I seen you, chile. Seen you and them other two. Seen you all good 'nuff to tell my Ro who it was she lookin' fo' down at Rockett's. And which'n she was to search out and bring me . . . no matter yo' foolin' dress."

"I wasn't ever headed to Mrs. Manning's, was I?"

"Yeah, 'deed you was; but by luck we held you. You don't want no piece of that place, not now, not with that man dyin' there, layed up and groanin' on."

"Mr. Hunt, do you mean?" (Of course, I hadn't yet learned the man's true name.)

Mammy Venus made a dismissive sound, something between a sigh and a hiss. "Hunt is what he *do*—hunt nigger girls—but it ain't his name. Bedloe. Tolliver Bedloe. And yes, he dyin'." Here she let go a low, rumbling laugh. "Though maybe it mo' right to say he bein' slow-murdered."

"By Melody? His . . ."

"Say it loud, chile: his *slave.* Celia: that her name. Melody what he calls her for his own pleasurin'."

"Is that why she's being held down by the market, in that pen?"

"No. She there when the sun high so's she won't run on. Nights they lockin' her in with Bedloe. He say he can't sleep lessen she at the foot o' the bed, layin' there like some ol' bitch dog."

"No one knows that she—"

"She know. I know. Now you know.

"See: she been months away with that man, and every night she be fixin' his special treat: a slow-roasted apple." I recalled the bushel I'd seen at Celia's feet. "But what he don't know is that when he sleepin', she be takin' a mirror down off'n its hook and scrapin' the quicksilver from its backside. Next day, come dessert time and he callin' fo' his sweet, she sprinkle that quicksilver down the hole of a cored apple, and roast it up just so and give it to him, watchin' while he eat it in quarters. And all the while her soul smilin' like Sunday."

"She's poisoned him?"

Her answer was indirect. "They says now the man can't talk 'cause of the headaches. Cain't keep nothin' on his stomach save his sweet apples and warm milk, li'l bit of pone. He sweat and he shiver and he shake. Tips of his mean fingers, they's cold as ice." She laughed again. "And don't nobody know what's at him save Celia, Mammy Venus . . . and you."

"Will he . . . die?"

"He will if ol' Eloise Manning don't quit doctorin' the man. What she feedin' him night and day but calomel? Same thing—mercury, it mostly is—that be killin' him! She gonna throw some laud'num into the mix, I s'pose; but that ain't but gonna make the man stupid."

"Is Celia a relation of yours?"

"Not by heart's blood; but yes, she related . . . 'deedy, yes."

Mammy Venus set to swaying again, suddenly in the throes of "sight."

More affirmation: "Oh yes, 'deedy yes. La, la, I *knew* you would, be you witch or waterfowl or what not. I knew you would."

"You knew I'd what?"

"I knew you'd help."

"Help with what?"

"The savin' of her, is what." Mammy Venus was slipping away. Her rounded shoulders slumped, and her ruined hands fell heavily onto her lap.

"Who? Who am I to save?"

When the Seeress lapsed into song, I knew I'd have no answers. Finally: "Go now, chile, and come back at cockshut."

At this she scattered the bones into the ash heap of the hearth. "We got a story fo' that book you keep," said she, slowly, so very slowly extending her leg to point with her slippered foot to where my *Book of Shadows* lay.

"A story?"

"'Deedy, yes. A story." And she swore to tell me just how it was she came to keep watch o'er both Celia and "them two po' chil'en." Of course, by "po'" I guessed she meant unmonied, or otherwise unfortunate. In fact, she'd simply spoken their name: Poe. Rosalie and Edgar.

7

The Commission Merchant

I LEFT Mammy Venus, intending to return at sunset—or "cockshut"—as commanded. Meanwhile, back amidst the homes of Shockoe Hill, what was I to do? Already I regretted having willed Rosalie away. On I wandered, half expecting, half hoping to encounter the girl at every turn.

I would not return to the market; more precisely, I would avoid Celia. Cowardice? Poltroonery? Perhaps. But was she a witch, or worse: a murderess? No: I'd not seek her out till I'd learned more from Mother-of-Venus. Instead, I'd wander away the late hours of the day.

At some point, I found myself seated in the octagonal core of Monumental Church. O, but churches were not the refuges they'd once been; and here was a hideous one besides, so inelegant, so puritanically plain. I verily pined for the grandeur of the cathedrals I'd seen all down the length of France.

Thusly was I led to ponder the recent past. Most disturbing were thoughts of my Mystic Sister, she who'd set me on this shadowed path: Sebastiana d'Azur—the premier portraitist of the royals, pet to Marie Antoinette, and a witch to whom this new, black-clad Cassandra could not compare.

So there I sat, alone, a sea separating me from the only language, the only land, and the only family I'd ever known. O, but I would not cry. Neither would I suffer so graceless a space a moment longer. I stood—so fast I felt light-headed, queasy; very odd—and quit the box pew I'd occupied for I knew not how long. Again I took to the streets, walking aggressively, as if to distance myself not only from the church and that dis-ease that had come over me whilst within it, but also from the saddening thoughts of all I'd lost.

It was then I remembered Edgar's offer, voiced before he'd left Bowler's so abruptly: he'd suggested I search him out at Ellis & Allan, Commission Merchants. His "penitentiary," he'd called it. At Thirteenth and Main. This I determined to do.

. . . But first, a confession of sorts:

Dismissed by Mammy Venus, about to quit that sepulchral den, I saw it aglint, deep in the *nécessaire:* gold. Sebastiana's bracelet, given her by the prince of Nassau whilst he wooed her in his fur-lined carriage, stilled on the banks of the breaking Neva in Catherine's Russia. *Ornez celle qui orne son siècle,* read the inscription. Adorn she who adorns her century.

Perhaps I suffered then a fit of longing for my lost Soror Mystica. Perhaps I was loath to leave something of such value amidst the spilled viscera of the *nécessaire.* Perhaps . . . nay, not perhaps; let me say it with certainty: I did not trust the veiled woman. And so, quick as a cat, I snatched the bracelet up when it seemed Mammy Venus's visionary fit had ceded to sleep. Sleep? I cannot say for certain; but from the chimney corner there came not a word.

I needed to acquire . . . *des choses quotidiennes;* and having bequeathed to the sea what other baubles I'd been given by my Sister—in a self-dramatizing fit of pique and pity, which already I regretted—I'd need to convert that golden bracelet to ready cash; and quickly, too.

So it was that I had the bracelet in hand when I sought out Edgar Poe. Now I will not, cannot, aver that I'd enjoyed his company earlier (or ever), but I knew no one else in the sphere of commerce. More: to Eddie I could speak French, and there was comfort in that, no matter the conversation's content.

A man at a downstairs counter—it was not John Allan; for, though I'd never meet him, I'd later hear Allan described: a big, burly Scot with red hair and hawk-like features— . . . a man nodded to a stairwell when I asked after Edgar, or Eddie rather, and with a subsequent shrug dismissed us both.

There Edgar sat, shirtsleeves rolled, reading; shoved aside were several ledgers—much more deserving of his efforts than the *Edinburgh Review* he then read, or any other such literary luxury, were one to ask his foster father—which no doubt detailed the recent affairs of Ellis & Allan; and were therefore of no interest to Edgar, who drew his passions not from the common spring.

At the landing I had to cough, though my tread up the stairs had been intentionally heavy. Finally, Edgar deigned to raise his head from the page. He trained his gray eyes upon me, said nothing, and returned to his reading. My regret at having come was surpassed only by my sudden discomfort. But then—and would that I could claim the move as tactical, and not merely instinctive—I spoke in my native tongue, excusing myself and turning to take my leave. Whereupon Edgar rose—so like a coiled spring he was—and bade me enter the storeroom, saying, "*Bonne journée, monsieur.* I see you've managed to shake my sister. No mean feat, that."

Seeing no seat, I leaned first against a burlap bag of cornmeal; and choked on the golden dust that came to coat my already stale and street-sullied pants. I removed to a barrel of nails, all the while feigning that manly nonchalance that I'd remarked among the mercantile men of Richmond. The first words from my mouth, though they were in the favored tongue of my interlocutor, were ill-chosen, and caused to rise up the unholy trinity of Edgar's eyebrows, blood, and temper. For I'd said that Rosalie had left me in the company of Mammy Venus.

"*Cette vieille femme!* How she haunts my every hour!" Edgar slammed his hand down on the well-nicked pine of the table. Taking up the *Review,* he seemed intent on wringing the words from off its pages. "She has a hold on my idiot sister that is regrettable, very much so."

Seeking a new avenue of conversation, I chose badly; and on I stumbled, in weak defense of Rosalie. "Your sister speaks highly of you," said I, though in fact Rosalie had not spoken a word on the subject; rather, I'd inferred her high opinion of her brother.

"She does, yes," said Edgar, "but rather as a washerwoman might speak of Niagara Falls, or a poulterer the phoenix. . . . Dear Rosalie is kind, but without wit; and her word is of little worth." Silence ensued; and within it my affection for the maligned girl grew. And so, reaching to strum the raw nerve, I asked in English:

"What of this Mother-of-Venus?"

Edgar put his incisors to purpose: a snarl; which spoiled his boyish features. He rocked back onto the chair's hind legs and, crossing well-knit arms upon his chest, appraised me. Opting not to take the bait, he asked, in measured tones, "Have you seen her by daylight?"

I said I had not. "Of course you have not," said he, "for bats shy from the light. Ah, but beware: they prosper by night."

He'd not scare me. I'd not allow it. "Why does she wear that veil?" I asked.

"The veil," said he, "is a courtesy." He laughed; there was no joy in the sound.

All around us were the stored wares of Ellis & Allan: stacked sacks of coffee, swollen to near bursting as the beans had drawn the summer's moisture from the air; tea, loose and in labeled jars; bottles of wine asleep on their sides, showing labels from all the world o'er. There were bolts of cloth leaning into the corners; and ready-made clothes folded onto shelves. I saw lute strings, kid gloves, hair powder, and purple-dyed feathers destined for ladies' hats. Too, there were farm tools which I could not have put to purpose had I tried. An alphabet of hardware, it was: awls and axes, braces and brads, cutting tools of every kind. There were wheeled and spoked and spiked things seeming destined for a torturer's den, and not the family farmstead. I shifted atop my barrel of nails—the proverbial bed, it might have been—and asked of Edgar, "But who is the woman? You speak of 'the hold' she has over Rosalie . . ." Already I understood that Rosalie knew more of Mammy Venus than Edgar; she must, for she evinced no fear in her presence, whilst Edgar was troubled by the mere mention of her name.

"I cannot say who or what she is," said he, "nor do I care to conjecture. But all our lives, *all* our lives, that woman has been near. Too near." Was he about to confer a confidence? It seemed so; but instead he withdrew to the *Review,* adding, "I want no one near. No one. Let Rosalie do as she will." . . . I had been dismissed.

It was then I resorted to the matter at hand, literally: I held out the bracelet of hammered gold and glittering stones. "How much?"

Edgar's eyes went wide. He sat weighing the bangle in silent appraisal whilst I told an altered story of its provenance, retaining the prince but replacing Sebastiana with a nameless "countess of my acquaintance." O, but Edgar heard not a word of it: already he'd descended into thoughts all his own. His stare was at once vacant and oddly active.

Finally, Edgar leapt up. He was halfway down the stairwell before I heard his command, "Come!" Had it not been for that command—duly obeyed—I'd have thought he meant to make off with my treasure, steal it. But no: worse: he'd hatched a plan.

8

Moldavia

I WAS no horseman. I could not even feign familiarity with the beast I was made to board that day. But the choice was simple: I could either hop up onto the sorrel nag with a hand from Edgar and settle behind him, or I could stand in the back doorway of Ellis & Allan and watch him ride away with my wealth.

Where we were going, and why we had to hurry, I'd no idea. Edgar said not a word on either subject; but he smiled broadly, and showed a lightness of mien he'd not yet evinced.

That horse: O, what a beast it seemed; though doubtless it was but some dray horse, incapable of the trot my memory attributes to it. Better is my recollection of holding fast to Edgar. This had struck me as inappropriate, though Edgar thought nothing of it, I'm sure. I remember his broad back, and the breaking sweat which caused his linen shirt to cling to it; lithe, lean, muscular, mysterious, and somehow mean, his body seems to me now a suitable metaphor for his speech, and the lucubrations I see in print nowadays; for Edgar is wont to review his fellow fictioneers with a pen of open flame, scorching the lot of them.

We rode on and on; or so it seemed. In truth, it could not have taken us but five or ten minutes to make our way from Ellis & Allan uphill and due west, to Moldavia.

From high upon its hill, Moldavia looked down in lordly, nay feudal fashion upon the city of commerce. Not two years prior to my arrival in Richmond, John Allan—newly among Virginia's wealthiest men, owing to the death of an uncle and an inheritance said to exceed five hundred thousand dollars—bought Moldavia for fifteen thousand of those dollars; and there he ensconced his wife, Frances Valentine, her sister, Nancy, and his ward, Edgar.

Moldavia had cultivated gardens sloping east toward the city proper, and south toward the river. On the eastern declivity vegetables grew, while the southerly slope showed fig trees, raspberry bushes, and arbors overgrown with grapevine. The exterior of the home had little to recommend it—to my eye at least—save for two galleries, downstairs and up, which gave onto the eastern verge.

Edgar having handed our mount to a stableman—whom he verily lashed with the horse's reins—we entered Moldavia, my companion calling out loudly for the home's mistress.

The front door, I recall, opened onto a great hall, to the right of which sat a morning parlor and a tearoom; to the left was a dining room of odd geometry, its appointments exquisite. On the second floor, above the dining room, a parlor large enough for dancing mimicked the dining area's angles. Other rooms abovestairs were reserved for the exclusive use of John Allan. The sisters Valentine had their suites as well, which I saw through open doors; for yes, I had occasion to explore.

Edgar had directed an old black woman to show me up to his room in the home's northeast corner whilst he continued to call out for his foster mother.

Frances Valentine Allan, born of one of Richmond's first and finest families, was of a delicate disposition, and was perhaps disinclined to satisfy John Allan in . . . in every wifely way. Perhaps, too, she'd simply come to dislike the man. After all, Edgar—indulged, nay worshiped from early childhood by Frances and her sister—bore for John Allan that species of hatred which renders the heart and brain mere organs of revenge. Indeed, Edgar would stop at nothing in avenging himself of the slights—real or imagined—he'd long suffered at the hands of John Allan.

Too, Edgar had come to resent Allan's all too public philandering, which shamed Frances. I suppose Edgar knew a similar shame; for I myself heard him reference—in acid tones—a certain Henry Collier, a bastard son of Allan's who'd shadowed Edgar all through his childhood and had become his daily devil. Allan's infidelity was further set in relief by his recent intervention in Edgar's affairs of the heart; for Allan, in league with the father of Edgar's beloved—Elmira Royster—had conspired to end an informal betrothal which they each thought unsuitable (as did Rosalie, who told the tale). Letters were confiscated, lies told; and when Edgar finally returned home from school—humbled, if not humiliated—it was to find Elmira Royster formally engaged to another.

Under John Allan's thumb as well as his roof, Edgar had little choice but to accept his consignment to commerce. Days were spent with those abhorred ledgers. Edgar found himself with detestable work to do; and he was left to read and write only at odd intervals. Perhaps his earliest efforts had already been published, I do not know. If so, they'd yet to earn him either recognition or remuneration. And so, suspended between penury (his own) and affluence (Allan's), with heartbreak his lot, Edgar endured, growing ever moodier, ever madder, ever more determined to effect his escape.

The day of my visit to Moldavia, John Allan was out. Neither was Rosalie present; for, of course, she resided at Duncan Lodge, the Mackenzie home.

Frances Allan was at home that day; and I recall her being rather plain, free of all pretense save one: perfume. She insisted on a scent made from a species of iris grown in distant Dalmatia. Orris root, it is commonly called; and its scent overwhelmed one in her presence. Also, it was evident from her bearing that money was not as new to Frances Valentine as it was to her husband, who'd come penniless from Scotland and now alternately deprived and indulged his household in treats such as ice cream—a Wedgwood bowl of which was brought up to me in Edgar's room.

Seated at Edgar's desk, I delected my first ice cream—ginger-flavored, I well recall—whilst taking care with the scattered pages of scribble strewn about. Of the books I remember but a volume or two of Byron. Surely John Allan—the man of Business—would have detested so rakish a figure as Lord Byron, whose poetry and exploits among the Greek revolutionaries were then regular features of the *Enquirer,* the more so since the poet's death two years prior. There is much to recommend Byron, *bien sûr;* but no doubt Edgar's admiration for the man rose in direct proportion to his foster father's disdain.

It was *Don Juan* I sat thumbing—or was it *Sardanapalus*?— . . . no matter; but as I scanned the verse I heard Edgar's voice, raised in supplication. I went, nay stole out onto the hall landing, the better to hear his words rising—as sickly-sweet as Mrs. Allan's scent—from belowstairs.

Before I could cull any sense from the distant conversation, I heard Edgar launch into the most effusive of thank-yous, praising his foster mother's every attribute. And I heard Frances Valentine opine, "Well, it *is* rather exquisite? 'A countess of Europe,' you say? . . . *Mais c'est très cher,* Edgar dear. Can you truly account for its value?" Edgar answered in the affirmative.

It all came clear to me then.

And not five minutes later Edgar came bounding upstairs, setting me to scramble gracelessly back to his room, where, atop his desk, he proceeded to count out bill upon bill upon bill. By the bulge in his waistband, I concluded he'd already secured his commission; but I said nothing of this; instead, I accepted with equanimity the loss of the bracelet and the gain of John Allan's cash. It was—even I knew it—quite a sum. A sum large enough to make John Allan very, very angry, thereby doubling, nay trebling the value of Edgar's commission.

His business done, I was led downstairs by Edgar and let to pass a moment with Mrs. Allan, who already wore the storied bangle. The parlor was set about with fine furnishings in the Empire style; among these was a secretary atop which sat a lockbox of rare woods and iron; and which no doubt contained the lady's accrued (and now depleted) household allowance. On the wall hung a poorly executed Scots landscape. In opposing corners, as if they might come forth to fight, sat two busts by Canova: *Dante* and *Mary Magdalene*. The latter, when remarked upon by me, innocently enough, caused Edgar to declaim, "Nonsense—we have no reason to believe Mary Magdalene ever sinned as supposed; nor that she is the person alluded to in the seventh chapter of Luke." At this, Mrs. Allan rolled her eyes and shrugged her delicate shoulders. Tea was offered, and declined on our mutual account by a quite restless Edgar. A moment later he leapt up, pecked Mrs. Allan upon the cheek, and shoveled me toward the door.

The same nag awaited us, seeming a bit fresher for having been hayed and watered. With nary a word to the stableman or myself, Edgar hurled himself atop the mount and . . . and rode off!

What could I do but bid the groom direct me toward the capitol? From which building (I hoped) I'd be able to make my way back to the Van Eyn mansion.

Seething, cursing Edgar, I set off.

The many clocks of the Dutchman's home were left unwound; but from within that deathful place I heard the distant tower tell the hour. Six, I suppose; perhaps seven. *Enfin,* the sun had nearly set. By its last light I wandered the dark hallways and dim rooms of the manse.

I'd arrived to find the cellar door shut; I'd report, simply, that it was locked, but never did I see the hardware that could have rendered it so. Pushing on the panel, as Rosalie had, I felt nothing, no give at all; I might have pushed on any patch of the foyer wall with equal effect. Knowing I was early—for I'd made my way from Moldavia with surprising ease, and had not gotten lost—I stopped worrying the cellar door, and told myself it would open in time. I did, however, ring the servants' bell, following the lead of Rosalie, whom still I expected to encounter at every turn.

Only then did I set out to explore, tentatively; for I imagined Mammy Venus plotting my rude progress by my footfall.

Through an open door at the end of a lightless hallway, I saw a lamp. To this I was drawn, like the proverbial moth: save it was not flame but the promise of books which drew me; for a wall of shelving could be seen as well.

The library was fitted out in mournful fashion. Drapes of deep chocolate were drawn to show straight-backed chairs of mahogany, their horsehair cushions covered in mud-colored damask. A settee seemed designed for discomfort. A rug lay under the whole collection, its design—a ghastly geometry of reds, bordered in gold braid—seemed to hint at some ancient spill of blood. A painted Cromwell supervised all from atop a marble mantel draped in crepe.

I might have backed from the room, from its mortuary aspect, save for those shelves, quite well stocked; and a most intriguing piece of furniture: a double desk placed dead center, and anchoring the room. At this, two people might work, facing each other across an expanse of mahogany, its edge worked with silk oak.

It was on the desk that I found a cold supper of salt fish and ham, set out on china rimmed with a dull-colored cornucopia: corn, pumpkins, and odd, misshapen squash. There was a bottle of Burgundy wine, too. As this had yet to be decanted, I deemed it safe, unlike the witch-made wine that had come from Sebastiana's cellar on a like occasion. The *vinum sabbati,* that was; a drink I'd come to both mistrust and crave.

Sated—and mindful to thank Rosalie; for it was she to whom I attributed the supper—I took to the shelves. By the last of the daylight I counted twenty-six volumes of Voltaire and nine of Swift. I took up the lamp and set about inventorying the shelves in earnest. There were volumes in French—*Gil Blas,* Fénélon's *Télémaque,* et cetera—and Dutch, of course. The classics of Greece and Rome found fair representation. Novels that I'd known as contraband stood proud: Sir Walter Scott (everywhere I went Americans showed themselves Scott-wild) and my beloved Mrs. Radcliffe. Other titles of a tenebrous cast teased me: *The Penitent of Godstow, Children of the Abbey, Trecothick Bower, The Victim of Magical Delusion,* and so on. These trivial volumes—for so they would have been dismissed by that same society that secretly sought them out—were redeemed by journaled accounts of Congress, Jefferson's *Manual of Parliamentary Practice,* Campbell's *Overland Journey to India,* et cetera: titles representative of a real and therefore worthier world.

I went at the volumes, taking them down two or three at a

time until—quite forgetting myself—I'd piled a range atop the desk. So in thrall was I to one in particular—Felt's *Annals of Salem from Its First Settlement*—I did not hear her approach.

Later events would lead me to conclude that Mother-of-Venus had come in silence; for she moved too slowly to generate sound, her every move penitential, her every step the very definition of pain. She may have stood outside the library a long while, I cannot say. O, but I started when finally she spoke. "Lower that lamp," said she, her voice seeming the distillation of all agony.

This I did, as soon as my hand proved sufficiently steady. And into the library, lit now by only the early moon, she came. O'er the wood of the threshold her step grated, as if her sandals had soles of sand.

Still she was veiled, shrouded head to toe in blackest bombazine. I'd taken a seat at the desk—as directed—and watched as Mother-of-Venus made her way slowly to its far side. Her stride was tight, as Celia's had been when I'd seen her shackled at the ankle; but by the silence, the utter silence, I knew that Mammy Venus wore no shackles—leastways none real enough to rattle. And she stooped: when finally she gained the desk's second chair, I saw that she stood not two heads higher than its caned back. Her own back was bowed, yes; and her arms appeared fixed in their position, like the wings of a trussed fowl. And when she turned to look this way or that, she moved stiffly from the waist; and it was by following her squared shoulders as much as that veil that one guessed the object of her regard.

Mammy Venus carried a scent, nearly as strong as Mrs. Allan's. But this scent was not so easily identified; though by night's end I'd know it to rise from a salve—concocted of honey and hemp—and applied by Mammy Venus not for vanity, no, but rather for the relief of pain. Too, all that long night she'd draw rolled leaves from a waxen pouch affixed to her skirt: cannabis, it was, rolled into plugs and steeped in red oil and honey. These she'd suck and chew, and swallow.

It took some time for Mammy Venus to settle into her chair. I could barely see her, though she sat not six feet from me. When finally she spoke—her words a rustling exhalation—it was to ask if I was ready.

"Ready . . . ready for what?"

"She comin'."

"Who's coming?" I asked. "Rosalie?"

Her low, rumbling laugh rose into words. "No'm. . . . Her mama."

Thusly was I introduced to Eliza Arnold Hopkins Poe; who'd already lain fifteen years in a most unquiet grave.

9

The Revenant

THERE came wind. There came rain. Distantly, the church bells counted out a dark hour.

I sat across from Mammy Venus, who'd devolved from silence to a deathly stillness. Only by the rustle of her veil did I know she breathed. Finally, unable to abide the darkness, I rose and—not petitioning for permission—set the lamp atop the desk. I raised it to a slow glow. It lit the books piled near its bronze base. Beyond its roseate chimney all was shadow. The shelves rose into utter darkness. A medallion made of horsehair and plaster shone like a moon at the center of the ceiling. And the library would have sunk even deeper into shadow had it not been for the literal, low-hung moon. Oranged, it was; sulfurous. Still, I was grateful for its off-color light, shining through the tall windows of wavery isinglass. Manifold panes, there were, rendering the windows a geometry of glass and delicate wood; all of which set to trembling as the wind rose.

The trees and shrubs of the yard could be heard. Somewhere a branch scratched at the casement: a sound akin to a child's cry crawled through the house. Rain—like gravel sprayed from a great hand—hit the glass behind me; too, it came down the chimney to land, dully, fatly, on the andiron and mounded ash.

Slowly, slowly, slowly, Mammy Venus raised her cicatrized hands to the desk's edge. Those hands, what a contrast to the delicate inlay of the wood: claw-like they were, brittle and stiff, the fingers skin-soldered one to the next, all eight fingers tipless, and only the thumbs intact. Her wrists were thin, the taut skin pale and thick as canvas. Between the wrists and the wide sleeves of her shift, blackness resumed.

I heard again her last cryptic words, seeming now to echo through the clock-struck silence (for the hour was eight): *the actress was coming*. I thought she'd meant to somehow speak for Eliza Arnold, lend her ruined voice to the dead woman—sufficiently unsettling, that would have been— . . . but no: worse: she'd spoken plainly: Eliza Arnold was coming. In the flesh; such as it was.

The wind now whistled through the house. Framed things clapped against the paneled and papered walls. Somewhere a windowpane gave way, falling in shards onto a hard floor. In the chimney—as shadow within shadow—I saw the ash rise and swirl and take tornadic shape. The crepe that overhung the mantel waved, and surely would have blown from its place had it not been anchored by candlesticks of brass. Then the window squarely at my back began to rattle; soon it shook so violently I shrank low in my chair, certain a spray of glass would come. This persisted till . . . till I turned to the window.

Far more frightening it was to find nothing there. Yet still the panes threatened implosion, still the wind whipped, still the rains came.

"Git it, now. . . . Git it!" repeated Mammy Venus. "Raise up that sash, chile; and be quick, lessen you want to bathe in glass this night!"

I'd already risen from my chair. I was backing from the window—a window so tall I might have passed through it to the parterre, to the gardens beyond—when Mammy Venus spoke a second time. The window, it was edging ever higher: up, and up, and up. Its frame could not long withstand the wind. Cracks and fractures were coming. And so—as directed—I rushed the window, fell to my knees, and with both hands threw it high. It flew up; and I fell back onto the rug. Through a mask made of my fingers I watched as the wet, inrushing wind brought . . .

In she came on the chilling current, slowly: a drifting Ophelia.

She passed o'er me where I lay on the blood-colored carpet, shuddering like a hillside aspen. I felt a bodily constriction: the skin of my nipples went icy-tight; my testes withdrew. The library felt cold, terribly so. This current would diffuse through the house; and from behind her, from beyond, there'd come a warmer and more seasonal wind hinting of the garden, of growth. But nothing, no scent could counter her stench.

Now she'd come, the wind lay down. The rain, too, ceased. And a mortuary silence presided.

At first I thought her tall, nearly as tall as I; but soon I knew my mistake: she was not earthbound, and so her height defied calculation or conjecture. She hung on the air, hovered near the hearth with a quite delicate elbow seeming to rest upon the mantel. The lamp was bright now: within its chimney a red tongue rose in fiery complaint. By this heightened light I saw her.

She'd eschewed all modesty; as the dead do.

Naked, she was. My eye roved to the black thatch below her belly. The hair there was of an excessive length and thickness, well matched to that greater ebon mass that overspread her shoulders, spilling down her back to her hips. Her breasts were firm and full and seemed to possess a weight the rest of her person lacked. Too—ruddy at their thimble-like tips, with pools of pink outspreading—her breasts showed color. Only her dark and changeable eyes were equally . . . alive, set beneath lustrous, expressive brows; brows which would arch when finally she'd deign to address us.

. . . O, yes: those hideous hands. When first I saw them my bowels went slack and I had to swallow back a swell of vomit. Was it merely the sight of her hands? Or was it her accompanying stink? Regardless, I retched. The feet? Atwin to the hands; and so I forbear to describe them. Vomit wells again at the mere recollection; and so I stay my pen to say instead:

Save for her hands and feet, there was beauty in her aspect; and this despite her death-state. In defiance of it, perhaps. Still evident were those charms which had rendered Eliza Arnold an idol of the stage; for this she'd been. That beauty was changed now, certainly: her flesh was bloodless and gray, and the angles of her body were no doubt far sharper than they'd been in life. Her skeleton showed itself, as if her skin were but a winding-sheet. The bones were especially peaked at her collar, and shadows pooled in the hollows there. The bones of her upper chest I will compare to stays set into a terraced yard. Her ribs? Conjure if you can staves without their barrel. Her stomach had sunk into concavity. Her hips were squared, and no longer supple. Her thighs had withered, and nearest to her sex they were a hand's width apart. Her legs were knobbed at the knee and ankle.

Her face? Its residual beauty was marred only by deeply sunken cheeks and eye sockets, and by that deathly pallor. Above the prominent cheekbones, her hazel eyes were afire. Her nose was slightly pug. Her mouth was full; the lips pale, nay pink as her nipples and seeming still to whisper of life.

The mouth itself—mobile, sly—defined her; the more so, unfortunately, when she opened it to speak. For the gums were but a bony ridge out of which rose teeth the color of butter gone bad. Their roots showed blackly. And there issued from that mouth not breath, but the most foul, the most fetid, the most fecal of scents. Indeed, this cold cologne issued from her every orifice. Plainly put: she'd rotted.

Still, no feature of the dead Eliza Arnold rivaled that of her hands and feet.

I'd noticed that her weight—if weight she bore—was tilted back, onto the pivot of her heels; for during her long tenancy in the earth, her toenails had grown into calcified curls, doubling back upon the soles and . . . and growing into and through the flesh of her foot to protrude, like spring shoots, through the top of tiny feet that had once trod the stage with grace. Heinous torsions they made, the nails cracked and filthy, blade-like and thickly yellowed.

I saw her hands closely when, readying to speak, she slid down the length of the mantel, nearer the desk, and caused the coldness to shift within the library. Again the ash spun into funnel shape. Again the lamplight complained.

She trained her eyes on me. I held her stare until she—with a nod, and something I'll deem a smile (for want of a better word)—issued me back to my seat at the desk. It was from that vantage that I saw Eliza Arnold near, and set her hands upon the bunched shoulders of Mammy Venus. O, too well did I see their ruination. Like the bound feet of a Chinawoman, the digits lay back against the palm, nearly flat, and the nails pierced the flesh at the palm's thickest point, exiting topside near the bony wrist. Such hands were, perforce, useless. They were as fists, and forever fixed. When Eliza Arnold used her hands, it was as an inverted claw of sorts: she would drag the jagged back of her hand across a surface and snag at it with the protruding nails. This she did presently, teasing the tulle of Mammy Venus's veil.

"Tell me," said she, "where are they?" She addressed Mammy Venus; my relief at this was extreme. I was too discomposed to speak; to a corpse, no less.

The question came again: Eliza Arnold sought news of her children; this I knew. "Speak of them!" she demanded, her girlish voice gone shrill. I heard her native England in her diction; and smelled Hell on her breath.

Mammy Venus sat immobile before the actress, who yet dragged her ragged nails o'er the veil. She made once or twice to swat at the pestering hands; either she missed—moving so slowly she was easily evaded—or her own ruined hands met those of the ghost without effect. I cannot say.

"Too rude, slave?" asked Eliza, in a simpering tone. "All right, then: please. Won't you *please* speak of my children?" Such menace in that faux politesse.

"Yo' chil'en ain't no worse than when last you came; and you know it, too, watchin' 'em like you do."

"No worse, you say?" Now the actress made to raise the slave's veil. She caught it with her claw, and success seemed imminent; for Mammy Venus did not, could not thwart her. In high dudgeon, Eliza Arnold spoke on, "No *worse*? But you were charged with bettering their lot, were you not?"

Mammy Venus let go a labored sigh, and tried again to throw off the ghost's prickled fists. Eliza Arnold laughed: it was a sound both mischievous and menacing: part giggling girl, part ghoul. Knowing no hope, Mammy Venus surrendered; and her stiffened arms sank to her sides. With foreshortened fingers she fumbled for a plug of hemp, had it, and set to sucking from it sweet relief. Eliza Arnold desisted and let fall the veil. Leaning nearer Mammy Venus, she asked—in the most stagy of whispers, meant for me to hear—"This *is* the witch of whom we spoke, is it not?"

Mammy Venus nodded.

Eliza Arnold dropped one bony shoulder and batted her

long, matted lashes. "Is it true, witch, that you've got both a cat and a mouse *là-bas*?" She waved one horrific hand toward my . . . toward my waist; or below. "How exquisitely French of you. Show me, do!"

Mammy Venus spoke in my defense; just what it was she said, I cannot recall. But now Eliza Arnold was riled; and her words came accompanied by a viscous, red-gray spray which settled atop the Mammy's dark shoulder, and glimmered 'neath the glow of the lamp, as she said, "Then let the curtain rise!" And slipping her hands beneath the veil, she raised it high—one swift, sweeping gesture—to show a thing, nay a woman whom I must labor to describe.

First let me report that I fell back from the desk. The chair overbalanced, and I went with it. I righted the chair, and I sat again; though this time I settled nearer the open window. My breathing was shallow. My blood coursed cold. My eyes teared at the sight; and I cried the more as fright evolved to sympathy.

Across the desk sat Mammy Venus, alone. (Eliza Arnold had surrendered the stage to slip, agiggle, into the shadows.) I stared at her, grateful for the scanty light; for I'd not have been able to sustain a fuller revelation of that face.

Something had. . . . Somehow there'd been. . . .

Horrid! Unknown in nature, this.

In the dimness, I saw her left and only eye well with water. The right side of her face was eyeless, yes; rather, that eye was but a mound beneath a concealing spread of skin, sclerotic skin burned to a bloodish black. It held an odd texture. What was it? What could adhere to flesh so fully? What had come, afire, to wrap her right side, to burn away the ear—naught but a shell-like curl remained—and blind the eye, and stretch tight the swollen lips to fix onto Mammy's face the snarl of a rabid animal?

The left side of the face . . . stay: the left side of *her* face showed the one dark, lidless, and flinty eye, an unafflicted nose and half mouth. There hung from the hairless right side of the skull a scarred drape of fabric and skin: the veil beneath the veil. Its creases and folds and slick, suppurating wounds hid the line of the jaw. Bunched at the neck, the skin was least smooth, and hinted of what had come. Some literal drape—scarlet, it had been—had seared itself onto the flesh, which showed still its texture, its nap and weave. Velvet, was it?

I say with shame that I turned from it. From her. From Mammy Venus.

"I sorry," I heard her say.

My hot tears fell anew. Steeling myself, I raised my eyes to look upon a woman who'd been burned beyond what any soul could suffer. Yet suffer it she had. Suffer it she did.

My mouth hung open; but speech seemed an insult, apology absurd.

"I sorry to show myself like this," said she; and I saw what constrained her speech: she could not part her lips, which were as withered roses: ruffled and black-edged, the flesh having blistered, split, and set. Neither was her tongue whole, nor supple enough for easy speech.

Eliza Arnold came fast from the shadows, as if on cue. "Voilà!" said she with a sweeping gesture; but she took her place clumsily and caught a corner of the desk with her hip. Though the skin snagged and bunched, she seemed not to notice. (More apt to say she tore herself, I suppose.) From the wound a brownish matter oozed, like sap from a tapped tree. Heedless, unhurt, she asked of Mammy Venus, "Have you brought them? Say you have, please do. Or I swear—"

"Hush now. They here. Fireside."

I was directed by the ghost to retrieve the objects in question: two paddle-like brushes better suited to a groomsman than a lady's maid. These I affixed, by means of buckles and leather straps, to the hands—like animate ash, they were—of Mammy Venus. This done, I retook my seat.

Eliza Arnold had mounted the desk, and now spread her naked length across it—the strangest of odalisques—till her black mane fell all atangle into the lap of Mammy Venus. She then kicked at the books I'd piled earlier, and—though contact was hard to discern—they fell onto the floor, alongside what first I took for strips and bits of paper, loosed from the volumes; but these fell too heavily, and were in fact chitinous chips of nail from off Eliza's kicking feet.

Prone, the actress turned, shifted just so; till finally she lay facing me. Those feet, wrapped in their heinous mail, were too near to where I sat. Too, the splay of her legs was open to me, showing within that thatch the coralline lips of her sex. So horridly ripe, she was; such that . . .

Mon Dieu. Out from her sex there crawled a white, death-fed worm, fat as a gouty finger.

Onto the windowsill I spilled my stomach. And as the shadow world spun on its axis, there I sat, in an all too literal state of upset.

"Let us tell the witch what we must," said Eliza Arnold, who'd taken my sickness for praise, of a sort. And with flair, she commanded Mammy Venus to begin. "Speak—albeit in your nigger gabble—of your salvation."

Whether from fear or the habit of service, Mammy Venus did speak. Already she'd begun to brush the black hair of Eliza Arnold; and I was grateful for this, for it seemed to settle and soothe the ghoul. Yes: all through the night she'd brush and brush and brush, whilst the two of them told a tale of fire. Transformative fire.

10

City of Pity

"Heap on wood, kindle the fire, consume the flesh,
and spice it well, and let the bones be burned. Then set it empty
upon the coals thereof, that the brass of it may be hot,
and may burn, and that the filthiness of it may be molten in it,
that the scum of it may be consumed."

—*Ezekiel 24:10–11*

THEY might've knowed it was comin'," said Mammy Venus.

I sat far back from the desk, the legs of my chair straddling the low, sullied sill of the open window. I might have slipped from my seat, from the Van Eyn library and gardens, save for one thing: already I knew that the dead do not suffer gladly such evasion.

"La, yes," said Mammy Venus—whose taut skin trembled when she spoke, like the struck skin of a drum—"there was hints all that fall, and into a winter cold like no other. A comet done already come; and not ten days 'fore the fire an earthquake come in the night to rattle folkses' dreams. . . . What the year was?"

The actress answered. "Eighteen-eleven, fool. One day after Christmas. Twenty-two days after I'd died. Died to be lain in a grave with no stone, deep in a dark and unvisited corner of St. John's Yard." The accent was arch, and spiced with spite.

1811, yes. Fifteen years prior to my arrival. The British were bedeviling the eastern seaboard, and the city's ten thousand citizens awaited the call to war; but Eliza Arnold Hopkins Poe—abandoned, destitute, dying—had no choice but to appeal to the charitable impulses of the good people, "the oh-so-very-good people of Richmond"; for there were the children to consider.

Henry, age five, remained in the care of his paternal grandfather in Baltimore. General Poe had, in a former and more glorious day, befriended no less a man than the great Lafayette. That generosity which had earned him Lafayette's *amitié* was the general's salient trait; indeed, he'd spent away all his money and was unable, therefore, to care for Henry's two siblings, Edgar and Rosalie. So it was the younger children went with their mother to Richmond in the summer of 1810, in advance of the theatrical season; for:

Eliza Poe was the brightest star in that constellation known as Monsieur Placide's Players. It was thought she'd play the ingenue for many years more. It was said she was capable—nay, quite a bit more than capable—in a repertoire of some two hundred roles; though she shone most brightly with the Bard: Cordelia, Ophelia, Juliet, and Miranda, et cetera.

A bride at fifteen, and widowed three years later, Eliza Arnold had turned to a fellow actor, David Poe. Together they traveled the Eastern theatrical circuit—from Boston south to Savannah—but Eliza's talents so outshone her husband's that he grew too used to the darkness, and took refuge in drink. In quick succession he disappeared first from the stage, and then from the lives of his wife and children. But Eliza pressed on, and with Placide & Co. arrived in Richmond; where—within two years—she'd die of consumption. The obituaries would state that the stage had been deprived of its chief ornament.

Too, Edgar and Rosalie—the boy not three, the girl still acrawl—found themselves deprived of their sole parent.

At first, the children were taken into the house of a Mr. and Mrs. Luke Usher, friends and protectors of Eliza's; but the Ushers were themselves actors, and therefore itinerant, and not ideally suited to the raising of children. From thence—and this within weeks of their mother's demise—brother and sister went, separately, to the homes of John Allan and William Mackenzie, men of affluence whose wives won the children in a churchly sort of lottery; and thereafter had resident in their homes, for all to see, the animate and unimpeachable proof of their high morals, open hands, and pure hearts.

Eliza Arnold sat upright, leaving long strands of black hair in the hands of Mammy Venus. This, evidently, caused the corpse no pain. "I was—" she began, before stopping to amend the verb, "I *am* twenty-four years old. And I was famous, too; well known, if not free."

"Woman, you don't know what *not* free is; so hush 'bout that now."

"Well then, to clarify: I hadn't funds sufficient enough to live independently; and though the options for dependence were plenty, I was unallied when I . . . when I began to die." She pulled a sad face, and mocked a mortal's crying. Yet true sadness could be heard when next she said, "I would die to leave my boys behind and—"

"Stop now," adjoined Mammy Venus. "It's three babies you done brought into this world."

"Yes, well, she *was* my issue, it's true."

" 'Deed she was."

"Though she be as bread that refuses to rise."

"She got her a heart, same as you," said Mammy Venus. " 'Deedy, hers be whole and beatin' on, and far better'n what you got."

They bickered on about Rosalie. With Eliza Arnold's unequal affection for her children laid bare—in short: she lamented loosing a wayfaring Henry to the larger world, greatly favored Edgar, and all but denied Rosalie—the tale telling resumed:

"Everybody knowed somebody who burned." Mammy Venus spoke with a detachment that belied her scars whilst Eliza Arnold returned to her earlier pose: supine, sprawled across the desk. With her tipless fingers, Mammy Venus worked from the revenant's mane a miscellany of leaves and twigs, clotted dirt, et cetera. Clumps of hair came away in the white bristles of the brush; these she shook to the floor.

"I suppose there is truth in that," opined the actress. I could not see her face now, but what I could see was most unsettling. I stood, walked around the desk to stand near the shelves. "Indeed, they were packed into the theater that night. Some seven hundred of them, I'd say." She spoke while staring up at the ceiling, and smiling; like a sweet dream, this recollecting seemed.

"Seven hundred folk. An' each with a soul; and someone who loved 'em well, and whose heart done broke 'cause you—"

"Bah!" said the actress. "Tell me then: who was it loved you? Who would have mourned you, had I let you slip away?"

"Woman, never you mind 'bout my life . . . 'bout my life that was. Your tongue be quick, but I knows the weight that sits upon your soul, heavy as a smithy's anvil. I sees it, even." The hair came away now full as horsetails.

"You 'sees' it," mocked the actress. "You are your damnable sight. You fancy you can see every- and anything. . . . Mind, Mammy, that sight is a gift I gave; and I can just as easily—"

"Go on, then. Take it away. Ain't no gift you gave me, woman. 'Deedy no. And who says was you gave it in the first place?" Mammy Venus made to return her veil to its place. Her trembling hands encumbered by the brushes, she could not. Before I knew it, I'd gone to her. I lifted the long veil and let it settle o'er her face. Ever so slightly, she pulled back from me, as if to spare me having to touch her; or perhaps my touch brought her pain. As for Eliza Arnold . . . pitiless, she seemed: she mocked Mammy's inabilities. This spurred the latter woman to say again, "Ain't no gift, nohow. And wasn't you done it. Was some . . . some *weirdness* of the Lord did it, right when I was like to die."

What was she, then, this Mother-of-Venus? An Enoch, who'd been swept up undead to see the Afterlife? A Daniel, graced with a prophet's sight? Whatever she was, I'd come to doubt she was a witch.

"The Lord? Well, as you wish it," said Eliza Arnold, dismissively, "but you people attribute altogether too much to that Lord of yours." She then propped herself up on her needling elbows, turned more fully to me, and said, in words that were as close as ever she'd come to apology, "It was only a few of the women I was after. The rest, I only hoped to scare. How was I to know the herd of them would . . . would *spook.*" Again, that girlish giggling. "And how was I to know the theater would so readily catch flame, that the whole of it would rise on a red wind?"

Seventy-two people died. And history holds no toll of the injured.

Eliza held that the house was full to capacity that December evening. It was a benefit for Monsieur Placide and his players, who'd been in Richmond the full season. Within that very week they were to strike their sets, pack their props, and head home to Charleston. As the Richmonders had enjoyed the fare, it was decided the players should leave the city with money enough to ensure their return. Too, the town still openly pitied the corps the loss of their star—the "widow"

Poe—for whom two benefits had been held in November, as her health worsened and death drew near.

It seems the admired and now consumptive actress was quite the cause that winter of 1811. Her two rooms in the Washington Tavern became the most fashionable place of resort. Cooks and nurses and lady's maids were dispatched to her deathbed. The ladies of the Dorcas Society came gaggled like geese, to flutter and cluck o'er the orphans-to-be. Certain men came—alone, at night—whilst both the children and society slept.

As the young mother's lungs began to fill and fail, the lottery began: who would rear the children, Edgar and Rosalie? By preacher, constable, lawyer, and ladies, the matter was soon decided. Eliza went unconsulted; though, with what strength remained to her, she seethed, in silence, at the show of false pride and piety.

"And so imagine my delight," said Eliza, laughing, "at discovering that the grave is oft an open place. From it I rose! High as the famed balloonists of France, who took to the skies in their baskets of wicker, fueled by the by-products of flame. Well, my body would be my vehicle; anger, my flame; and vengeance, my destination."

"Lord alive," said Mammy Venus, "she ain't never gone come off that stage she on. She need the drama like a sow need slops."

Eliza, ignoring her, raised high her right hand—she would have made a fist, had she been able—and acted on, vowing again, "Vengeance!"

"On the Mackenzies?" I asked. "On the Allans?"

"Thereby achieving what?" she countered. "Orphaning my children a second time? No. Neither the Mackenzies nor the Allans were at the theater that night. I'd seen to it."

"So you knew, then," I concluded, "you knew what you would do that night?"

The actress overspoke my lines. "Vengeance, I'd sworn!

And vengeance I'd have upon God's good people, who'd come to my deathbed to finagle for my children. The wives who'd come to call upon death, not me; and who'd left whispering of my 'laxity.' Vengeance, too, upon their husbands, some of whom had come earlier to my rooms, for . . . for visitations of the private sort."

"Do you mean . . . ?" It was a sentence that neither propriety nor Eliza Arnold would let me finish; for, when the indelicacy of the enquiry gave me pause, the specter spun herself sideways in a swirl of wet and lashing air, and came to kneel upon the desk in an animalian stance of attack. As her watery weight (such as it was) fell forward, onto her hands, I saw her nails press up further through the gangrenous flesh of her hands. "You, too, witch, presume to deem me a whore?"

"No," said I, "I do not."

Eliza Arnold backed down. Still, caustic was her tone when next she spoke: "A woman does what she can," said she, summarily. "A woman alone, with children, does what she must."

Was Rosalie the issue of . . . the unplanned-for progeny of . . . was she the child of some man Eliza Arnold had favored for cash, or sustenance of some other kind? I did not ask, no; but one had only to hear Eliza Arnold speak of Edgar and Rosalie—the former adored, the latter scorned—to conclude that she had stewed the two in separate pots, as Mammy Venus would later say, without elaboration. Regardless of the calendar of conception, it seems likely Rosalie shared but one parent with Henry and Edgar. Who would doubt it, seeing the half siblings? Rosalie: daft but educable, kindly but dim, hard-favored in every way. And Edgar: hard-hearted and cruel, yet with a mind uncommonly capacious and knowing no end of refinement. She: clumsy, long-limbed, and limber. He: with every muscle—of both body and mind—ever in flex.

In late years, when John Allan sought to sport with Edgar,

he'd refer to Rosalie's bastardy, seeking not to lower the girl but rather cut to the quick his foster son; for Edgar worshipped his dead mother.

Eliza Arnold returned to the ministrations of Mammy Venus. The ghost sat cross-legged atop a corner of the desk. She bade Mammy Venus stand, and return to her chore: brushing the black hair all down its length. Well tended though it was, that hair remained lusterless; and though it came away in clumps and whip-like lengths, still the mane seemed full.

"I rose from the grave with an ease that would astound you," said Eliza Arnold.

"Perhaps," said I. "Perhaps not."

Tilting her head to the side, Eliza asked of Mammy Venus, "She's acquainted with the dead, then?"

"Seems so," came the response. In a lowered voice she further observed, "Leastways, she don't seem too impressed with you."

"Magnifique!" exclaimed Eliza. "We may dispense with the explication of a great many mysteries, *non*?"

"Oui," said I with some relief; for it wasn't the dark that begged explication, but rather the light: Who were these women, presently? And what did they want with me?

Eliza raised high her arms, and began, "And so I rose, with vengeance my aim; and I—"

"La, la, chile! Ain't nobody here payin' to hear you proclaim and prance about. Tell the tale plain-like; and then get on back to where it is the dead belong."

At this I expected Eliza to cause the wind to whip anew, the sky to rant and cry down its rain; but she simply ignored Mammy Venus. Perhaps she was duly chastised; for she did proceed in plainer tones:

"A scare," said she. "That's all I intended: a simple scaring."

Mammy Venus made a dismissive sound. "A scare—simple or no—don't burn the blameless down to ash."

Eliza Arnold sat in contemplative silence. Mammy Venus worked on. I stood flush against the shelves. Beyond, the night air was cool, calm now. The aroma of ghoul-risen rain lingered; too, there came on the breeze the scents of mown grass, of coal turned from the earth, of tobacco set in store, of the river-lapped shore. . . . O, but nothing, nothing could counter the stench of death that came as the actress declaimed the facts:

A Thursday, the twenty-sixth of December. Two new plays were to be presented: the first, Diderot's *The Father; or Family Feuds,* was to be followed by *Raymond and Agnes; or The Bleeding Nun of Lindenberg*. At the entr'acte, there were to be performed two songs, a dance and a hornpipe.

All went reasonably well; or so said Eliza Arnold. "Save for Placide's daughter, who danced—as ever—like the hindquarters of a cow."

"You were there?" I asked.

"Witch," said she, "there are ghosts in every theater. . . . Yes, of course I was there."

It was during the first act of *Raymond and Agnes*—which she disparaged as "a blood-and-thunder pantomime"—that something seized Eliza. "I'd come before, yes; but that night, standing in the wings, well. . . ."

In the stalls she saw women who'd crowded her rooms, scented kerchiefs clasped to their mouths. "They'd thought I was too sick to hear," said Eliza, "but I heard every word. They might as well have been at market, picking over my children as though they were produce. Oh yes, I heard it all; and it seemed I heard that cold commentary again that night in the theater. Suddenly, I was brimful of hate, hate for those women, for their denying husbands, for the whole City of Pity!"

And so Eliza Arnold set herself upon a stagehand as the curtain came down on the first act of the pantomime. This stagehand—"a boy, he was," said she, "luscious, warm with life; and showing all the meaty hues of the hale"—this stagehand came too near Eliza. Unseen, still she caused the boy to shudder and quake, and "abdicate the throne of his responsibilities"; till there she stood, in possession of the rope he'd held; which led to a chain from which depended the chandelier that had lit the robbers' den of the first act. The boy had extinguished but one of its two oil lamps.

"Next I knew, I'd begun to hoist the flaming thing. (These hands were yet whole.) And hoist it I did, high up into the rafters, where hung our company's backdrops, each oil-treated and thick with paint. The rope snagged. Pulling it harder, I set the chandelier to swinging and. . . ."

Here Eliza Arnold smiled her ingenue's smile and waved her horrid hands, rolled each from the wrist as if to dismiss death with a simple gesture. "And thusly did the end begin," said she, "whilst on the far side of the forestage curtain a fiddler fiddled."

11

City of Pain

"At first," said Eliza Arnold, "the fools took the embers falling down to the forestage for some new lighting effect. They oohed and they aahed and they clapped; and they kept at it, even when Hopkins—the talentless lech who was playing Raymond—bounded onstage to announce, *'The house is on fire!'* Still they sat, awestruck, watching the falling fire and waiting for what amazement would follow."

"We thought it was playactin', is all," said Mammy Venus from behind her veil.

She had gone to the theater early, with two friends in tow. "Fanny," remembered Mammy Venus, "and Pleasants, too. . . . La, yes, Pleasants. Chile, you ain't never seen a gal pretty as Pleasants.

"They came with me to the theater ahead the Starkes 'cause I'd work to do. See, I was with the Granville Starkes then, who kep' a house in the city. Was better than bein' in the country, in fields workin' from cain't see to cain't see: cotton or whatnot. I was maid to the missus, who treated me right fair, mos' times."

"Fairly!" exclaimed Eliza. "Who treated you *fairly.*" She'd wheeled on Mammy Venus; now she turned back to me. "Is it not galling, and does it not abuse the ear, this nigger gabble? It distresses me so! Truly, it does. . . . But go on, Venus; do."

Mammy Venus had been sent to the theater in advance of the Starke party. Her mistress, Sofia Starke, was hosting that evening, and all had to be in exquisite readiness—the velvet seats of the chairs were to be brushed, shawls of satin and lace neatly set out on same; rosewater was to be sprayed at the last possible moment; and pans of warming coals were to sit on each seat till the warmth settled deeply into the cushions.

In these chores, Mammy Venus was helped by Fanny and Pleasants. "La, yes, we was skylarkin' that day, with Pleasants sittin' up front the box, actin' all grand and such. And Fanny goin' on 'bout Lord knows what."

When the first theatergoers came, Fanny and Pleasants had to quit the theater proper by a side door. They then ascended an outdoor staircase to the gallery, high in the theater's eaves, where they were to meet the rest of their party. Mammy Venus had longed to join them there, said she.

"Yes," said Eliza, "for there you'd have met up with your man."

"Hush now," countered Mammy Venus; but Eliza spoke on:

"Our mammy had a beau, she did. Name of Mason; and brother to this Pleasants she speaks of. I suppose they'd have 'jumped the broom,' in the way of their kind, if only. . . . I mean to say they'd have married."

"Hush," said Mammy Venus; but now that his name had been spoken, Mammy Venus told more of Mason: said he was the middle child of five, and hired out to a man named

Crittenden who ran a sawmill down at the riverside. Mason kept the man's accounts; this Mammy reported with pride.

Eliza told more of the joy the couple had known; for she fell to miming their favored dance. I'd no idea what the ghoul was up to as she spat out a rhythm and brought her hands to her shoulders and knees, knocking the latter like a bellows, such that the foulest of air rose from between her legs. "The juba," said she. "No darkies danced the juba like Mother-of-Venus and her handsome Mason."

Mammy Venus had petitioned her mistress to let her ascend to the gallery when all was in readiness; but the night was to be a social triumph for Sofia Starke, what with the attendance of gallant young Lieutenant Gibbon—son of a hero of the Revolution, and himself a hero of the war with Tripoli—and Jacob and Suze Van Eyn, who'd finally accepted the oft-proffered invitation to sit in the Starke box. No, Mammy was to remain at the ready, attendant upon the family's guests. Too, she was to watch young Master George Starke, aged twelve, wont to fidget and ever ready should some means of mischief avail itself. "If'n she'd let me go to the gal'ry with the others, I might've got out that theater more'n halfway dead."

There was no ceiling on the theater: the rosin-soaked shingles of the roof were nailed directly to the pine framing. At the fore of the theater, as seen from Academy Square, and high up on the third story, just above the gallery, there was a decorative window, an *oeil-de-boeuf* that drew the flames as a furnace would. The fire swept up from the stage—where scraps of falling canvas had caught the wardrobes and props, adding to the pyre—and raced along the roofline to rage out that single window. So it was that those in the gallery were the first to see the fire rising; and the first to flee.

Mammy Venus explained further: the slaves and servants of the gallery—nearly all of them—would survive. The first to see the flames catch the pendant scenery, they'd quickly and safely descend that very staircase built to separate them from white society.

Oddly, Mammy Venus and Eliza then turned their talk to the performance proper, as if they were hesitant to speak further of the fire. I prodded; and it was Mammy who took up the narrative in its particulars:

In the pit and the three tiers of boxes, the people lingered: last to see the rising flames, they clung to their collective disbelief, given o'er as they were to the magic of the theater. Only when that scarlet curtain caught flame did the audience rise. Screams were soon heard. Through the side windows could be seen the slaves' and servants' exodus from the gallery; which was, by dint of design, well ordered: that is, the narrow stairway affixed to the theater's outer wall of brick allowed no person to pass another. Inside the theater, disorder would reign. Chaos would come.

The majority of the audience—certainly all those in the pit—had come into the theater by its front door; and so it was through this door they sought to flee. Quickly it became impassable, as did the theater's two side doors: the press of people against the doors, which opened inward, prohibited their use. And at the doors the dead would be found piled: hot bone and ash. As for those in the boxes ringing the theater, they discharged into narrow hallways, which fed to even narrower stairwells, braced, yes, but not built to withstand such a rush. Duly, the stairways caved; the second collapsing onto the first, and the third falling twice as far, to the ground floor. Those spared the crush of the stairs were now stranded, and had no option but the windows, which they broke by the launching of chairs. The opened windows fed the hungering flames.

Those who had made it out of the theater stood in the safety of the yard, staring aghast at the silhouettes of those at the windows, stilled, more afraid of the fall than the coming flames. Others could be seen behind them, afire. The panicked were pushed from the windows, landing to break arms and wrists, backs and legs; some, crawling from the building, were struck by burning bodies and smothered beneath them.

Bells rang all through the city. Richmonders rushed in from every ward. Soon bucket brigades were at work; vainly so: the fire was so hot thrown water evaporated before it could find flame. The building itself was fuel, yes, and the scenery; but also the chairs of the boxes, which were famously restyled each season by the dip method, and so were thick with paint. Too, the boxes were separated one from another by papered and painted boards, their ceilings draped with fabric and canvas. It all went up as there issued from within the flames a howling, a death-song which devolved to a sound for which no eyewitnesses were to find words. Indeed, rumors would rise that there'd been animals backstage; for no one who heard the sound would, or could, accept that it came from the citizenry, caged in flame.

Meanwhile, Mammy Venus and all those in the Starke party had leapt from their first-tier box to the lip of the stage: a fall of six or eight feet, said she. Sofia Starke had had to be shoved by her husband; and she'd badly twisted an ankle as she fell into the arms of Lieutenant Gibbon. Granville Starke made it down to the stage—which was beginning to burn, its planking of untreated pine catching fast—and when last seen by Mammy Venus, he was moving toward the main door of the theater; his wife hobbled ahead of him whilst he held tightly to young George. In the still-hot ash of the next day, within the charred outline of the theater that had been, there would be found two bodies—one large, one small—fused together; only by the father's initialed cuff links—brushed nickel, rendered purple by the heat—would Granville and George Starke be identified. Sofia Starke would remain massed amidst the anonymous ash. Lieutenant Gibbon would escape, only to die within days of his burns. It was he who helped Mammy Venus, the last to leap from box to stage; and speaking of the soldier, she paused to mourn.

As for Suze Van Eyn, she, too, had been forced to leap, dislodging a hip as she landed. No one save Mammy Venus heard her cries; for Jacob Van Eyn had been fast in fleeing. Indeed, owing to an instinct that would corrode his soul, Jacob Van Eyn ran from the theater; and only when he gained safety did he turn back to the fire with a thought for his wife of long years.

Mammy Venus escaped the fire, once. Standing, stupefied, o'er a prone Suze Van Eyn, she'd felt a tug, and turned to find Mason. He all but dragged her through a half door set below the stage, used for storage and the odd effect. ("Oh, how droll!" said Eliza Arnold. "You must have used the same trap as the ghost in our *Hamlet*. Ironical, that.") The stage burned just above their hunched backs. Mason's shirt was torn, and Mammy Venus watched the whip-scarred flesh of his back blister and weep. The hair on his head singed, sparked from off his skull. Surely Mammy Venus had suffered similarly.

Safe in the yard, Mason beside her, a bedazed Mammy Venus was set upon by Jacob Van Eyn, asking after his wife. "I hear it now, I do," said Mammy Venus. "In the Hell of that yard, with the night lit red, that man comin' at us askin' after his wife like she was ours to keep.

"I tol' the man she was there, up on that stage, callin' out for him. And . . . and next I knew we was back under that stage—me and Mason both—like bones that done slipped through a grill. . . . *Damn* that man! He done come all close to us both, takin' me by the shoulders—pressin' my dress into my skin, where scraps of it stay till this day—and he tells me, whisperin' all the while so's nobody can hear him for the coward he is, he tells me I gots to go get her. I cain't say that he spoke a threat; but he sho' *meant* to. And then he turns me back to that Hellfire and shoves at me, whisperin', 'Go. *Go on now!*'

"And I, like some bitch told to fetch, I do it. I do it! La, what a fool I was fo' that white man! And Mason, what a kindly fool he was for me; 'cause he came behind, back into that burnin' place, its legs of brick already trembling like a foal's."

Mammy Venus had been brushing Eliza's hair with a ferocity to match her tale telling, but now her tight arms fell still. Eliza Arnold made no complaint.

"We went in just like we come out. The stage wasn't yet burnt up, not total-like. But the roof was gone, so wasn't nothin' stoppin' the smoke from risin' up and out; out it went in gray waves; waves rollin' faster than any water ever rolled. Whippin' round, it was, with a whooshin' sound. Wind like I ain't never heard, 'fore or since. Don't never *want* to hear its like, neither. . . . There was screamin' so pitiful. The people they was dyin' not from smotherin'—'cause that smoke, mostly it rose up and away—but from the fire itself; they was burnin', all bunched up by the doors—I saw 'em scratchin' like cats in a sack—and under the stairs that timbered down. They was standin', some of 'em, watchin' they own selves burn up. La, it was like turkeys in a rainstorm, starin' up to drown. . . . Some was already swelled up pregnant-like—man, woman, no matter which. One man—I knew him by eye, but not name; a white man—he layin' under a beam that done cracked his head like an egg, and I . . . I saw his brains runnin' slow as winter syrup. His eyes was open, and they followed me to the stage where old lady Van Eyn layin', like on a funeral fire.

"First, I think she dead. Gots to be. And I'm fixin' to make my way out a second time, 'fore the whole stage fall in. But then I sees . . . well, I sees her movin' up there. First I think it's the flame catchin' her skirt; but no, it ain't. She *movin';*

she movin' strange-like, but she movin'. I go close as I can. Starin' through flame, I see her face ain't her face no mo'. Raised up on that stage, the heat be bakin' her; and as I watchin' I sees her jeweled ears shrivel, till the clips fall from 'em. Them fancy combs she wore in her piled hair—which is like to gone, burnt up—they meltin' to her scalp, so's that the swelled skin glistenin' like it's greased. Her nose is turnin' up like a pig snout. Her lips is swelled to twice they size, and tightenin', pullin' back in a toothy smile, like she pleasurin'. Now I know there ain't no truth, no how, but that she dead! But she *movin'* still! I sees her legs crook-up quick, knee to chest. And then, with the heat bakin' the big muscles first, her arms do the same; so that now she look like she fixin' to fight!

"Strange, yes; 'deed it was. She be movin' like a boxin' man, but she dead and gone. And I cain't get no nearer to her, lessen I climb up on that stage; but that ain't no plan at all, for here goes the stage now, fallin' down entire. *Whoosh!*

"I standin' there now. No smoke; but heat, heat like the back side of the sun. And I callin' out for Mason. Or *tryin'* to call out, but cain't, 'cause the air is hot beyond breathin'. Cain't take none of it in, for the burnin' it brings. Cain't see, for the sting in my eyes. Cain't think none too clear, neither, 'cept to think I'm like to die, and soon.

"And then . . . there she be. All naked and pale behind a wavin' sheet of heat, black hair snakin' on the air. She smilin' like Satan's wife, come to fetch him home for supper." (This description of herself Eliza Arnold thought particularly rich.) "And she pointin' down at me. 'Course I ain't got no reason to think she anythin' but livin', 'cause death ain't yet had time to grow on her them dragon claws. . . . Yes'm, there she be, all calm and sass, like she ain't up there but for to take a bow.

"What I do? I walks to her. Don't know why; just do. I *knows* her. She that actress they all been talkin' 'bout, sayin' how sad it was she leavin' two babies behind. Dyin'? La, yes. Was then I knowed I was lookin' through flame at a dead woman. But I wasn't scared none. I wasn't. Through the cracklin' heat I walked at her thinkin', *This be death.* And save for the pain—the pain was somethin' now, chile—save for the pain, death was somethin' simple.

" 'Course, I wasn't dead. *She* was, but I wasn't."

This I heard with relief. "So you aren't . . . you aren't dead?" Truly, I didn't know. Was I facing one ghost or two?

"No'm," said Mammy Venus, "I ain't dead. Jus' as close as the livin' can git." Whereupon, she took the tale to its end:

It was a rain of timber, flesh, and flame. The stench of seared flesh made her retch, and blood rose up her burning throat. Still, she walked toward the actress, who seemed to float; indeed, had to be afloat, for there was no longer a stage on which to stand.

Suddenly, the flaming velvet drapes stageside fell from their supports, fast fluttering down to surround Mammy Venus. Wings of blood they were, beating toward her. The last she remembered was that enveloping flame. And a voice. Speaking of salvation.

12

The Penny Slave

AFTER the fire, two slaves were sold: Mother-of-Venus went for a penny, and Pleasants was sold away with her surviving siblings.

"Mason?" I enquired.

The black veil moved side to side, slowly. *No.*

And I knew that Mason had not walked from the flames.

"What about . . . How did you . . . ?" I stuttered the question to completion, asking how Mammy Venus had survived.

"Cain't say, not rightly or in full. Best I can tell it, I was found long after the walls come down, beside a tumbled bunch of hot brick. Likely the first folks done found me took me fo' dead. My clothes was all burnt off, and that flamin' drape had wrapped me round like a swaddlin' sheet sewn of blood. Likely, too, them folks left me layin' there, and fell to tendin' white folk. See, dead black folk was a low concern, comin' after *dyin'* black folk, who came after *dead* white folk, who came after *dyin'* white folk, hear?"

At some point, I recall, I addressed Eliza Arnold directly: "Was it you who carried her from the theater?" I would wait out her response; this she knew, and she delighted in the delaying of same.

"I suspect she don't know much more'n me 'bout what happened that night," said Mammy Venus. "She just won't say so." And then, on cue, seeming bored by it all, by us, Eliza Arnold turned away and set to running the ragged backs of her hands through her hair, tasking herself with what knots and snags remained. Soon she'd entangled herself. Mammy Venus rose to her aid.

"Don't know what words was said, if any," reported Mammy Venus, "but somehow I knowed what was meant, what was on offer, hear?

"And next I knew, I was wakin' to pain, havin' promised to watch out for the chil'en of that red angel." She laughed. "'Deedy yes: there I was, mo' dead than not, thinkin' some angel had come down from off the Seat to save me. An angel. *Pish.*"

Mammy Venus spoke that night of soaking in tannic baths, copper tubs full of steeping tea. Beside the baths and soft, soft bandaging, there wasn't much could be done. Or so it was told to Fanny, who took to caring for her friend.

"Was it Fanny who . . . who bought you?"

"No, chile. Fanny wasn't no mo' free than me. She couldn't buy me, not even fo' a penny." With effort, Mammy Venus raised her arms and made to wave them. She meant the motion to take in the whole of our surrounds: the mansion; and by extension, its owner. "Was this here Dutchman bought me when I didn't even know I was fo' sale.

"There I was, asleep in my soakin' tub—and chile, ain't no language for pain bad as that was— . . . there I was, soakin' and shiverin' and wonderin' at the ways of the Lord, when there comes a white man to Fanny's door. A man you knows, leastways by name."

"Me? I know no one."

"La, yes. It was that big, red-hair'd, hard John Allan, lookin' like a knife just come from cuttin'. Worse, he was, then; befo' all that money fell on him. La, yes. Was young John Allan done hunted me down fo' his uncle—Galt, by name—who traded in slaves out the back door of his store, all quiet-like. And so here come John Allan talkin' to Fanny 'bout how he and that rich uncle of his be sellin' off all the Starkes owned. 'Cause they all dead, with no kin comin' on to press a claim. And so Allan, he tells Fanny she gots to do what he says, 'cause she 'harborin' a fugitive,' and whatnot. Harborin', hear? Like I'm some ship that be settin' to sail. Me: who cain't hardly open my one eye to see if'n it's sun or stars above."

"'Says who?' Fanny wants to know. 'Course, I hears all this, layin' as I am in my tub, behind a screen set near the fire.

"'Mother-of-Venus Starke,' says John Allan, usin' a name that wasn't never mine, 'has been sold to one'—and I hear the man thumbin' some papers—' . . . to one Jacob Van Eyn.' And then, sudden-like, he's askin' for Fanny's signature. Why? I cain't say."

"Now, Fanny, she ain't got no writin' either, but still she makes a mark where that red Scot tells her—be it trick or no—'cause what else she gonna do?"

"A penny slave," sneered Eliza Arnold.

"A penny, 'deedy yes; and sol' in a deal done by your boy's Mas'r Allan. La, I *do* wonder what like hardnesses your Edgar be learnin' in that house?"

The actress found herself with no line.

"So's it is I sit here, live here. In this big house owned by a man done paid a penny to hide me away and keep me quiet."

"Is that why he bought you?"

"I s'pose; but I cain't say fo' true, seein' as how we ain't never spoken, not rightly. But he couldn't no ways pretend he bought me for service. One look at me tol' it true: I wasn't fit for no work, nohow. Couldn't hardly rise by daylight, what with the sun burnin' my bad skin and stingin' red my eye. I couldn't hardly rise to tend to my own self, lessen Fanny come to help me. Which she did."

"Pleasants, too?" I asked.

"Pleasants? No, chile. She didn't come round. Wasn't free to—new mas'r held her tight—even if'n it was her will to."

"Which it wasn't," added Eliza Arnold.

Mammy Venus resumed: "La, no; that Dutchman he wasn't but storin' me in the cold and quiet of the cellar, like some ol' root veg'table. Jus' like he hoped, I set to shrinkin' and shrivelin' in the shadows, and was silent, too. But we wasn't under this roof but one month—me and the Dutchman—befo' both his heart and head went wrong: like tops that won't spin, won't wobble true."

"Oh," said Eliza, "he wobbled all right. I saw to that."

"There she be, braggin' on. I don't know what she did to the man, if'n she did anything at all. Don't want to know, neither. I think it was the guilt got to him, like . . . like grave rot."

"Hmmph." Thusly did the ghoul disdain the simile.

"La, yes, that guilt done got the man good. He wasn't a bad man, no; just a man who done a bad thing, forcin' me and Mason back into the flames. And I ain't sayin' he ought to have gone his own self—every critter gonna lick its own wounds first, hear?—but he sure 'nuff ought *not* to have made me go.

"But it's no nevermind now. What *is,* is this: soon after I come here, the Dutchman he up and head off to the woods or shore or such-like, leavin' behind all this"—again, the slow wave—"and leavin' law words, too, what make it safe for me to stay. Cain't nobody make me leave, long as I live on."

"And in return you've kept Van Eyn's secret?" I asked. "About what he made you and Mason do?"

"Kep' it? I s'pose I have; but only 'cause ain't nobody ever asked." She thought on. "Kep' his secret? La, what I care about some white man's burden o' shame? *Pish.*"

"Don't think he conferred this house upon her from the goodness of his heart," said the actress. "*Mais non!* He'd but brokered a deal—and a bargain to boot—by which he'd soothe his conscience and secure the silence of the one living witness to his cowardice. Well done, say I. . . . Of course, old Van Eyn thought his fried slave would die. And doubtless he thought he'd retain his wits a while longer. Sadly"—Eliza sighed—"neither act eventuated." And unbidden, she soliloquized on the subject of guilt:

"Guilt," said she, "hmm, yes. Van Eyn's guilt was surely more acute than most, and it was the door by which I entered his soul; but let me tell you, witch, the city entire was beset by that most banal of emotions. Rather like a rocking chair, guilt is: something to do, and locomotive, yes; but it gets you nowhere in the end."

Eliza Arnold told how the city of Richmond set to punishing itself—"a puritanical impulse," she deemed it—whilst still the ruins on Academy Square sat smoldering. With the dead as yet unsorted, with ashes yet unsifted, all business in the city ceased. It was decreed that no dance hall or other place of amusement could open its doors before four months had passed; to do so was to incur the demoniacal fine of $6.66, billed against every hour of mirth and merriment.

When it was seen that the dead could not be discerned one from another, a mass grave was called for. Too, a monument was in order. "And what but a church," asked Eliza Arnold, "could redeem the scene of such theatrical debauch?"

Quoth she: "'Is not the Playhouse the very exchange of

harlots? The Players, generally speaking, who are they? Loose, amoral types!'"

There came a grumbling from Mammy Venus. Laughter, it was; and within it I heard her affirm it: "Gen'rally speakin', yes'm."

Eliza rose to float nearer the hearth, to hover o'er the ash that had spun and drifted to darken the golden tassels of the rug. "'A visitation,' they called it. Preachers here, there, and everywhere said the fire was divine retribution against a too-worldly city. Ha! Richmond? Worldly? But never mind. It was deemed a sin and an offense to attend the theater. And we—its populace—were called clowns, harlots, and whores."

"Godless, too," said Mammy Venus. "Don't be forgettin' that."

Eliza declaimed further: "'Criminal in its nature,' was the theater, and 'mischievous in its effects.' Such idiocy! Till finally there came this: 'May such haunts of vice and dissipation be consecrated to the purpose of adoration and worship of the sovereign Lord of the Universe.' They would cap the charred ground with a church!"

A maleficent wind blew open the books Eliza Arnold had kicked to the floor. Their pages were riffled by her bluster. The oil lamp guttered and spat. The windows trembled. A wet wind whistled up the chimney. A light rain fell upon the yard, came as a chorus to back what more the ghoul had to say:

"It was John Marshall and his ilk—the *grandees* of this pitiful city—who decreed a church be erected. And beneath it, at the church's fore, they'd set the great mahogany box into which the ashen dead had been shoveled. There they sit still"—and here Eliza raised her inverted claw toward the window, toward (I knew it) that very church in which I'd sat earlier—"beneath Monumental Church, where now the Episcopalians preen. An abomination, it all is!"

With that opinion I was inclined to agree; but of course Eliza referred to more than the church's architecture, done up in angles to pain Pythagoras. But I said nothing; and waited out the actress, who summarized thusly:

"So it was that the theater came to be deemed Satan's place; and so it was that the site of theatrical artistry in this city was sealed by a church. With nary a production mounted, not for eight years' time."

"And po' you, stuck ghoulin' about with no place to go, not knowin' who or what to haunt besides that boy of yours. La, I like it. Rich, that is!"

"So brave you are now, slave! But shall I speak of the even greater ruin you once were, and tell this . . . this witch-thing who it was trembled, who it was pissed and shat herself when next I came? Shall I?"

The actress floated fast across the library, perching atop the divan's curved back. She set her talons on its horsehair cushion. Her heels dented the divan, just so. Her feet she angled upward, to both spare and show the ingrowth of nail. She'd cross and uncross her legs, knowing the splay of her legs and the show of her sex had unsettled me earlier. When finally she spoke, it was to say, "I waited a long while to show myself again."

"And why not? You gots all the world's time to wait, woman."

"I waited, and I wondered if I'd chosen rashly; for I feared I'd have her God-sentiments to counter." She nodded at Mammy Venus. "She'd not listen to me if she thought me Satan-sent. More to the point, I wondered what practical use she'd be as a surrogate. Perhaps I'd not dragged her fast enough from the flames, and ruined as she was—"

"So it *was* you who got her out of the theater?"

Doubtless Eliza Arnold had dealt with worse hecklers in her living past. Said she, icily, "Rescue is not at issue. I speak now of salvation; and I shall resume, if let to do so."

I nodded; and indeed she did resume:

"I had only to visit Van Eyn twice, thrice perhaps, before I had him teetering on the brink of the abyss. Yes: easily I ruffled that old Holland bird. Quite inspired it was, choosing to play the wife from Hell, damning the coward and cursing him as he half slept. Finally, he absorbed the city's shame; and that, when alloyed to his own, well . . . he was quite done for. Off to the shore of the Chesapeake I sent him, and there he remains, never to darken these doors again. Off he went, yes; but not before I—in the ghastly guise of the not-so-dearly-departed Suze Van Eyn—told him to 'settle the gracious darky who tried to save me from the inferno.'" This last Eliza recited in a voice that was unsettling, truly. "Thusly was our Mammy Venus installed in this place, to live out her long, long years. But have I been thanked? Never, I tell you. Not once. But no matter. . . ."

"Pish," said Mammy Venus. "Wasn't right, you drivin' that man from both his mind and his house, specially when some ol' shack down riverside would've served me jus' fine."

"Base ingrate!"

And on it went, till there came a truce born of exhaustion; only then did the two—by turns—take the tale to its end.

Years passed before Eliza Arnold returned.

"I'd been a long while gettin' used to the gift of fo'sight that had come from the fire. Some's born with a caul and the gift of sight; but I done got mine different-like. I knew things, is all. Saw 'em befo' they came to pass? But not much came to pass, 'cause I wasn't much more'n a corpse outside its coffin, hear? Life wasn't nothin' but the waitin' on that angel I done seen. And then here she come: no angel at all, no'm.

"But it wasn't her came first. No. Was Rosalie.

"One day I look up and see a gangle-girl out in the yard, tendin' to this'n that like she s'posed to be out there. A young'un she was; for I'm talkin' back some years, hear?

"I called to her, and into the house she come, not fearin'

me nohow. I got used to the girl right quick. And soon she comin' mo' and mo'; 'cause Fanny, well. . . . The carin' fo' me done worn her down, till she wishin' me dead. Not harsh like, no. Was mo' a kindly wish, and I cain't blame her none, 'cause it's a long time I been wishin' the same.

"Then Fanny went off for good: sol' down to Petersburg. What choice I had then but to rise up, run my own tea baths, hunt that there yard lookin' for things to pot up and cook? Wasn't long after that Rosalie—sweet Rosalie, my Rosalie—started comin' round to do for me reg'lar, tho' she wasn't but a pup. Nine, mayhap ten years ol'."

"She came alongside . . . you?" I asked of Eliza Arnold; but it was Mammy Venus who answered, without elaboration:

"No'm."

"But it was I who sent the girl," said Eliza, as if speaking of a stranger, not a daughter.

"You . . . speak to her?"

"'Speak to her'? Not quite."

"Anyways," said Mammy Venus, "the girl, she done come and I was glad of it; but never did I think she was Devil-sent, or the one I was tol' to watch fo'. Then, one day, I knowed this one here was comin'. The notion of it settled on me like a sick-headache that cups and cups of juniper-berry tea couldn't cure. I knowed, too, that it wasn't no angel fixin' to visit; for the forebodin' of it came dark as dark is. 'Deedy, I was mo' scared of the fo'sight than the *true* sight of her. Mo' scared to know she be comin' than of seein' her come, hear?"

I said I understood; for indeed I did.

I asked Eliza why she'd waited so long to return.

"Chile," said Mammy Venus, "that answer is plain; and I can give it: she didn't need me, 'cause her Edgar was back here in Richmond and livin' jus' fine. As for her Rosalie, well . . ."

Eliza spoke for herself. "The girl," said she, "was here all the while, in Richmond. So, too, was Edgar, at first; but then sadly, sadly, he sailed for England with the Allans, to be schooled there as the Scot tried and failed to establish a branch of his business. And I'd not see my beloved, my blessed and brilliant Edgar for five years! But, Mammy, did not my Edgar return a right angel, so refined?"

"He did, missus. . . . If'n you say he did."

"And Rosalie?" I asked.

"Schooled by the Mackenzie women, she was; and is still, I suppose." Eliza then turned her talk to Henry, who'd quit Baltimore at an early age to wander the world, she knew not where. "All I know of my dear Henry is what I glean from the letters he sends Edgar; but there have never been more than one or two in any year, at least not that I can find." Sickening, to know I'd sat at that same desk which Eliza regularly rifled. I imagined her—with useless hands—prying open the folded sheets of Henry's letters with her teeth, blowing apart the pages with her wet breath of rot. And all the while the Allans knew not that their house was haunted.

Fanny was gone. Mason was dead. "What of Pleasants?" I asked.

"Pleasants, she grieved hard for my Mason," said Mammy Venus. "And took to blamin' me. Cain't blame her; 'cause Mason, he done walked from that fire one time, and one time would have been 'nuff but for me, and him followin' me back in and—"

"But you were made to go—" I began, only to be hushed.

"Pleasants. Well, she done lost a lovin' brother; and with him went her heart and her good looks, too. Leastways, her mas'r thought so. Him it was said she'd gone ugly with grief. And he meant to sell her off. La, how she done fought and pled to take her siblings with her. And how she'd come to wish she hadn't; 'cause they all. . . . La, it hurts to speak of it, still.

"Pleasants, see," said Mammy, finally, "she was a beauty like no other, and there wasn't no heart's ugliness could spoil them features of hers, not whole and true. . . . Now don't go thinkin' I'm speakin' of a blessin', chile, 'cause I ain't. A curse is what it was. And a curse it *still* is, hear?"

Pleasants and her siblings had been parentless. Rather, they'd a mother who'd met a hard end, having borne five children by two fathers. "The black one she loved, yes'm; but that white one? No, 'deed not. Was rough usage, that.

"The boys—Mason and two teens: Eustis and January—they was dark as their daddy; but Pleasants and the littl'un, them girls had white blood showin'. They'd go at a good price. But Pleasants, she said she'd cut herself, ruin the sale if'n she didn't go to the block with her brothers and her sister beside her. And so she did. Sol' as a lot, they was. The boys, they went into the fields. But Pleasants and the girl—still some years away from bleedin' reg'lar, she was—they fetched well, 'cause they was bought for . . . other purposes, hear? The young'un, she was hothouse'd: a flower to be plucked in time."

"Plucked indeed," said Eliza, lazing back to laugh, such that she nearly overbalanced. Righting herself, she asked of me, "Can't you name her yet? Isn't it plain?"

From behind the black veil the explanation came: "Eustis and January, they was bought for the fields, like I says. But Pleasants and young Celia, they was bought for the bedroom. Of Augustin Bedloe. Father to Tolliver: the man you met as Mr. Hunt."

13

I Ascend, in Search of Sleep

By the time I retired, the hour was striking small: one, it was; perhaps two.

Mammy Venus had said I would find an upstairs room in readiness. I was to sleep—if sleep I could: it seemed to me a most unlikely prospect—in the room at the southeastern corner of the second story, where the windows gave out onto the yard behind and the street beside the Van Eyn mansion. This news I heard with relief; for I'd begun to dread the descent into the cellar. Far better, thought I, to ascend to some long-untenanted room abovestairs. Far better to sleep alone than to bunk beside the Seeress in the cellar. O, but when Eliza Arnold rose and offered to lead me to my sleep, I all but longed for the bondwoman's bed.

"Go on now, chile," urged Mammy Venus, seeing me stall at the library's door. "Sleep till you rise." She nodded toward

Eliza, as if to assure me I'd be safe in her company, that I should follow her lead.

"Tomorrow starts it all," Mammy Venus went on. "I's set to break that rapin' chain that ought never to have been forged. I gonna free that girl been too long abused by the Bedloe boy. Too late, might be, for Pleasants; but that sister of hers I *can* save, and will." Mammy Venus lowered the lamp to a dim glow before taking it up. "We gonna turn all force toward it; and quick-like, too, hear? . . . Sleep now. Go on." And she shuffled into the shadowed hall, leaving me alone with Eliza Arnold.

Up the winding stairway we went. I breathed shallowly against the ghoul's stench, which broke upon me like the wake from Charon's ferry.

I kept to the wide side of the angled, fanning stairs. Eliza drifted up nearer the banister, where the stairs' angle was most acute. Her hands hung lankly at her sides; lank, too, were her feet, and her toes sounded *thump, thump, thump* against each carpeted stair: a metronome, marking the time of our ascent. Bits of nail broke from her feet and shone like streambed gold upon the stairs.

In an alcove of the stairwell there sat a black Madonna, one hand raised in supplication.

On the second story, the hall showed a runner—turf-like: thick and deeply green—bordered by the bare, heart-of-pine floor. No gasoliers were lit. No artwork was hung. Below the wainscot the walls were powdery blue; indigo or black above. A watery corridor, it was; and the silence was that of the deepest sea.

I followed Eliza down the hall to an arched door at its end. Here was my room. I knew it; for a lamp had been lit within: light seeped under the door.

At that door Eliza stopped. She did not turn back to me where I stood, three, perhaps four paces behind, marveling at the bony set of her shoulders, the show of her ribs, and the slight sag of her buttocks. By the scant light, her skin appeared blue, like that of one come in from the cold. Or perhaps she leeched the tints from off the walls?

Why had she stopped? Was someone or some*thing* within the chamber? Had Rosalie returned to rendezvous with her dead mother? This last thought quite chilled me; and pondering same, I saw Eliza try to turn the glass knob of the door. Simply, she hadn't hands suited to the task.

Could she have passed into the room unimpeded? Perhaps. Could she have drawn herself down to vapor, and slid to the door's far side? Perhaps. But instead she stepped back, and bade me turn the knob. And so I was the first to step into the corner chamber to find . . .

No one. And nothing; save:

A square and unfurnished room with walls of unpainted plaster. By daylight, they'd show themselves elaborately cracked and patched. The floor was laid of long, thick planking, like those a shipwright might use; and these were patterned with scratches and scuffs that showed where once furniture had sat. No furniture now; not a stick. No adornment at all, save for the thick trim of the windows, their oxblood paint peeling, great scabs of it fallen to the floor.

In a corner of the room sat the lit lamp. I took it up, and turned to see Eliza Arnold . . . gone. Or so it seemed.

There, to the right of the door, was a curtained alcove, cut into the wall. Across it was drawn a drape of dark blue damask, fringed in silver. Such fabric would have been hung against the daylight; and so it was I knew a bed lay hidden within.

Curled like a cat, she was, on a corner of a bed that could accommodate two. A bed stuffed not with straw, but with down; and made up with musty linen.

Eliza sat with her legs half folded beneath her, her feet sticking out from beside her hip; a hip which showed itself deeply hollowed and shadowed despite the lamp I now raised to her. She cocked her chin toward her shoulder. Ever the ingenue, she may even have batted her long black lashes.

"Do you sleep here?" I asked. Absurd, the question was; and she let it be known:

"'Sleep,' you'd call it? You papists are so quaint." She passed the back of her hand o'er the coverlet, patted it as best she could. Invitingly. "*Non, enfant,* I do not 'sleep' here. It is you who will sleep here."

"Ah then," said I, holding high the drape to convey, *Please go.*

I had hoped to be led to a basin and full ewer, to a fresh smock, to a glass in which I might gauge the state of my dishabille. Instead: a bed, only. Still, into it I'd fall once I'd exorcised it of its present occupant.

"Will you return to the earth this night?" I asked, rather pointedly.

"I think not," said Eliza Arnold. "I've a mother's work to do. And so I leave you to your peace, such as it is." And with that there came a chilling gust—wind from off the very wings of death—and the drape blew from my grasp. I nearly lost hold of the lamp, too.

I looked to the four corners of the room. Nowhere did I see Eliza Arnold; but I knew she was present, still. I was cold, bone-thoroughly so. And O, how I pitied the Poes their . . . their maternal malingerer.

I addressed the air. "Do they know . . . ? Can they see you?"

The answer came from near the door, which had blown shut as Eliza quit the alcove. I will not say it was speech I heard, no; but regardless, an answer came. As ever, Eliza Arnold disdained the plural as well as the feminine pronoun; and spoke only of Edgar:

"He does not know. He cannot see me."

I turned toward the ghost—I felt her, just there—and saw her coalesce. Was she made of mere . . . coldness? The windows and door shivered in their frames; as did I.

Then: "Do you know my Edgar?"

"I do; though not well."

"His is a rare genius, you know."

I made no response; for none came readily. Unwise, it would have been, to speak truthfully. Had I been pressed to give my opinion of Edgar, well, his mother would not have been pleased. This Eliza knew; for she heard as much in my silence; and countered with:

"No, of course not." It was even colder now. I all but wrapped myself in the fringed drapery. "Genius knows but its own. And you, my Hercule, my Herculine, are but a witch. A sport of nature. . . . Slight genius in that, I should think."

"Is it genius one needs to rise rotted from the grave?" I asked, my words fast born of insult.

At this the actress went rigid . . . rather, *more* rigid. She tossed her black mane, haughtily, and arched her back. (Her spine extended audibly.) Her hands found purchase on her hips as she stated, flatly, that she'd shown genius in her day. Tired, cold and oddly bold, and wanting to rid the room of the ghoul, I countered her claim as cruelly as I could. I dismissed both her own genius and that of her boy by asking, simply:

"And Rosalie? What of Rosalie?"

A wet and lashing wind rose. Quickly, I stepped to the shut door and opened it; for I'd let nothing impede the revenant's exit. When the wind lay down, I closed and latched the door.

Silence. Stillness. The fading breath of death.

Yes: she'd gone. No doubt to worship at the bed of her dreaming Edgar.

The crowing of a lone cock woke me.

It was dark behind the drape, but daylight fired the silver fringe. Again: that excited stutter from the yard.

I swung my stockinged legs o'er the side of the bed and

stood. Bitter was the taste of waking, coffee-like it came. Dust drifted down from the disused drape; and my unfresh clothes, my unwashed person, rendered me as stale as the long-unslept bed. I crossed the cool wood of the floor, wondering would I see the river beyond. I did; but also I saw Mammy Venus, there, down in the walled yard, at work.

A breeze brought the riverine air through the window, from which several panes had fallen, or been blown. Cool, this Sunday morning of an oncoming autumn. Cloudless the sky. I knelt, careful of the glass, and watched Mammy Venus and the black hens that circled her blacker skirt.

With a long stick, the Seeress was scratching circles in the dirt before the henhouse door. As she did this, the hens fell still. Only the roosters roamed freely; and among these, only the one crowed, tossing back his comb to complain of the risen sun.

Three circles drawn—they were perhaps five, six feet in diameter—Mammy Venus quartered the first two and halved the third. She scratched . . . something into each compartment thusly made: a word, symbol or sign. I could not tell. Carefully, she set a single kernel of corn beside each mark. This done, she tucked the stick under her crabbed arm and shuffled toward the too-attentive hens. Drawing more feed from her pocket, she tempted the fowl forward, toward her.

And she struck. Sprang like a snake. O, what clucking came! In an instant she had in hand a scrawny specimen.

The chosen fowl was so perfectly black it shone blue beneath the sun. I was, I confess it, somewhat shamed; for these were the same hens that had so unnerved me when first I'd come through the hedge with Rosalie. So docile they were now, almost dumbly so; for the spared hens had quieted, and only the roosters scratched and scampered about.

Mammy Venus walked each circle, hen in hand. Whether she spoke or not, I cannot say. I heard nothing; and of course she wore that concealing veil. Finally, with speed that surely must have pained her, she threw high the hen. It came down in a flutter, all acluck; and immediately took to the circles, pecking along their perimeters.

From each circle the hen took a single kernel and returned to Mammy Venus; who picked her up. Slowly, she circled to read the hen-writ prophecy.

Frenzy; for Mammy Venus scattered the contents of her pocket. The hens scratched, smothered one another in search of food. Two flew at each other and met—apeck—in the air. On came the roosters; and soon dark feathers shone, slick with drawn blood. Mammy Venus stood watching the violent show.

O, but then she showed violence of her own; for:

She switched her coddling grip upon the hen she held, took it by its neck, and swung it. Swung it to snap its spine. Now its neck and head hung like the lace of an undone boot.

The hens and roosters scratched away the circles. For surety, Mammy Venus parted the pecking lot of birds, dragging her feet to erase all signs of her art. Center all, she stopped.

I swallowed hard when up, up the black veil tilted; and I knew I'd been seen.

14

Prophecy

It's no trick at all, the haunting of a house. This I learned that first morning in the Van Eyn manse; for, turning from the window through which I'd witnessed the Prophetess at work, I moved to another—which gave out onto the side street—and there saw a redheaded boy in short pants, staring up. Perhaps he'd seen me pass the window earlier. Perhaps he'd seen the lamplight of the night before. Regardless, he watched me now; and I must have appeared quite ghoulish: sleep-tossed, shocked, and sidling into view through that upper window of what was, surely, a most storied place.

We stood thusly—staring, immobile—for a long while; till finally the boy broke, and ran away. I smiled, and could not help pitying him; not for the sight he'd seen—it was only me, after all—but rather that he'd no one to corroborate the sighting. I hoped for his sake he'd keep his secret, and seek no converts. "Far easier for you that way," said I; my breath fogged the glass pane, sun-shimmering and thick with the dust of years.

So: I, too, was a ghoul. I'd fed the legend. At this I smiled; for I was a fool.

. . . To resume:

I descended, quit that chamber in search of simple things: a water closet, clean clothing, breakfast of some sort . . . ; and also my odd hostess, who'd already set about ordering our third day of action.

Curious, I tried the knobs of several shut doors of the second floor. Some were glass, and deeply faceted; others plumply white and porcelain. One came off in my hand as its twin fell to the floor on the far side of the door. There I stood, the knob like a picked fruit in my hand; and I thought of Eliza Arnold. Where was she now? Would I know her only by night, raising a wind to huff and suck and trouble the house and its tenants?

I pushed open the plank door to disclose a room equal in size to the one I knew. Indeed, it seemed to mirror that other room, save its windows gave out onto the front yard. Far smaller than the rear yard, the weed-grown front was bordered by pickets that sat like bad stitching. Beyond, there spread the street, sloping to gutters o'er which the occasional plank had been set. Across the street were stables: horseless, defunct; I knew it from first sight.

This room was full of furniture, all of it pushed into corners and draped in white cloth. A snowscape, it seemed: the peaks of a four-poster bed, the plains of low bureaus, and the valleys of cushionless chairs. I bumped a drifted mound of white: a rocking chair set to rocking, its song creaking away the silence. I lifted a sheet—loosing puffs of dust—and found two chandeliers, retired from their chains. The headboard of a narrow bed lay propped against a wall, its finials carved into pineapple shapes: the timeworn sign of Welcome. But who had felt, or could ever feel welcome in such a place?

Finally, I descended.

On a nail within the three-seat necessary there hung an *Enquirer* dated July the ninth. It had yellowed, but its mourning borders of black remained crisp. I read it—though it hung there for plainer purposes—and remember well the wondering headline: how might the Ruler of Events, it asked, have better shown His support of the American Experiment than by taking Two of its Authors at the Very Same Hour? Still it was conjecture (wrote the editor), but word had come from Quincy, Mass., that John Adams had expired in time with his successor, Jefferson, on the very day of Jubilee, the fiftieth Fourth of July. Surely these deaths bespoke some Heavenly Sanction, surely America was God-Marked. . . . *Or ghoul-marked,* thought I. And having done what needed doing, I returned to the house; wherein I found Rosalie.

She was seated at the dining-room table, fingering its runner of mourning crepe. She'd donned a bright red blouse for the day, though it appeared her skirt of brown homespun, as well as her stockings and shoes, had been worn through the night, wrinkled, baggy, and scuffed as they were. At the end of her long, thin braids she'd affixed two wide ribbons of a calico print; and do not think me petty, but to give a better picture of Rosalie Mackenzie I must needs say that the ribbons matched neither her blouse nor skirt.

She bade me good morning. I rejoined with the like, or rather I made to: before I could finish Rosalie reported in mournful tones, "Mammy Venus says you are to make your way southward."

"Does she now?" I stopped. I stood gripping (rather tightly, I suppose) the bowed back of a chair. Would I have reacted similarly had I heard this news from Mammy Venus herself? I think so, yes; for madness—mere anger, not madness of a lunatic order—was but my manifest emotion. That is, I no doubt *appeared* angered; but I was, in fact, disappointed, saddened. Profoundly so. True: I'd had no expectations of Richmond, and my hours there had shown me all species of strangeness; yet I'd hoped to stay. I'd hoped to know it as home.

Now here came word I was to leave. Was I surprised? I think not; for I'd heard well the revelations of the night before. There was a plan; and I was but a pawn within it. . . . Yes: I supposed I knew, deep down, that I'd be leaving Richmond. And experience had taught me I'd likely do so in haste, and hidden from the common eye.

"Yes," said Rosalie, "southward. Dearest Herculine, won't I miss you so?"

Rosalie had not meant to dominate me, nor in any way wound me with so graceless a pronouncement. Simply, she'd blurted out words as she'd heard them. And now was sad. And tearful. Genuinely so. There went my anger; but still I knew a bitterness, and I fear it flavored what next I said:

"And this directive has come from the hens, I presume."

On Rosalie's face no answer was written. She knew nothing of what I alluded to. This I knew for certain when suddenly her eyes caught light, her colorless lips twisted into a smile, and she said, "Hens cannot speak. They can only cluck. Silly Herculine!" Whereupon she tipped into hysteria, her laugh rather much for my morning ears.

"What I meant," I began, speaking more to curb her laughter than explain myself, ". . . I simply meant to say that this morning I saw—"

And with that there came a crashing noise. I fell silent; for that was Mammy Venus's intent, of course, when she, nearby but as yet unseen, tipped to the floor a vase of Eastern origin. (I'd see it later, a puzzle in porcelain, its pieces painted red, gold, and green.) I understood: Rosalie knew the hens as hens, and nothing more.

Duly chastised, I sat unspeaking. Rosalie, as sometimes

she did, set to humming. This was in no way tuneful; no: rather more like the thrum of a simple machine. And soon I heard that now familiar shuffling.

Into the room came Mother-of-Venus. In her right hand she held a bowl of delft, in which were mounded blue-shaded eggs. With her left hand she clutched to her breast—blessedly!—a change of clothes.

"Mornin'," said she. The veil met me squarely, and lingered too long: my eyes fell from it.

"Good morning." I was contrite. Wordlessly, I let it be known: with Rosalie present, I would measure my words.

"The hens," said Mammy Venus, "they done spared these in the night. For you." She motioned me to sit. I did; and she set the bowl before me. The eggs steamed, were still hot from boiling. The blue of the delft was nothing compared to the blues of the eggs themselves. I wondered if they'd been dyed; and worried that they hadn't.

"Can . . . can these be eaten?"

Rosalie giggled. With spindly fingers, she tried to stifle herself; in truth, she seemed about to stuff her fingers *in* her mouth. Happily, Mammy Venus precluded same by setting the folded clothes beside me and saying I'd Rosalie to thank for the warm iron they'd met.

Thank her I did; only to watch her flush, and bow her head as if I were a suitor come in search of her hand.

"Change of clothes is called fo', that so?"

"Yes indeed," I said, "thank you." I saw that these were my own clothes, taken from the *nécessaire*.

"We gots some water, too, warmin' up. Eat now, hear? Wash up after."

There we were: Rosalie and I on either side of the long table with its cloth of grief; and Mammy Venus at its head. Cruciform, it is, in my mind's eye.

Mammy Venus asked Rosalie to retrieve from the pantry

the loaf she'd find cooling there. This Rosalie did, obediently, as would a gundog.

With Rosalie away, Mammy Venus confirmed what already I knew: "The hens," said she, "they done spoke."

I stared down into the bowl of blue eggs. I raised a finger to one, felt the warmth of its smooth shell. I was hungry, yes, but didn't know if I'd be able to eat.

Mammy Venus rose and approached. In the time it took her, I felt tears welling. From the dry weight of her hands on my shoulders I would have flinched, a day earlier; but now her touch was welcome. I swallowed back my tears to ask, "Will I go alone?"

"No'm," said she.

And then she took an egg from the bowl and began rolling it, rolling it ever so gently atop the table, pressing it beneath her scarred palm. The shell gave. Cracks came. She passed the egg back to me for peeling. This I did; and doing so, asked further, "Will I . . . will I be with Celia?"

"Yes'm, you will."

Surprised I was, to feel the welling tears, to hear my hammering heart.

I split the first of the peeled eggs. The yolk was common: chalky, sun-colored, and delicious. The second egg I ate as well. But the third I peeled and proffered to Mammy Venus, watching as up it went behind the nodding veil.

15

Monumental Church

ROSALIE returned bearing a silver tray which badly wanted polishing. On it was a heel of bread, a deep-bellied spoon, and a bowl of steaming broth. From Duncan Lodge she'd brought a wedge of Cheddar, "deliciously old," which had come as a great wheel from the Mackenzies' Northern relations. I ate my fill. The off-color eggs had deterred me somewhat, but down it all went.

While eating, and with our speech proscribed by Rosalie's presence, I watched as Mammy Venus gathered up the eggshells. She held the lot of them in hand—calciferous chips and slivers and chunks—and I wondered would she read them, as she had the bones and hen-circles? I found I'd a thought to spare for the strangled black hen, whose fate had worsened of late: doubtless she sat aboil in some kettle (I won't say cauldron), her body and bones being poached apart, the body destined for a fricassee and the bones for that barrel of beetles belowstairs.

"You serve the Lord His due this day, like that good Missus Mackenzie ask you to?" Mammy Venus asked this of Rosalie.

"Yes, Mammy. I knelt upon waking, and I prayed." She added, in a whisper, "For Herculine"; but she did not turn to me.

"Yo' heart is large, chile."

"And I'll pray again when I meet Miss Jane at mass."

"Do that," said Mammy Venus. "Cain't hurt none, I s'pose."

Silence again; broken only when Rosalie received the day's orders:

"Ro, listen now." Rosalie went rigid, was rapt. Her eyes were wide, grotesquely so.

"Today," came the words from behind the veil, "we gots to sell that harp sits yonder," and Mammy Venus raised a stunted forefinger to point toward the wall, and the music room beyond it. Rosalie followed the finger, and stared too long at the wall. "That man sells pianos and such, down Cary Street; what his name?"

"Mr. Wickham, do you mean? Wasn't it he bought the piano, some years back? Surely it was, yes! Why, I remember—for it wasn't but two winters ago—. . . we asked Eddie to come, and he came, and the men—three men, plus Eddie—they took the pianoforte away." Rosalie turned to me, and continued: "They had to take it sideways through the parlor windows. A piano through a parlor window? I mean, Herculine, have you *ever*? And at night, no less; for Mammy, do you recall, you'd insisted that—"

"Chile," interrupted Mammy Venus, "seek out that same man that come then, for the piano. Tell him it's the harp that's goin', and quick-like. Cash money. I won't be bargainin' or barterin' nothin'. And I knows a fair price, too, hear?"

"Yes, Mammy."

"And it's this night or no night a'tall. When the clock say six. The front door won't have no bar, tell him. They's to come in, set cash atop this table"—she patted the hardwood—"and take the harp, hear? Simple as pie."

"Yes, Mammy."

Rosalie stood now at the dining-room door, tense as an arrow pulled back on its bow. "Stay, chile," said Mammy Venus, "and hear me: fix things at the lodge so's that you's here, this night, for Wickham and after. Come 'n go, if need be; but be here to watch over ol' Wickham and them ham-headed boys of his, make sure nothin' else leaves out this place. And be here when the clock lets fall eight chimes, hear?"

Rosalie tugged at her two braids and asked, "May I lie, Mammy?"

"You may, chile, this one time."

The nodding that followed set the girl's braids to bobbing. Her hands she clasped before her, at the height of her heart.

"And Ro, your Edgar, he be comin', too."

Rosalie stared. Her mouth opened to a rigid *O*, yet somehow she spoke: "But how? However will you . . . ? Eddie *never*—"

"Never you mind," said Mammy Venus, "and not a word 'bout it to the boy, hear? Be gone now, and do good."

"Yes, Mammy." And Rosalie left us, quick and simple. I waited for it, but she did not set the house bells to chiming. I heard only the screen door slam.

Two things I understood, then: Eliza Arnold would come again at eight, as she had the night before; and Edgar Poe steered clear of the Van Eyn house unless . . . unless commanded to come by some extraordinary means. And so I echoed Rosalie's question: "Yes, however will you—?"

"Never you mind, neither," came the response; the words were kindly, not at all censorious. In fact, Mammy laughed as she added, "That boy, he brusque-like, but still he do what his momma tells him."

It being Sunday, the bells of Richmond tolled *sans cesse*, calling congregants and marking the hours in quarters and halves. Thusly do I know that not an hour passed before I'd washed, changed, and quit the Van Eyn house by back door and bush.

I would make my way to church. Such was my inclination, bred of long years' habit; but also I'd been told to go by Mammy Venus. I'd begun to ask questions: Why southward? What else had the hens "to say"? Et cetera. But the Auguress had said, simply, "Monumental. There's a lesson waitin' on you there."

So it was I returned to Monumental Church, knowing the story of the fire, knowing the church had been built upon a pyre. Even the architecture of the place was somewhat redeemed, now I knew the story of the site.

I knew, too, that Mammy Venus had a plan; but she'd not speak of it that morning at table. Was she in league with Eliza Arnold? I thought so; but all I knew for certain was what I'd been told as I left the house: I was to avoid the market square; and Celia, particularly.

I understand, now, that the success of the plan depended on no Richmonder associating me with Celia. Therefore, I could not hurry to her ramshackle cell, as I was wont to do, now I knew her story. . . . O, but just because *I* knew Celia's story, that did not mean she knew it.

Enfin, I obeyed Mammy, skirted the market, and made my way to Monumental Church.

At Academy Square, I found chains closing off the streets. I'd seen these before a second house of worship as well; and as I stood before them their purpose came clear: they were in place to preclude any worshiper's being disturbed by hackneys or hansom cabs or, more pointedly, the hooves of the horses that drew them. Quite civilized, this; or so I thought as I stepped o'er the chains and approached the church by its less conspicuous side door; for mass had begun. I did not ascend the front stoop, and gave but a glance to the stony monument thereon, though now I'd have known several of the inscribed names.

With my hand upon the door's handle of brass—gone green from too much touch—I thought of the theater's side doors, and how the dead had fallen so near where I stood. For a moment . . . well, I thought I felt something. Nay, *saw* something. A blinding flash, it was; but this I quickly attributed to my eyes adjusting to the darkness within the church.

No one turned; rather, I saw no one turn and deem my entrance disruptive.

There sat the congregation in boxy pews. Above was a balcony, quite full. I thought then of the gallery high, high in the theater, where Mason and Fanny and Pleasants had sat. The second tier of the theater's boxes would have been on a level with the church's balcony. Below this would have been the Starkes' first-tier box, set quite near the present altar.

The altar. It wasn't the type to which I was accustomed. I recall only a high pulpit of Puritan design, from which an old man preached down upon the people.

His manner did not suit me, not at all. (That said, I admit it: already I'd come to prefer my churches empty.) Yet still, talentless as the man was—his oration flat, his rhetoric simple—I came soon to wonder if the effect of his sermon upon me was not somehow . . . bodily. In short: from my very first step into mass-crowded Monumental Church, I grew sickly. Ever more so; till finally it was all I could do to steal along the curved walls of the church to its fore, just inside the main door, and there excuse myself into a pew to sit, to steady myself.

The wooden door of the pen-like pew slammed shut behind me, and thusly did I cause the ruction I'd sought to avoid. Indeed, center all, from where he sat with his long, Hessian-booted legs in the aisle, a gray-haired elder turned, with undue drama. At this, all turned. Toward me. Even the priest, the preacher, the pulpiteer gave pause.

There were whispers; and from within the sussuration I drew—like a splinter from skin—a single name: Marshall. John Marshall. Indeed, it was he; and I say now: if one is to be judged, then let it be by the land's foremost.

O, but then, beset as I was, I could not care that I'd disturbed the service; for truly, I was ill.

My brain was fevered. Within me one thought resounded, as though it were a clapper and my skull a bell. As I sat—sweating, shivering, shaking, knowing the woman beside me sought to help me yet unable to answer her—that thought devolved to a voice. One voice. Its words—if words they were—I could not discern; but its begging tone was all too clear. Then the one voice shattered like glass—inconceivable that no congregant could hear this—and there came many voices in its stead. Male, female; and the most plaintive cries of children. All of them dying; dead. Burning; burned.

And trapped beneath me where I sat. In the church's cellar. The lot of them, entombed.

Somehow I mastered myself. Opening my eyes, I feared I'd see the theater's dead. I did not. I saw only that I'd disturbed those seated nearest to me; yet, thankfully, the service had resumed. I accepted from my kindly neighbor her kerchief of silk, and with it mopped my sodden brow. I deferred all other offers of assistance, and did so as demurely as I could. What I mean to say is this: still the dead sounded in my head, and no doubt I all but shouted when spoken to in churchly whispers. Indeed, I saw a woman many pews distant turn and twist her thin lips into a puckering *shush*.

I had to absent myself, and quickly.

Yet when I made to rise . . . well, I found, confusedly, that still I was seated. I'd moved not at all. Again, I willed myself up, up. But my limbs were not my own, and still I sat.

Tears came streaming, and I could not even raise the kerchief to my cheeks. These were not tears of sadness, but rather pain. . . . O, what a headache came!

Still the voices spoke: words or nonsense, I cannot say; but I knew what it was the dead sought: egress. Now.

I knew then a fear greater than any I'd known before, a fear too great for earthly measure. Yet within that deathly din I congressed with the dead. *O, but how was I to heed their wants, do what they willed?*

Understand: I'd met the dead before, yes; but never had they affected me so. Was it the *mass* of them that sickened me? Had they a strength born of their numbers, of the suffering of so many?

Disruption be damned, I'd launch myself from Monumental Church by all means necessary. I clutched at her who'd proffered her kerchief, meaning to say, *Walk me from this place*. What I said, in actuality, I cannot here record; but it had its effect, and soon I stood, aided by two men who'd hurried from a neighboring pew. Sons, I presume, of the kindly "M.S.," whom I'd never know by more than her initials, monogrammed onto the kerchief she'd pressed upon me.

I heard one of the men make horrid reference to my eyes; but I knew not what he meant. I could see clearly, though still the headache raged. I feared that if I reached to touch my throbbing head I'd find my skull cracking, my every sense seeping forth.

Those abetting men must have been strong; for I removed from Monumental though my muscles were not my own. My heart sputtered and lurched like a coal-choked engine. My step was slapping and graceless. I felt lesser muscles fall to twitching: my eyes blinked wildly, my fingers unfurled from fists I'd not meant to make. My tongue pressed itself to the roof of my mouth. And my sex went rigid, showed its shape behind my squared, four-button fly.

High in the pulpit the preaching had stopped, and the black-robed man looked down upon me not unkindly. Neither were the celebrants unduly cruel. I watched mutely as the mouths of men moved, offering assistance. But the two sons of M.S. had me, each with an arm hooked under mine, and we progressed, sloppily but surely, toward the church's main door. Where my situation worsened:

For, as we stepped o'er the entombed I suffered a most terrific blow, akin to a horse's kick; and this lifted me some inches off the floor. Not once, but repeatedly; till it must have seemed I'd determined to dance from the holy precinct in Saint Vitus–style.

Glad those men were, I'm sure, when finally we made our way to the far side of the church's door; for there I sank against that great four-sided monument. Well I recall that cold stone against my cheek. How long I sat thusly, I cannot say; but in time my strength returned. My senses, too; for the dead fell silent as I raised my fingers to the inscribed stone.

Could it be that the dead wanted naught but to be known? For though they were still present, they'd calmed; but still there was no peace beneath me.

Was it I who'd riled them? If so, how had I entered the church Saturday without like event? Perhaps it was the mass that maddened them. Or the combining of both: a witch present at the reading of age-old rites.

. . . I dismissed my escorts. I said that I'd a most unfortunate malady, and was prone to fits. I said I'd sit out the spell, that soon a friend would come. As indeed one did:

For I stood when I was able, and walked the stone's four sides. On the south-facing side I found the one name: MASON.

With a forefinger I traced the cut letters. And I heard myself speak words of apology. A far greater surprise it was to hear what next I said to the dead: to Mammy's Mason I made a promise: to save his baby sister.

16

The Spirits of the Dead

I LEFT the church. I descended to Broad Street. I raised my face to the buttery sun, smelled the salted air, and listened. Once I knew my direction to be true, I took to those declivitous streets and coursed toward the river, as would rain freshly fallen.

There I sat, through to the dimming of the day; for I'd not walk about the city and risk encountering Edgar, or Rosalie as she ran her errands; and I'd been told to keep from Celia. I worried where I sat, and with good reason: I'd just met the disquieted dead. I'd learned I was to run. Was I to run on forever, knowing no home and doing the bidding of ghouls?

Warm beneath the westering sun, and lulled by riversound, I acceded to a state midway between panic and prayer. I soothed myself by watching swans and their cygnets, all downy and dumb. Gulls cut the silty air. Clouds were stretched thin on the light wind. . . . The water rippling in the wake of the swans, the gulls angling above, the clouds in their formations . . . : were these signs that Mammy Venus might see? Was the day itself a book I hadn't the eyes to read? *Pish,* said I, telling myself I'd read too many Books, had heard too much talk of divining dreams, of sisters who read the dregs of teacups and the slick entrails of birds, split and splayed upon hot rocks. *Pish,* indeed.

In time I determined that seven would be the hour of my return to the Van Eyn house; thusly I'd not involve myself in the business of the harp, yet I'd have time enough to prepare myself for the coming of Eliza Arnold at eight. Eliza Arnold and her children, mind.

Pondering how best to "prepare" for what awaited—a séance; or at least the strangest of soirees, with some of us living and others dead, some of us "sighted" and others blind . . . *enfin,* this would be no parlorish night of pinochle and claret punch— . . . pondering, yes, I came to appreciate the lesson of Monumental Church. It was not that I could see or sense the dead; for already I knew this. Rather, Mammy Venus had meant to remind me that others could not. Others, such as the congregants who'd sat unmoved; but more particularly, the Poes.

Returning to the house, I found candles and lamps set about: the Dutchman's manse was aglow. And silent. The marble of the foyer seemed a frozen lake, its veins showing as cracks beneath the great chandelier; which had been lowered on its chain and lit some hours past, so now its candles wept both wax and light. Too, the front door had been unbarred. And the harp was gone. On the dining table I found half-eagle coins, spilling from a leather purse.

I returned to the foyer; for there sat the cellar door.

It appeared open, slightly so. Would I try it, see if . . . ? It was then he spoke and I turned, nay spun. *There:* on the stairs: beneath the black Madonna: the glittering gray eyes of Edgar Poe.

"It was you, was it not?" asked he.

My heart was slow to recover from the start. Seen through the finely turned spindles of the banister, Edgar seemed a caged thing. I stepped to where I could see him at length, asprawl upon the fifth or sixth step.

"All the city is speaking of the traveler who took a fit in Monumental Church. It was you, was it not?"

I owed no answer, and so gave none. Instead I asked, "Have you come with your sister?"

He smiled. "I knew it," said he. "I knew it was you."

"Is Rosalie here?"

"Is not madness to great wit always allied? Yes, she's here. Down there," said he with a nod toward the cellar door.

"She's with—"

"*Nigrum, nigrius, nigro.* Yes."

"Why aren't you—"

"The question you ought to ask is why ever am I here at all, in this infernal abode. *That* is the question."

"Bon. D'accord," said I. "Why ever are you—?"

"I don't know," said Edgar. "*Disons que* . . . let us say that . . . that I am here, period; and let that suffice." With this Edgar drew himself up tightly, knees to chest. Around his knees he wrapped his arms. His rolled sleeves showed the ropy muscles of his forearms. His fingertips were dirty; no: night-dark with ink. So, too, did his lower lip bear a smear of indigo.

"Was it Rosalie told you to come?"

Edgar sported a long scarf of brown wool, and one end of this he took up and threw o'er his shoulder. Leaning to set his sharp chin atop his knee, he said through clenched teeth, "I do not take orders from my sister, monsieur."

"No," said I, "I suppose not." I gestured to the cellar door, and took a step toward it. "Are we to descend?"

"No," said Edgar; yet still I moved nearer the door, and was reaching to push upon it, to spring it open (if open it was), when Edgar repeated, rather more emphatically, "No! We . . . we are to wait, I believe. . . . Yes, I believe we are to wait."

He'd stood to speak; but now he retook his pose upon the stair.

His face showed the want of sleep. His eyes were weighty, dark, and bagged beneath. Though his hair was disheveled, still that dark forelock fell to its place.

At the best of times, neither Edgar nor I was inclined to idle chatter; and—this being decidedly *not* the best of times—no chatter came. O, how I willed a clock to strike, a stair to creak, Eliza's foul wind to rise.

Instead, improbably, there came a poem; for, like a duelist drawing his weapon, Edgar took from a hip pocket a sheet he'd folded into quarters. With confidence he read: confidence in his art, I suppose; and confidence born of his supposing that I cared to hear it applied.

(Though I've both an ear and an affinity for poetry, it is not from memory that I transcribe what follows. Rather, Rosalie, for some years to follow, would keep me subscribed to the *Southern Literary Messenger;* and therein I'd read the poem at a later date, and with a shudder recall it from its first recitation.)

As preface, Edgar said the poem had been "astew" for some time; but the night prior—"whilst asleep," said he—it assumed its "eternal" shape; which is this:

Thy soul shall find itself alone
'Mid dark thoughts of the gray tomb-stone;
Not one, of all the crowd, to pry
Into thine hour of secrecy.

"Very nice," said I, making to applaud.

"*Attendez!*" said he, hotly. "I'm not done."

Be silent in that solitude,
Which is not loneliness—for then
The Spirits of the Dead, who stood
In life before thee, are again
In death around thee, and their will
Shall overshadow thee; be still.

If only he knew, thought I, who it was stood around him, overshadowed him; and how near it was to the hour of her coming.

On he went:

The night, though clear, shall frown,
And the stars shall not look down
From their high thrones in the Heaven
With light like hope to mortals given,
But their red orbs, without beam,
To thy weariness shall seam
As a burning and a fever
Which would cling to thee for ever.

Now are thoughts thou shalt not banish,
Now are visions ne'er to vanish;
From thy spirit shall they pass
No more, like dew-drop from the grass.

I heard steps upon the cellar stairs. Edgar heard them, too; for he sped to the poem's end, his voice suddenly reedy and thin.

The breeze, the breath of God, is still,
And the mist upon the hill
Shadowy, shadowy, yet unbroken,
Is a symbol and a token.

How it hangs upon the trees,
A mystery of mysteries!

Edgar, *le pauvre*. He barely made it through his recitation. With the footfall rising, rising, he looked to me not for appraisal of his poem—quickly he tucked the paper away—but rather for comfort, for company, for consolation.

The hall panel popped open.

Here came Rosalie, lamp in hand.

When Mammy Venus showed herself—"shadowy, shadowy, yet unbroken"—and shuffled o'er the marble to stand beside Rosalie at the foot of the stairs, silent all the while, Edgar. . . . Well, Edgar had all but pressed himself flat to the curved wall of the stairwell. He'd have hidden behind the black Madonna, had her niche been roomy enough. I watched as he clasped that scarf to his face, covering his mouth and nose. Still his eyes glittered, but now they seemed run through with some ancient ore.

There we were: the oddest of assemblies. Yet not all were present.

Then: the first of eight chimes fell; and O, how well I recall the fall of seven more.

Now was the hour of Eliza's coming. And slowly, slowly, with increasing strength and surety, a breeze came aborning. A breeze that was not "the breath of God."

17

La Muse Malade

TWO tongues were spoken: those of the living and the dead.

Mammy Venus and I heard all present, as did Eliza Arnold; but Edgar and Rosalie could not hear their mother. Neither could they see her; yet somehow they knew her, of that I'm certain. Edgar, especially.

Eliza's scent was not as strong as it had been earlier; for she came not at full force. She was . . . dissolvent; so much so that she hung behind Edgar, quite near, and it seemed he knew only a sudden, inexplicable chill, and that death-hinting scent against which he breathed into his scarf. To call him a coward would be unfair, patently so; yet his actions must bear the adjective *cowardly,* for so they were: he trembled, and his cheeks were alternately blood-flushed and blanched. Finally, he withdrew as best he could, tightened his body into a ball, there upon the stairs, and looked not at

Mammy Venus—it was to her that he attributed the chill and the stink—nor at Rosalie, but at me. All the while he sought only the night, and the fastest path to liquor.

When first she'd come, Eliza Arnold had shown a minimum of attributes. The wind had risen, yes, and the odd window was heard to rattle; but that was all. Perhaps she'd come earlier, before my return, and had bided her time in the top floors of the house. Perhaps, coming as she did—faintly, vaporously, holding but tenuously to the body that had been hers in life—she hadn't strength enough to rile the night: she brought no storm. Nonetheless, she made an entrance: with the clock striking eight, and the four of us in place, she appeared at the top of the stairs and hovered there.

I did not take the actress in fully; for I was too conscious of my gaze. Mammy Venus's eyes were veiled: if she looked to Eliza, no one would know it. Edgar's eyes of moonstone were yet trained on me; and I thought it best to return his worried, wondering stare. As for Rosalie, she turned her gaze this way and that, and found no focus.

It was Edgar who spoke first. Raising an ink-tipped finger to point at Mammy Venus, he said, "Scented of the sepulcher, she's always been. . . . it is air that has seeped from an opened tomb, I swear it! And I cannot abide it. I cannot!"

"But abide it you must, my darling," said Eliza Arnold.

Edgar had not heard her, not as I had; this was clear. But still he fell silent, and backed up the stairs slowly, away from Mammy Venus and toward his unseen mother. At this Eliza smiled, and descended nearer her beloved. Just when she seemed about to speak again, however, Edgar erupted; thusly:

"Rose, come from there! Step away from her. Come from that death-stinking thing."

Rosalie made a shushing sound. "Eddie, Eddie," said she, with no fear in her tone, "I smell something, yes; but it is *not*

Mammy Venus. It is not! I know it. It is, perhaps . . . well, the Harvies have recently plowed, have they not? Or perhaps—"

"Idiot. *Idiot!* Never have the three of us been together," said Edgar to his sister, "without the coming of that smell. If it's turned earth, then it's earth that has been turned by worms. Vile, it is. *Vile!* And never have you conceded what is plain: it rises from that Negress!" Again Edgar raised an accusing finger to point down the stairs to Mammy Venus, standing now at the first step, with Rosalie beside and slightly behind her. As for Eliza, she descended to where her face was level with the great chandelier; and I saw her too clearly. On her face was a commiserating look to mock the black Madonna's. Down she floated, nearer Edgar. Would she surrender to some maternal urge and touch him? If so, would he know it?

. . . Maternal? Hardly; for all the while Eliza Arnold did not look upon her daughter. Not once did she deign to regard, address, or even acknowledge Rosalie. Not even when the girl spoke, as then she did:

"Darling Edgar," said she, edging out from behind Mammy Venus, "I've spent countless hours here, have I not?"

"You have," answered Edgar, "against all good sense."

"Well then, I can assure you, that scent—and I smell it, too, I do—it comes not from Mammy but . . ."

"But what? Speak!"

The tears welling in Rosalie's wide eyes were rendered diamantine by the lamp held high in her trembling hand. Still, she resumed: "Eddie," said she, "the smell—and forgive me, but I must say it, I must—the smell comes only when you do."

This Edgar dismissed with a sharp hiss, as a cat dismisses a dog. And he let go his madman's laugh, adding, "Worse has been said of me, *ma soeur*."

"And worse be comin' on you, too, lessen you mend your mean ways." Mammy Venus had tried to hold her tongue and only now did she fail. Too, she may have wanted to change the subject; for surely she did not want the siblings to argue the question of the stench at length. After all, she knew who it was stank, as did I. And there the culpable party was, looking down upon us all.

"Fie on you, nigger," was Edgar's rejoinder to Mammy Venus.

"Eddie, no!" pled Rosalie.

Edgar stood then, and it seemed certain he'd bolt. Down the stairs and out of the house. Somehow—I knew not how, of course—we needed him; and so it was Mammy Venus who spoke, saying (to Eliza Arnold):

"Speak to him. Speak to the boy."

Rosalie and Edgar both wheeled on me, thinking it was I who'd been addressed. The veil turned, too. And then I knew: I had to speak, say something under cover of which Eliza could do her dark work.

In French, I rambled on. Couldn't we all get along, lay all blame aside, et cetera? Meanwhile, Eliza drifted down to Edgar, bent, and began whispering in his ear. I pitied the boy, huddled there, so cold, the abhorred stench at its strongest. Still I spoke on; but I might as well have sung "La Marseillaise"; for Edgar heard not a word I said.

What did his mother—his *muse malade*—say to him? I know not. She whispered, as I say; and her words went unheard by all but Edgar Poe.

Whatever her words, Eliza Arnold spoke to some effect. Edgar sat stunned; and was, henceforth, naught but nods and acquiescence. We'd won him to our side; albeit mysteriously, meanly, and by the machinations of his dead mother.

As for Eliza Arnold, well. . . . She all but bowed before moving to straddle the banister. Her lips were a sickly twist: a smile, she'd have called it. She looked down at me; for she knew I strained not to stare, lest her children deem me odder than already they did. But stare I did, yes; and with revulsion saw Eliza Arnold spread her stick-like legs and thrust her pelvis out and down, toward me, *at* me, flaunting again her wasted sex. So coldly blue she appeared. Faint, she was; though not so faint I could not see her for what she was: a mix of trollop and *tragédienne.*

I cursed her in French: *"Abhorrée! Démon!"*

Edgar looked to me. Doubtless he thought I'd taken his side and cursed Mammy Venus. From this confusion I extricated myself, somehow, with words in the tongue he loved. I begged his forbearance. I'd said we'd work to do. "The Lord's work," said I. I don't know why I said it—where was the Lord in all this?—but when I did, well . . .

Eliza Arnold threw back her head and let loose a laugh. The resultant chill that blew through the foyer—her breath, was it?—set to tinkling the crystals of the chandelier. I thought then that the actress had betrayed herself. Good, thought I; let Edgar know her, see some sign of her. O, what a sickly pietà would ensue! . . . *Mais non.* Soon I withdrew my wish; for I wouldn't will such dark knowledge upon Edgar, nor upon Rosalie. (There are spectral burdens no mere mortal should suffer.)

Myself, I ignored Eliza's show as best I could. This was not difficult to do; for the light was dim, and Eliza dared not loose too big a bluster upon us. And that decrepit cologne was sufferable as long as she did not draw from the night what it was would render her stronger; be it moisture, moonstrength, or whatnot.

Finally, I turned to Mammy Venus. By the tilt of her veil I saw she watched Eliza, waiting. But I drew her attention with a cough, or some such trick, and to the slow-turning veil conveyed my message: *May we please begin this planning, the sooner to conclude?*

Mammy consented with a nod; and spoke:

"Listen here. There's a slave girl sits in the marketplace pen. We gonna spare her. Save her. Set her to runnin' befo' her mas'r passes and she's sold down into Sugar or falls to kin that's like to use her hard."

Rosalie was alight, shining more brightly than her lamp.

For his part, Edgar stared down at Mammy Venus. He lowered his woolly, breath-wet scarf to ask, "What do I care about the plight—or the flight—of some ashen wench?" . . . O poor, hateful Edgar Poe, with a viper's tongue atwist within his mouth. Indeed, he chose his words with devilish facility: "ashen," he'd said: to connote fire.

"You don't care nothin' fo' the girl, that much I knows. You talk yo' verses and such-like, but yo' heart is cobbled of coin, just like yo' daddy's."

Edgar seethed. "John Allan is not my father," said he.

Mammy Venus leaned nearer the boy, setting a slippered foot upon the first stair. "Proof of yo' better blood is what's wanted, right here, right now."

"Proof?"

"Yes'm. . . . Show me, show *us* you ain't no Allan. Show us you better'n him."

"You're a wise one, woman," said Eliza Arnold. Her breasts went pendulous as she bent forward, whispering to Mammy Venus, "Well done. You've hung before my colt the one carrot that will cause him to run: his hatred of John Allan."

The actress turned to address me whilst Edgar weighed his two hatreds—Mammy Venus and John Allan—one against the other. "Had you anything to do with this ever thickening plot, witch? If so, bravo. Or rather, brava."

"Speak," said Edgar, finally. "What it is you want of me." He addressed Mammy Venus; but the next words heard were mine:

"Cooperation," said I, surprised I'd done so. "When and how it's wanted."

Edgar considered. His thoughts, I'd imagine, featured words such as *slave, fugitive, infamy* . . . ; and no doubt he conjured a red-faced and shamed John Allan. He cared not to offer proof of his truer heart, his better blood; but he'd cut John Allan if he could. There remained but one point on which to satisfy himself.

"La, yes, boy," said Mammy, anticipating Edgar's question, "there's coin to be had."

I thought of the off-sold harp.

"Cooperation," said I, again, hoping to spur Edgar to assent, and thus hurry the night to its end.

"What stake have you in all this, *mon ami*?" asked Edgar. The French was spoken snidely; for now Edgar knew to whom I was allied.

I gave no answer. Edgar stared. In the silence, I heard Eliza Arnold: "You'll have his cooperation, when and how it's wanted. Leave the means to me. . . . I've an idea; and I'll broach it in the night, *this* night. Now, send him from here."

Thus prompted, I said to Edgar, "Never you mind"; and added, cruelly, "Go now, poet. And take care to listen for more night-whispers." Worse: I quoted back a line he'd read from his "Spirits of the Dead." Said I, "'Those who stood in life before thee, are again in death around thee.' Now, *vas-y*. Go from here!"

And go he did. Indeed, he came scurrying down the stairs. It was I whom he avoided now, leaving a wide berth between us, as one would when walking behind an ornery horse. And I admit it: at this I smiled.

Edgar told, nay commanded Mammy Venus to send word of what she wanted with Rosalie. Opening the unbarred door, he turned to add, "And send coin enough to secure it." Whereupon he kicked the iron bar from where it stood propped beside the door. It fell to the marble with a crash and clang that caused poor Rosalie to fumble her lamp. Its chimney tipped to the floor. Red glass shone like blood at her feet. And she, holding open flame, ran to her brother, who raised a sturdy arm; into this she ran, such that I heard the breath rush from her lungs.

Mammy Venus neared Edgar, and quickly, too. I worried what she'd do. From Eliza Arnold there came only, "Tsk, tsk."

"Go now," said I to Edgar, stepping between him and Mammy.

Rosalie stood upon the red glass, weeping. Mammy Venus took her into the darkness of her dress.

It was I who barred the door behind Edgar.

When finally her breath came regularly, and her tears had all fallen, Rosalie went home. We'd consoled her as best we could; and I thought it sweet that she'd brook no criticism of her brother. This Eliza Arnold feigned not hearing, though she hung directly overhead. She'd floated from the stairs to the chandelier, and there began to pass her hands through the candle flame. I stole a glance up at her, and saw she evinced no pain; but the act did add something . . . unpleasant to her usual death-essence.

With Rosalie gone—smiling, she was, when finally she left, going out her usual way and setting the servants' bells to ringing—Eliza, still playing upon the fire, opined, absently, "I wish I'd burned." It seemed to be scarring—that carrion that clung to the bones of wrist and forearm—even as she asked, "Where's the pain in burning? I feel no pain at all."

"La, woman," said Mammy Venus, her veil upturned, "how I wish you could. How I *wish* it, 'deedy yes."

Eliza Arnold, observing the effects of flame upon her flesh, ignored Mammy Venus; and the latter soon returned to the working of her plan:

"What you gonna have that boy do?" asked Mammy Venus. "Left to it, he won't act in no int'rest but his own."

"Fear not," said Eliza. She hovered above us still. Her feet hung at the level of my head; and from them I backed away. "I'll . . . I'll inspire him. It's a distraction you seek, is it not?"

"It is. Tomorrow. At the noon hour," said Mammy Venus. "We need the townfolk turned away from the runnin', hear?"

"Tomorrow?" I echoed.

"Yes, chile: tomorrow." And thusly did I learn when it was I'd leave Richmond. *Flee* Richmond, I should say.

Not long after this revelation, a wind rose within the house, and in the foyer the death-scent strengthened and swirled. Down from on high came Eliza, holding to a nearly full form. Said she to me, "I've a bone to pick with you, witch."

"I hope it's not one of your own," said I.

Mammy Venus rumbled with laughter.

Eliza Arnold had learned of Edgar's commission, and accused me of conspiring with her boy. Soon, said she, he'd have funds enough to actuate a plan from which she'd failed to dissuade him: he would quit Richmond. This Eliza did not want; a fact made plain by her rant.

She berated me with what seemed a prepared speech. With the coins he'd gotten from me—from Frances Allan, in fact—Edgar was slowly cobbling the road he'd take north, for Boston was his dreamed-of destination: a city of lettered men, men who knew the worth of a poem well-wrought.

"Stay away from him," warned Eliza Arnold, "or your dark amour will rot in her pen. . . . Do you know what I could arrange when Tolliver Bedloe 'passes,' as the living so unctuously say? Why, I could have your precious Cecile—"

"Celia," said I. "Her name is Celia."

"I care not what the wench's name is! I say I could arrange for her to be sold into a most determined concubinage." Eliza set to scratching her pudenda with the back side of her fist; and, as earlier, the liquefaction of her slow-rotting self flowed from the snagged and torn skin. A nut brown effluence, it was. She ripped the ruddy lips of her sex, yet did not flinch, did not drop her eyes from mine. "Tolliver Bedloe has a brother. Did you know? Some years younger, he is, this Sebastian Bedloe; but already he's discovered he prefers the blade to the brand. And I could easily—"

"The Devil knows you by name, don't he, woman? La,

yes, I know he do." Mammy Venus stood now between Eliza and myself, and spoke on: "Go from here, ghoul. Fetch that boy of yours from out the grogshop befo' he pickle himself so's he won't be of no use on the morrow. Go now."

"You stay from him," said Eliza Arnold, again. She was quite near me now, as if somehow she'd passed *through* Mammy Venus. "Stay from him, do you hear?" It was then I learned that Eliza Arnold did in fact breathe: I smelled and felt it, cold against my chin. Perhaps it was the wind and water, and the soul-matter of which she was composed. Perhaps it was naught but the air that trailed her from the tomb. Regardless, there issued from her a force as putrid and repellent as she.

I nodded and said, "I've no stake in your Edgar's future. Let him do what he will, once he's helped us." And I wondered: did she not know I'd be gone from Richmond before the sun set again?

. . . Blessedly, Eliza Arnold set off in search of her son.

Leaving the chandelier's candles to burn to blackness, Mammy Venus and I quit the foyer and descended to the cellar. There we traded Rosalie's naked lamp for a most welcome fire, which soon I'd stoked to a roar.

That night I catalogued for Mammy Venus the contents of the *nécessaire*. With questions, she assessed the import of all I'd brought from France. I knew not why. But once she'd made plain our plan, I understood: I'd not be taking any of my things with me. Rather, I'd have to choose among them, sparingly; and consign the rest to the care of Mammy Venus. For a fugitive I'd be; and fugitives must run lightly.

18

The Night-mare

HOURS passed as we sat within that cellar. We spoke, yes; but not idly so. Mammy Venus conceded some points of the plan, but she said, too, that it would be best to set the pieces of the puzzle in place one at a time. There was no arguing the point; and I suspected she was right. After all, I was . . . unsteadied, at best; and the whole of the scheme would surely have overwhelmed me, had I heard it then. So it was that we tasked ourselves instead with a witch's inventory:

Scattered on the dirt floor of the cellar, and atop Mammy's table of deal, were the contents of the *nécessaire*. She sat chewing her hemp, fingering certain things and asking questions now and again: Did I prefer men's dress? (I did, then.) Who was it I'd left behind? (I spoke of Sebastiana only.) Was it true that French witches busied themselves with the boiling down of baby's fat? It came clear to me then, with that question: somehow Mammy Venus had been reading in our *Books of Shadows*—Sebastiana's or mine; the former bound in black leather, the latter red. This I asked her.

"La, chile," answered she, "I gots no letters."

"So then," said I, without guile, "if you cannot read, how . . . ?" But I had an answer before I'd voiced the question; and I said it aloud: "Rosalie. Rosalie? . . . *Rosalie!*"

The black veil tilted forward, affirmatively; and Mammy Venus clarified: "I knows some words by sighten' 'em; but yes'm, it's Rosalie been readin' out the rest."

"But these," said I, taking up the two Books, "these are not meant to be . . . these are not suited for . . ."

"La, chile, rest yo'self. Ro, she think it's stories you collectin' and writin' up, all fancy-like. She—po' chile—she be readin' and readin' and never once will she raise up that head of hers to wonder what's real and what's worse 'n real. Ain't much real to Rosalie, hear? No'm: real and unreal: two parts of a land with no borders drawn; and *that's* where Rosalie wanders. Always has. And those books of yours, they ain't no ways worse than them stories that whoreson brother of hers been teasin' her with since she could crawl. . . . No'm; don't you worry 'bout my Rosalie. You leaves that to me, hear?"

"But you and she, you've read through—"

"No, chile, not all the way through. La, look at there! Them books is big. But we *gonna* read 'em through, 'deedy yes. They's got answers I been waitin' on a long while."

"But how," I began, ". . . if I'm to leave tomorrow, how will you manage to . . ."

Again, I knew the answer before it came: I'd not be taking the Books.

I protested. O yes, there were tears and pleas; for those Books were all I had of Sebastiana, and the sole record of my escape from the convent school, and . . . *alors,* they were all I had to learn from, all I had to anchor me in this new world.

"Herculine," said Mammy Venus, "La, Herculine." She

made a great effort to pronounce my name properly. Too, her tone was broadly sympathetic, and sincere; and I knew she sought not to rob me of the Books. She spoke on; and I listened to the points and promises she made.

Firstly, asked she, how was I to run with two volumes in tow, each as heavy as a six-month pig?

Secondly, she needed the Books as much as I did. This she swore. Further, she proposed a trade:

"Look here, chile," said she, "I ain't in the habit of gatherin' up somethin' for nothin'. No'm. I's gonna read, or leastways hear what secrets is writ within"—she placed her palms upon the Books, which we'd set on that table of deep-nicked pine—"and I's gonna share with you in return, hear?" Her voice fell to a whisper as she added what was plain:

"I knows some things, too, witch."

She, with Rosalie's aid, would write me. ("La, you ever seen the pen that chile pushes? Her writin', I mean? Pretty as a picture, it is; and careful as a clock. But you think *I*'s slow? La, I says to her, 'Ro, what you usin' for ink. Molasses? Hurry on. Hurry on.' But it ain't no use, never and no ways.") So: we'd stay in touch by post. In time, the Books—both of them—would be returned to me. Such was the plan.

The matter of the Books settled—and I was told in no uncertain terms that it was—Mammy Venus said I'd best decide what it was I could not live without. The rest of my things I could reclaim in time.

"When I return to Richmond, do you mean?"

She hesitated; and finally said, "I looked for that, chile, I did. But I cain't see it."

"Have you seen where it is I will go? Have you seen . . . ?" O, but even then I knew to cut short the questions, lest answers come: I did not want to know what she'd seen.

Mammy Venus said I'd no need to choose those things most convertible to cash; for she'd sold the harp, and had supplementary funds besides. Too, she knew of the bracelet's sale to Frances Allan.

I was left to inventory my few possessions. Mammy Venus took to her cot, eventually; and I watched the slow and painful process by which she did so. Finally, she lay at rest, her veil in place, smoothed atop her chest. Her hands she tucked into her pockets after she'd drawn forth a last lozenge of honeyed hemp. This she'd set upon her tongue as though it were the Host.

"The risin' day looks to be long," said she, counseling rest.

I stumbled to a sagging cot in another of the cellar's tiny rooms. I'd taken up the bare lamp and turned low its light; now I set it on the milking stool beside the bed. I'd lie upon the moldy mattress for but a few minutes. A respite. A nap, perhaps; but nothing more.

I'd dreamed that I'd fallen from the *Ceremaju,* and was drowning.

Half waking, I found the cellar as dark and silent and cold as the deep sea of my dream. My wide-opened eyes showed me nothing. And I feared drawing any breath at all, though my body begged of me, *Breathe, breathe!* A suffocating weight—water; surely it was water—had settled atop my chest. But the weight was not water.

. . . It was Eliza Arnold. And here was wakefulness of the worse sort.

Indeed, Eliza's weight was akin to water; for wasn't she made of same, and much mystery besides? And having her atop me—atop me, yes—brought a smothering sensation akin to flooded lungs; or so I imagine. She was not at full form—and so she only half reeked of rot—but still she'd come with shape and weight enough to wake me.

As the dark dissolved—none too readily; for I'd slept a long while, and the lamp had drunk away its oil—I saw Eliza by star- and moonlight. In a naked crouch. Atop my chest. I say again she was but half solid; and I saw her as through a theatrical scrim of gauze, felt her grow weightier as she took shape.

Both fear and the actress's stance stilled me. Soon I knew I could breathe; and I did so, deeply, fearing not water but Eliza's redolence and . . .

Stay; let me say this: Sleep does sometimes slip from us in a watery way, *non*? And waking, we do sometimes reclaim ourselves slowly. . . . Well, I could not wake, not fully; for I suffered then a want of sense, a want of self and . . .

To explain: I inventoried my self as earlier Mammy and I had inventoried the trunk. I knew my innards by their state of upset: my stomach swirled like a drain. And now here were my eyes, outstaring, and a nose and mouth resisting the sudden stink, and legs one and two at length—from wriggling toes up to my hips—and arms, and hands. And on the hands fingers, which then I twitched. First the right hand, then the left; but I ran afoul of sense when I found upon myself a . . . a supernumerary limb: a third hand.

Set upon my forehead with its fingers curling down to shadow my right eye. I willed it to move: nothing. Perhaps . . . perhaps it was one of the two hands I knew, *my* hands, which now seemed not my own because it slept on, pinned and needled from its odd positioning. A not uncommon experience, this.

But no:

For just then Eliza Arnold explained, smiling to say:

"I've come to lend a hand."

She played the line for laughs; but the only laughter heard was hers. It tolled like a rusted bell; and resounded the more as she took on weight.

With a prickly fist she reached up and tipped the hand onto my face. It—cold, hard, blue, with black hairs and swelled joints—tumbled to the hollow of my throat. As if to strangle me. But there it lay. Lifeless. Dead, to put it precisely; dead and dissevered from its owner at two, perhaps three inches up the wrist.

Explanations and apologies were in order, surely. The former came grudgingly from Eliza Arnold. The latter were heartfelt, and flowed fast from behind the black veil; for Mammy Venus, roused by my scream, had risen and come as fast as she could, lamp in hand, to settle the commotion.

Soon I understood that Mammy Venus—with Rosalie's assistance—had read of the Hands of Glory.

They'd read either the copied extract in my Book, or the original tale as told by Sebastiana; who—at her Parisian esbat, on the eve of the Revolution—had endured a hag by the name of Sofia: a burgling witch resident in the Bois de Boulogne who'd long used the Hands to ensure her safe in- and egress of the homes of Paris, picking to the bone those few that were treasure-fat.

With a dictionary purloined from Edgar, and with Rosalie's quite rudimentary knowledge of French, Mammy and she had puzzled out the entry; and the former struck upon a most excellent idea (so she held), which then she incorporated into her plan. But one thing remained: the harvesting of a murderer's hand. For help with this, she applied to . . . well, guess who?

Once I'd steadied myself—I'd tried in vain to throw off the ghost, flailing at her to no effect, receiving naught for my efforts but arms wet to the elbow—I leapt up from the cot. Eliza decamped to a dark corner, where she suffered quite well the curses of Mammy Venus. I retrieved my Book, threw it open, and began to list the reasons why we should not, *could* not fashion a Hand of Glory; not the least of which was my disinclination to do so.

"La, chile," observed Mammy Venus, after I'd spoken at

length in the language of my dreams, "you soundin' all red. Like you talkin' with an Injun's tongue."

"That is French, you fool," said Eliza Arnold. "The language of France."

"Mayhap; but *you* hear any sense in it?"

"Not at that rattling speed, no," admitted the actress.

Calmer now, I reasoned in English:

"Firstly," said I, "what's needed is a murderer's hand, harvested at the moon's eclipse. Has there been an eclipse of late?" Awaiting no answer, I spoke on. "And I doubt this . . . this relic," by which I referenced that putrid appendage which had fallen to the cellar floor, "is a murderer's hand."

"Ah, but it is, witch," said Eliza Arnold. "Dead but one month; and having taken the life of his own mother no less. Voilà!"

"His own mother?" said I to Eliza. "Understandable in the odd case, I suppose."

Mammy snorted out a short laugh; and in her own defense added that Rosalie had read—and rightly, too—that an eclipse is preferred, but not requisite to a Hand's success.

"Yes," said I, "but such a thing. . . . *Alors, écoutez,*" and I took up my own Book to recite:

"'Pickle the Hand in an earthenware jar, with salt, long peppers, and saltpeter; let it sit two weeks.'"

"La alive, *two* weeks?"

"Yes," said I. "Two weeks. And there's more: 'Then dry the Hand in an oven with vervain; or better, set it out beneath the summer sun.'"

"La, chile, we done missed that part about the sun; and that ver—"

"Vervain," said I. "And the candles needed are to be made from the murderer's fat—'from a slab sliced from his buttock or thigh'—with wicks twisted of his hair."

It was the ghoul who contributed to the confusion now.

Would that I could say she spoke; but no, instead she sped from out the dark, bent double, and . . . and coughed up, as a cat would, what hair she'd chewed from off the matricide's skull.

I looked to Mammy Venus. Her hunched shoulders rose once and fell.

Said Eliza, the lumpen mass balanced aback her hand, "Here's the hair. As for the fat, well . . . even if I had the hands for the task, this fellow had no fat, on his buttocks or elsewhere. Worms, I'm afraid, have made fast work of him."

"Mon Dieu," was all I managed before sinking onto the cot. Doubtless my complexion had sunken to a swampy green; for Eliza adjured:

"Come now, witch. Is it the worms? They tickle a bit, is all; and only at the beginning. Nowadays they bother me not at all."

I had my Book—open to Sofia's recipe—on the cot beside me. Eliza set the severed hand nearby. The hairs? There it lay upon the linen, a massed and masticated, oblong and loggish thing resembling . . . *alors,* resembling that which is carried fast from the bedchambers of a fine house. The hairs were twisted and slick, coated with whatever had come from deep within Eliza Arnold. . . . And loath though I am to admit it, my thoughts then turned to practical matters: How would wicks be made of the hairs? Who would separate the strands and . . . And I'll say no more than this: I did it.

O, how I despaired, bent to so horrid a chore; but who besides me had the hands for it? To distract myself—from the stench, from the texture of that gut-borne ingredient—I asked of Mammy Venus, "Why, *why* would you want to fashion such a thing as a Hand of Glory?"

"How else you gonna get Celia out the Manning house?"

Eliza Arnold laughed, and deemed Mammy's idea "rich."

"Hush now, hag."

"You're calling *me* a hag, you brittle, barbecued—"

"Arretez!" said I to both women; for I needed silence in which to work, and think.

The sun would soon rise. Yes: the hour of action was near, that much I knew. I knew as well that it was I who'd sneak through the streets of the city to rescue Celia. And Mammy Venus was right: I'd need every advantage that came to . . . hand.

Blessed be! What had I become? Evidently, I wondered this aloud as I labored with the Seeress at my side; for I recall she answered me, said, "You becomin' what you always been, is all."

So it was I came to stand in the backyard of Eloise Manning's boardinghouse, with the malformed hand of a murderer as my makeshift key.

The sun hadn't yet risen, but the sky showed violet. Still the grass beneath my boots was wet with dew. And still—O, how I hoped it!—most Richmonders slept.

. . . See me: crouched, atremble behind a gnarled oak. O but how, *how* would I step from the comfort of the shadows, cross the lawn, and take to the marble steps of the stoop—one, two, three—to turn ever so slowly the door's silver latch and. . . . I doubted I could do it. Nay, I knew I could not; for I'd scant faith in the shriveled, five-fingered "key" I carried.

But I thought then of Celia, who lay within. And I rethought our plan, which had come to this pass. So: out of the shadows I stepped and—one, two, three—up those marble stairs I crept.

19

Escape

A FINE house it was, Mrs. Manning's: three stories of Federalist persuasion, not unlike the Van Eyn mansion; but here the lawn was laid in turf and gravel, and all was well tended: the hedges clipped, the paint not let to peel, the washed marble of the forestoop agleam. A wonder it was that the garden gate creaked so; O, but then again everything creaks in the hours betwixt midnight and morn.

I'd set off through the city, climbing hill to hill with the Hand clapping against my thigh; for Mammy Venus had dropped it into a sack—sewn of leather and not much bigger than a glove, in fact—which I'd then roped about my waist. Mammy Venus had seen that Tolliver Bedloe would die 'neath the light of that night's moon; which still was in retreat. . . . So it was I had to wait.

Strict were my orders: enter the house by the first light of day, *not* the last light of night. It was the risen sun would shine on the corpse. O, but the moon and sun do sometimes share and confuse the sky, no? So, too, was I confused; for I needed the residents of the house asleep, but needed a dead Bedloe as well.

Understand: with Celia's master dead—the mercury and calomel having maddened him; and the emetics, enemas, and leeches having had but deleterious effect—her fate would worsen. If such a thing were possible. She'd pass to kin—that younger brother Sebastian, who'd long lain in wait—or, worse still, the newly widowed Mrs. Bedloe would intervene, as had her mother-in-law when Augustin Bedloe had grown too fond of his pet, Pleasants.

Mammy Venus had told the tale earlier, in a rage-quavering voice. How Augustin had impregnated Pleasants. How, when Pleasants had begun to show, Lucy Bedloe—Tolliver's mother—had ordered an overseer to bend Pleasants backward o'er a stump and beat her with cowhide and birch till she lost first the baby and then her life. . . . From the folds of her black frock, Mammy Venus had drawn forth a length of timeworn leather from which there depended a locket of pressed tin. In it were hairs not from Pleasants, nor from the mother she shared with Celia. No: these were hairs from Celia's *grand*mother, passed down from woman to woman when death or sale had come to steer the course of their lives. Pleasants had worn the locket since the death of her mother. How Mammy came to possess it upon Pleasants's demise, I cannot say; but Celia would know the locket, certainly; and so it was given to me, lest I need to prove to her our good faith.

I had the locket tied around my own neck when finally I stepped from behind the oak—the Hand afire behind me, the sky muddling to blue—and crossed the lawn, took to the stoop, and reached to touch the filigreed silver of the door handle. Which gave with soundless ease.

I knew we'd not made the Hand by the recipe, as written; and so it was with little confidence that I'd drawn it forth when finally I reached the Manning property, stepping—creakily—through that gate of white picketry. Still, I righted the Hand, and set it with its stiff fingers splayed in a low crotch of the oak. With a sulfur match I lit the thin twists of candle we'd made from common lard. First I lit the candle closest to the thumb, for protection; so the witch Sofia had directed. Then I lit the candle that leaned against the first finger, to still the wind. I heard and smelled the hair-wicks as they caught flame.

Finally, there the thing sat, burning on. I hoped it sat too high to interest any cats. And I worried about extinguishing it; for the Book held that mother's milk was the sole substance that could quiet a Hand once lit. As this was in short supply among us three weird sisters in the Van Eyn cellar, we'd let the question lay.

Thirteen rooms there were at Mrs. Manning's: unluckily, one would have thought. This reconnaissance we had from Rosalie, whose daftness was oft interpreted as discretion; which is to say, people convinced themselves they could confide in her. Too, Rosalie had brought back from Mrs. Manning's maid-of-all-work, Flutie, this item: Tolliver Bedloe was resident within the far southern chamber of the first floor, known since '24 as the Marquis' Suite; for Lafayette had slept within whilst touring. Doubtless Eloise Manning despaired at present; for impending death—time was all it would take, said Rosalie, quoting Flutie, who in turn had overheard a doctor—had already driven from her door one Mr. McKay, an Irishman rich from the manufacture of rope. Worse still, word had gotten out that Eloise Manning was letting that dissolute Bedloe boy keep his slave girl with him at all times, in the very same chamber. And though his indiscretions were scandalizing her house and name, Tolliver Bedloe had indeed pressed money enough into the fleshy hand of Mrs. Manning to secure not only her best room but the right to do as he pleased. Now, though, the woman wished he'd go—"to Heaven, Hell, or the country," quoth Flutie—before he tainted her house further.

Rosalie did well: I found Celia as directed. Asleep in that south-facing suite. Not upon the cot that had been set in the parlor of the suite—for her, surely—but rather at the foot of the great iron bed in which Tolliver Bedloe slept the sleep of the dead.

Whether by Mammy Venus or her hen, I know not; but the clock of death had been rightly read. There lay Bedloe. Still. With a chest that would not rise no matter how hard I stared. His blood, newly stopped in its course, yet rendered his flesh in reddish tones; nay, better to say it was pink-going-gray, like worms turned out into the light. From him there radiated neither warmth nor that death-chill I knew too well; but his bowels had begun to seep, and the two rooms of the suite reeked. His eyes were sunken yet wide open. At first, I thought to search out two coins: I'd close his eyes and weight the lids thusly, with what money he'd need—so custom holds—to pay the ferryman for his passage Beyond. Then, thinking better of it—and thinking less of Bedloe, now I knew his peccadilloes and predilections, his perfidies and perversions—I left him wide-eyed and watching, waiting for whatever might come. Coins for the ferryman? Nay. Let the villain swim the river Styx.

I woke her with a shake to the shoulder. A shoulder so beautifully bare; for her robe had slipped from it in sleep. "Yes, yes," said she, "what it is, Tolliver?" Accustomed to wading in the shallows of sleep, she rose fast to full awareness. So it was she curled into herself and scooted back against the bed frame, clutching an appliquéd shawl to her chest. She asked, nay demanded to know who I was, what it was I wanted. She said her master lay just there, mere feet from us; and I thought she sought to wake him with her words.

"No," was all I said. "Stay," and, kneeling at her side like a proposing suitor, I set a hand upon her shoulder.

It was then she saw and knew me.

"What . . . ?" she began, knowing now to whisper. "What are you doing here?" So confused was she that she let fall the shawl, and her shift of thin cotton fell as well to show her shoulders and the honeyed downslope of her chest. This I saw by light that shone from both the moon and sun; which, married, sifted through drawn curtains. Dawn: I'd have to act fast.

"I'm to take you," said I, awkwardly; for, in Celia's presence, my tongue went dumb and knew but a fraction of the English with which I'd have credited my brain.

"What are you saying? You'll take me nowhere," and she stood, doubtless thinking she'd appeal to Bedloe himself. "My master—"

"Your master is a man of mean appetites; and I know how he's marked you."

At this Celia drew the shawl and shift into place. "I . . . I don't understand," said she, finally.

"Yes, you do," said I, taking hold of her hand. "We're to run. You must dress."

I stepped to the armoire, o'er the open door of which hung that yellow dress of hers. "Please," said I, handing the dress to her, and taking care to whisper—as though Bedloe had living ears to hear—and positioning myself between Celia and Bedloe; lest she learn the man had passed.

When next she looked at me, imploringly, I blurted out what it was I knew of her life and our plan. Mere words, I muttered; nonsense. "Dead," I began, "no, *dying,* I mean. Yes, dying. And when he passes. . . . Never mind. You and I must run, now. From here to . . . I don't know where, exactly. I mean, there's a place, yes. And a woman who knows you. Knows *of* you. . . . Near here."

"Who knows me? Say the name."

"A slave," said I, regretting it instantly.

"'Slave' is no name."

"Mother-of-Venus," said I.

"I know no one by that name. And if you think I'll risk running in order to satisfy some—"

She fell silent; for I'd drawn the locket out from under my shirt and held it now as a mesmerist might. No further words were wanted.

I had her by the elbow. We were nearing the door of the suite.

It was then she turned back to Bedloe, and saw his death-wide eyes.

Something overcame her. She tore from me. She crossed the room in a golden blur. I watched from where I stood, one hand on the door's latch, listening for the sounds of wakefulness beyond. The scene was dimly lit; but the scene was this:

Celia, bedside, staring down at a man she'd known from boyhood. Beside whom she'd been educated. With whom she'd been reared. By whom she'd been kept. And badly used.

She raised her hands to her face. She stifled tears; and sundry emotions I shan't presume to list. Too, it may have dawned on her then: Bedloe's death made of her a murderess. This she'd never intended: she'd meant only to lay him low, and run when he was weak.

Her shoulders rose and fell. Her hands fell from her face.

"Come," called I from across the room. And just as I made to say it a second time, she struck:

From off the bedside table she took a glass pitcher, the contents of which she splashed onto Bedloe's face. As if to wake him. This done, she stood staring. Too still. And then . . . then she brought the pitcher down upon a corner of the table to break it. In her hand she held but its handle, attached to which was . . .

I reached her just as she stuck the jagged glass into Bedloe's neck.

No blood came from the chilling corpse; leastways not whilst we stood above it. I recall naught upon the pallid neck but a gash, not deep but wide as a smile.

Celia shivered and shook in my arms. I held her as tightly as I could, counseled her toward calm. She surrendered the weapon; and I set it on the floor bedside, as if Bedloe had broken the pitcher himself as the last act of his life. When I understood that there'd be no concealing his cut neck, I understood this, too: we had better run, and presently.

All I recall is stealing through the dining room of the house, where a long table of dark and undoubtedly rare wood had already been set for breakfast. The china and silver and crystal shuddered in place as we passed. Still I can see a decanter of cut crystal on the sideboard, its bellyful of brandy set to sloshing by our hurried passage.

Out we went, into daylight: the sun had risen. I forgot the Hand; and cannot but smile at the thought of cats or climbing children puzzling o'er such a find.

We ran when it seemed we could. Much more difficult it was to walk when it seemed we ought: as a horseman passed, as house lamps were lit . . . .

I sought to avoid the wharves, and the market; for I knew such were the first parts of any city to wake. So, with a measure of confusion that needs no description, I led Celia up this hill and down that: in a word, I was lost. It was Celia who remarked upon it as we passed some places twice; but I assured her I knew the way. (Which was a lie. In truth, I all but prayed.) Finally: Shockoe Hill. And the dilapidated Van Eyn mansion; wherein we'd further our plan. Whatever it was.

All the while we'd run, Celia had stopped but once. Breathing deeply, with tears of fear streaming, she set to ask who I was, really, and why I'd come, and would we retake to the *Ceremaju* or run by road, and . . .

And to all and every question I could only shake my head and answer, *"Je ne sais pas."* For I didn't know how we'd run, or why I'd come, or even who I was, really.

20

Plans into Action

POOR Edgar Poe.

As Celia and I stole through the streets, Edgar would have just fallen asleep. Always, said Rosalie, her brother resisted the night, and sleep; and when he slept insisted on a bedside lamp burning bright, and a tiny brazier of incense—orris root, had from his living mother—or fagged aromatics thrown onto the fire. He said he knew coldness in the night, and that sometimes the smell and very sight of death descended upon him.

As indeed it did those two nights: first with a poem, then with a plan.

Eliza Arnold would no doubt try to hold to as indistinct a shape as she could; for I doubt she sought to frighten Edgar. . . . I wonder still, did she siphon from the night moisture enough to take shape, and show herself? Did Edgar half wake to write as she bade him write, do as she bade him do? Or, born of dew, redolent of rot, did she invade his dreams?

All I know for certain is that, on the night in question, Eliza Arnold carried to her son what seemed to her a brilliant plan; brilliant in that it furthered her ends as much as ours. Of course, neither Mammy nor I believed Eliza when she'd sworn her pure assistance. The best we could hope for—from Eliza and Edgar both—was that their plans would contribute to the success of ours. In fairness, I will say that neither were we wholly selfless. Mammy Venus sought to right old wrongs, and win for herself a sort of absolution. I sought Celia, of course; and she in her turn sought freedom. Only Rosalie was true; but, sad to say, she had no self to assert.

As for Eliza Arnold and Edgar Poe, the plan they actuated must have seemed to them sublime.

Eliza had told Mammy Venus that she would spur, nay "inspire" Edgar to create on his own a most useful diversion the Monday morning of our escape. When pressed, she'd say nothing further. But she was excited—O, the stench of it!—and late the night of our strange séance she'd waited with impatience for Edgar to tumble from the Court House Tavern. Eliza had spied him there, and left him to drink away his demons. (Or so he thought.) Said she, once she'd returned to the cellar, "It's best to let him pickle himself, for then he's quite susceptible to . . . to dreams." I wondered how a mother could smile at the thought of haunting her own son; but smile she did. "And what's more, he'll wake suffering the aftershocks of drink, and—despising himself so—he'll turn to our task with all the ardor of an ox. Splendid!" Not long after this, she returned to Moldavia, to the bedstead of her Edgar—or, as she was wont to call him, her "poet"—and there set to work.

Eliza's plan was a dangerous one; and it might well lead to the end of Edgar Poe. Thusly was it sublime, to her way of thinking. . . . To explain: should Edgar succeed at his feat he'd win for himself a measure of renown, and anger John Allan in the process. More: his faithless Elmira Royster would regret having spurned so strong, so celebrated a suitor. . . . O but, too, he ran the risk of drowning; for the particulars of the plan were these:

Knowing Edgar enamored of Byron, and knowing John Allan disdainful of the dead poet's dissolute and too-showy ways, Eliza Arnold had struck upon her scheme: she'd "speak" to Edgar of a swim to rival his idol's swimming from Abydos to Sestos in Turkey, in imitation of Leander.

Wouldn't this cause quite the stir riverside? She'd see to it. And Celia and I could steal away under cover of the commotion. Thusly would Eliza Arnold appease Mammy Venus, too; and this—for reasons I cannot enumerate—she desired to do.

Brilliant? Who am I to say otherwise? Surely the plan succeeded on some counts—the papers would write of the strength and derring-do of the younger Mr. Allan, "Richmond's collegian and poet," thus angering the elder—even if Eliza did not realize her highest hope: a dead Edgar, whose ghost would rise to walk beside her.

To swim the James seemed to me a devil's chore. (Aptly so, in Edgar's case.) Most swimmers opted for Shockoe Creek, as the James was always rather cold—coming down as it did from the mountains—and there were those rocks and rapids set therein, and a sinister undertow, even well downriver from the falls proper.

Still, in Edgar went. At Ludlum's Wharf. And on he'd swim—he was broad-backed and strong: to that I'll attest—and he'd not turn to the shore for six miles. At Warwick he'd quit the water, with a sun-blistered back and neck, swollen hands, and a swiveling tongue; for, though duly exhausted, quick he was to speak of Byron, pronouncing that he (Edgar) would have swum the Hellespont and thought nothing of it.

Much more was said by young Master Allan, and reported by those who walked the six miles back to the city at his side; for the swimmer—in an added show of strength—disdained conveyance on horseback or cart.

Of course, by the time Edgar and his entourage returned—with the hero hailed and huzzahed—Celia and I had slipped away. Unseen; if not unsought.

We'd arrived at the Van Eyn home in silence. Finally, I'd gotten Celia to desist with her questioning; for, upset though she was, she understood that to risk being heard in the streets was to risk everything.

Through the hedge I led her, and—with the hens present, still and silent: mere silhouettes they were, shadows within shadows—down the treed alley we went, up and into the house.

I would deliver Celia to Mammy Venus. That was all I knew to do.

She sat in the cellar, fireside. On either side of her were two traveling bags. Packed. On the table and floor was spread all the rest of what I would not take.

Celia saw this odd array. Rather, let me say she did *not* see Mammy Venus; for when the older woman spoke, the younger started. Stepping to my side, staring down the dark, Celia asked, "Who . . . who are you?" Of me she asked, "Who is that, *there*?"

Silence; broken by the Seeress, who said: "That there locket . . ." Celia wore it now. "I done waited long years to see it where it ought to be. Mother-of-Venus, I is. All one word, strung-up like; but you can call me Mammy, or Mammy Venus. Don't much matter."

I felt the tension slip from Celia's shoulders; it seemed as real as that shawl sewn with rosettes that had slipped similarly when I woke her, suddenly. Woke her to all this strangeness.

"You knew my grand-mama?"

"La, no, chile. I ain't no Methuselah now."

"My mother, then?" Celia seemed untroubled by Mammy Venus's speech.

"No'm. I knew yo' sister, Pleasants. And it was Fanny got hold that locket when . . ." Mammy Venus let go the end of that sentence, kindly so.

Celia turned to me. "I knew of a Fanny," said she; for she'd begun to believe, to trust. Returning her gaze to the darksome corner, she asked, "How did you know Pleasants?"

"Like'n you'd guess, chile. Wasn't we all fish in the same barrel? Mason, too. I knowed yo' brother, I did. Fine man, he was. But maybe you too young to remember Mason. He—"

"He died. When I was but a girl; but I remember. It was—"

"It was fire, chile. Mason, he done died at my side. A good man, he was, 'deedy yes. Inside and out: fine-hearted and handsome. We . . . me and him . . . we was fixin' to fetch up, to marry, as best any bonded folk can. . . . He was shy, Mason was; but I . . . well, believe me when I says, Miss Celia, that yo' brother and I, we would've made a life if'n he hadn't—"

"If he hadn't gone into that theater a second time. To save *you*?" Celia's questioning voice had gone cold. "I've heard that story told, yes. Many times." Again, her shoulders tensed. Her lips were thin and tight. Celia held Mammy Venus accountable for her brother's death, and likely her sister's, too.

"You've not heard the whole story," I whispered to Celia. . . . Indeed, she hadn't.

Celia did not hear me; or if she did, still she stammered an accusatory, "You . . . you . . ." at Mammy Venus.

"She," said I, "has arranged for you to run. With me." Celia was confused, of course; and quieted.

"Ain't no runnin' on just yet, hear?" And Mammy Venus

asked of me, "You get her out that house quiet-like? How's that Hand of yours?"

Celia, calmed, looked to each of my hands, wonderingly.

"Never mind," said I, hiding my hands away. (I was still quite conscious of them, then: large, long-fingered, and slim they were, best suited to pockets and gloves.)

Mammy Venus would not slip a second time, would speak no more of witchery. Instead, she turned to the plan proper, and said, "Dawn's comin' on, but you gots a few hours to pass befo' you can go."

"Go where?" asked Celia. Confusion, indeed; for at once she knew anger, accusation, fear, gratitude, and much else besides.

"Away, chile," was all Mammy said. That night she'd deal out the plan as a sharper does cards: calmly, confidently, her every move weighty with consequence. And, too, she'd resort to simpler matters, rising slowly to say, "Come on upstairs with me, chil'en. Ain't no tellin' when yo' next meal will come; so there's victualin' to do, hear?"

How she did it—with tipless fingers and arms all but soldered to her sides—I cannot say; but upstairs, in a windowless pantry off the dining room (where we could light a lamp that would not show without) we, Celia and I, were served chicken (the oracular one, I suppose) alongside bitter but delicious greens, pot liquor, corn pone, and cider. There was cold ham, too; salted. And I wonder now if Mammy Venus didn't busy us with food the better to crowd from our mouths our many questions.

One question I did manage was this: What next?

"There's the printer's boy, Joe, who's scared and cain't see right and . . ."

"I know him," said Celia. "Runs the printer's boat."

"Used to. He run a packet now, reg'lar-like 'tween here and Norfolk. With the mails and such."

"What of him?" asked Celia.

"He gonna meet you on the far side of Mayo's Island."

"Norfolk?" said I, some steps behind.

"Norfolk," said Mammy.

"But . . ." I began.

"You right. They ain't lettin' no boats into Norfolk, for fear of the fever. But Joe, he ain't—"

"All the way to Norfolk on a packet boat," said Celia, "and with a fever raging there." I wasn't sure if her tone were one of complaint or confusion; but Mammy met it with:

Silence. Then this: "You rather gonna sit on the stoop of Missus Eloise and wait fo' them Bedloes to come from the country, now Tolliver's gone? Maybe he could keep 'em from knowin' you all was back from France; but, chile, there's a corpse now and a corpse cain't tell no mo' lies, hear? . . . 'Deedy, yes, they be comin' on soon. And what then?"

"Go on," said Celia.

"I will, thank you please," said Mammy. "Joe gonna get you downriver a spill, is all. Down 'bout the Bermuda Hundred. There a man gonna search you out riverside, where a lane of dogwood be runnin' white and pink 'bout now, hear? Lark: that the name. He hires out onto a snag boat that runs the steamer routes. This day there won't be but him on the boat. So's it Joe to Lark, then Lark to Norfolk. They's both run folk befo'."

"Still," said I, "there's risk in it."

"Risk? La, chile, you could say so, yes. . . . Risk, and plenty of it."

"Norfolk it is," said I, finally.

"Norfolk, yes'm," said Mammy Venus. "After that, I cain't see no mo'." Celia, of course, knew not what she meant. I did. And it scared me. I sought distraction in a wedge of corn pone, which crumbled beneath my buttering knife; for my hands were atremble, terribly so.

* * *

We ate our fill, for certain; then we repaired to the cellar to sit before a new-kindled fire.

Talk was of Mason and Pleasants and "days that was." Celia and I asked questions appertaining to then, not now; and were happy to forget our fugitive state. Still and safe, well fed and warm, we forgot—for whole minutes at a time—that already we'd begun to run.

What I most remember is watching as Celia warmed to Mammy Venus; and in so doing granted that long-sought absolution. Celia's enmity dissolved as Mammy spoke from behind her veil—she would never raise it for Celia—and in speaking brought back to Celia those siblings who'd long been storied figures, half remembered. Mammy Venus spoke of them lightly, telling tales of their younger years: Mason making clumsy love to Venus, as he'd called her, trying too hard to shine and looking silly, "like nothin' but a mess of love." Of Pleasants, Mammy Venus said, "All mens, *all* mens betimes, came at that girl bug-eyed and lollin' 'bout, liken they just swallowed down two jugs of tanglefoot."

I watched in silence as the dead returned—I speak figuratively, for once—and the two women gifted each other with smiles, quiet laughter, and not a few tears.

But the sweetness of the sharing ended abruptly; for, with the hour still early, Rosalie arrived and set the house bells to ringing. At this Celia started, terrifically. Mammy Venus and I set her at ease. Rosalie, I said, could be trusted. Which truth I hadn't known until I heard myself speak it; but yes, it was true.

I mounted the cellar stairs and sprang the door for Rosalie. She came bearing a bundle of clothes. From these we'd fashion a sort of disguise for Celia. She'd need to appear less fancy than was her custom. With homespun and drab cloth and a head rag we dulled her down, as one would roll a diamond in dust to disguise it as glass. Likewise, I had to dress as far *up* as Celia did down; for I was to play Celia's foreign master, a man of means. And so we drew from the *nécessaire* the last of the fashions forced upon me by Sebastiana. So dandified was I—in my knee breeches of cream broadcloth; in a frock coat had from Van Eyn's closet; in a cap trimmed in swansdown— . . . well, I might as well have resorted to woman's wear. I felt the fool. And looked it, too.

Sometime in the course of these preparations—done in the darkness, the silence of the cellar, which had now a churchly solemnity—Rosalie burst forth with, "Mammy, Mammy, may I look?" Standing before Celia—so close she swayed back, the better to stare—Rosalie raised a stub of candle to Celia's face, and proclaimed, "Mammy, you were right! Why, I declare it for truth: her eyes are as purple as all things Easter. They are indeed! Never have I seen a more beautiful woman, never." Rosalie then spun back to Mammy Venus to exclaim, "Such beauty, Mammy!" and to ask, "What matter the color of it?"

It was from Rosalie that we learned of Edgar's plan.

As always she did, she devolved to near hysteria—born of adoration and fear, I think—when speaking of Edgar. Most significantly, she told us the timing of his swim. Edgar—looking, said Rosalie, haggard and "all afire"—had come to Duncan Lodge not an hour earlier, pushing past Miss Jane to wake Rosalie and enlist her in his plan. (Which plan "came to him in the night," said Rosalie; "*poured* at him like a poem!") He commanded his sister to meet him at the market square at half past nine. "He needs me," said she, pridefully. "He said so." Rosalie was dumb to the danger Edgar would be in; for—with a swirl and half skip—she said, "Our Eddie can swim and swim and swim."

As soon as Rosalie had spread the word—to Messieurs Allan and Royster, especially; and Mr. Ritchie of the *En-*

quirer; and Elmira, too—she was to summon a common crowd. This she'd do by flying about the city proper. When all parties were in place—be they angered or awed, cursing or curious—Edgar would wade into the James at Ludlum's Wharf. Noon, it would be.

By then, we—Celia and I—would need to be upon the far shore of Mayo's Island. There we'd board Joe's packet and slip into the flotilla that was sure to accompany Edgar. Indeed, Rosalie had taken it upon herself to alert her foster brother, Jack; and he, said she, was already loading a flatboat with illicit brew. To pole the boat he'd get his "trouble buddy," a boy whose name I can recall, and so here record: Ebenezer Burling.

Of course, by the time Edgar took his first stroke, Eloise Manning—or some member of her corps—would have found Tolliver Bedloe dead in his bed. And Celia would be deemed missing once she was searched out in the house, the pen, and all places between. The wound in Bedloe's neck would speed the search, surely.

With luck, we'd have crossed to Mayo's Island before word of Celia's absconding reached the ferryman; for, said Mammy Venus, he was a black man with white ears and a fondness for coin. . . . Indeed, at this we did succeed. We'd make it onto Mayo's Island—which sat centered in the James—with the ferryman seeing naught but a Frenchman and his girl.

. . . But before that came to pass, we'd had to bid goodbye to Mammy Venus.

Celia did so first, saying she'd always pray Mammy's name, no matter what came. Mammy, in turn, shuffled nearer Celia; raising a ruined hand to the locket at her neck, she said, "Git yo'self free, girl, hear?"

Me? I'm afraid I showed rather less grace in my goodbye. Once it was stated—yet again—that we'd write via a most willing Rosalie, I all but lunged at Mammy Venus, and hugged her. Hard. Audible, it was: the pain I caused her. But she suffered it well, waving away my apology; and when she turned just so, in that cellar now lit by a suffusing sun, I thought I saw, behind layers of blackest tulle, a smile.

"Go now," said she, all but shooing us from the cellar. "Run on. Run on!"

Rosalie left us on the far side of the Van Eyn hedge. When next I saw her she'd be standing downriver, on the bank of the James; and we'd be aboard the packet, with Joe poling in search of the current.

The sun had climbed to its height; but there clung to the water a swirling mist, and there'd fall a sun shower, quite out of season. I've long wondered if those water forms—the mist, the rain that fell to pock the river—wasn't a watchful Eliza Arnold; for:

Edgar was aswim. Boats had come to bob beside him; and cheers rose up from within these as well as from the crowd that crawled along bankside. It was among that mass—fifty persons, I'd have hazarded, though the newsmen would toll one hundred or more—that I saw Rosalie. She stood at the back of the pack, her long arms bare and upraised. Others, too, were gesturing and pointing and waving Edgar on, but as they moved downriver, Rosalie remained in place. Soon the crowd pulled from her, as we in turn pulled ahead of Edgar; and away. Turning back, I saw Rosalie standing there, still; . . . till suddenly, with her arms akimbo, it seemed she'd fly from off the shore. But it was a wave only.

And though I knew it to be unwise, I raised high my right hand—slowly, slowly at first, then so quickly it seemed I sought the sun itself—and I waved thanks and good-bye to Rosalie Poe Mackenzie, Sister to the Poet. Whereupon she broke at the knee, sinking into a curtsy deep as the sea.

21

The Vomito Negro

NORFOLK: a most mortiferous place, all but emptied by the fear of fever.

Lark it was who'd sent us in search of a Mrs. Harmsford's. A fine-enough house, he'd said, wherein questions would be few. But at said establishment the door was opened by a man name of Plume, who looked none too well. Worse: he was chatty, and too curious for my comfort. . . . How was it we'd arrived? By packet, or were they letting larger boats into port? Was quarantine lifted, then? Or, asked he, in conspiring tones, had I bought a way in for me and "my black"?

From this Plume we learned that Mrs. Harmsford and company had decamped to the country and would not return to Norfolk till the first frost settled the fever. It seemed some thirty-odd persons had succumbed to "the *vomito negro*" in the days prior to our arrival. (We snuck into the city with no trouble at all: Lark rowed us ashore in a jolly boat, kept tethered astern of the snag.) Such mortality was considered supportable, I suppose; and it was not this outburst of fever that drove the citizenry from the city, but rather the too fresh memory of '21, when nearly two hundred people had passed after a sweet boat had come from Point Peter, Guadeloupe, with sugar, rum, and the pox in its hold.

We walked from Plume, from Mrs. Harmsford's, and followed what few people we found in the streets; and thusly were we led waterside, and across Back Creek. This was where those without means waited out the fever. A shambles, it was, of wharves and taverns, of whoring and faro playing; but all of it was eerily quiet now and seemed but a dream of dissolution, not dissolution itself.

The waters of Back Creek were in recess, and the stink was extreme. Celia clutched a kerchief to her face: to hide herself, I supposed; but then I saw others doing the same: every drawn breath was a risk. Finally, though it smacked of unsavory types—we had to step o'er a sailor's extended leg to enter; and in a corner a fleshy woman sat with one breast bared—we ducked into the Lion d'Or, tucked up Woodside's Lane.

There was a long bar and a mud-caked floor meant for dancing, or fun of the fistic sort. Upstairs there were rooms. We let ours from a woman we had to rouse at her counter. Whilst speaking to us she tangled her tawny hair till it seemed a nest topside her head; this same act showed the underflesh of her arms—slack as windless sails—and breasts that shook like unset puddings. She, too, was off-color: sick; as Plume had seemed. Squinting her suspicion, she asked from whence we'd come. I lost my way amidst her English; so it was Celia who responded.

"No, we ain't comin' from the islands, missus," dissembled she. "We's in from the country, is all."

What new show was this? I may have smiled, at first; but I desisted when our hostess said, "I don't sleep no niggers here."

Celia stepped behind me. Already I'd learned to resort to French when in trouble. *"Madame,"* said I, whilst slapping coin onto the rum-wet counter, *"si, par hasard, vous avez une chambre . . ."*

"All right, all right," said she, going at the coin with filthy fingers. "One night, eh?" She smacked down a key the size of a shinbone.

Our relief was profound; for now we'd a closed door behind which to hide. . . . Soon word would spread of Celia's absconding. Adverts would be seen. And when this came to pass, we'd not want some hard-lucker—trapped in a fevered port, and spurred by a posted reward—remembering the violet-eyed slave he'd seen near Woodside's Lane.

Although, in point of fact, we'd taken precautions:

Sailing in silence aboard Joe's packet—with Edgar miles behind us—I'd spied in the boat's tiny cuddy, or house, a pair of spectacles. These, rather brazenly, I begged of Joe; all the while I dared not look at him directly, for unnerving and saddening it was to see his right eye loll about its socket, bobbing like a boat badly moored. A scar beside the eye testified that once it had sat straight, and seen.

My idea was this: we'd hide Celia's eyes; for Joe had made sunshades of the spectacles by wrapping strips of indigo-dyed gauze around the clear lenses. Joe himself commended my plan, saying we were wise to hide Celia's "white-lady eyes." He went on to call me brave; and when I demurred, he spoke of the risks I ran, the laws I was breaking as an aider and abettor. Now I knew these laws—draconian, indeed—I'd no wish to sit in consideration of same. Scared, was I? Yes. Surprised? No; for such laws stand to reason in a society wherein people are the most valuable property of other people.

I took to the streets of Norfolk that early evening with no fear of the fever. Celia remained in our room, behind a locked door, listening for the agreed-upon knock—two long, three short—that would signal my having returned with food and fresh water. Or so it was hoped.

Celia, of course, would have been much more efficient if it had been she who'd taken to the streets. Doubtless she'd have returned to me with more than the half gallon of fresh water I found, had for a half cent off a tea cart being trundled through the streets. And doubtless Celia would have secured fare far more savory than the hog's jowls, collards, bread with no butter, and toddy I procured for a ninepence and a few fips. (I knew not the words the vendor used. Indeed, I thought I'd bought bacon; so when Celia explained the porcine provenance of the meat, I was unable to eat it, hungry though I was.) But, of course, I could not risk sending Celia out into the streets. She might be found; if not by the first of the catchers who'd come, then by the plague.

I, on the other hand, knew how I'd die.

The death of every witch is the same, in kind if not circumstance. We die of the Blood; assuming, that is, that we find no more violent fate: bullet or blade. Something there is that boils in our blood. Our powers, perhaps? Our talents? . . . But it is that same blood that will rise to betray us; and a witch's "natural" end—horribly anticipated; for somehow the Blood tells of its rising—is a red mess; and none who witness it are likely to forget the sight: blood seeping, spewing, spurting from every orifice.

As a child no more than six, I'd seen my mother die the Red Death. (Witch begets witch; but did my mother know her own nature? I cannot say.) Some years later I began to sense the Blood within me; for I was witness to its potency, its power when the infirmarian—Sister Clothilde, the keeper of herbs, lancets, leeches, and the like—was directed by Sister Claire de Sazilly to bleed me. Perhaps, said the cunning, conniving Sister Claire, a bleeding would relieve me of my "bad humors." So it was I suffered five leeches upon my inner arm.

I watched them suck and swell till they seemed the gouty fingers of a fiend. And when Sister Clothilde returned and retrieved them—stunned, she was—and dropped them into the jar from which they'd come, still they grew, till finally they were as fat and purple as eggplants. They burst that glass vessel, and fell to scarlet shards upon the floor. Now, as to what the infirmarian reported to Sister Claire, I cannot say; but surely I fell further out of favor with her till finally, finally she struck, she who'd long lain in wait. And I was but a weapon in a war waged for the rule of the holy house; and the usurper—Sister Claire—plied me against my sole supporter, the mother superior, Marie-des-Anges, and the end began.

Yes, the Blood . . . ; in it lies our sisterly strength, and in it lies our demise. This (need I say it?) was not the happiest lesson I'd learned at Sebastiana's side; and I shan't dwell upon it here, save to add this: it was a strange relief to know the Blood awaited me, and that I was safe from disease, from pestilence, from plague.

Thusly, I walked the streets of Norfolk that night with impunity. And proud I was when I'd procured not only water and food, but a fast way south.

Yes, south: as directed by Mammy Venus. Indeed, I was insistent when Celia and I spoke, as briefly we did, of our destination. Surely it would have made more sense to set out for Ohio, or the North. So said Celia; and I agreed. Still, I'd no choice but to counter her every sensible suggestion with mere and no doubt maddening insistence. South it had to be; but how could I convince Celia of this? Tell her that the veiled Seeress had appealed to her poultry? That the same hen Celia had met upon a plate had determined her fate? No. So, I simply insisted: south.

My insistence was met with tears. Of frustration, of fear. Anger, too. I felt terrible; such that finally I had to leave our room. Doing so, I said to Celia, in what must have seemed a mock-heroic tone, "Let me see what I can find."

I made my way wharfside. The sun hung low, was near to setting; the sky was striate, banded in grays and pinks, pearlescent shades. Blue clouds nudged the white ones away. Beautiful, it might have been; but still the city stank from the recessed tide.

It was dark by the time I found Isham Lowry.

He was a man quite responsive to coin; and who ran a coastal sloop on the Ashepoo, sometimes slipping from port to port, all up and down the seaboard. After the requisite preliminaries, Mr. Lowry asked where it was I hoped to go. He was almost mine, I knew; for, cagily, he'd led me to a streetlamp, in the dim glow of which he looked me up and down. It was the swansdown that decided him, I think. But just then—his question hanging in the fetid air—I panicked, and fell silent; for I could not recall the name of a single American city south of where we stood. I stalled with French; and, thankfully, not put off by my Gallic gamesmanship, Mr. Lowry offered this:

"Charleston?"

"Charleston, *oui,*" I enthused. "*C'est ça.* Yes, Charlestown. In Carolina south, *non*?" (I laid it on rather thick, I'm afraid.)

When I'd managed to spit out a few more particulars, Isham Lowry smiled—rather too slyly for my liking—and said he'd take me on if I stood dockside at dawn. With "my girl."

Knock. Knock. Knock-knock-knock.

Celia opened the door. Seeing me, she could but smile and ask what had happened; for I was mud-covered, caked to the knees.

See, I'd practically skipped up from the port, so proud was I of having secured our passage. (Not once did it occur to me that Isham Lowry might—if he were more than merely sly—take my half payment and sail from Norfolk in the night. Without us.) Flush with success, I walked from the wharves and soon secured the water and food. All this in hand, I hurried back to the Lion d'Or. But, apparently, lamp attendants are no more immune to the fear of fever than others: most streets were let to fall dark; and a scythe of moon was no help at all. So it was that I fell headlong o'er bricks left piled in the street by a mason of sinister bent. Yes: I fell to measure my length in a muddy gutter. The water and food flew from my hands; luckily, they landed well, far better than I: the water jug still stoppered, the food yet wrapped.

Need I say my step was less hurried after the fall? But I made it back to the room. Abashed. My lower half brown as a bull's.

Surely it was naught but habit that caused Celia to do what next she did.

She led me from the doorway, and secured the door behind us. I saw that she'd tempered the squalor of our surrounds. Simply, she'd draped her red head rag from a hook before the lamp, rendering the room roseate. Too, she'd raised up a fire; which—though we needed not the warmth—did succeed in burning back the stink of the city. As the two chairs of our chamber were rickety, and would bear but a child's weight, Celia led me to the bed. The lumpy mattress she'd shaken out; and she'd smoothed the thin quilt sewn of flannels, chamois, and refuse cotton. The mattress on its iron strappings sagged; and the whole of it sang out rustily as I sat.

Celia sank down before me, and busied herself with my boots. All the while I watched her work.

Unaccustomed to touch, I trembled. I stilled my lower lip by biting it.

Celia had hiked up her skirts to kneel upon the plankwood floor. Beside her lay a braided rug, well-worn, and so filthy I could discern pattern, but no color. Onto this she knocked and tapped and scraped the mud which fell in clots from off my boots; this done, she unbuttoned the boots and removed them.

When she stood it was to walk to the fire. She'd folded up the rug and now she cast the caked mud onto the fire, whereon clods of it popped and broke and smoked. I sat transfixed. The drabness of her dress was no distraction at all; it deprived my eye of no delight. Her skin shimmered; for the work she'd taken on had set her to perspiring. Those violet eyes were weaponry: with them she stilled me; and into them I stared, when I dared.

She returned to kneel before me, without benefit of the rug. Up through the floorboards there came harmonica song: too melancholic a tune, all out of keeping with what I felt as Celia . . . Well. She'd brought back to the bed a knocked-about basin of white tin, and into this she poured water from the half gallon I'd secured. The mud had insinuated itself beyond my boots, my stockings and breeches; and so: Celia rolled my stockings low, pushed my pants high, and with the ample hem of her skirt set to wiping the grime from off my skin.

"Your legs," said she, "they're . . . like a lady's; but better made; muscular." She looked up, afraid she'd offended me. "Quite muscular."

It seemed Celia was as nervous as I. Or perhaps this was the role she'd long played. An aggressive acquiescence: looking out from under lowered lashes, tilting her shoulders this way and that, shyly; with her laces seeming to undo themselves, her blouse falling open to show the downslope of her breasts. . . . I accuse Celia not of dissembling; it was perhaps a habit, is all, and one long allied to her survival: I was naught but another white man expecting service and pleasure.

Of course, all the while I feared Celia would discover that I was quite *other* than I seemed. Still, what could I do but sit in tremulous silence and watch her work?

She rolled my stockings off. I demurred. She insisted, as earlier I'd insisted on our taking a southern route; and so I thought it best to maintain silence. Of course, it helped that the pleasure I knew in being laved was extreme. When, unintentionally, she tickled me, I withdrew. Celia looked up, smiling, and soothed me with her eyes.

I was no Christ figure, no; but here knelt Martha and Mary both: the very soul of service, of selflessness. Blessedly, Celia hadn't oils with which to anoint me, hadn't hair long enough to dry my feet, as had those sisters of Lazarus.

Up through the floor came barroom conversation, lurching and loud. We, in our turn, whispered. Up came music, too: a fiddle, following hard on the slow harmonica. Celia now hummed as she worked, wiping and wringing the dirt from her skirt into the basin.

The room, if it had been hot before, was now stiflingly so. But, as the fire had been lit to fight fever, we kept it at a roar; and did not crack the alley-side window. Simply, we sweated. Celia wiped at her neck and bosom with a clean corner of her skirt. In so doing she showed a woman's geometry: those slopes and shapes and soft angles I'd come to admire, and coveted. Celia's breasts were all but free now, sitting in cups made of stays and lace, whilst mine were yet bound by swaddling; lest they betray me.

"Henri," said Celia, drawing me from my sensory stupor. She spoke on then, but I heard not a word. *Henri? Qui, ça?* O but Henri was me! Yes: I remembered. Within the Van Eyn cellar, I'd been asked my name by Celia. Mammy Venus and Rosalie had stood quietly by as I fished for one, not wanting to lie but knowing Herculine would not suffice. Hercule, I'd been on occasion, as it . . . suited. But no: now I'd be Henri. Worse: I found a last name, too, christening myself Henri Collier. Rosalie stifled a snort, with little success; and I understood: the name had come to me so quickly because I'd heard Edgar say it. Henry Collier was that bastard son of

John Allan's who'd so bedeviled Edgar's youth. Of course, I could not retract my own name once I'd spoken it; so Henri I was, and Henri I would long remain.

O, but let me say that poor Henri had other worries, just then. Celia's touch was such that . . . well, pardon me the indelicacy of saying . . . . *Enfin,* my sex rose, strained against the thin fabric of my pants. But before I was thusly embarrassed, betrayed, I saw . . . something. Something unfamiliar in Celia's hand. Nay not *in* it, but on it.

I took her hands. Slowly, I turned them toward the light. What first I'd taken for some species of pestilence—ants, mosquitoes, or mites—showed themselves as . . .

"What are these?" I asked. Celia resisted, made to withdraw her hands from mine. But again I was insistent, asking the question a second time as I trailed my fingertip along the fleshy curve of her palm, from the base of her thumb across the lined pink plane to her tiniest finger, feeling . . . Shame. I felt shame for the whole family of man as I . . . as I traced the tiny brands Tolliver Bedloe had laid into his slave's hands.

Both hands. So small were the forged irons that their marks might well have gone unnoticed, if singly set; but no; o'er the years—scarification showed this to be the work of long years—Bedloe had set his marks all across Celia's palms, both palms, identically. Till now it appeared as though ants, indeed, or some other steady insects, had been frozen in their course.

In my horror, I held Celia's hands quite tightly. Perhaps I forgot—for how could it be so?—that I held the hands of a woman. *This* woman. Who sat with her jeweled eyes cast down, her profile tucked toward her shoulder.

Celia showed me where Tolliver Bedloe had first signed her: just under the fifth finger of her left hand. I had to look closely to read the brands: T—O—L. "Tol," said Celia. "They called him that when he was a boy, and I was a girl."

"He's been doing this to you since you were children?" I

took care to speak of Bedloe in present tenses; for Celia needed no reminding of his demise. Earlier she'd wondered aloud what would happen to those she'd rendered masterless. To whom would they pass? Would they be put to auction? Speaking of her two surviving brothers—Eustis and January—she'd begun to cry. They'd suffer for what she'd done, though they'd be happy she'd run, and they'd urge her on in their prayers. This she knew; yet still she said, "I meant to slow him, not kill him. Slow him so I could run. If we returned home, he was . . . he was building me a cabin. He was set to stow me away—far from all the others—and . . . and *use* me in privacy, as his father used Pleasants. . . . I couldn't. I couldn't!"

Bedloe's plan was plain; and I saw it too clearly when Celia showed me the rest of his handiwork. His branding was a progression of pain; and I care not to contemplate the path his perversions would have taken had he lived, had he secreted himself away in a cabin stocked for his own pleasure, with Celia naught but an instrument of same.

Celia sat back to unbuckle her own boots, the soles of which were worn through. I did not press her; it was she who persisted with the sickening show. Her right foot bared, she fell back onto her elbows and set her heel atop my knee. "The heel," said she; and I turned her foot this way and that, toward the light, till I saw the ornate brand, big as a bottle top. It was blurred, but I read ABED.

"It was Tolliver's father marked me first. I wasn't but four when he bought us all. After the fire."

"If you were four . . ." said I.

"Tolliver wasn't but a boy, still," said she. "Fourteen."

They'd been children together. Had been taught together by tutors. Augustin Bedloe had raised Celia to be the boon companion to his boy. She'd known some perversion of privilege; and the field slaves had hated her and Pleasants both. As had the white women of the house, from whom they were kept. When Celia had had her first blood, she'd been presented to Tolliver. He was twenty-one; and she was a gift meant to mark his maturity. On her he began to practice his branding; and other perversions learned at his father's knee.

How could she not revel in his end? And so I said it:

"He's dead. It's done."

I'd hoped to stop her show. I was unsettled, deeply so. But no: she continued: . . . it seemed she had to.

The brands tracked the soles of her feet as they did her hands: a tight line from heel to the fifth toe, just where the delicate pink instep met the firmer flesh of her feet. The pain would have been extreme. So, too, the shame of suffering it without recourse.

Celia stood.

"No," said I, "please no"; but she turned, and raised her skirt to show brands set behind her knees.

Turning again to face me, she shrugged her blouse from her shoulders. It fell to her waist. Her breasts: bared. Too beautiful. Full. From them I had to turn away. But Celia took me by the chin, gently, and turned me back. To see. To watch as she raised the heft of each breast to show what dark work had been done beneath them. There, just there—I raised a finger to touch it—was the still-swelled, livid brand I knew had been burned upon her aboard the *Ceremaju*. Twenty, thirty, *fifty* brands of like design I counted, there, beneath her breasts.

Celia took my hand in hers and . . . and I found the weight of her breast in my hand. And she moved nearer me, or I moved nearer her; so that it simply occurred: I kissed the ruined flesh. Kissed, too, the fullness of each breast.

In time, I'd find and be shown more brands. When she was naked, they barely showed upon her body; for Tolliver had hidden them all, and hidden them well. This, surely, his father had recommended: what if he should have to sell her? Best not to spoil her looks. Fine, though, to spoil her soul.

. . . Yes: Tolliver Bedloe's brands had known total license. They'd found their way to the most indelicate, shaming spots upon her person. One hundred and sixty-two, total. Celia knew each, could count them unseen; as I suppose Christ could count the steps to Calvary.

That night in the Lion d'Or the show of Celia's pain went no further than her hands, her feet, her breasts and legs; for I could suffer no more of the sickening show.

Indeed, it was Celia who ended up comforting *me*. She assured me the physical pain was long past; and with tears, a smile, and a childlike shrug, she supposed that Tolliver Bedloe would bother her no more. "Unless he walks in death."

I said nothing at this; for she thought it the strangest of suppositions.

Celia sought to convince me that she would be well, *was* well. And she sought to thank me, too. This she did in the only way she knew: by granting, by gifting her very self. She knew no currency but her beauty; and this—from long and sordid habit—she meant to spend.

I could not allow it. O, I *wanted* to, yes. I admit as much. And I might well have indulged if I'd not had my own secrets to keep. What's more: the love I bore for Celia could suffer no such show, no matter my needs and wants, my dreams and desires. If ever she were to love me as I loved her, then . . .

O, what plans I had. O, what a future this fool presumed.

. . . *Enfin,* I resisted. Both Celia and myself. I saw the smooth plane of her back, slick with perspiration, its slow sloping to her buttocks. The shape of her calves was enough to. . . . Let this suffice: I went slick here, stiffened there. . . . But now was not the time, no; for who knew but that forces of law stood on the far side of our door? I said nothing of this, of course. Nor did I make any protestations of love.

In my denying Celia, I was but a gentleman. Or so Celia

thought; and when finally it seemed she understood my tacit refusal of her favors as a kindness, not a denial, well . . . I knew then more pleasure than any bodily commune could ever provide.

We settled on the floor, between the foot of the bed and the fire.

Once we'd settled, and Celia had redressed, she'd sent me downstairs in search of vinegar. See, I'd suffered badly the mosquitoes we'd met waiting riverside. The vinegar was easily had. (Harder it would have been to find in the Lion d'Or a drink that was *not* vinegar.) With the vinegar and warm ashes combed from the hearth, Celia made a poultice; which then she applied to the pox upon my lower legs, my hands, my neck, and even my face. The pinkish welts were swelling still, and stung. But there was relief: the remedy worked, even as it rendered me quite the sight: rather polka-dotted, I suppose.

As she worked, I stared at the designs upon Celia's hands. Once, twice I dared to raise her hands to my lips, hoping my kiss might suffice; for I knew no words.

Now we were tired. Spent; utterly.

Returning with the vinegar, I'd wedged a slat-backed chair beneath the door's knob. No one in Norfolk, or downstairs at the Lion d'Or had taken undue notice of us. It seemed we were safe, secure enough to sleep; and so we settled somewhat. We lay on the floor, not speaking. (We'd fears no talk could tame.) Celia leaned into me, into the crook made of my raised arm. I worried she'd feel the mass of my bound breast; but otherwise, I daresay I was content, with Celia beside me. In time, she hummed; and sang a song that served as lullaby.

Indeed, sleep would creep upon us. But I'd not surrender to it; for I needed to watch the grimed window for signs of first light. I insisted Celia take the bed. She, in turn, insisted I take it. In the end, the bed knew neither of us. At its foot, before the fire, we lay, curled as familiarly as siblings. We'd been sincere: our mutual insistence was no show; for neither of us—then—felt entitled to more than the floor.

Part Two

22

Fernandina

STILLNESS and fear. That's what I recall of the running. . . . Stillness and fear.

Isham Lowry was true to his word, and awaited us at the wharf. We slunk from the harbor at dawn, and Lowry set his course: south, from Norfolk. Though the wind was steady, the going was slow; terribly so.

Though often we were within musket shot of the shore, still Celia and I ventured topside. To breathe. To let the breeze lick the salt-sweat from our limbs; salt, too, I saw on Celia's cheeks. I thought then that Celia ran the greatest risk of us all, despite what I'd heard from Lark. Every port we'd put in at sat in a slaveholding state; and Celia was an absconder who'd left a dead planter in her wake. What's more: she was property, and precious to her owners. If we were discovered, Celia would be driven home; by sea, if she were lucky; by land if she were not. And at the hands of drovers she'd doubtless be abused. As for what might attend her back in Virginia, well . . . such thoughts I forced from my mind. As to Isham Lowry and myself: Would we be let to surrender our charge with a shrug and apologies? Hardly. Shackles there'd have been, and lashes and a shame that would spread in advance of our names. In a word: ruination. . . . O I was ignorant indeed; and blessedly so.

We'd no choice but to run on, now we'd begun. But how would we know when we'd arrived? Where were we headed? So much was unknown. In truth, all I knew for certain was this: I feared the loss of Celia, and would do whatever I could to prevent it.

Charleston. Savannah. We achieved these, and lesser ports as well.

Always, Lowry was well met. Still and fearful in the humid hold, we listened to his wharfside dealings as best we could.

Lowry seemed engaged in no particular trade; and I cannot say what it was boxed beside Celia and me as we huddled in the hold of his boat. Notions, I suppose, making their slow way south to supplement his trade in those roots, fruits, and vegetables which we found basketed and busheled all about, and which sustained us. Soon it came to seem that our captain was a man amenable to any plan, at a price. So it was that somewhere among the islands of Georgia, Lowry agreed to take aboard a great clock—crated in a coffin—destined for a family of means somewhere in Middle Florida. At news of this, Celia started. She grabbed at my hand. We dared not speak—the deal was being struck too near—but when again the word came, *Florida,* Celia tightened her hold on my hand. Her eyes were wide. She nodded with such force that beads of sweat flew from her brow. She huddled so near I could verily taste her sweat, smell her hope as earlier I'd caught too well the scent of her fear.

Florida: a haven. She'd long heard the stories.

Back at sea, I conferred with our captain. It was decided: when he took to the port at Fernandina—on Amelia Island, at the mouth of the river St. Mary's, and just o'er the Georgian border—we'd disembark, first waiting for night to fall.

Afterward? Afterward would come; and I supposed we'd know it when it did.

Midday, it was, when we made the Florida port; wherein we abandoned the one particular of our plan: we'd not wait for nightfall before debarking.

It was intolerably hot in the hold, the air so close I feared for Celia's health. She made no complaint, of course; but once—as we sat listening to the dissonant port-song, and willing away the hours—I saw her sway. Her shoulders went slack, and she broke at the waist. This was something more than sleep; and O, the dread with which I watched Celia for the first signs of fever.

I'd already squared with Lowry, and he'd been off for an hour or more on matters of custom. Or so I presumed. It was then I suffered a weighty thought, one that dragged my soul to the very depths. What merchant would not seek to profit twice on the sale of the same product? Though I'd paid for our transport—and paid well—mightn't our captain, however kind he seemed, be right now scheming to surrender us outlaws? Surely the reward would be steep; and Lowry would profit well from any suspicions he'd long tended. Surely he'd not be surprised to learn that Celia was a bonded woman; O, but a murderess to boot! There'd be certain money in that. And I . . . what was I? Alas, whatever I was, of this I was certain: I stood in violation of innumerable laws, natural and otherwise; and it'd be best if I were not found out.

So off the ship we crept.

Still Celia wore her obscuring spectacles; for, when a stevedore in Charleston ceased his flirtations—suddenly, thinking an unresponsive Celia blind—we both of us knew ours to be a solid ruse, and one we would maintain whilst we ran; for it might earn us measures of pity and deference, and let us proceed free of suspicion. So: Celia played blind, and I feigned distemper at her extreme dependence. In truth, her steady hold of my elbow anchored me; for it was I who stumbled wharfside, nearly tipping into the drink as the full force of Florida fell upon me. . . . O Florida: an inferno; but I was no brave Virgil.

The sun was a sizzling disk; and seemed to hang so low that I—in my sudden near-delirium—made to swat it away. The swat being the unofficial salute of the Florida territory—wherein multiform species swarm and buzz and bother and bite, by day and night—this was not remarked, not unduly. As for the Florida air, it hung in denial of its proper state: it rendered itself a liquid, and through it one had to wade, not walk. It swelled the flesh, osmotically, till fingers bunched as full as stalked bananas. Hair rebelled: it was as though one had pulled Spanish moss from the low-leaning oaks and piled it atop one's head. The tongue of the sun lapped at my pink skin, which seemed to sizzle like fatback thrown agriddle. All I wished, elementally—that is, without regard to custom or courtesy, or long-kept secrets—was to strip to my First Suit and leap to the cool relief of the water. I did not, of course. In fact, as terribly conscious of my body as I was upon that wharf—owing to its great discomfort—I tightened fast my waistcoat: no one, least of all Celia, should see my sweat-defined silhouette; for it would deem me sister to the man I seemed.

From an old woman the color of honey I secured a hat folded of palm fronds; this, I say with no exaggeration, was lifesaving. Its brim gave shade to my face and neck; and out from under it I could peer here and there, keeping watch for "a way." (How I longed then for some of Mammy Venus's rude prophecy! Happily I'd have turned a forked stick to the earth, or sought clues in the dregs of a teacup or kettle.) Said woman kept a cart and stool not far from the wharf; at this she sold sundries woven by her own hands, as well as tiny pies and tomatoes. Huge tomatoes, I might add; which she kept in cool water and sold—sliced and salted—for a picayune. Rich as meat, they were; sublime! And as I revived, losing myself in the taste of tomato— . . . the red flush that followed upon the first bite, and washed back the flake and taste of the ham pie I'd bought—Celia rose onto tiptoe to whisper, "See what she's set down. There." She nodded to a corner of the cart, and took care to look away; for of course we meant for her to seem sightless.

The cagey old crone had laid down a fan, folded of fronds like the hat; expertly made, it opened as gracefully as anything seen at the courts of old. This I knew when the woman raised a like fan to her own face, putting it to purpose. She showed an excessive relief; but still the fan was demonstrably . . . needed. Celia must have one. I'd thought of purchasing her a hat of her own, but had adjudged it too showy, too telling a luxury. It would mark her as unaccustomed to the heat, to the discomfort that was a slave's lot. A fan she could sport with greater discretion. I asked its price, and heard spoken a sum I cannot recall; but I do know the seller offered change; for it was that transaction which betrayed us.

I, distracted by the smooth workings of the fan, did not see the proffered change; and so it was Celia who reached to take the coin from the woman. Too late, she knew her mistake. Their two hands hung in suspension, their fingers nearly touching, and there was communicated . . . something; something which seemed to charge the very air. . . . The cartwoman's long and crooked fingers. Celia's smooth and upturned palm, pink yet showing Bedloe's dark artistry. Finally the woman stood to a great height, and let fall a single coin into Celia's hand. This Celia passed to me, dutifully, and in resumption of her role. We both of us sought words; but were preempted when the woman asked:

"You come a far ways?" She addressed Celia. Stay: it was more than that; for as she spoke she came around to the front side of her cart, squinting into Celia's queer spectacles. On she came steadily, by inches. She'd not stop till she gained the far side of those spectacles: Celia herself, that is.

Celia looked this way and that; and then raised a crooked fingertip to pull the obscuring glasses down onto the bridge of her nose, to show her eyes in all their splendor. Said she, "Far, yes. Very far."

We were running. And not a hundred yards ashore, we'd been found out.

It was then that I spoke up, begging the vendor not to—

The woman stopped me by snapping her fan to its widest spread. From behind this she took me in. Up and down; deeply. She circled me, predatorily. Her bare feet showed beneath a skirt of gray homespun; and on these she moved smoothly, easefully.

Aged, she was, yes; but quick as a cat:

Snatching the hat from off my head, she said not a word. I fell to choking on the last of the tomato, which I'd let to well in my mouth since the proffering of the coin and the sudden end of our charade.

I stood ready to run. I had hold of Celia's elbow; but I steadied somewhat when I saw that she was calm, and that she and the woman stared at each other. Could they have spoken, and I'd not heard their words?

The woman retook her stool in silence. From a sort of quiver beside her, she drew a fresh frond. From under her cart there came a machete. She looked at me. I stepped back. But then she took up a smaller knife, better suited to the delicate task at hand; which was the fashioning of a band for my hat.

And when I reset the hat upon my head, it fit better; it fit perfectly: as if I'd worn it a lifetime.

. . . All around us the townspeople milled. There'd have been no escape if the woman had betrayed us; and already I've spoken of reward—significant, surely, to a seller of ham pies and tomatoes.

Before standing to return the hat to me, the vendor took up a stub of pencil. She had a square of brown paper, on the foreside of which she'd figured her till: it was thick with ticks and cross marks. On the reverse of this she wrote something. She then pressed the paper into my hat's crown, and smoothed it while saying, "The heat is supreme. This here paper will cool you some." I smiled at this kindness; but before setting the hat in its place, I glanced within and saw half of the word she'd written, and knew the letters only. I looked up, quizzically; and she answered with, "Set it up there now; and leave it sit a while."

Turning to Celia, she added, "That hat might see you both through, might keep you both cool. Mind me now, and go."

We walked stiffly down the street and dared not turn back. Once, Celia stumbled, nearly going down on one knee. Again I feared the onset of fever; but I relaxed when I understood that she'd but retaken her role: the unsighted slave. Meanwhile, it was all I could do to set one booted foot before the other.

Midway down the street, Celia drew me into the shade thrown by an inn. She directed me to take off the hat and hand it to her, showily, and mop my brow with my shirtsleeve. "Pay me no mind," said she; which order I followed as best I could whilst Celia, slyly, read the paper, still in the bowl of the hat.

It was a name: Travers. Celia raised her violet eyes o'er the steel rim of the spectacles. Her eyes found mine, and she repeated the name. "Travers," said she. "Travers will see us through."

Soon we'd stepped from the shade, Celia leading me back out into the blaze. Her step bespoke a plan, a purpose; and this she actuated before the post office, once we'd found it, outside of which we waited a long while; or so it seemed, now we kept to a runner's clock. Finally, Celia asked of a black man did he know anyone by the name of Travers. She'd an uncle by that name on the island; he was supposed to meet her dockside; her master (me) was effecting a transfer, as she had recently suffered a loss of sight and—

And the man cared not a whit for her woes; but still he made our man: Isaac Travers. He'd land some miles out. We'd get there by keeping to the road on which we stood presently, and turning right at what remained of the old mill. The man made to leave us; but Celia reached suddenly for his arm. "He has land, you say? He's . . . he's free, then?"

"Out that way," said the man, nodding us on. "On foot, be an hour." He looked at me in appraisal, and added, "Maybe more'n an hour." Returning to Celia, he closed with this: "If'n he's yo' uncle, seems like you'd know he's free. Ain't that so?" And he tipped his straw hat, gullied down the middle and ragged around its edge. Too, I think he winked; but of that I am not certain.

We set off in silence, both of us listening behind for whoever might come.

23

A Night's Refuge

OLD Isaac Travers was free, indeed, and possessed of eighty-one acres and a wife named Lottie who shared his Quaker-like ways. It was Lottie who stepped out onto the sagging porch to call off the dogs and greet us as friends, and Lottie who served us a most welcome meal of ash cake and fried bacon. Later, when Isaac had come in from his indigo—meeting us with kindness, and few questions—Lottie took from the sill a still-warm pie of mixed fruits; and when she set it center all atop the table of pine at which we four sat, and cut into the bronzed crust, and loosed steam as sweet and light as a thrush's song . . . well, it was then I thought Celia and I might truly, truly make it away, to live free.

That table of deal was inlaid with delicate tile, chipped from years of hard use. Its edges were nicked where knives had slipped. All else in the kitchen was simple, save for a lamp with a ruby shade and a lone geranium that sat upon a second sill. Heat shimmered from the stove set in a corner. Through the kitchen's windows and walls—the planks of which had warped, and spat their clotting clay to the ground—I saw day give way to dusk; but not until night had fallen did we speak of things of import.

Blessedly, no questions bore on the past. Where we had come from. How we had traveled. Why we had run; for surely it was understood by the Traverses that we were runners, both. No: all talk was of the near future, and where next we'd go. And when our hosts spoke, our eventual freedom was implied. Such talk soothed both Celia and myself.

"You'd best not be stayin' here," whispered Isaac, moving to close the kitchen windows, lest enemy ears had come near. Thereafter the kitchen grew hot, hotter than the blue evening beyond. "No," he repeated, "that wouldn't be wise."

Lottie laid her hand on Celia's and explained: "Every port city's a tattler's town. Secrets come and go on every ship."

Celia had set aside her eyeshades, and I could see her eyes shining kindly as she took up the work-worn hand of Lottie Travers. "We'll not stay the night," said she. "There's danger in it for you, and I . . . *we* wouldn't want—"

"Hush, now," said Lottie. "When ain't there danger in doing the right work of the Lord? You'll stay tonight. And you'll leave out of here at first light."

Lottie spoke on: "Seems no one saw you come. Let it be that no one sees you go. That way you'll take all the danger with you, 'longside our prayers." She sat back in a caned chair that worried beneath her weight; for Lottie Travers was a woman big of heart and body both. "Was Banana May sent you, wasn't it?"

Yes, said I, it was. Though she'd not given her name, and I'd seen no bananas beside her cart, surely the woman we'd met had been Banana May. Lottie had taken my hat from me with a knowing look when first I'd passed into her home.

This after we'd walked some bright and dusty miles, eyes trained on the scrub for the remnants of a mill. When hooves were heard behind us, we started. We each of us thought to take to the brush; but the road was long and straight and already we'd been seen. Our blood cooled when an old cartman came up beside us. Of him, we asked the way to the Travers stead. Fifty paces more and we'd see the mill, said he; and so it came to pass.

Already we were known on Amelia Island. Isham Lowry, of course; but also Banana May, and the two men of whom we'd asked directions. Friendly or no, caring or no, they all knew that a white man and a black girl had set out landward. The girl was blind, or nearly so. The man was thin and tall, with a foreigner's tongue and a bloodless face. Should questions be asked, by anyone, we'd come quickly to mind.

Two maps were brought down from a can set high upon a shelf. On these were markings in many colors, which I took for proof that the Traverses had helped others, had shown them the way as now they'd show us.

Isaac had marked his own acreage on the map, and spoke of it pridefully. "I's had this here land—with *paper* rights, mind—since eighteen-hundred three. Bought it before them Spaniards said no Americans could. And me and Lottie, we's held it through raids come down from 'cross the border—them Georgia men calling themselves patriots, when they ain't but pirates—through the Spanish fall and whatnot." Lottie nodded at the map, urging her husband back to the business at hand.

Isaac sighed; and doing so, showed his age. Bodily, he seemed strong, despite the stoop of his shoulders and the bow of his back; but that sigh had shown his soul, and it was laden. Said he, "Find you a boat that's goin', I say."

"The overland routes," said I. "What of them?"

"Nah," put down Isaac. "Where you gonna head? Out into Middle Florida?" He said Florida as *Fla-dah,* with both *A*s soft as gossamer satin. "Ain't nothin' but planters out that way, grabbin' at the land."

"And," added Lottie, "you'd be twenty-eight, thirty days overland to Pensacola. Half that to Tall-hassee. And that's if you had horses twice as good as any we got to give. And Isaac, he's right: there's nothing in the midlands but more of what you're running from, like as not. . . . Cotton going in. Plantations spreading like wildfire. I'm agreeing with my Isaac: go from here by boat. Shore-ride down to the mouth of the St. John's, maybe ride the river to the Cowford."

"That's right," said a nodding Isaac, tracing the route with his finger. I saw that already it had been marked in red. "There's the way. And from someways along down the river—right about here, say—*then* you go overland. Get onto the King's Road and make yo' way south."

"Is there . . . is there more South than this?" It seemed to me we'd been days and nights sailing to World's End.

"There is." Isaac laughed. "I ain't been; but yes, sir, we got more South if'n you want it."

We all laughed. Perhaps my release was sweetest: Isaac Travers had called me sir.

Talk returned to the King's Road, which the British had built down along the Eastern coast. It was then the Traverses turned to each other, nodded, and said—in unison, almost theatrically, and in the Spanish style—"San Agustin."

Simple as that, our way was set.

Again the maps were consulted. At night's end they were tucked safely away.

I slept that night in the wide, downstairs hallway of the Travers house. "The better to catch what breeze may come," said Lottie. I had a blanket to spread beneath me, and a second to roll and bunch beneath my head. Lottie asked did I have all I needed. I said I did; but I saw who it was I most needed, wanted, and lacked as Lottie led my helpmate away: she and Celia would share an upstairs space.

Doors with screened windows were set at either end of the hallway; and that night a breeze did blow, bearing the throaty croak of frogs, the chirp and chortle of insects I did not care to encounter. Unable to sleep, I rose onto tired legs and tiptoed to the front door. I meant to take in the moon. It was full, or nearly so. . . . Now it's true: the sisterhood attributes too much to the moon; but still I'd felt its strength at Les Baux, and since the ascendance of the dead at Monumental Church, well, I felt somehow . . . stronger. And so now I wonder: did I hope to siphon more strength from the moon, to draw it down? Perhaps.

Instead, I saw the moon had cast its blue o'er the black land. And I saw upon the shadowed porch a glint of silvered steel: a shotgun, cradled in the arms of Isaac Travers. He kept watch in an uncushioned rocker, two hounds at heel. . . . Sister-work? I cannot say. Prayer? Perhaps. All I know is that I asked the moon and its Maker to bless the man.

I retook to the floor, unseen. Sleep would come, fitfully; and at dawn I'd wake not knowing where I was.

24

Into the Territory

In St. Augustine, I'd begin to dream in English. Not at first, no, but some months after we arrived. Simple dreams, these; odd in the ordinary way. Not witchly. Not conjured dreams, no.

Jarring, it was, to wake having dreamed for the first time in a secondary tongue. I knew English, of course; albeit from books. And English was of course the shared tongue of Celia and myself, though she'd acquired much French in her months abroad with Bedloe. And when I grew tired or upset or scared, I would revert to French; though always Celia—for want of confidence—would answer me in English. Too, English was the language of our escape; and much came to depend upon my facility with a tongue that first sounded blocky and overly broad, lacking the nuance and nicety of French.

Though my dreams would turn to the language I was living, I cannot say that I settled too readily into English. For the St. Augustine we found knew many tongues, and my ear was often confused. In time I'd acquire—through study and witch-trickery, too—knowledge of most all the speech that spiced the city's stew: Creek and Catalan, Mandingo and Muskogee, et cetera. And yes, Spanish, of course.

Upon our arrival in the city, the Spanish had been gone but seven, eight years. The treaty which bears the names of Adams (J.Q.) and Onis had been signed in '21; whereupon Florida—both East and West—were annexed to America. Territories, they were, are; though lately talk has turned to statehood.

It was the Spanish who'd made a haven of the peninsula, who'd sheltered slaves slipping down from the Southern states. (Such were the stories Celia had heard.) Americans, however, favored the British model of slavery; and thus suffered not well the lenient ways set down by the Spanish, whose paternal approach had allowed runaways to live freely, with access to law and land, as long as they swore allegiance to a pope who must have seemed as distant as God Himself.

It was a pope, of course—in collusion with a king—who'd first sent the Spanish unto the peninsula. Thereafter came a band of Church- and crown-blessed men whose mellifluous names belie their savage deeds:

I go back to Ponce. Juan Ponce de León, who took these shores early in the sixteenth century, and named the place for the flora that abounded: *La Florida.* So, too, did the Calusa abound; and Juan Ponce found not the fabled Fountain of Youth, no, but instead found the air thick with the natives' cane arrows, tipped with flint, fish bone, and shell; all of which split upon impact and slivered through gaps in the Spaniards' armor. Juan Ponce de León returned to Cuba to die of his wounds, his fountain unfound.

Pánfilo de Narváez, who gained the bay of Espíritu Santo on the western coast, later came to march his men among the Timucua, demanding tribute and allegiance. Within a half year, these conquistadores would retake to the Gulf, ruined, sailing off in hastily built boats: the bottoms caulked with palmetto fiber, the sails stitched of clothing, the rigging woven from the tails and manes of the horses they'd had to eat.

One of Narváez's men—Cabeza de Vaca—made his way home to speak of La Florida's savages, its sand-strewn wastes, its snakes. . . . He deemed it a luckless land, best let alone; meanwhile, he plotted its plundering, and sought the patronage that would allow it. O, but pity poor Cabeza; for the title of *adelantando* was granted instead to:

Hernando de Soto; who, having brought low the Inca in Peru, sailed from Havana in 1539 with a complement of six hundred men settled onto nine ships.

De Soto explored West Florida, gathering pearls aplenty; but it was gold he sought. Only gold would satisfy. So it was his men tortured tribesmen, certain they could trail their speech toward cached gold, hidden, hoarded in the midland hills. Fever felled de Soto—a failure—in 1542.

Thereafter came a priest—Luis Cáncer de Barbastro—who'd but martyr himself to the Tocobaga. And Tristan de Luna, who'd sought with de Soto the Seven Cities of Gold. His five hundred men, who'd soon turn mutinous, crossed from Cuba to find the Coosa plague-stricken; for the Spaniards preceding them had left behind the pox.

Midway through the sixteenth century, the Spaniards despaired of mining La Florida. In supplication they raised their empty hands, and let the Indians alone.

A short reprieve it would be; for, in 1562, Spanish interest revived when La Habana burned with rumors: Frenchmen, it was said, had dared to sail inland on the River of May—the Spaniards' San Juan, and our St. John's.

* * *

Owing to unexpected kindnesses and excess of coin, Celia and I made our way onto that same river St. John's the Spanish and French fought for some two hundred and fifty years ago. On it we sailed, unquestioned, aboard a midsize mail packet we'd hired onto in Fernandina. Again we played the roles of Planter and Blind Concubine; this time doing so to full effect.

We sailed the St. John's at dusk, our boat so low on the water that the crocodilians lounging bankside looked down upon us. Never, never will I forget first seeing their eyes, lit to a sulfurous orange by knots of pinewood burning their turpentine atop the pilothouse, hot and bright in their brazier of steel. The saurians massed at our approach, slithered into the black water and came to scrape their plated selves against our hull.

The cypresses shone silver by our light, and silver, too, were the crowns of swamp bay and the water lilies bobbing all about. Four-legged creatures crashed through the cane. Birds fluttered from our fire. All was steeped in a most eerie silence.

Happy we were to reach the Cowford, where—by prior arrangement—our pilot poled us ashore. Cowford they called it; for there the river shoaled, and cattle could cross. Of course, now the Americans have renamed it Jacksonville, shaming the place with the name of that militarist who sits athrone in Washington.

From the Cowford we proceeded by hired cart to the banks of Black Creek, itself navigable for some miles; but as we'd no boat of our own, it was decided—after a converse that had its hard edges, owing to fear on both our parts—we'd pass the night in an old blockhouse we found. Its walls were timeworn, but its roof was true. Vines had overgrown the whole, and this curtain of green kept the moonglow from its few rooms, featureless and without furniture. Where the light was brightest—neither had we a lamp, of course—

Celia and I settled atop some hastily gathered moss. In the quiet, we heard snakes aslither, creatures acrawl. And surely it was some admixture of fear and fatigue that let us sleep, seated, shoulder to shoulder, our backs flush to the cool coquina wall.

I woke to an unfamiliar sound. The quarried shell and timber all about me seemed to shiver. The sun was yet low; the hour early. Nearer, nearer came the noise till finally I heard within it . . . hoofbeats.

Oxen. And a rude cart whose wheels stood tall as a man. Tall as . . . me.

We'd no choice but to hurry from our shelter and hail the trap. This we did, too hastily; for as we rushed from the brush the startled driver raised high his whip and sought beneath his seat for some greater means of defense.

"No, no," I hastened. "Friends." I pointed to Celia and myself, and back to him.

The man relaxed somewhat as I told a fast tale about a foreigner and his friend, nay slave, who'd lost their way as night fell. The slave was ill, and poorly sighted, and the foreigner had brought her from Middle Florida in search of St. Augustine and *un médecin* therein. "Pray," said I, "are we near the place?"

"Hop up," said he whilst still I made our case. He nodded to the bed of his cart, wherein were set several stumps newly drawn from the ground; and which looked like rotted teeth as they rolled, their roots outreaching. "First, see, I thought you was a band of red men comin' from out the woods. With tommy-hawks and whatnot. I liked to stripe my draws, speakin' plain." He laughed with relief, and I could see that he cared not at all for the particulars of my story. Neither did he show his empty palm, as others had.

Celia nudged me to silence; and I desisted from my storytelling as we stepped to the back of the cart. I helped Celia up, and settled myself beside her. Soon I moved to where I could converse with the cartman; for this he wished to do. Unfortunately, he fell to using words that offended, tossing them o'er his shoulder like offal. (He spoke of Celia as though she were not present.) Soon I let my English devolve to shrugs and simple queries, and the man abandoned hope of my good company. But neither could I speak to Celia, now; and so the three of us rode on in silence as the day rose to a boil.

Be he mean, malicious, or merely a fool, I cannot say; but the cartman we'd waylaid led us astray.

We were an eternity in the ox-drawn bed, alternately bumping o'er dry road and slogging through wet. The shade was inconstant, at best. We were hot and hungry, and in dire need of natural relief. (I would loose my water roadside, choosing to do so as a man does; for, though Celia turned away, decorously, still she was near.) Too, we were exhausted; and so we both of us dozed, deeply, despite our discomfort. Waking, we discovered that already we'd traveled some distance south of the city.

Our pilot was en route to some southerly settlement, where he'd take to the Indian path and make his slow way westward to trade with the outlying natives. Only then would he return to St. Augustine proper. Now, with the day advancing, I sewed together the scraps of his narrative, saw his plan, and protested, mightily so.

Thusly did we find ourselves stranded long, long miles south of the city, at the headwaters of the Cawcaw Swamp; from whence we made our way—through scrub, mind, with nary a path to guide us—onto the banks of Moses Creek. Reasoning that water wants itself, we followed said creek hoping it would lead us oceanward.

The way was indirect, and we wandered south as well as east. To a second body of water. Not the ocean, mind; but rather that creek I now know to call Pellicer's. From there the way was easier; though still we trod o'er scrub and hammock, Celia singing to alert snakes and whatnot to our coming.

Eventually, we gained a road passable to wagons as well as horses; here, luck led us further. Though we procured no ride, we followed the road to the western bank of the largest body of water we'd yet seen: the river Matanzas, which wends its way northward, to St. Augustine.

Still we were well south of the city; for St. Augustine sits some fifteen miles or more north of the location I describe. Between the river and ocean lies Anastasia Island, and it was at this island's southernmost tip that Celia and I found ourselves. The tidal waters being then in recess, we were able to achieve the far Matanzan bank, thus trading scrubland for sand. Opting for river over ocean, we walked on, watching for watercraft: anything that would afford us faster passage into the city.

At first, I thought it was the purple beautyberries I'd dared to pluck and eat, starved as I was. (I'd seen a shorebird do the same.) Then I thought the swarming mosquitoes had siphoned off too much of my blood, leaving me light-headed. Perhaps it was the sun. Nerves, too, could complicate things; this my bowels told me time and again. *Enfin,* as we made our slow way northward, I fell into a state of upset the like of which I'd known but once before: in Richmond, when the unquiet dead bricked beneath Monumental Church had sought to summon me.

I told myself, nay I insisted that I was sick; and simply so. O, but I knew better; for I suffered not a loss of strength, as would seem sensible; but rather I . . . changed. My limbs were supple, my step resolute; but my innards were achurn and I felt reason forsake me, time and again. I would mark a site—a tree of distinct shape, say—and then, some fifty steps on, I'd turn to see the tree and not recall a single one of those fifty steps.

Celia begged me to slow down, and I thought I complied; but I'd turn to find her far behind me. Once I wandered off the strand, onto dune; and found thereon a path overgrown in greens and browns. On this I ran, *ran,* drawn on so strongly I didn't feel the palmetto snagging at my stockings, sawing through cloth to cut and bloody my skin. I heard Celia calling; but I was not free to stop.

I crossed that dune to the ocean, spreading blue beneath a bluer sky that showed no clouds. The salt air was invigorating; but nothing could counter what it was I suffered as I fell to my knees in the sands and let spill all my stomach could spare. Bile, it was; too, some of the beautyberries bounded up whole. My body was no less confused than my brain; but somehow I rose again to run.

Celia followed. And soon we came upon company. But they'd not carry us northward, no. They were in no condition; for they were dead; and had been for centuries.

Celia would later say my eyes rolled white. That I tipped back like a plank, flatly, onto the Matanzan sands. In my head I heard naught but murmuring—there was French within it; of that I was certain—till again my senses ran riot and I suffered the full effect of a history I'd yet to learn:

1562. Huguenots—French Protestants—have dared to colonize upon the St. John's in defiance of the Catholic king of Spain.

From their Fort Caroline, the French attack Spanish treasure ships. Worse: these corsairs are *Luteranos;* this the Spanish king cannot, will not abide. He sends Pedro Menendez de Avilés to route the infidels. Menendez sails from Spain with eight hundred men and arrives to overtake a Timucuan settlement on the coast, renaming it San Agustin.

Whilst the Spanish settle, the French settlers set to attacking. Five hundred Frenchmen—under Jean Ribault—sail southward in five ships; but a hurricane seizes the ships, setting them ashore well south of St. Augustine. The very day of the wreck, the Spanish—on a forced march, through torrential rains—arrive at an unguarded Fort Caroline and slay the one hundred and thirty Frenchmen resident within, renaming the redoubt Fort San Mateo. And lest the French misread the blood-message, Menendez's men string the dead through the trees and stake in the sand a scroll which reads: WE DO THIS NOT AS TO FRENCHMEN, BUT AS TO LUTHERANS.

Returning to St. Augustine, Menendez receives word from his Indian scouts that the shipwrecked French sit ashore some miles south. He sails with but fifty Spaniards to discover the French stranded, stalled by an inlet of the sea. The French surrender; and Menendez—promising the soldiers safe passage back to a fort they do not know has fallen—binds them hand and foot, and ferries them across the inlet in groups of ten. Catholics are bade to step forward; and artisans needed in St. Augustine are culled from the lot, carpenters and caulkers and such. The remaining French are drawn deeper into the dunes, where—on the orders of Menendez—their heads are dissevered. One hundred men die in ten groups of ten.

Later, a like number of remnant French struggle to the same inlet. This group—Ribault among them—meets the same red fate. In toto, some two hundred heads fall to the sands at that inlet the Spanish will come to call *Matanzas:* "massacre."

The very same at which I'd fall.

Two years after the massacre, a Spanish-loathing mercenary, Dominique de Gourges, is dispatched by Catherine de Medici, who has sworn vengeance upon the Spanish king (her despised son-in-law). De Gourges lands on the peninsula's northeastern shore with one hundred arquebusiers and eight sailors. He allies himself to those Indians whom the Spanish have betrayed, and soon Fort San Mateo sits a shambles. O'er the slaughtered Spanish are set signs: WE DO THIS NOT AS TO SPANIARDS, BUT AS TO TRAITORS, ROBBERS, AND MURDERERS. The avenged French sail off, leaving the land and their Indian allies at the mercy of the Spanish at St. Augustine, where Menendez sits as the city's founder.

In time, the rulers of Spain and France will seek and grant forgiveness, mutually. Such are the rules of conquest, I suppose. . . . But the dead have rules all their own; and the Frenchmen who'd been surprised by knives knew all too much of time and nothing of forgiveness. O'er the bloodied shore their residual souls lingered, for two hundred and fifty-odd years. So frustrated was their life force, so full their death-strength, that I—drawn to it—fell aswoon; not into death, but a state akin to it.

A night was passed on those death-strewn dunes. A confused Celia took *me* for dead; for she could find no trace of my blood's coursing, nor could she discern breath: my chest, she would swear, moved not at all. And though it must have been cold comfort, Celia curled up beside me that night. I, upon hearing this, would wonder: Did she know . . . ? Had she seen . . . ? What secrets had I shown in that deathly sleep?

But no: Celia would say only that she'd cried, that she'd despaired. And that she'd been rather more than surprised when, at dawn, my eyes had opened to show—she swore it—my pupils slowly, slowly retaking their rightful shape.

I'd not recover for some days; by which time we'd gained St. Augustine. A fisherman had been waved ashore by Celia. I can report no more of the particulars; for—having again met the massed and disquieted dead—I suffered a loss of sense and a lassitude many times greater than that which I'd known in Richmond. . . . No. All I can record—begging excuse of my morbidity—is this: upon waking from that first Matanzan interlude, I began, merely *began* to understand that which now I know:

Of all witchly traits I suffer the strangest: I am death-allied.

How was it I knew the dead as I did? When, from whom had I learned the language they speak? Perhaps from the succubus, Madeleine, who'd spoken . . . nay, it was not speech proper; for it came through a throat from which she'd torn her tongue. Yes, sense and blood both pulsed from that ancillary mouth, above which her girlish lips were still. Father Louis, then? The incubus-priest, her paramour? Or was this alliance an affinity borne on the blood of certain sisters, a talent akin to scrying or forevision or such? I cannot say. I do not know.

Let this suffice: I am somehow allied to the unquiet dead. If I am the wick, they are as wax surrounding me: it is their moribund *press* that fuels me, that lets me burn as I do.

Though already I sensed this, still I was left to wonder how, how, *how* to make a life among my guardian dead? Among such obverted angels as those hovering south of the city, amidst the Matanzan dunes, who'd gifted me with . . . something—strength, I will call it—in proportion to the terror they'd known at life's end, and suffered still; for indeed, once I'd recovered, I knew myself changed. Stronger; yes.

I woke in a hot white room. I was prone; and it was with relief I saw that I wore my clothes, filthy from days of running. I'd no memory of coming to this place. Water: I remembered water: sailing from the Matanzan inlet. After that: nothing.

. . . A boardinghouse, in the northwest quadrant of the city.

Celia had secured the two rooms that composed the whole of the second story. On the first floor lived the owner, a free woman who sold soaps from the door of a house that was hers by rights unassailable. It was a lean-to affair of tabbia and timber, and our rooms had a stunted balcony overlooking the cobbled street, quiet save for when sailors or a horse cart came clamoring past.

Therein, we let the past recede. We read, nay scoured newspapers, some from as far north as New York. In these we found no mention of ourselves. No adverts. This was welcome news, indeed. Still it was a struggle to stave off thoughts of discovery, of debasement, of lashed backs and darker things beyond; for I'd learned the territorial penalty for what I'd done: death. As for Celia, well . . . her thoughts I cannot here record; for she'd speak of such things only when pressed; and I did not press.

Soon, our store of funds was depleted. Celia had begun to help our aged landlady in the making and vending of her soaps; but to our purse she could add but pennies. It was time for me to rise, to do what . . . what a man must.

The Spaniards had left behind a skein of land grants, the disentangling of which greatly complicated American settlement of the Floridas. St. Augustine—being the East Florida capital—was no exception.

In theory, land could be had on such terms as these: cash; first come first served; with a minimum purchase of a quarter section—one hundred and sixty acres—at a price fixed at $1.25 per acre. With the help of usurers, speculators, and scouts—all happy to acquaint me with the ins and outs of credit—I sought a smaller parcel for ourselves, an arable slice of some greater pie. The problem, then, was not so much the financing of a homestead as the finding of one.

I shopped; and spoke ad nauseam of hillocks and hammocks, sea cotton and such. I sought a tract suitable for citrus—I'd opted for citrus o'er silkworms: a whim—and searched as far north as the mouth of the river St. John's, as far south as Twelve-Mile Swamp, and from the coast to the

Cowford ferry. I was partial to the Diego Plains, and a particular parcel sitting on Pablo Creek. This was not far from the King's Road, and therefore I might more easily avail myself of the biweekly post. Alas, further discovery disqualified said parcel, which yet belonged to a man who'd returned to Havana with the outgoing Spanish. I could have made application to Congress, the Spanish king, or the Havanese himself; but no approach was promising. So it was I determined I'd no business as a planter. I'd cleave to the city, Celia beside me.

But what, precisely, would my business be?

That very same land mess that deprived me of my plot on the plains presented me with an opportunity, some months later.

I met a Frenchman resident in the city, a man in American employ. He—Public Translator and Interpreter of French and Spanish Languages, was his title— . . . he had tired of translating the contested land grants and would quit his position once he secured a hoped-for commission to chart the upper Keys. . . . Territorial Translator? . . . French? Of course. English, yes. Spanish, yes. There'd be a bit of guesswork, and much thumbing of dictionaries; but I could do the job. Of this I was convinced (more by Celia than myself). And when my compatriot's commission came through, he presented me to Governor Duval as his successor; and all was set.

There came with the post not only remuneration—$275 per annum: a sum seeming more than fair—but also a home not far from the city's parade, or central plaza. The house, *our* house, sat on Hospital Street; and O, how I hoped we'd make of it a home.

Its two stories were of timber and coquina, quarried from across the harbor, on Anastasia Island. Fossilized matter, this, showing the whorl and curl of shells. How I came to love its texture, the way it glittered pink beneath the morning sun, and shone blue by moonlight. Even our roof spoke to the senses; for it was tiled in the Spanish style, with terra-cotta plates molded o'er the thighs of women.

The L-shaped house showed its shuttered back to the street. Within were rooms aplenty, a surfeit of rooms, opening onto gallery or courtyard, which latter showed long years' worth of experimentation in plantings: orange, lemon, peach, and pomegranate trees sat alongside bamboo, chinaberry, and sundry palms. There was fig and a single live oak. The kitchen, safely distant from the main house, sat in the shade of a Spanish chestnut, the yield from which we roasted and ate with as fine a wine as we could afford.

The intimacies of Norfolk were not repeated, and indeed seemed forgotten (by Celia, if not myself). Our duties were set. This we achieved through common sense, and without recourse to debate. Things civil were mine to handle. I was the man, after all, albeit one of scant consequence. That is, I'd not yet reached my maturity—I supposed I was approaching twenty-one, or may even have passed it; but easily, plausibly, I drew forward my date of birth, and claimed to be in my twentieth year—and therefore, though I was privy to territorial business, I was accorded no vote. But neither was I obliged to contribute my twelve days a year to the building and maintenance of the territorial roadways—a requirement I would have been expected to meet, surely, by the hiring of slaves; for I'd no slaves of my own. Save for Celia, of course, whom I had to put forth, time and again, as my property, on censuses and the like. (One day, in so doing, I renamed her: she was Liddy, thenceforth.) This pose of ours pained me. But it was agreed that we'd lie to ensure our safety, and keep what secrets we shared.

Celia's profile was, perforce, even more humble than mine; and if the larger world were my sphere—which manly role I did not covet—Celia held sway on Hospital Street. At first, she seemed to enjoy housekeeping; for she'd not done it before. Bedloe had kept her pure for his own purposes:

creaming and gloving her hands each night before sleep; trimming and buffing her nails himself, the dainty work done with tortoiseshell accessories. (Celia would suffer no tortoiseshell in the house.) . . . I will not say Celia fussed, not overly so; but our house was comfortable, quite. Flowers were brought indoors, and spiders chased out—even though Celia seemed not to equate a spider with its web, and cobwebbed corners were all but sacred: spun churches she would not destroy. Our linens were ever fresh; for she boiled and I pressed them. As for our meals . . . alas, I'd exiled myself from the kitchen, knowing it to be for the best—and Celia herself suffered her share of trial and error, some of the "error" so appalling that we nearly choked, if not on the food itself then on the laughter it elicited. In time, Celia mastered the basics; and later devised a fish stew that surely would have won her fame, if ever we'd opened our doors to the world beyond.

Though she was as unfamiliar with the ways of commerce as I, Celia did our marketing, too; had she not, it would have seemed suspicious. She would arrive at the parade early or late, when other shoppers were few. She befriended no one among the populace, be they bonded or free. Of course, she was remarked. (As beauty will be.) And we'd been living on Hospital Street but a short while when a bondman came to the door—rather boldly for my tastes—and asked after Celia. I was rude to my rival. When next a barber named George began nosing around, I dealt with him even more peremptorily. Among Celia's would-be suitors, her master was deemed mean. This Celia thought quite funny; but my actions had the desired effect. Soon no one came to our door. No one save the Indian who carted in our wood, weekly, from somewhere beyond the city proper. He was ruined, humbled to the dust, and was already astagger, asway when seen at midday; for he vended wood only to keep full his silver flask. No one save this Seminole—Yahalla, was his name—ever shared a meal with us on Hospital Street. Celia invited him on occasion; for—from their very first meeting—there existed a bond between them, one I shan't presume to define.

At first, I feared a too-steady stream of messengers bringing documents I'd not be able to decipher. I worried needlessly: I was well nigh two months in the post before asked to act; and then it was a letter come from Spain, and all I had to do was post it on to its addressee in Havana.

Indeed, a great benefit of my position as translator was easy access to the post, and the territory's official portmanteau. By one or the other, I wrote both to France and Virginia. Writing to Rosalie—as I'd sworn I would—I kept things simple, and discreet. I bade her write me back in care of the governor's residence, to use two seals, and to make no mention of Celia in our correspondence. As for Sebastiana, I procured a short novel—*The Castilian,* by Truesay Cosio—which was available as newsprint, and I set about ciphering a long letter to my Mystic Sister, whom I missed terribly. I posted first the newspaper novella, then the letter; and awaited her reply. Ciphering tried my patience—writing *this* word when one meant *that,* and organizing the mathematics of it all—but I knew Sebastiana would insist on cipher, for our correspondence was of a sensitive nature, indeed, and the French share not the American notion of a "silent," or inviolable post.

I'd hours to devote to my correspondence. My official duties were few; and soon I grew secure in the post; for I proved myself capable of translating all that came my way. This was owing to my self-schooling, a most extensive library of reference material, and . . . a certain aptitude I'd soon develop. By "aptitude" I mean, of course, Craft-work; to which I did return in time. Only to suffer consequences not even Mammy Venus could have foreseen.

25

The Translator

SEBASTIANA remained silent a long, long while. Rosalie, though, wrote regularly.

Miss Mackenzie's missives showed that absurdly steady and deliberate hand Mammy Venus had spoken of. Indeed, Rosalie wrote with a chirurgical precision, and must have used a ruler to achieve so straight a line. Sadly, the stability of her hand was not matched by that of her mind. I mean no cruelty, of course. Mere amanuensis to Mammy Venus, Rosalie gave no wit to the words she wrote; simply, she did as directed, copying out this or that passage, be it spell, secret, or some divinatory direction.

Mammy Venus retained possession of both Sebastiana's Book and my own, but soon I'd set to compiling a second *Book of Shadows* and into this I'd copy all that came to me from Virginia. This I did behind locked doors, secreted in my upstairs study. . . . Study? Nay; for it would devolve to a witch's den.

At first, I was frustrated; for Rosalie wrote of herbs, of fruits and vegetables. It was as though I'd written to ask, *What should a witch plant?* A long while it would be before I understood what Mammy Venus knew, having read between the lines of Sebastiana's Book: the Craft rises from the earth, and a sister is naught without her garden.

Within a cycle of seasons, I'd cleared our gardens of purslane and pigweed, wood sorrel and pokeweed, and planted beds that provided us with much in the way of foodstuffs: fruits, the vegetables Celia tended, the herbs I'd plant without explanation.

I now had in writing those spells that had let Sebastiana's gardens at Ravndal grow without regard to the seasons; but these spells I cast sparingly in St. Augustine. Once, having witch-fiddled with our garden, I caused the tomatoes to grow to the size of infants' heads, so large they snapped their stakes and fell to the ground. When questioned by Celia—who'd been house-bred by the Bedloes, and knew little of nature—I attributed the excess growth to Florida's general fecundity, and to certain secrets I'd carried from France; and there the matter lay. . . . Dangerous, this; for of course Celia knew nothing of *my* nature. To her I was but a man, and all my attributes—such as they were—were evident. A witch? No. And *sur*-sexed besides? No again. She knew nothing of *me*.

I tried to convey to Celia what news I had from Mammy Venus, though I hid from her the regularity as well as the fuller content of our correspondence. I'd asked Mammy Venus if she could "see" anyone in pursuit of us. She said she saw no one; but added that the sight had not come clearly: she could not be certain. And I heard from her—in couched terms, the better to keep Rosalie from questioning our role in the affair—that Bedloe had been interred quickly, with his fellow planters of the opinion that he'd met a just reward. His widow had called off the law; for she was content with having both Celia and her husband gone for good, no matter the means. Which good news was followed by bad: though the authorities sought us not, slavers did; for the Bedloe heirs—unconcerned with justice, but ever mindful of Mammon—were disinclined to cede the two or three thousand dollars Celia would earn at sale. This last bit I kept from Celia; for what would the sharing of such news have achieved? We could not have lived with greater care. Still, this keeping of secrets was saddening; and soon it would render our contentment specious.

Rosalie must have pored o'er the Books I'd left behind, reading aloud to Mammy Venus; who, no doubt, sat listening in the soothing dark, at times uttering, "La, la, yes; 'deedy, yes. *That* what she want. Send it on now, girl. Write it down and post it on." Thusly were those letters composed, I'm sure of it. Three sheets, they were, always, covered in Rosalie's too-precise hand, folded into quarters, addressed, and double-sealed. Weighty, they were: expensive; costing as much as seventy-five cents to redeem; for Rosalie never prepaid her post.

O, but I oughtn't to complain; for Sebastiana and the many sisters of her acquaintance rose from the pages of those letters, like scent from a flower, with offerings such as this:

". . . harvest yarrow, certainly. . . . Sacred to the Horned God. Hang it on a sill or fix it to a pane each Midsummer's Eve, to protect a house and the witch within."

"Huckleberry will be needed, betimes, for the breaking of a hex."

Bedstraw and burdock, cowslip and crocus came the list—alphabetized, I knew, by young Miss Mackenzie; who believed still that I was engaged in the crafting of some fictitious work. At other times, it seemed Rosalie fancied herself contributing to a cookbook, or a history, or a botanical miscellany. Poor Rosalie Poe: her head and her heart broken into bits at birth, and seeming never to recompose. Sad, yes; but fortuitous, too. For without Rosalie as vessel, nay conduit—I cannot call her a vessel, even; for I doubt she ever "contained" any of a letter's content—I might not have been privy to such whatnot as:

". . . plant raspberries, if the sun allows; for the brambles are tea-suited, the berries best for parfaits and pies." Slyly, I sent off for seeds, which I then sowed in accordance with the moon's calendar. (Seeds sown when the moon is waning will fail; those planted when a pewter moon shines full will prosper.) I made tinctures, and let them dry to flakes in the marble mortar I'd bought off the town's apothecary. (If it can be said that I had a friend in St. Augustine, it was he: the apothecary: Erasmus Foot, by name.) I whispered spells to myself at night, and tried them first on ants, then cats, and finally a flop-eared dog that ambled down Cardova Street each day at dawn, as if he'd a standing appointment to keep. Mind, I sought to cause no harm: these spells were silly—witchly commands akin to "sit" and "fetch"—and, what's more, they were without effect. The ants marched on unimpeded. The cats stretched languidly upon their warm sills. The dog would stop, lick my hand, listen to my nonsense, and shy off to his appointment.

Dear Rosalie even set to rhyming at times, thusly: "Lemons and lime prove useful over time / And roses, too, must surround you." Further, on the subject of roses, she wrote, "the petals are for puddings and powdering, and the hips can curry love." Just how to curry love . . . well, it was not told; and so I wrote to Sebastiana seeking rose-specific advice as well as seeds from her *roseraie*. As I heard nothing back, I planted what I could, careful to set a climbing variety of rose along our outer fence to dissuade the clambering children of a house further down Hospital Street.

Sebastiana? No. Nothing. . . . But rarely did a week pass without a letter from Virginia. Rosalie copied Sebastiana's

Book in its entirety. Mammy Venus continued to sell off the Van Eyn estate in pieces; and—with the proceeds from two candlesticks of Bavarian glass—Rosalie bought books on subjects Mammy Venus thought would interest me. From these Rosalie copied long extracts, rather than entrust them to a porter or private carrier.

Of course, I set to compiling a library of my own. From habit, I arranged these books spine-in upon my shelves; but they were of no interest to Celia, for whom I procured other volumes. (She was inclined to novels, and read *The Scottish Chiefs* five times if she read it once.) I got my books from traveling merchants, and left standing orders with the town's few booksellers: they were to buy on my behalf any and all books pertaining to certain . . . "ancient arts," I think I called them.

Books were easily come by at the port, too. It was there I got a calf-bound Galen off a South Seas captain who knew not what he had. Other tomes—old and salted, and some new-pressed, with their pages uncut—were had from crews eager to trade their tired libraries for racier fare. Thusly did I swap certain "French" novels for books on astronomy, folkways, history, and, especially, herbcraft. (Dried herbs make up nine-tenths of a ship's *materia medica,* and the healing talents of certain sea captains would shame many a sister.)

From my sailing acquaintances I acquired cuttings and seeds as well. What other paraphernalia I needed I got from Erasmus, or ordered through the mails. From the apothecary I bought those many jars which soon I'd labeled in accordance with their contents, the which I gained by means above-mentioned. I identified in cipher the more "delicate" substances: ground bird wing, bee stingers, snake eggs, and such. And throughout the house I hung herbs to dry (decoration, said I to a questioning Celia).

My return to witchery was slow, if steady; and when first I

plied the Craft in earnest, I did so for the common good. Only later would I stray and . . .

Stay. Let me stall that confession, that shame, and instead tell how it was I used my talents to benefit both the territory and myself:

I found that with a few words from the Galen and tea brewed of betony and lemon, I could induce a trance state and . . . Well, I would doze; and when I woke—if I'd had a document in hand: open upon my left palm, to be specific—all I'd need do was transcribe its sense, which had made itself known to me, somehow, no matter the language of the original. This was an aspect of the Craft rather easily achieved, and therefore I shan't record here the details of my first, failed attempts. (Note: some sisters rightly advocate gota cola to induce such sight; others say skullcap, or maddog-weed: neither worked for me.) The rub, though, was this: I could not work my translative trick in company, and dared not risk discovery whilst in a trance; for, though I never witnessed my own descent, I venture to say it was not a pleasant sight. I imagine my eyes backrolling to their whites, my tongue lolling forth, lizard-like, to "speak" the sense of the document I worked; but all I know for certain is that, of a sudden, I'd slip the trance, take up pen and parchment, and spew out the sense thusly culled. Then: sleep; for such work was exhausting. Waking, I'd write a fair copy and destroy those first pages, marked by scratch and ink spill.

In this fashion, I succeeded in translating Spanish, but also Dutch, German, Sicilian, Catalan, Cherokee, Italian, Greek, Swedish, and sundry other tongues. Soon the governor deemed me indispensable—albeit aloof, and strange in my ways—and raised my salary to $300 per annum. Still, the work came infrequently; and so I took on non-territorial matters, and found myself translating letters of love, loss, threat, et cetera, in exchange for coin, baked goods, bottles of port, and the promise of skilled labor of all sorts, if ever I should need it. (Thusly did I have a Minorcan expand the root cellar of our kitchen, much to Celia's delight; for it meant she had to venture to market less often: still she kept to herself, ever fearful of discovery.)

Emboldened by the success of my *thé de traduction,* as I came to call the concoction, I turned the Craft elsewhere. Shone it on Celia like a beacon, blinding her to what love she might have come to feel for me, naturally; for between us there was a sympathy—born primarily of circumstance, perhaps, yes—that I cannot, will not deny, even now.

. . . Alas, what I did was this: I sent two directives: Tell me, wrote I to Rosalie and Sebastiana both, what say the Books on the subject of Love Spells? Worse: I insisted on specifics.

26

From Longing unto Lust

WEEKS passed before Rosalie wrote in direct response. From Sebastiana, nothing: it seemed she'd forsaken me.

Rosalie's letter was long, and showed those characteristics I too well recall: there was the steady hand, yes, but also well-wrought sentences showing great lapses in logic—like presents with their bows undone. Still, it was with a quickened pulse that I slipped the letter from my cubby at the post office: *C,* for Henri, or Henry Collier.

She began, as ever, with news of Edgar. This was welcome, though I cared not a whit what the boy had written, nor who'd deemed it publishable. All I wanted to know was that Edgar Poe was far from Richmond, far from John Allan; to whom I worried he'd betray us, if for no better reason than to goad the older man. (No one save Edgar Poe could, or would, betray us.) With relief I'd read earlier of Edgar's exploits in Boston, to which place he'd hied shortly after our escape, putting out to port on his profits from the sale of Sebastiana's bracelet. There—lying as to his name and age—he'd enlisted in some branch of the service; something maritime, if memory serves. Of course, I wondered if Eliza Arnold had haunted her boy northward. Or was she bound to her grave in St. John's Yard? To have gained answers to such questions from Mammy Venus would have required too great a delicacy on both our parts; for Rosalie might well have roused herself at the mention of her mother or brother, or caught coded words related to either. And so, in my correspondence, never did I commit a sentence to paper which might alarm, dismay, or disappoint Rosalie. Much went unasked, unanswered.

Finally, in this latest letter, after news of Edgar—he'd been discharged from service (the facts of which were well glossed by his sister), had returned from points north, was living with family in Baltimore, and had achieved "renown" with *Tamerlane,* poems printed at his own expense (John Allan having refused him the funds)— . . . finally, Rosalie answered my most direct question. What follows I read in my noon-shadowed den, the sun sieving in through the shutters, my heart high in my throat; and all the while, I recall, Celia's song rose up from the courtyard garden.

To bind the beloved, wrote Rosalie—thinking who knew what?—one ought to extract, sun-dry, and powder the liver of a black cat; and make of this a tea, steeped in water poured from a cast-iron kettle. . . . Indeed.

Or: one could roast the heart of a hummingbird and grind it down with cubeb berries, musk oil, ambergris, honey, and oils pressed from the seeds of the marshmallow plant. (This from a Creole, once resident in Paris, and quoted late in Sebastiana's Book.)

Or this: a particularly loathsome approach to love's procurement: Hang a black toad by its heels for three days and gather its gall into an oyster shell; add to this—when next the moon wanes—a quart of ale, three marigolds, and a measure of rosemary balm. Brew; and cool. Finally—and can you not hear Rosalie giggling as she writes?—rub the dregs onto the breasts and genitals of the love object. . . . Would that I might, thought I; but if I'd access to the breasts and genitals of the love object, I'd have no need of such a potion!

O, how my heart darkened as I read the ridiculousness in Rosalie's letter; for surely solitude was my lot, sadness my ever-state. I'd find no love, not even by means magical.

Alas, there were things of use within that and subsequent letters treating of the same topic; and so here I record the following:

A list of herbs requisite to a lover's herbarium: mandrake and lovage, absinthe and spikenard, vervain and dragon's blood, dill seed, dulse, Beth root, quassia, and heart's ease; all of which found place of precedence in our garden.

And though I refrained from casting spells o'er the animals of our surrounds, and forwent all vivisection—blessedly; at least for the cats, rats, and bats whose body parts were called for—I did try a charm or two composed of things organic. I took to carrying in my left hip pocket a heart-shaped piece of lemon peel (dried by the sun for seven days), as well as five pumpkin seeds sewn into a honey-soaked bag of white cotton. In my right pocket I had always a pinch of vervain, purported to dispel the pain of unrequited love. (Note: Mark said charm a failure.) Too, I scoured the shore—steering clear of the Matanzan strip, mind, though it drew me mightily—until I found a water-worn pebble through which a string could pass; this I twinned with a piece of pink corral, and wore as a necklace. . . . But still Celia smiled at me as one would a sibling, and seemed as likely to climb into my bed as to clamber onto the roof and cockle-doodle-do the dawn.

. . . I grew ever more desperate. Having Celia so near, so

terribly near, rendered me tenfold more lonely than ever I'd been before. Even Celia remarked my melancholy; but how could I explain it away? It was as though I'd taken some saddening poison, and had now to search out its antidote, or die. O, I was dumb from love, heartsore and sick; and so:

Into our table wine went powdered juniper berries and a pinch of dried basil. Worse: I slipped into our dining room one morning whilst Celia marketed, took up that same bottle—which we'd decant that very night—and o'er it imprecated, thusly:

"Venus's wine, bubble and churn,
Passion burn, passion burn*!"*

Such was my state that I knew no embarrassment in so doing. And that night—with the wine complementing venison steaks, stewed plums, and bitter greens—we, nay I achieved naught but drunkenness; and the next day was without end as I heard in my ruined head the throbbing refrain, *Failure, failure, lovelorn forever.*

I'd desisted in my efforts somewhat when Celia came to me with a sachet she'd swept from under her bed—verbena, lemon, serpentaria root, and elder flowers, tied into red wool with a red string—asking, lightly, if I'd resorted to conjuration in achieving the state's business. "This is no official business," said I, taking the sachet, *"je t'assure."*

"What then?" she asked.

"I read somewhere that such a poppet keeps crawling things from off one's bedposts." This was cruel, but effective: Celia snatched back the sachet and resettled it 'neath her bed.

Celia—who doubtless felt increasingly free as months fell from the calendar—seemed . . . if not happy, happier. And though we lived in steady accord, with nary a harsh word spoken, there was nothing from her—no look, no touch—

that told of love, or love's slow approach. Meanwhile, my love, my longing, my lust was as milk in a jug: it turned, it curdled, till not even I knew what it had become.

Perhaps it was the half pants I wore that made me think myself all-man. Was it my post, my role as governor's pet? Or the salary, perhaps, that rendered me superior? Had I caught the Skin Fever of the South, and come to think myself white-entitled? Or was it simply Love and her lesser sister, Lust, left too long to war within me? Regardless, no reasoning will dissolve the shame that came.

. . . Eagerly I'd awaited our first winter. And indeed, the days did cool; and on occasion one could deem them "cold." But in the Florida territory winter looked a great deal like spring—save for the occasional frosts: the white and much-feared black, which could blast crops—and autumn offered scant respite from summer. Seasonal change was subtle; the calendar, confused.

We—Celia and I—had caught but a hint of the heat when first we'd run: that autumnal heat had been as naught compared to the dog days that descended when we'd been in the territory nearly a year. And worse still was our second summer; indeed, they say it is one's second summer in the South that lays one low, and to that truth I can attest.

That summer of '29 settled like a mantle o'er the city; wetly, closely it clung. At the post office, all talk turned to the dreaded twins of summer: fever and hurricane. Of fever I'd no fear, not for myself. Hurricanes? *Pish,* I might have said. At home, Celia and I let our prepared food go cold, not wanting it hot. We opened our shutters to the street the better to catch every last bit of breeze; and, secretive as we'd been, our neighbors—a brazen bunch, they were—poked their heads o'er the sills, to yoo-hoo and hullo. (Which temerity I checked by the hiring of a rat terrier, who charged the least distraction, teeth bared and barking.)

Too, in summer, we took to sleeping on the galleries—unsheeted, and beneath mosquito netting—myself above- and Celia belowstairs. It was either that or forfeit sleep altogether. Shortly, Celia professed again her fear of snakes and such, creatures that she believed could not trouble her if only she slept upstairs and not down, where she was practically in the yard proper. I could not counter her logic; for she did not pretend to present a "logical" argument. What could I do? . . . I admit it: I thought to dissuade her by introducing into an upstairs room a certain indigo snake that favored an old stump not far from our home. Such chicanery is illustrative of how profoundly I feared the loss of privacy.

What if I uncovered myself whilst sleeping? Showed my parts in sum? My den I could keep locked, and my ever growing Book I could tie tightly with ribbon, and hide. But no curiosity—I knew it to be true—was greater than my *self*.

Yet I relented: Celia and I moved her bedstead to the second-floor gallery. Pleading modesty, propriety, and such, I insisted we place it far from mine, so that she would sleep at one end of the L and I at the other. Too, I erected screens, and strung enough silks to do a seraglio proud.

Between our beds were thirty-one paces, and each pained me as I dreamed of taking them, singly, and nearing Celia. Nearing those delights of which I dreamed. Yes: I dreamed of taking that night-walk; taking, too, the treasure at its end. Thirty-one steps, and there lay all I longed for. Thirty-one steps, and there lay my dream.

. . . I say it plainly: I knew little of love, and lust had teased me terribly. There'd been the elementals, yes, and all they'd sex-taught me. Far better it had been with Sebastiana's boy, Roméo. And the courtesan, Arlesienne, well met in Avignon. But since then there'd been only that night in a fevered Norfolk, the memory of which I'd worn thin. Now I wanted more. For too long I'd wanted more. *I would have more.*

I stewed in my secrets, and treated love's fever with self-abuse. At this I became quite adept. Nay: expert. With Celia otherwise occupied, quietly I'd turn the key in my door and . . . and I'd set to it. I'd take down from its hook the gilt-edged mirror that hung above my washbasin. I'd arrange it just so, propped against a bedpost. Out from my cabinet would come a balm I'd concocted: oil thrice-pressed from olives; cantharides, or ground beetle, the aphrodisiacal qualities of which were espoused by no less than Cleopatra; cinnamon, which added a certain . . . sting; a hint of clove; and honey to smooth it all. And then, with all in readiness, I'd . . . well, I suppose the rest is plain.

. . . Perhaps not; for, built as I am, the feat was, is, a two-handed chore. With my right fist I'd pump at the prick whilst with the fingers of my left hand I'd pry the pearl from its shell of flesh. The resultant release brings twice the pleasure any man or woman might feel; of that I've since grown certain. To quiet myself I'd bite down on a length of leather kept 'neath my mattress for that purpose; and without which I'd have alerted all of Hospital Street to my pleasure. And pleasure it was. My sole pleasure, I will call it, those first years in the territory. A pleasure I would have forsworn, too, or traded away for one night, *one night* walking hand in hand with my beloved upon some moon-cooled beach.

In time, I acted. Did I take those thirty-one steps? Did I profess my love? No; nothing as bold, as brave as that. No indeed. Instead I brought Celia to me. And I committed deeds that cannot now be undone; for time holds to the truth, and makes of it that most immutable thing: history.

27

Matanzas

RIDE *the Madison dead.*

These words I discovered—in an unfamiliar scrawl, most decidedly not from the precise pen of Rosalie Poe—on the back side of a letter that arrived when I knew desperation too acute to suffer. This riddle—and a riddle it seemed; for what was the sense of it?—had been committed to paper in lead, and the writer had pushed the pencil without conviction. Light, so light were the words; nearly illegible.

The main of the letter—written by Rosalie—made no mention of the extra, nonsensical sentence. Her pages held news of Edgar, of course. Indeed, she'd torn "To Helen" from the *Southern Literary Messenger.* Only in a postscript did she write, "And, oh yes—dearest H.—do turn this Recto-

Verso to see that our Black Mammy has tried her hand. A delight and wondrous, don't you think? She commits hereon some words she heard in a dream—"

Mammy Venus had written? Extraordinary. And words "heard in a dream"? Had she divined something I needed to know, the specifics of which she could not entrust to Rosalie? O, but one sentence, and a sentence devoid of sense? Maddening, this.

O'er the course of our correspondence, Rosalie had sometimes written of things oracular. Pages in my Book were dedicated to the induction of dreams, though I was (and remain) disinclined to try my hand at same. But never, not once had the letters mentioned Mammy Venus's divining anything herself; till finally I supposed she sought to conceal her gift, her sight, from Rosalie. So: it was Mammy who'd written the words, not Rosalie.

Ride the Madison dead. How might the words relate to love's procurement, which was all I cared about, and the point I pressed in my letters? I sat with that letter for days; till finally it dawned on me: I'd dealt with seeming nonsense before, had I not, as translator?

I set to brewing my *thé de traduction.* If it had worked on Swedish and Muskogee, surely I could put it to purpose on a single, confused line of English!

. . . See me: sitting in shadow, sipping. Atop my trembling left palm sits the letter in question. And I got it, I did.

Mammy's words bore no relation at all to the fourth American president, as I'd thought they might. No: instead she referenced that massed presence I'd encountered when first I'd approached St. Augustine: those southerly spirits I'd long denied.

Rile the Matanzan dead, was what she'd heard in her dream. Surely it had come as nonsense to her, too; for she knew not the word *Matanzas*—how could she have?—and so had resorted to what seemed, what sounded like its closest relation: Madison. Too: *rile* not *ride*.

. . . An idea? Recommendation? Command? Regardless, I'd resort to the dead. My days of denial were done.

When next the moon was full—the moon again, of course; but it *is* true: better she be waxing than waning—I sailed south from St. Augustine on the river Matanzas. The tides and current were kind; too, the wind blew from behind, so that—in a boat rigged simply, with one sail—soon I achieved the inlet.

I kept watch for those dunes I'd never revisited, and wondered what I'd find there. I did not worry what I'd find, no; for even then I supposed the dead kind—confused, but kindly; and meaning me no harm. Still, would I have gone again to the strand if not sent by the Seeress? If I'd not been lovelorn and lusting, lost? No: I would not have: too fresh were the strange effects I'd suffered when first I'd stumbled upon the dunes.

The night sky shone a bluer blue, nearly black. And the dead Frenchmen made weather at my approach:

The clouds sank low, were as one with the wind whipping the sands, the rushes, the reeds, and the saw palmetto. Species—rabbits, turtles, birds . . . —skittered o'er the shore with what speed they could muster: scared, they were. The wind went chill and swirled, till it seemed the very sands might rise. Waves in the river tufted to white. Seaward, o'er the dune, the greater waves of the ocean ground shell unto shell till it sounded as though a sea-beast had risen to gnash and gnaw the land.

The river tide was high and rising still. The boat seemed drawn ashore. I let fall its black anchor, leapt thigh-high into the wintry water, and waded ashore.

I had with me a sack; for there are things, tried and true,

that quiet the dead, and these I'd taken care to carry: milk, honey, and blood, to be precise. Cow, bee, and me, we'd all contributed.

Trusting to sisterly instinct, I'd twined around each ankle five tiny bells of brass; ten total; for brass bells call the dead. This I knew from my dealings with the elementals. . . . Silence; save for the wind, the waves and the brassy tinkle of my tread.

I cast off a coat of skins and stripped to a simple tunic. So blessedly free, I felt, without that swaddling I'd come to detest. So free, in fact, that soon I'd stripped off the tunic to stand sky-clad—naked—a thing I'd never been before, not in nature. Thusly, I walked the shore, stepping my weight into the loam, letting the river suck at my soles. I was roused by the wind's caress: the tips of my breasts went hard, as did my member; slick were the lips of my sex. But only the moon watched; for no fisherman or sailor would pass the inlet at so late an hour, and the nearby fort—British-built, to guard the inlet and defend St. Augustine from a riverside assault—had long sat derelict.

I turned to face the rolling dune. I walked beachward, up, up to where the sands were thick and powder smooth. It was then I saw a red shadow spread. From the dune and down, down onto the beach. I knew it meant to mock the great exsanguination, the blood-loss of centuries past. *Here,* said the shadow. *Here fell the French.* Here their spirits were resident still. So, too, their bodies, devolved to bone.

The shadow seeped to where I stood, and spread to surround me. This was no trick of the moon's; for I felt it. Felt the ancient blood, arisen. The smooth sands made of themselves a cold and bloody mud, so cold my feet soon ached. And the blood rose further, rose to still the tongues of the bells and . . . No: it was not rising. I was sinking.

Knowing this, I knew, too, that I was unafraid; for something inside me had stilled. I sank to my knees, fell onto all fours, and surrendered to the sands. . . . Only then did they speak.

Within the wind could be heard the moaning of men. Falling forward, I felt them, too. And soon saw them: their bones rose to glow, blued by the moon. Bones, bones all about me. A bed of bones.

I sank lower, further; all was colder. Knowledge now was extrasensory: I saw not with my eyes, heard not with my ears, felt not with my fingers. I all but abandoned my body as I sank away, completely. Down beyond the bones to the dissevered heads; within which were the residual souls of the soldiers.

Menendez's men—their blades blunted by hacking through the vine-tied land—had not killed all the Frenchmen, no. And they'd cast the half dead into this tomb of dune with their heads not wholly off, but clinging redly to their bodies by string and strand. Many had fallen to suffer death slowly, their blood pulsing into the sands. And into the sands—where they lay cold-pressed and still, salted by the proximate sea—there'd come some ungodly alchemy. Till now here were the Frenchmen, conferring upon me, *me,* the mass, the very matter of the lives they'd not lost entirely.

Some pled for their lives in the French of the living; these were those whose half-fleshed heads were still attached to their skeletons. O, how they must have suffered! Not the worst of it was the *masticatio mortuorum:* in contact with their bodies, these men had devoured their own digits, proceeding on to their lips and tongues when fingers and hands had been whittled to bone. There were those whose souls, or spirits, were yet resident in their skulls; and it was they who spoke to me in a language the living know nothing of. This comes from . . . Beyond; and is composed not of words but of pure sound, pure sense. . . . Only now do I recall my French saviors—Sebastiana and the lot—speaking of the guillotined dead, and the severed heads that had spoken on after they'd fallen into the baskets of bran set to catch them, begging the executioner to stay a blade that had already fallen.

When finally I'd quit that moribund beach, taking with me its secrets—inchoate, these were, *are,* and I cannot here record them; for they defy transcription—I'd return to St. Augustine, to Celia, well changed. Understand: I was no better a man or woman; but as a witch I was tenfold worse. No: not worse: stronger. And worse, yes; for I applied that death-dealt strength selfishly, ruinously.

Of course, before I'd return three days would fall from the common calendar. Yes: two midnights and three noons I'd pass in the sands, amidst the dead.

. . . To explain, as best I can: it was Aristotle who spoke of a tripartite death. He believed every being was made of both body and soul; and that the soul could not exist without its bodily host. Perforce, the death of the body meant the death of the soul. Further, there were three aspects of the Aristotelian soul: the vegetative soul (which kept the body vital, or saw to such mechanics as breath and heartbeat); the animative soul (by which we move, and exercise our senses); and the rational soul (simply: the mind). The rational soul might expire without compromising the vegetative—as in cases of coma—but the death of the vegetative soul, or the cessation of the body's functioning, causes, always and without exception, death of the animative and rational souls. Or: utter death.

O, but not so, Aristotle; for though I was *bodily* dead those three days, never was I more alive. I did not breathe, and my heart hammered not; but my every sense was somehow engaged in taking, taking, taking what life force remained to the Frenchmen, till finally they were free—released from life: dead—and I was full of what effluvia had come from those two hundred souls. In a word: I was stronger. . . . As my argument is with Aristotle, I'll leave off; and take this up with the togaed one if ever we meet in a world beyond this.

Indeed, had one unearthed me then, doubtless they'd have deemed me dead; for I appeared to be in accord with those deathly indicators put forth from time immemorial, since Hippocrates penned his *Prognostikon,* and on through Pliny and Cornelius Celsus and . . . No. Stay. Was it not Pliny himself who wrote in his *Natural History* of the Romans Acilius Aviola and Lucius Lamia, both of whom rose up when lain atop their funeral pyres? Yes. And Plato, too, wrote of those returned from death. As did my physician of preference—the Greek, Galen—whose *De locis affectis* quotes one Heraclides of Pontus to tell of a woman thirty days dead of uterine suffocation who rose up and walked.

And lest one dismiss this belief in a temporal life after death as solely a classical concern, know that I'd turn in time to the Europeans; and there—in Kornmann's *De miraculis mortuorum,* in Garmann's treatise of the same title, in Bacon's *Historia vitae et mortis* . . . —I'd find proof aplenty; nay not proof, per se, but all told tales of those who'd come back from Beyond. Alas, nowhere, nowhere did I find word the first of a commune the like of which I'd known.

When I'd rise—the sands all but belched me forth—I was cadaverous. Pounds of flesh had fallen away. It was a quarter hour or more before I could open my eyes to the sun. And sand had packed my body, as the Egyptians packed the every orifice of their mummies. I huddled in the dunes that midday—no longer red, or shadowed—and I spat sand, shat sand, picked it from my nose and ears. This done, I dragged myself to the shore and floated in the river; which odd baptism revived me somewhat. I wanted washing as well; for I'd voided, utterly, when first I'd fallen. Not from fear, but rather as the dead do. Too, my sex had gone rigid; and rigid it was when I rose, though I knew I'd committed my seed to the sands.

Finally, I struggled into the boat, still sitting at anchor. Neither the wind nor the current cared a whit for my predicament; and slowly, slowly I poled my way into deeper water, where I sat watching the slackened sail with despair. I thought not of recourse to witchly locomotion; though surely, if Shakespeare's Weird Sisters had sailed the seas in eggshells, I might well have struck upon some means of getting a sound-bodied boat back up to St. Augustine.

When finally I achieved the city, it was to find Celia standing shoreside. Distraught. . . . Strange, this. Very strange. But then I saw something stranger still: here was not the Celia I'd known but days before. O no: worse: here was the Celia I'd long sought.

28

Bewitchment; and Worse

ALL the magic I'd done had fast found effect: Celia was bewitched.

Shrunken, starved, and blistered by the sun, I returned to Hospital Street in that coat sewn of light pelts, and wore beneath it naught but the shift I'd recovered from the sands. Still my eyes shied from the afternoon sunlight. My tongue felt like a strip of salt beef. My throat? Parched; for surely I'd swallowed sand. Which is to say, yes, I must have appeared quite the fright as I sidled ashore. Regardless, Celia rushed me.

"Henry," said she, "O, thank God, Henry, you're home. Where have you been? I was so worried. The governor's man came two days ago, and I had to lie, say you were . . . I don't know *what* I said, truly. I only knew I couldn't say you'd gone missing, that I was worried sick and feared that—" She threw her arms around me. She kissed me.

Her words fell off; but well I knew her fear, her frustration. I hadn't thought I'd be gone three days, of course; but still I'd left her all alone, when long ago we'd determined to stick together, to keep from all authority, no matter our need. Thusly had our loveless marriage evolved.

I made to answer her—lies, I would have told; for I'd no choice—but I tasted blood where some membranes had split in my throat or mouth, perhaps atop my tongue. Best not to speak; but I managed one word more: a whispered, "Celia."

She helped me home. We kept to the lesser streets; and soon I settled in a cane-backed chair set in the shade cast by our kitchen. With water from the *tinajone* Celia washed my face and neck, my hands; and I thought of Norfolk, years ago; and of the love, the life that had not come to pass thereafter. Ever fearful of discovery, I would not surrender that tatterdemalion coat; which was far too heavy for the day. I shivered, absurdly so.

As Celia busied herself in heating water for my bath and fixing a cold supper, I excused myself and climbed to my den. Suffice to say I was exhausted; though that scarcely summarizes the state I found myself in. I'd changed. This I knew. I was somehow stronger, but not in a bodily sense. In a soul or spirit sense, I suppose. And so I was eager to see what it was I'd gained; and supposed—rightly—that the change would show in what witch-work I did. . . . O that sinking within; for it was then I knew it:

And when Celia came to my door to say she'd drawn my bath, I saw it:

I'd changed, yes; and so, too, had she.

She rapped lightly at my locked door. I'd donned a robe, beneath which I was naked; for I wanted but to bathe.

It showed in those amethyst eyes we'd had to hide. They

shone in that shuttered room, dark from the dying of the day. I lit a lamp; and saw what I'd feared: tears. Tears and something else besides.

She said she'd missed me. I apologized, said I'd have felt as hidebound as she, not being able to summon help or organize a search, for fear of discovery. Yet I wondered why she cried, and why it was she seemed . . . off keel, as I'd never seen her before. A Stoic, she'd always been. Celia: who sang only when she thought herself unheard. Celia: who never spoke of times past, of loved ones lost. Now here she stood, teary, atremble. There'd come a change, indeed; though still I did not know myself responsible. Soon I would:

For, announcing that my bathwater sat warm in the downstairs tub, and that supper was on the table, Celia came to me. Not since Norfolk had she come so close. She did so with intent: she touched me. On the hand. I stepped back. She came on. To fall against my chest and kiss me, fully, on the mouth. When I opened my eyes, I saw the truth in hers, and it was then I knew it for true. I sickened to see what I'd done.

The potions and poppets, the spells and chants. . . . They'd all seemed ineffectual when first I'd tried them. O, but I was no longer the witch I'd been. Meeting the Matanzan dead had rendered me . . . more. And it was this—the death-alliance—that gave sudden, strong effect to what Craft I'd worked.

After that kiss, I recomposed myself. Or tried to. And I let Celia summon Erasmus Foot; for she was insistent. No doctor, he: the prognosis was vague; yet sleep was prescribed. Certain pills and potions—soporifics—were given me. And sleep I did; till late in the cool night, when I woke to a familiar tread upon the outer gallery. By moonlight I saw the slow turn of the doorknob, of cut and faceted glass. Its light shattered: a kaleidoscope, it seemed.

Again she tried the knob, so violently its light split and spun within my room. She did not knock; but neither did she walk away. And early the next morning I opened my door to find her opposite, acurl, asleep, tears having tracked her cheeks.

I did not ask after her behavior. And she offered only this: she'd worried about me in the night, had sought to check my health. "Nothing more," said she.

Shamefully, I say this: the next night I took no precautions. That is: I left my door unlocked. And resisted sleep, waiting for the scene to unfold similarly; as it did:

Again: her tread. Again: the turning of the diamantine doorknob. And . . . and there she stood, ten paces from my bed.

Her nightshirt was undone, its laces loose upon her bosom.

I feigned a deep sleep, yet I parted the netting that overhung my bed; and, shifting, drew back the sheets the better to accommodate my long-sought company.

Ten paces. Nine, eight, seven . . .

Though I knew little of love, and less of lust, I was expert at subterfuge.

And so, as part of my plans—O yes, I know it: there is naught but shame in this—I'd bound my breasts beneath my shift and donned half trousers that unbuttoned at the fore. I'd show myself as the man Celia believed me to be. But I deceived myself, nearly as badly as I'd deceive Celia; for I'd forgotten the . . . the processes of pleasure.

Understand: with Sebastiana's Roméo the sex had been sudden; splendid, but too sudden to recall in its particulars; and I hadn't had to hide myself. Neither had I dissembled with Arlesienne. As for the incubus and succubus—Father Louis and Madeleine—they'd diluted my desire with dread. More: one doesn't love a sex-specter—the iciness of the love act precludes this—one merely partakes, or is partaken of. And so this simple subtraction of my few partners renders down to the sum of one; and she's a one I've not yet mentioned: Peronette Gaudillon. Niece to the mother superior of the convent school. That girl of devilish gifts—truly—who'd nearly caused my ruin; for she'd slunk to my bed one stormy night, claiming fear, and I . . . I'd surrendered to instinct, and did to her what I'd seen dogs in the churchyard do. I knew no more of the frictive act than that. Still, I'd taken her, brought on her hymenal blood by use of my member. She *knew* me, yes.

Innocently—is not all instinct innocent?—I'd shamed Peronette. Perhaps I'd even ruined her; for along with her maidenhead went the prospect of marriage to a titled or landed man, indeed any man save one with a shame to twin her own: poverty, ugliness, or a lowly trade. And so she betrayed me, said to all and everyone that I'd seduced and used her, and that I'd done so with the Devil's help. She spoke of my sexes, said only a handmaiden of Satan could have borne such a being, said . . . *Enfin,* she—whom I'd loved in spite of all sense—helped speed me to judgment, and condemnation at the hands of Sister Claire. Condemned? I was, summarily so. As for Peronette, she escaped C—— with naught but her coal-dark conscience. . . . Often I've wondered where she went.

So, to prevent Celia's discovering my true nature, as Peronette had—it would take but a hand falling onto my bound breast, or a finger finding the split of my girl-sex where it sat beneath my scrotal sac—I . . . I bound her hands. Yes: with Celia beneath me, with my prick distended, whilst battling the buttons of my half pants, I panicked and pinned Celia's hands to the thick, moss-stuffed mattress. I bent to kiss her, and took her kiss in return. Nearly delirious I was, from the onrush of my every sense. I wanted to free my own hands yet worried where hers would wander. I thought, nay I *thought* not at all. I merely acted; and with that tulle we'd hung in lengths to stave off mosquitoes, I tied fast Celia's wrists to the bedposts.

At this she let go a sound so surprising I hear it still. Like that of an animal in a trap: a whimper, a whine; but then—whilst kissing her, whilst laying bare her body and taking what it was I sought, there amidst the darks and the pinks of her delights—I heard a change within the sound she made. Now it seemed a pleasure-song, and she sang it the more as I . . . as I bucked. O yes, I bucked. . . . A beast near dead of thirst, I drank down the trough entire. And only then untied her.

On successive nights we refined that most common of sins. I took pleasure, and gave same whilst staving off the question that came:

Was I not a slaver, no better than Tolliver Bedloe?

29

Ruination

FAIR and accurate it is to say: we were not ourselves.

We each were ever at the ready; and with our bodies—hers naked, mine artfully clothed—we buffed every tabletop in that house on Hospital Street. The rough deal of the kitchen. The mahogany of the dining room, which had come from the governor's residence in West Florida, in Pensacola; where Jackson had dined upon it (which fact—I must admit—pleases me, perversely). Too, we busted a delicate table in the east-facing parlor; after which act we lay sated atop the splintered mass.

In those first weeks I came to know Celia's body well; for she made it mine to work and wander o'er. I was a pilgrim, searching out and worshiping at her every point of pleasure; whereupon I retired behind a locked door to explore my own correspondent or complementary part.

I would not sleep with Celia, and this grieved her. In sleep I could not be cautious; and I would not risk discovery, no. Indeed, all through the throes of those shaming days, I heard but one refrain. I heard it when we were together. And when we were apart. When I spied Celia from the upper gallery as she worked the garden below. When I attended her at her toilette and bath. When we walked the bayside by moonlight, me fancying myself a true suitor. Always, I heard it; and the refrain was this: *If only she knew . . .*

What witchery would bind her to me if she knew? Knew me for a witch. Knew me for more than a man. Knew . . . me.

And what was I? Rather, what had I become? A satyr, for certain; but pleasure soon ceded to shame; for I'd reduced Celia, lowered her to what she'd been for Bedloe from his boyhood: a toy, which he'd broken. Of this I found much evidence; for Bedloe had laid his brands into Celia's every secret spot. These I found: under her arms, on the incurves of her buttocks, even on the most tender flesh-folds of her sex. I found them all, those whorls and curls of scar. O, what pain he'd pleasured in! I hoped he'd met its like in Hell. . . . But I was using Celia, too, was I not? And though I'd not hurt her as he had—I told myself I hadn't—surely I'd not helped her heal.

By the time I understood what it was I'd done, it was too late: already we'd drunk deeply from the well of pleasure, not knowing it polluted.

One late-winter morning I woke to find Celia busy in the kitchen. This in itself was not uncommon. She was always the first to wake; and it was a kindness I'd come to count on that she'd set out for me those preserves we'd bought or put by in seasons prior: quince or pear or apricot. This morning there were none. Neither was her hair done: the bun broken, its netting of close-worked lace gone. A new and different wildness shone in her eye. She said nothing as she sat working on . . . With a sickening chill I saw it: she was crafting a crop. Before her sat a basket into which she'd gathered Spanish moss and—I looked closely, but dared not ask for confirmation—hair. Black: hers. And blond: mine; for I'd let my tresses grow, and wore a plait tied back with a leather thong. How she'd gathered strands of my hair I'd no idea. More worrisome was this: she made no effort to hide having done so. These hairs—*our* hairs, stiffened by the addition of the moss—she was weaving into a whip of sorts: smaller, suppler, but nonetheless a whip; and I knew, on sight, that she'd put the finished thing into my hand one night. I knew, too, that I could not, *would* not do what she'd ask me to do.

That was the morning I saw the signs I'd heretofore ignored:

Celia's ringed eyes had sunken into her skull; for rarely did she eat. She'd shed weight, yes; and her skin had lost its luster. Her hair had gone brittle, and broke in my hands. Indeed, I could deny it no longer: she was sick, in body and soul. Still, I denied it was I had made her so.

She would see neither the doctor nor Erasmus Foot. And so I'd but one option left: I'd make her well. Was I not stronger than when first I'd bewitched her? Therefore, it stood to reason I could undo what I'd done. And if she no longer loved me, well . . . In truth, she had never loved me. This I came to admit; and I reminded myself of it daily; for Celia continued to present evidence quite to the contrary.

. . . O, but the breaking of spells is a different thing altogether, far harder than the casting of them.

I wrote to Rosalie, and asked Mammy Venus to "see what she could see." In my fiction (said I) my heroine had come to a terrible impasse, and I feared I'd not be able to write on till I learned how she'd break a love spell she'd too blithely cast.

I wrote as well to Sebastiana; though years had passed without a word from my Mystic Sister. Years! And not a word. This upset me terribly, and angered me, too; but what could I do but write and wait, wait for her to save me a second time?

There came from Virginia nothing of use. Rosalie, *la pauvre,* thinking she and Mammy Venus were aiding me in the novelist's art, offered this and that, drawn from that oddest of libraries in the Van Eyn cellar. (Quoting no less a sister than Téotocchi, Rosalie suggested I have my regretful heroine read Sappho backward by the light of black candles; which I did. It was but a waste of time and wax.) Yes, Rosalie read both Books—Sebastiana's and mine—as fiction (which was forbidden her by the Mackenzies), and thrilled to do so. And never did she seem to sense the urgency of the words, the truths the Seeress and I shared in our correspondence, though each letter passed through Rosalie, perforce, as stones through water fall. Worse: Rosalie reported that Mammy Venus "could not see what was to be done." Meanwhile, months passed; and Celia grew ever more rangy and wild-eyed. And . . . and it was all I could do to sate her in the night, all I could do to forget myself and act as she bade me act. Understand: she'd grown insistent, quite. And I was helpless before her. The worst of it was this: she slept at the foot of my bed, upon the bare boards, as she'd long done with Bedloe. And so we'd do what we did every night, *every* night; and then I'd free Celia—she insisted, too, upon restraints; and I bound her without complaint, ever mindful of my guise—and she'd all but slide to the floor, spent, her shame not nearly the equal of mine. O yes, yes indeed: Celia insisted on those shaming deeds to which she'd been bred by Bedloe. And whilst early on I'd partaken in these—ever less aroused, I was; though there's scant redemption in that, I know—now I began to refuse; for we'd progressed from sex to acts which muddied the heart and mind, left sullied the soul.

Celia met my refusals with supplication, with tears, with tirades; such that I relented; and let myself be urged onto greater degradations, till finally I dreaded the fall of night; for at night I knew, nay practiced a most active shame.

By daylight I redoubled my efforts to break the spell. I verily flailed at the Craft, all to no effect; none. All else fell by the wayside; till finally I had words of warning from the governor. I'd mislaid a Dutchman's letter, and had made mistakes on documents pertaining to the Arredondo grant, which confused further the ownership of some thousand-plus acres upon the Alachua plains. I let it be known I'd take greater care, but still I gave scant attention to my office.

. . . Was it the bewitched wine that had worked? Was it the amulets I'd worn? Perhaps it was the cake I'd baked, bearing anise seed and sweat wrung from both our blouses. I did not know. *I did not know!* All my efforts at undoing the unknown spell failed; though time and again my increased strength was evinced; and I had to take care, lest I afflict Celia further.

Finally, I perceived a slight change in Celia. She ate again; though not with a natural appetite. The flesh that had fallen slack was fuller. I did not know if I had effected this; but neither did it signify; for still Celia's will was not her own. Still she was beholden to me. Still she sought my . . . attentions.

In time—despairing of ever finding a solution of the supernatural sort—I thought I might at least distract Celia; and in so doing get out from under the governor's thumb, as it seemed I ought; for sanction came ever more frequently and our house—the translator's house—was now a shambles; and suitably so, as within it we lived as lambs ambling toward slaughter.

I'd set aside some money; and when I heard tell of a certain house for sale on the far side of the parade, I drew a bill of exchange—$891 was the odd price insisted upon—and secured the two-story home built of coquina. We would move. Perhaps I could convince Celia to occupy herself with the outfitting of our new house.

But no: she'd no interest in this. She did as I bade her do, and set up house; but in our daily dealings I saw her slackened will. I busied myself as best I could; but as to household matters, well, I did not know where one went for such and such a trifle, nor what one should pay for a crate of Liverpool china. Neither could I force myself to care; for I'd other concerns. Thusly our days were spent apart, in new rooms either empty or chockablock with furnishings left by the last tenant. By now, I'd compiled quite a bit of paraphernalia; the which I set up in a studio cum laboratory, keeping the key to same on a cord worn around my neck. By day I did Craftwork—no success to record—or assuaged my guilt and shame by absenting myself from our new abode; for I knew Celia was too fearful to wander in search of me, be she spellbound or no. (We'd seen no adverts; but still Edgar and the Bedloe heirs were uncertainties: the former driven by cruelty, the latter by coin. And though Celia wore her blue spectacles and carried a pass—written for "Liddy," and signed by me—slavers are common in port cities, and kidnappings not unknown.) . . . At night, Celia came to me; and—I will not deny it—always I complied, in the manner of old.

Celia's pleasure in pain grew ever more disproportionate to my willfully granting same. O, never, never was there a less willing sadist. What once I'd done for pleasure, now was penance. There were bruises, there were bites; but I drew the line at blades. Neither could I say what she wished me to say. Abysmally I played what roles she assigned me. (Eliza Arnold would have let go her stinking laughter, surely, had she witnessed this.) It was my sickly luck that Celia sought restraint, always; for still I heard that refrain, *If only she knew . . .*

All the while I begged relief of the Virginians, to no avail. Begged it, too, of Sebastiana. . . . Nothing. *Rien de tout.*

Then, one day, it came. Rather, he came: the post rider. And the minute I heard his tin horn, I knew it: he carried a letter for me. (Such presentiments had come more and more frequently, and accurately, since my return from the Matanzan dune.)

Sure enough, there I found it. In the post office. In the *C* alphabet. Yes: the letter was from she. Sebastiana! Finally. O, what a rush of love I felt then, forgiving my sister for having forsaken me. Now here was word from her—advice, some illustrative story, spells to reverse what I'd effected?—when it was most needed.

I scurried to the shade behind the postman's shop, and I held the letter in trembling hands. Quite large, it was. And showing her seal, and the familiar toad sketched on the fore, sitting fatly beneath a name that had come to seem mine.

Presentiment, indeed: I knew, *knew* that with the advent of this long-awaited letter all would change. So it was that tears welled when I slit the seal, unfolded the parchment, and read what few words she'd written. It was Sebastiana's hand, yes. And blessedly, she'd not used cipher. O, but why cipher what already was cryptic? For Sebastiana had committed to paper naught but an address:

No. 55, Leonard Street. Man-hattan.

And her signature:

S.

30

Northward

I RAN as only a coward can.

And I was one oxcart, two barks, and a stage away from St. Augustine before I began to understand the enormity of what I had done. For I'd run, yes. In the night. Leaving naught but a note behind.

I told myself I hied northward to see my Soror Mystica, now she'd broken her long silence. (And this was true, though not the truth entire.) I thought Sebastiana—who'd saved me, who'd shown me so much, who'd answered the first of my many, many questions— . . . I thought Sebastiana, and Sebastiana alone, could extricate me from what it was I'd wrought. I would go to New York as the Greeks had gone to Delphi, even though *my* oracle was a witch who'd all but abandoned me. Once she'd promised to follow me o'er the sea, to find me and host an esbat in my honor—such is the responsibility of a discovering sister—but then she hadn't even written me. I'd come to fear she'd suffered the Blood. But no: now I knew she was in New York. She'd come! And I'd have crawled up the seaboard to see her. . . . Yes, here was all the reason I needed to leave St. Augustine, and Celia. *To flee.*

And indeed I left suddenly—hushed and rushed was my departure from the territory—for I knew not what to do with Celia, and wanted only to deny what I'd done.

For too long, and lucklessly, I'd tried to break the bond I'd cast. And the house on St. George Street (so it sits, yes) proved not the distraction I'd hoped it would. Neither of us took to it, not really, though it was sturdy and well more than serviceable. The seller had added to our contract, at no great cost, that odd lot of furniture; and this included two portraits of (I supposed) his forebears. Though I thought this ancestral abandoning peculiar, it came to seem right that the doughty couple remained, overhanging the mess I'd made of things, staring condemnatorily down from within their frames of unworked poplar.

There'd been a day—now long past—when Celia and I would have decanted our best Madeira and settled before the portraits to name them, to bestow upon them a history of our own devising. Such were the inanities Celia and I had sometimes played, when first we'd arrived in the territory: pass-times, indeed. We'd have drunk, laughed, and made of our imaginings a night's sport. As things were, Celia said not a word about the portraits. I cannot aver that she even noticed them, though they covered a half wall in the upstairs salon. No: Celia had fallen too deeply for such drollery. She'd eyes only for me, my maintenance and usage.

Such was the state of our affairs when—in the spring of 1830—Sebastiana's letter arrived. So, yes: I ran.

I set cash and three passes (for "Liddy") atop my desk, the drawers of which I locked; for I'd leave much behind, none of which I'd want discovered. My study I secured, too, as it was replete with things requisite to the practice of the Craft, things that would have worried anyone but another witch.

Into a single bag went my Book, and clothes sufficient for a fortnight; for I'd travel to Manhattan as directly as possible, without dalliance. Surely I'd gain the isle within two weeks' time. My return? Well, in that note—and O, how I labored o'er those few lines—I said I'd sudden business in the North. Said it pertained to family, though I'd mentioned nary a relation (having none). Said I'd a heart ill-suited to farewells. (True, though no excuse.) Said I'd return by summer's onset, if not sooner.

Though I'd recoursed to the stage's timetables, as printed, I bungled the matter; thusly did I thwart my own progress. I went seaward from Cowford by barkantine—no steamer standing at the ready—and would not avail myself of a stage until we'd put in at a port of the Chesapeake; by which time I'd passed the best route to Richmond. I might well have returned there, but for this: I feared discovery, still; I wanted no haunting at the hands (O those hands!) of Eliza Arnold; and sought with fair desperation my Mystic Sister. So: northward. *No. 55 Leonard Street.* (I held to that address, and to S's letter as though it were a compass, or some other instrument requisite to a sure and steady passage.) I was in the Maryland port not three hours before hiring onto a mail stage bound for Philadelphia.

We achieved the City of Brotherly Love—which strange appellation struck me, when first I heard it—by nightfall. I was tired; for—as figured—I'd been well nigh two weeks upon the go. And so I resolved to fall abed in the first hotel I found. But no:

In Philadelphia, our driver set down two pouches of post, took up three others, traded his horses for fresh ones of Virginian stock, lit two torches of larch, and retook the road. I, to my great regret, was with him: the lone passenger; for he'd promised we'd find New York (Sebastiana!) by sunrise. I ought to have been suspicious when my fellow travelers declined to travel through the night; the more so when one—a matronly sort, with a hen's high bosom—bade me "Good luck, and Godspeed!"

Too soon I saw I'd no need of extra speed—God's or another's; for I had beneath me the hooves and wheels, the whip and will of a mail driver.

"Hardy, are you?" he'd asked, having given a fast hand and a faster farewell to my co-travelers as they descended the stage.

"I am . . . I suppose." Knowing not why he'd asked the question, I reasoned my response could cause me little harm. But that night I discovered "hardy" high, very high atop the long list of things I was not.

"Good," the driver had rejoined, "for we gots a carryin' contract set for renewal, and Mr. Bristed—he owns this rig, and more—he says there's coin in it for me if I ride her fast and well." He went on, speaking of the post as a husband might his well-loved but demanding wife. In truth, the driver was wedded to an idea, or ideal; which was this: the surety, the celerity of the mail; three bags of which he'd deposit in Gotham at sunrise, at any cost.

In short: the night was ruinous. And the object of stage travel—if one were hardy, nay *fool*hardy enough to "follow the mails"—seemed the separation of the traveler's bones, one from another, by means of the bounce, the lurch, the tip, and the spill. Of this I grew certain. Stay: I overtell it; for the best of drivers (doubtless mine was of this class) cause their carriages not to spill, or overturn entirely—whereupon, surely, he'd abandon all travelers roadside and proceed with the mails in his hands, or strapped aback, or clenched atooth—but rather they tip their stages side to side in repeated *near* spills, thusly wearing out the great wheels evenly whilst hastening on at Hell's speed, upsetting not the much-loved mails—no, no; fie and forfend!—but only the stomachs of those misfortunate few who accompany them.

See me: seated, nay trying to keep my seat in the full darkness of the coach—dark, yes; for I'd taken it upon myself to snuff the coach's two lamps, lest they, too, spill forth their stomachs and set fire to the banquette. My arms are upraised to crown my head. I have forgone balance, deeming it better—no: less worse—to be buffeted side to side than risk the shattering of my skull when the coach encounters stone or stump and launches me roofward. My feet, when serendipitously they find the floor, dance a palsied dance, the like of which would see any mummer tomato'd off the stage. . . . O, I swear it: my every sense was forfeit, my every organ unmoored and aswim in the stew of my self.

Despite the best efforts of my coachman, I survived; and arrived. I might have taken issue with the means of my delivery—for which I'd paid, mind—had not my eyes, when next they found focus, settled upon dawn-lit cliffs rising from the river Hudson. Owing to the stygian night just passed, it might well have been the very scape of Hell I saw, and not Gotham. . . . But no: here was Manhattan. And now my heart gladdened as down the Bloomingdale Road we hurtled, hooves and whip-crack waking the city in which, I thought, my Sebastiana slept.

My desire, my want for Sebastiana, was not sexual, no, but it was extreme; for it had grown in proportion to the shame occasioned by my misuse of Celia—a shame which receded as I rode toward my sister, my Sebastiana. Simply: it seemed I might trade my shame for salvation. . . . O, what a fool I was.

I sue not for sympathy, but rather say it plain: from the coach I fell, verily fell into the arms of the driver. He—who'd sought to sacrifice me upon the altar of Saint Post—was amused. This I knew when he laughed (not unkindly, no) and spoke a sentence of which I heard but the one word: *hardy.* Still, I'd have clung to him longer, leastways till the earth ceased its whirl-and-turn, but for this: my breasts, though bound, were flush to his broad chest; for he'd undone his cravat and unbuttoned his vest (both of a fiery red, and complementing that infernal coach). I pushed off him, and tried to steady myself. For long moments, my success was uncertain. The smiling driver seemed a buoy beside me. When finally I insisted he stand still, his pity was complete; and next I knew it he'd set me and my bag into a one-horse hansom, hired with his own coin. I heard him tell the driver to convey me—"slowly," said he—to that address I repeated from the far side of coherence.

Off we set for Leonard Street. I'd no occasion to thank, curse, or bid adieu to my Bristed coachman. I did, however, send thanks skyward for that most inadequate nag then towing me at something blessedly less than a trot.

31

Cyprian House

No. 55 Leonard Street.

Up the stoop of a dozen steps I went. Still my legs, nay my whole self was shaken from the night's transport: I felt like an uncooked custard. My heart beat hard. And surely I smiled; for wasn't I due to see again my Soror Mystica, my Sebastiana?

A sturdy, most impressive town house, this; all brick, with white sills and shuttered windows running four across on all four stories. The door was painted to match the shutters: black, and shimmering as if freshly tarred. Above it spread a glazed fanlight, rather like a spiderweb; for its woodwork was black-painted as well. Beside the door stood three-quarter columns, and sidelights through which I dared not peer.

I pushed the bell; rather, I pushed upon a brassy naval set beside the door, but heard neither bell nor chime. Beside the door—held to the brick by four screws—there was affixed a brass plaque; perhaps five inches long by two wide: tiny, in comparison to the house it meant to identify:

CYPRIAN HOUSE. The letters struck me as vaguely ancient. Romanesque.

My hand fell fast to my side; for I'd raised it, and was reaching again toward the doorbell when I heard within an insistent footfall. . . . Sebastiana? Was I finally to find my . . .

No. The door was opened by a girl dark as night but dressed in dawn-shades: a dress sewn of beiges, whites, and pale, pale yellows. She was young, perhaps younger than I. And though she was not as beautiful as Celia, it was to Celia that my thoughts hied; such that I stammered, "Hello. Yes. . . . Sebastiana? Is Sebastiana here, presently?"

The girl said nothing in response, but her smile steadied me. She stepped aside, and invited me into the first foyer, which was tiny but debouched into one much larger.

She shot past me, out onto the stoop to take up the bag I'd left there, forgotten. In my attempt to relieve her of it, I made of our two bodies a tangle of arms and legs. We knocked foreheads, in fact; the aftereffect of which was laughter.

I liked the girl; though that mattered not at all when next she spoke, saying, "I don't know of any Sebastiana, but perhaps the Duchess does. You, sir, are . . . ?"

Before me there hung an outstretched hand. "Henry," said I. "Henry Collier"; and I took her hand in manly fashion; that is: I squeezed it absurdly hard. She covered her wince with a smile. This I saw whilst still I held to her hand: a bird's wing, it was: delicate, sturdily made, and light, but long put to hard purpose: the pale pads of the palm were callused, the nails cut short.

Sarah was her name. After this introduction, I knew not what to say. Dumbly, I took in the surrounds.

The house opened off to my left as well as my right, an architectural fact belied by its facade. But it was plain to me soon enough: here were two houses made one. This explained the grand scale of the foyer, with its two staircases rising at either side and meeting—upon a landing well suited to Juliet Capulet—in an embrace of dark woods and fine detail: the banister, surely, was hand wrought, so, too, its spokes and finials. The stairs were carpeted in a mossy green, insewn with golden arabesques; and rods of gold held the carpet fast to each stair. Center all there hung a gasolier of brass and blown glass; and beneath this there sat a carpet of forested greens, golds, and browns, with lion's-tail tassels at its four corners. That square of rug could well have accommodated a roomful of furniture; but it bore a single round table of mahogany, with marquetry telling of an artisan's hand. Atop this sat a vase of cranberry glass, from which tropical blooms abounded. These put me in mind of the territory; from which saddening thought I was recalled by my companion. Again she spoke of this Duchess of whom I knew nothing:

". . . but if not the Duchess," said she, "then perhaps it is one of the girls, in particular, whom you wished to visit? They're all asleep still, of course; but if you'd like to return tonight, you can leave your card with me and the Duchess will consider it, and send a porter with her response."

"No, no," said I, confused. Fearing I'd be shown out, I added, "The Duchess, yes. I am here to see the Duchess." . . . A duchess, for true? Was Sebastiana the guest of some exiled duchess and her daughters? Wondering this, I found I'd a smile to spare.

"All right, then," said Sarah; but *her* smile belied her suspicions. Still, she did not show me the door. Rather, having stowed my bag in a closet set under the stairwell, she led me toward the right-side parlor. And sliding back pocket doors, she disclosed to me a room befitting . . . royalty, yes.

"Take your ease, Mr. Collier. The Duchess will be back by the nine-stroke—she always is—and then you can ask after your . . . who now?"

"Sebastiana. Sebastiana d'Azur."

Sarah wrinkled her nose, the better to recollect, it seemed; but this show devolved to a simple shrug as she said, "The name rings no bells. But the Duchess will be back shortly, as I say. You watch that clock, and dang'd I'll be if she and Eli don't hit that stoop before the ninth chime falls." The clock in question was a grandfatherly affair, square-headed, with its Swiss innards visible behind a belly of glass. "You've traveled hard, I see," said Sarah. "Some tea?"

"Yes, please," I said; whereupon she nodded and was gone.

The parlor was a perfect square, and solidly purple. That is: the divans, sofas, chairs, and ottomans, all were covered in purple velvet, and piped, tasseled, and braided in black. The frames of same were ebony. So, too, was the floor; rather, its wood had been stained black to match the furniture. A small carpet—purple, yes, but showing spots of a lighter violet; which were, in fact, the eponymous flowers themselves, thread-depicted and fine—sat beneath this suite of furniture. All other accessories, of which there were many, admitted but two finishes: silver or mirror.

Silver, too, was the tea set Sarah carried into the parlor. Its pieces were polished to a sheen, and were so numerous it seemed a sort of culinary chess set. Sarah bade me help myself; she hoped I understood, but she'd work to do. "Oh, yes," said I. "Yes, absolutely." Whereupon I thanked her for her kindnesses shown to a stranger.

"No one visiting Cyprian House stays a stranger for long," said she, excusing herself a second time.

I let the tea steep and set upon the iced cakes instead. *Tick tock* went the tall clock, as I waited for the fall of nine chimes.

The purple parlor was full of lesser timepieces, too: tiny

ones hung from ribbons, and silver mechanisms sat atop the mantel beneath bell jars. Proceeding with my inventory, I got no farther than a painting reflected in a mirror—huge, doubtlessly quite heavy, and, I knew, *very* expensive—which hung upon the forewall, its surface smooth and unblemished, the whole of it tipped just slightly down, the better to reflect the goings-on in the parlor. The painting itself must hang behind me, above me where I sat. Turning to take in its actuality, I nearly choked on the last of the cakes; for the beauty of the thing was . . . bold, let me say.

From where I'd sat—sunk deeply into the royal divan—I could read the painting's silver tag; for it was in keeping with the scale of the work: a canvas seven feet long by five or six wide. Ariadne, she was: *Ariadne Abandoned on the Isle of Naxos.* The artist was a Dutchman (presumably), named Vanderlyn. The date of composition, recent.

I stared up at this woman, well nigh life-size and wondrously naked, or nearly so: a diaphanous veil had blown on the winds of Convenience or Propriety and come to cover her crotch, the thatch of which shone through to complement the black curls falling beside her breasts. Supine, she was, with arms splayed overhead to frame a goddess's face, bespeaking sweet exhaustion and a deep, dreamless sleep. O, but if the subject did not dream, the beholder surely did. Namely: me; for I had to sip some tea to rewet my lips, which had dried as my mouth hung open in admiration of . . . of the art, of course. The art which showed a woman's legs supplely bent, her belly white as cream, her breasts as delectable as the cakes I'd eaten (and seemingly tipped with sugar roses, too). Indeed, I was quite . . . stirred by my Ariadne (yes: already she was mine); such that I had to shift myself within my trousers and would not, could not have stood if the Queen of All Countries had then come into the parlor *en parade.*

But my ardor cooled as I took in the parlor's secondary art; for it was thematic—bluntly so—and featured sundry

Judiths holding high the heads of Holofernes. John the Baptist was represented, too, as a naked Salome danced with his severed and salvered head. . . . Gore to offset the glories of Ariadne? This I sat pondering as the first of the nine chimes fell and, concomitantly, there came voices rising up from streetside.

32

The Duchess

I FLEW to the parlor's windows, and gracelessly pulled back the heavy drapes of purple damask, pendant from rods of wrought iron. . . . There she stood.

Not Sebastiana, but another. In an ensemble of burgundy and burnt-orange silks, showing that same panoply of shades that brandy will when held up to the light. Finely attired, she was; and quite fully attired, too, given the early hour. She spoke and gestured broadly across Leonard Street to a neighbor: the carriage maker, Von Hessel, whose works stood, between town homes as seemingly quiet and refined as Cyprian House.

She—the Duchess—had attendant at her side a man, a young man not much beyond boyhood: though he was tall and broad, the pale light of day betrayed him, shining as it did on a cheek yet unsullied by beard. As I watched, this boy—Eli, surely—took the stoop two steps at a time. From the door, he looked back, and waited for the Duchess to conclude her chat. He was well turned out, too: in heeled boots, chocolate pants, and a plum-colored coat. From off his head he took a floppy cap, cut from the same cloth as his coat. Loose curls fell o'er his brow; and beneath this black fringe there shone eyes . . . O, such eyes as Eliphalet's!

I could see his eyes, yes; for he stood but an arm's width away. We might have touched, but for the pane between us. As he'd not yet noticed me—I'd fallen back, and stood now within the folds of the draperies—I'd time to take him in. . . . The eyes: gray-green: the color of what smoke would rise from jade, if jade could catch flame.

Suddenly, he turned. He stared. As did I. Rather, I tried; but my eyes were drawn back to the Duchess, who now ascended. I let fall the drapes; and waited, anxiously, within the parlor.

Two people, only. Duchess and . . . duke?

Into the parlor she came, accompanied by that susurrus, that sibilance that is particular to rushing silk.

If her fortieth year had come, it had done so kindly. *She is younger than Sebastiana,* was my first thought. *And equally beautiful,* my second. For the Duchess showed a mass of jetty hair piled high atop her head, ringlets falling to frame a face beautiful but for its extreme pallor. From her *ferronnière*—a sort of tiara, the most of it unseen—a single gem depended: a ruby; which elicited the reds from her dress. This ruby seemed a third eye of sorts; for it hung just above and between her own, which of course . . . Stay. To her eyes I shall return.

I watched her lips—rubicund, too—and waited for her to speak. She did not. She smiled only. And approached me with her hands extended. Those ten fingers showed fifteen, perhaps twenty rings. I'd never seen a woman so adorned.

Behind the Duchess, I saw her consort unbuttoning his

coat. His look was a leer. Sarah had come to stand beside him in the foyer. She showed him no deference at all. Instead, she stared at me, as did he. As did the Duchess; who summoned her attendants forth, tacitly. Both girl and boy approached, till all three stood in a half circle before me.

Still not a word had been spoken. Still I held to the Duchess's gem-set hands. Still we all stared. When I could suffer this pose not a moment more, I asked, simply, "Sebastiana?"

The Duchess cocked her head, smiling still; but quickly, too quickly, her smile slipped away; for she spoke to Sarah of a straight pin gone astray within the ruffle of black that covered her bosom. "Who, dear?" asked the Duchess of me; but from me her attention had been taken.

"Sebastiana," said I. "Sebastiana d'Azur."

"No, no," said she, with heat; and I swallowed hard, fearing she spoke to me. No: she spoke—in terms ever more red—to her attendants, both of whom now sought that pin the Duchess swore would bleed her dry. "Excuse me, won't you, dear," said she, her English infused with a continental cadence. "I'm afraid we are all . . . rather . . . distracted by my . . . décolletage." Indeed. Six hands worked that precinct with impunity.

Finally, huffily, the Duchess showed me her back; for she turned in a swirl of silk and stamped out to the foyer, the others following. Still they struggled with that same troublesome element of the Duchess's ensemble. There was much conferring; and finally, success. Of a kind.

With her back to me—her shoulders (pale as her face) had been bared by the release of the offending mantle, and the pin within it—the Duchess dismissed Sarah and Eli both with directions I could not discern.

"Pardon me, *madame,*" said I, all impatience, "but is Sebastiana here? Perhaps known by another name? Asleep upstairs? For Sarah said that—"

Suddenly, to quote Sarah seemed absurd; for the Duchess had turned back toward me, and I could do naught but stare as she approached; for:

The removal of that bothersome fabric had laid bare not only the Duchess's shoulders but her breasts as well. And here she came, those breasts—well formed, firm—spilling from the stiff half cups of her scarlet bodice. To their tips she raised her beringed fingers and twirled, yes twirled, the protuberant nipples, flushed pink as the painted Ariadne's but hardening under my eye to a purple well suited to the parlor. Need I report that I fell back from her approach, aghast, appalled? Aroused. By her nakedness, yes; but also by her eyes. For it seemed the Duchess showed two smiles then: that of her lacquered lips, and another of her eyes, which had turned *crapaud.*

Somehow I managed to say it a final time: "Sebastiana."

I'd not utter one word more.

I stood shocked and stilled, but again the Duchess gained my hands. She held them, as she held my gaze. In tones appropriate to a child, a pet, or perhaps an idiot—doubtless I displayed aspects of all three—she said, "Sebastiana? You must refer to the sister who sent the trunk. It has sat upstairs—*en haut,* as you French would have it—for some weeks; but I'm afraid I all but stopped expecting you. Terribly rude of me, that; *terribly* rude. And now here I stand," said she, with a self-critical *tsk-tsk,* "showing you the Eye, willy-nilly, as if you're accustomed to it. Evidently, dear, you are not."

Yes: her ice-blue eyes showed the sister-sign in full. *L'oeil de crapaud.* The pupils pushing into the blue irises, shaping themselves in seeming imitation of a toad's splayed and globose toes. I'd only ever seen this done by . . . "Seb . . ." I stammered. "Sebasti . . ." came the second attempt.

"Oh my," said the Duchess, letting fall my hands and raising her own to a mouth shaped to a perfect, despairing *O.*

"You . . . you thought . . . . Oh dear, I'm so very sorry. *Desolée,* rather. You thought your sister was here. No, no, *no.* I know your Sebastiana d'Azur by reputation only, I'm afraid.

"But, as I say, the trunk she sent you from Paris has been here a month or more. And unless I'm much mistaken, there was a letter addressed to you. For you must be . . . ?"

"H." I breathed it in the French style, my own name a mere aspiration: *Ahsh.*

"Yes," said she, flatly. "Well then. . . . The letter. Sarah will have seen it, surely. My Sarah, yes; rather, let us hope it was not Eliphalet found it first, for he's a jealous cub." She leaned nearer to whisper what followed: "Of course I tamed and trained him some years ago."

Those are the last of the Duchess's words I can recall from that first encounter; for, as I watched her cross the parlor to tug at a tasseled black cord hanging in the corner—thusly summoning her Sarah, her Eli, and whomever else—my senses flooded from me and I fell back upon the divan. There I lay in mimicry of the sylvan nymph Ariadne, who hung above me. Both of us: abandoned.

33

The Letter

UNFORTUNATELY, I am inclined to fainting; worse: I cannot always attribute this to the proximate dead. Would that I could. I do all I can to forestall my falling, of course; the more so when in men's dress, as this—stupid, but true—very much increases my embarrassment. In my efforts at retaining consciousness, I oftimes fail. And so I did that day, my first in Manhattan.

I woke in a room that was not the last I'd seen. This one was nested in the eaves of an attic. It was decorated with great delicacy. Late-day light sifted through its one peaked window; and by this I saw I'd fallen (as feared) and had slept away the midday hours.

I lay on a comfortable cot, made up in white linen. I was dressed—blessedly—as I'd been when first I'd arrived at

Cyprian House. My shoes . . . whoever had laid me abed had removed only my shoes. Had I been led or carried to bed? I could not recall. But there was no one around now, and all was silence.

A *papier peint* of rambling roses covered walls which angled in toward the ceiling, itself papered. An oil lamp sat unlit on the bedside table. Upon a low bureau were a washbasin and ewer; later, beneath the cot I'd discover a bedpan of similar design: all white porcelain, patterned to complement the wallpaper: florals, in shades of red and palest green. Behind the head of the cot there hung a gauzy drape; this served as the fourth wall of my niche—hardly a room, this—and separated it from the larger space beyond: the attic proper. This drape had been dyed red, a shade rendered pink by the pass-through of light; and it afforded little privacy. As for the main of the attic, I might have explored it then—for it seemed a laboratory of sorts; most intriguing—save for this: beside me on the bed there'd been set a square of parchment, sealed still, its front artfully addressed: to me: *H.*

"Dear H., dear heart," began the unciphered letter.

"You are upset with me," wrote Sebastiana. "This I know." In time I'd rise, take to a wide sill which gave onto the yard and gardens, far below, and read on by the brighter light from without:

> I shan't put forth a profusion of apology, though I am inclined to do so, dearest, I am. But rather let me say that I understand your upset, as it is a state well known to me. I, too, in times past, sought those Sisters, any Sisters whom I thought might set my life aright. My Book shows it well: I, too, erred, and fell into the Slough of Despond. Would a witch come to show the way out, to show the way up? If so, who? When? And

if not, why? Where, *where* was the Saving Sister? You take me for such a one, as I saved you from that Breton horde. But heart, mark me: you err. I write to tell you that the Saving Sister is within you, and nowhere else.

Cry, do; for you have strayed, have caused hurt and left pain in your wake. Do not think me cold, *mon enfant.* Were I there, you'd avail yourself of my shoulder, and bathe it in tears. This I would let you do. . . . Indeed, a salt tide of tears rises within me as I write—I love you still, H., and would assuage you, would show you the way if only I knew it.

Do you know where it is I sit, now, as I write? You cannot, of course; but read on and imagine it well. I am on the beach, below my Ravndal. It is eventide, and the water laps at my legs as well as those of the escritoire I've had the boys carry down and set upon the strand. I wanted to write you in sight of the sea; for when I look to the sea, I see you on its far side. Not literally, dear, no; though, as you may know, I did watch you as you crossed. Watched you for some while; till, when you reached the Virginian port, I let you pass on unseen. I called back my Maluenda—bird, she'd been; then shipboard rat; and now, returned to cat, she sits atop my lap—and abandoned all eyes but my own.

For—let me say it plain—you made me mad, my H.

My jewels, heart? Into the sea? What idiocy! I did not bequeathe them to you in order to see them conferred unto the Deep, along with the bones of Madeleine? *Mais non!* How often I have woken—angry—from dreams akin to those of Clarence, brother to Shakespeare's bad Richard:

Methoughts I saw a thousand fearful wracks;
A thousand men that fish gnaw'd upon;

Wedges of gold, great anchors, heaps of pearl,
Inestimable stones, unvalued jewels,
All scatt'red in the bottom of the sea:
Some lay in dead men's skulls, and in the holes
Where eyes did once inhabit, there were crept
(As 'twere in scorn of eyes) reflecting gems,
That woo'd the slimy bottom of the deep,
And mock'd the dead bones that lay scatt'red by.

O, H.! Such folly it was! Such foolery! You sought to live by your own lights, this I know. (Though you had no means but mine, if I recall.) Your intent was admirable; but dearest, let us hope you've since learned to distinguish between metaphor and madness, and that you'll not spend what money I now send—in this trunk you'll find a store of it—on the wind, or pin it to trees for birds to pluck. Please, leave such romantic show as you committed amidships to our beloved Bard, or his Brethren of the Boards. *Invest,* my dear! One cannot count on coin always coming round. This—and many things besides—I hope for you to learn at the Duchess's side.

. . . H., I confess it: I have had to set my pen down these last moments; for still the anger rises within me—an Eye-turning anger, it is—and I understand why it was I forsook you. As indeed I did. O, but I can calm myself, as now I have—and as Asmodei cannot—still he rages when your name is spoken; for he has never reconciled himself to your many . . . gifts— . . . I *can* calm myself, yes, to summon naught but well-wishes for you. . . . I am asked—just now, just here, beachside—to convey to you a hug and grand hello from Roméo. It is he and his Ganymede who've set my writing table strandside, where now they splash in thigh-high water.

Yes, H., your Roméo is another's now. . . . Truer to say both boys are mine. And two are twice the fun of one. But that is simple arithmetic, *non,* well known to every witch since Lilith?

His name is Derich, and Asmodei found him in the Ardennes, where his mother—I did not know her—fell to the Blood. He brought the boy back to Ravndal, and all but tied a bow onto him. I've since passed him on to Roméo, as I've not the energy to practice upon a second pet, especially one who knows not my . . . preferences. It is so wearying, the training of consorts.

Sister, I've not the strength I once had. My pens sit as still as my brushes long have, and I've abandoned my Book along with my canvases. *Bref:* the tide of life, I fear, is in recess. My powers wane. The body has donned a drape of age. Life seems a weight that has fallen all at once, like that Blade that fell so steadily in the Paris of yore, my Paris, to dissever me from the city of my dreams, the city of my success. It was that Blade—this you know—that all but banished me to this stony pile set high ashore. . . . *Hélas,* the coming of the Blood cannot be far off.

And so, what need have I for this sex-athlete, this Belgian boy of doggish appetite? None. I let Roméo do with Derich what he pleases; and—as it pleases me—I partake. Of their bodies, not of their love, which is exclusive. . . . Love? I haven't the need, not anymore.

But you, my H., have you love? Have you held to what love you found? It was the Negress alongside whom you sailed, *non*? Your letters offered not the particulars of your plight. You compelled love, did you not? You sought to bind the love object to you by spellcraft? You did, *oui.* Take heart, dear—among the Sorority, since time immemorial, no mistake has been more commonly made.

Yet, as common a conundrum as it is, I must needs say I know no way to undo what it is you've done. But if any witch does know a way, it is the Duchess. Therefore, it is to her care I have consigned you.

. . . I owe you an esbat. This I know. It is the duty of every Mystic Sister to convene a coven for the benefit of those whom she discovers or saves. As Téotocchi did for me, long years ago. If I cannot—I will try, this I swear but cannot promise— . . . If I cannot come, if I do not come, then perhaps your time spent with the Duchess will prove sufficient, and I shan't be deemed wholly derelict in my duties.

Alors, oui: the Duchess. I know of her from tales told by a witch resident on the Isle of Skye. The two attended an esbat, years past, in the shadows cast by Edinburgh Castle. This was when the Duchess was but Lenore, lovely but lowborn, seeking fame and finding infamy astride the sidewalks and gentlemen of London's lesser precincts. But she is kindly, I am told, and surely her profession has rendered her . . . accommodating.

What next I read in the letter made my stomach lurch, as it had not since I'd quit the mail coach:

I've written the Duchess of your particulars. Surely there's little she's not seen, engaged as she's been in the bodily trade all these years. Still, I adjure you, H.: set aside your self—and here I assume you are still the witch you were: easily abashed, sweet yet overly prone to shame—and be with the Duchess who you are.

She closed with "Adieu," thusly conferring me unto God's care when, in fact, she'd laid me bare before a most rude Aphrodite. A witch-whore whom she barely knew. Further, she'd the temerity to sign my warrant—for I saw it as such—

with her token S, and sketched, rather shabbily, that toad that is ever asquat within its lower curve. Yes: there it sat, seeming real enough to leap from that page which I'd have cast aside or crumpled, had it not been for a postscript containing these particulars:

Sebastiana had hired a factor in Paris, and charged him with shipping to Leonard Street the aforementioned trunk, wherein she'd laid two letters—one for me, another for the Duchess (who'd evidently discovered hers)—as well as those few effects I'd left at Ravndal. Too, I'd find within several Books that Sebastiana knew would interest me. (They did, and my hard regard for her softened.) There was cash aplenty: a "store" indeed, which somehow she'd converted to American specie and promissory notes. (The notes were rolled into a ribbon-bound length of parchment, upon which Sebastiana had written: "Commit these not unto the Deep, dearest H.") There were other sundries, too, the lot of which is best described as "sumptuous." Finally, I found in the bottom of the trunk a rolled canvas, a portrait of some lesser signatory to the Treaty of Paris, which the Duchess was to sell or hang, as she wished; and what proceeded—be it cash or satisfaction—was meant as recompense for my upkeep; or "novitiate," as Sebastiana deemed it.

I hadn't strength enough for anger; but I sat upon the sill, crying none too quietly; such that I had not heard the Duchess approach.

There she stood. In the darkened attic. Behind the now blood-colored scrim. The shadows at her back seemed alive; and soon I saw that in fact they were: for there, in triangulated array behind the Duchess, stood the women of Cyprian House. I counted seven. The two nearest the Duchess reached a hand forward to touch, to work the living centers of the Duchess's breasts. Others drew back the diaphanous drape. Dim though it was within the attic, I saw the

Duchess's eyes again turn *crapaud.* Saw, too, that the fourteen eyes of the corps followed suit.

. . . "Supper?" asked the Duchess.

I nodded my assent. And whatever their cue—my smile, or words unheard by me—the sisters then rushed me. It was as though a witchly dam had given way. In they came, washing o'er me in kisses and kindnesses the like of which I cannot describe. Beyond these sisters—tugging at my travel-worn suit, offering clothes as fine as any I'd seen, speaking of baths and balms and fresh-brewed emollients—beyond their welcoming play, I saw the Duchess in the attic, in her atelier, lighting candles to stave off the dark. Seeing me, she smiled, broadly, beautifully; and with the wave of a hand, descended. Leaving me in the care of her minions: the women, nay the witches of Cyprian House.

34

The Cyprians

I WELCOMED it: the women's dress. It had been a long while, yes, but immediately I reveled in the restraint of a proper dress: a corset, stays, and such.

With some creativity, two of the girls managed to make for me a coiffure. They—the sisters Fanny and Jen—borrowed a length of false hair from the house's other blonde. Its ringlets I thought ridiculous, and so I demurred; but they would brook no complaint, and soon proved, by applying a mirror of carved hardwoods, that yes, I supposed I did look "fetching," as they put it.

Others of the sorority would disappear, down the attic stairs, only to return with accessories. Soon my *petite chambre* was aglint with silver, gold, and shining stones, aswirl with shawls and scarves. It seemed I was to be readied for some grand affair; and indeed I was: a typical night at Cyprian House.

Happily, another of the inmates—Eugénie, a light-skinned Creole up from New Orleans—stood as tall as I; and it was she who proffered a lime-colored dress of Swiss muslin, trimmed in white satin, and shoes dyed to match. The shoes pinched somewhat, but from this lesser pain I was distracted by a greater; for—as Eugénie was full in places where I was not—the company took in the dress with a battery of straight pins, till I wondered if the Creole's goal was to render me a voodoo doll, so sticked and (*pardon*) pricked was I.

Earlier I'd been stripped of my travel-worn clothes and handed a bathing shift of sheer cambric; which, when wet, clings as a second skin. Led to a far, dark corner of the attic by one of the sisters, I bathed in haste, though the water was warm, the sea sponges and violet soaps a delight. I did not wish to be discovered; or—as Sebastiana had put it—show "my particulars" to those present. Though they might know me for a witch, they'd no need to know of my . . .

But as I returned to the corps of costumers, a tiny witch asked in an accent telling of elsewhere, "Which do you fancy more? Your cunny or your Long Tom?"

Several others chided their sister—known as Li'l Belt, so tiny was her waist—yet there they all stood, attending my answer.

"Two sides of a coin, I suppose," was all I managed to say.

"Aye," said Li'l Belt, in the jaunty tones of Eire, "if it's coin that concerns ye, ye've come to the right place; for the Duchess can teach ye how to make two coins from one. A shrewd one, she is." This met with a chorus of laughing assent; and, simple as that, the topic turned from my anatomy to the Duchess's pecuniary acumen. I was free of my two secrets: stones, they'd been, boulders set upon planks pressing down upon me, smothering my soul as the Puritans had smothered Salemites of old. Freed of my secrets, I . . . yes: again I cried. Indeed, here came a great show; and well I might have carried on—for the sisters encouraged my release—had it not been for the corset and stays, which rendered my crying, my convulsing, a painful affair.

Soon, every eye in that attic showed a tear. Kerchiefs of lace were drawn and passed about; and laughter ensued when we recoursed to their monograms in order to return them to their owners. Several of the sisters showed the witch's eye. Among this number were the sisters—Fanny and Jen—but also a redheaded beauty whose black pupils had nearly overspread the whole of her apple green irises. I refer to Lydia Smash, or La Rousse, who had a temper to match her talents. Indeed, I'd learn she was in arrears to the Duchess for a porcelain tea set she'd caused to fly—not thrown, but *caused to fly*—at some dandified jackass who'd "made amorous" with her in ways which offended.

The two remaining girls—after Fanny and Jen, Eugénie, Li'l Belt, and Lydia—were named Cinderella (the blonde, who answered to Cindy) and Adaline. The latter was young, quite, and her arrival from Augusta, Maine, had preceded my own by a few weeks. This Adaline had the aspect of a bird freshly fallen from the nest; but she'd beauty in abundance: a piquant brunette with skin which defied the lily. The former—Cindy—was a dizzified flirt with a well-salted tongue whom I liked nonetheless; and this despite her groping for my "Long Tom" whilst pretending to arrange my petticoats.

On went this show, till finally we were distracted by the arrival in the attic of Eliphalet, the Duchess's Eli. He announced supper. And the girls trailed from me (with kisses) and past Eli (with kisses) to reassemble in the dining room.

There remained no one in the attic save Eli and myself. There he stood, before the parted curtain. He wore now a befurbelowed blouse of white lawn; downright piratical, it was, with its puffed sleeves and low-laced front. Whereas earlier, Eli had seemed wary of me—and here my pen wants the word *rude;* but I deny it, owing to courtesies later shown me by the boy—now he was solicitous and all but bowed. "I prefer you like this," said he, having taken in my attire.

I was inclined to thank him, and state my own contentment at having returned to such feminine fripperies; but instead—as if suddenly my senses ceded to the requisites of my dress—I turned coquette, saying, "And I prefer that a gentleman keep his opinion private, if his compliment is not pure."

"My apologies," said he whilst offering me his elbow; upon which I descended from attic to dining room, speaking not one word more.

Down the length of the dining room there ran a thrice-braced table of dark woods at which twenty, nay thirty could comfortably sit. The chairs were delicate. And sconces showed the walls papered o'er with South Sea adventures: nude natives attendant upon Captain Cook and his men. As for my first meal at the Duchess's table, well . . .

The fare was eccentric, the wine witch-fixed. Not as strong as the *vinum sabbati* I'd known at Ravndal, no; but neither was it the mere effluence of pressed grapes. Aside from those roasted meats and legumes I could identify, there came plates—carried by Sarah and Eli—which caused my new sisters to groan and press forth the tips of their tongues. Evidently, the Duchess had brought with her to these shores a taste for the treats of home; and was wont to serve up such dishes as larded rabbit, pastries topped with spinach, and mincemeat pies. ("'Tis what's left when the good parts are gone," said my informant, Li'l Belt, of the latter.) But in fact, I accepted a slice of pie, and found that the raisins and spices within very nearly redeemed it. The Duchess relished the retarding of our appetites with such show; and that first night I amused her by raising my plate when seconds were on offer; for I was hungry.

As the wine was her work, it was Cinderella whom the Duchess elected to toast my arrival. This she did—with suitable delicacy—before appending a secondary toast:

"And here," said she, raising high her glass, ". . . here's to our parts that go wet when tickled, and tickle when they're wet." To which we all drank.

"I've one, aye I do," said an excited Li'l Belt. The Duchess conceded; and the Irish witch all but sang:

"Here's to the whore from Peru, who filled her cunny with glue.
Said she, 'If they pay to get in, let 'em pay to get out, too.'"

Turning to the Duchess, at whose right hand I sat, I saw her roll her eyes of ice; but I saw too that she sought to hide her smile by sipping, at length, from her goblet of cut cranberry glass. Indeed, all the glass was cranberry-colored, and set amidst a surfeit of silver and china showing the Duchess's own pattern: reds and greens, silver-edged and Grecian; with a design which first I took for an abstraction. O, but upon closer inspection I saw that my own plate was painted o'er in . . . in genitalia. A vagina, center all; with little silver penises aflutter, winging about the plate's fluted edge. Surprised, shocked? I was not; for there sat the Duchess, breasts bared.

Dinner progressed amidst much banter. As no one addressed my situation, and no questions were asked of me, I wondered what it was the witches knew of my lot.

After dessert—marzipan and port wine, with grapes and a blue-veined cheese besides—Eli handed the Duchess a ledger, bound in green morocco, which he referred to as her calendar. "My dears," said she, eyes melting o'er the page before her, "so many cards and notes have come today, and in days past, that it must have seemed to our poor Sarah that every porter in town, every horse-drawn conveyance, had been dispatched to our door and—"

"And huzzah for our sweet Sarah," rose the cry, begun by Lydia Smash. Sarah took the compliment with grace from where she sat: upon the lap of Eugénie.

"Yes, yes," seconded the Duchess. "Where would we be without our Sarah?"

"But where would I be without you, Duchess?" rejoined Sarah.

"Thank you, dear. But do remember to take from the market till a shilling—no: two, three, or as many as you wish! And remind me to find for you that recipe of which we spoke, written by the Witch of Damascus. You'll take to it, rightly, I'm sure. And—no offense, dear—it has been too long since I tasted cake as fine as that."

"Yes, Duchess," said Sarah.

"Right, then," said the Duchess, returning to the calendar. "It's to be a full house tonight, sisters."

Applause. To which the Duchess responded with a toast of her own, or perhaps an admonition; which went something like this:

"Your Blood is pure, sisters, so pay it heed.
Man's, in his loins, is turned to seed;
Which, by the Beloved Channel, is transmitted
Into those places by Nature for it fitted.

"My dears, we've pleasure to impart this night; and specie and seed to gather. So let us proceed posthaste." With a doubly-ringed forefinger she traced the page. "Tonight, your sparks will fly as follows:

"Ah, yes. I see here we are to be visited again by the brothers from Cincinnati—dealers in silk, are they not?—

who request the company of . . . the sisters, yes. Makes sense, in its way. Fanny and Jen, what say you? Do you accept their suit?"

The sisters, seated shoulder to shoulder, spun toward each other. Hands were clasped, fingers fluttered o'er their hearts. "I should think so," said Fanny. She was the elder by a year, and often spoke for her sister. "They were kindly last time, and sister here," at which Jen flushed, "sister quite favored the younger of the two."

"Accepted," said the Duchess, absently; and from somewhere in her coiffure she drew down a pencil, to make a tick beside the brothers' names.

"Oh yes, please," sputtered Jen, such that all present fell to giggling, and goading the shyer of the sisters; who excused themselves to ready their rooms, and themselves.

Li'l Belt was to see her "bawcock," a printer's clerk named Burtis; who, apparently, had sued to spend the night with his beloved. At this, Li'l Belt blanched; and soon I understood why, for the Duchess admonished her. "My dear, you must tell your Burtis," which name she all but spat, "that, should he persist in his attempts to pass the night here, he will find himself denied your company completely." She hesitated before addressing the corps: "Do we not have rules, and are they not well known?" *We do,* came the choral response; *they are.* Whereupon the Duchess, turning to me, elaborated: "None stay the night. It is far too dangerous."

"I'll tell him," said Li'l Belt. "Again."

"Thank you, dear. He's a hardheaded one, your Burtis?"

"Aye," said Li'l Belt, excusing herself, "but—blessed be—both his heads are hard."

As Li'l Belt took her leave, Eugénie spoke. *"Pardon?"* said she, in the French manner.

"Oui, ma chère?" rejoined the Duchess.

"I wish to pass the night *toute seule,* Duchess. Alone, yes; save for Sarah, whose assistance I could use in the atelier, when her duties are done."

"Craft-work?" asked the Duchess.

"Oui."

"*Très bien.* But, Sarah, as you know, is much needed in the parlor. Will Eli suffice?"

"*Non, madame.* Thank you; but it is a witch that is wanted."

"Ah! Our new Henriette, then?" (Thusly was I granted a new name.) "Word comes to us from a much-respected sister in France that she is strong, *très forte,*" at which she flexed a biceps.

Eugénie smiled and looked to her hands, in which she coddled Sarah's. Nodding to me, respectfully, she proceeded to address the Duchess. "The new witch is welcome," said she, "assuredly; *mais, je vous en prie,* it is Sarah I request, if and when she can be spared."

"D'accord," said the Duchess. "Sarah it shall be." The Duchess then returned to her calendar, adding, "But I see here, Eugénie, that I've a request from Mr. Levy, the . . . the amalgamationist, shall I say? He's a friend of our mayor's, as you know, and he's offered to pay handsomely for your company—yours, specifically."

"I know of whom you speak," said Eugénie. "A planter, is he not? I was introduced to him at the Park Theater; and even there—in public—he showed too well his Southern ways."

"He treated you ill, my dear? And you did not tell me? The mayor, Eugénie, is a man very much in my debt, very much . . . beholden. Shall I have our Mr. Levy shown to the door of the city, as it were?"

"No need, *madame,*" said Eugénie. "But I decline his suit."

"Indeed," said the Duchess; and setting her pencil to the

page as though it were a blade, she cut from the calendar the name of Levy. "Not in my house," said she. "Away with you, Mr. Levy!"

Eugénie rose, and left us. Sarah and Eli tended to the spent dishes of those who'd already absented themselves. Three remained: Lydia Smash, Cinderella, and Adaline.

The first, Lydia, anticipated her charge. "Frank, will it be?"

The Duchess nodded. "At nine," said she. "But, La Rousse, can you first accommodate a boy whose sixteenth birthday it is? He's sure to be well-bred. Indeed, I know the father well. . . . There's five dollars on offer."

Lydia assented. "A dollar a minute," said she, winking my way.

Cinderella was to be matched to a twosome, well known at Cyprian House. "But oh," said she upon receiving the news, "you know, Duchess, it's each other they want, those boys. I am but a buffer of flesh, a thing they set betwixt their fears."

"The rate is double, dear, as always it is."

"So, too, is the boredom double," said Cindy, laid low by the night's prospect.

"Task yourself, dear. Take charge! And if you know what it is they want—even if they do not; or haven't the words for it—give it to them. Effect a three-party kiss. Turn low the lamp and touch their members, tip to tip. Play Comparison upon them, dear. Come, come, need I detail all that might be done?"

Cinderella seemed charged anew; and off she went—with much thanks and a kiss to the Duchess's bosom—to prepare for her tandem men.

None remained but Adaline and myself. To the former the Duchess now turned.

"Adaline, dear?"

Roseate shades overspread the lily of Adaline's complexion. Said she, "I think not, Duchess. Not yet. Do you mind, terribly?"

"I mind not at all, dear. This I've told you since first you arrived. You'll do as you please whilst here. And the same holds true for you, Henriette, *tu comprends*?"

"Oui," said I: I understood.

"Partake or not, as you please. But remember: there is money to be made, and lessons to learn. You'll be let to forgo the former, but not the latter."

The Duchess set her calendar aside, and stood. Eli, coming from an adjoining pantry, was charged with the delivery of the night's notes; for, throughout the Empire City, men awaited word from Cyprian House.

Her business seen to, the Duchess set to playing with, set to pinching and pulling at the distended tips of her breasts. This she did absently, as others might twiddle their thumbs. Her pupils turned Toad, but fast retook their common shape as she returned to herself and spoke. "So then," said she. "I've two to stand attendant, two to walk beside me this night: my Adaline, my Henriette. Splendid!"

And she quit the room in a swish of silk.

"Walk?" asked I of Adaline. "Outside?"

"No, no," said Adaline. Porcelain, she seemed: a doll. "We walk within the house. We walk, and we watch."

"Come," said she. "I will show you." Soon we were hand in hand, rushing down to the kitchen; from whence we made our way up a second set of stairs that accessed the shadowed interior, the secreted structure of Cyprian House.

35

The Parlor; Wherein Tribute Is Paid

CYPRIAN House—consecrated, as it were, to the isle of Cyprus, whereon ruled Aphrodite—had been redone to suit the Duchess, and to better serve the witches resident within, each sent by an elder—typically their Mystic Sister; and the point of this novitiate was the rounding-off of one's education, witchly, worldly, and otherwise.

The Duchess housed the witches—seven, preferably—in two-room suites; but there was room enough for others (such as your diarist) in the manse, which had been built some years before. The Duchess—who'd ascended as if by divine right; hence, her sobriquet—had acquired capital enough by 1824 to purchase the house for some $3,000. "And a deal it was," said she; for never did the Duchess shy from the topic of profit.

Four stories of brick on the north side of Leonard Street,

if my inner compass is correct; between Church and Chapel, well situated amidst the town homes of the affluent and the corridors of culture. Its situation set Cyprian House and the other brothels of the Fifth Ward apart from the iniquitous sinks some blocks southwesterly, in Five Points and the Bowery.

Indeed, the Duchess ran a fine and private house—open by appointment only. Of course, none knew the secret of its residents. But all knew that the women within Cyprian House were well tended, happy, and, as once I heard it put, "the upper breed of whoredom." And the Duchess—none called her Lenore; though many knew her from earlier days, days spent elsewhere in the ward—had achieved that mix by which a sister thrives in community: she was known, respected, needed, and feared. . . . Feared, yes: for young Lenore had once offset the violent advances of a suitor by pouring the man some whiskey from that flask she kept ever near; but O, the surprise when he drank it down: mixed with oil of vitriol, it was; a spray of which she cast into his eyes for good measure. And still the man—all but blinded, but daring not to appeal to the law—had begged Lenore's forgiveness, begged, too, to see her again. This she agreed to, albeit at a price thrice raised.

To her Leonard Street home the Duchess later added the property adjacent, its wall in common with her western one. These mirroring town homes—each with a lot spreading some sixty feet northward and beset, by the time of my arrival, with arbors and gardens and Grecian statuary—she'd had redone as one; hence the grand foyer and twin staircases. Walls had been brought down, and rooms adjoined. Most interestingly, the Duchess had designed an inner warren of halls, a maze of lath and timber that seemed to mock the homes' original architecture. That is: the upstairs suites of Cyprian House were framed by passageways, unseen from the house proper, by which the rooms communicated. It was from within these hallways that the Duchess watched o'er the workings of her house; for each room could be seen into via eyeholes artfully concealed. These were called "masks," and their locations were known to every resident of Cyprian House but never, never shown to the sparks who visited.

It was within this watchers' warren—the halls narrow, and perforce dim; yet finely fitted out—that my own education would commence the night of my arrival; for within this espial spot Adaline and I lingered, at length.

The hours of their appointments had been communicated to all the clients, and cabs of every sort crowded our door in the quarter hours preceding seven and nine; others were let to come at their convenience. Sarah opened the doors to them, receiving their capes and canes, et cetera. In the larger foyer, Eli stood sentinel; and it was he who'd usher the men right or left, to the purple or red parlor, depending. Within the night's chosen parlor—more often it was the purple—the Duchess sat, attendant upon the tribute due her.

Initiates—those new to the house, or out-of-towners drummed up by businessmen with whom the Duchess "had arrangements"—typically brought gifts. These the Duchess would hand off to whoever was near. The night of my arrival, Adaline and I both attended the Duchess at parlor, before returning to our study at the masks. We'd helped Sarah ready the house, and we'd helped the girls ready themselves. Thereafter, we took our seats beside the Duchess on that same divan onto which I'd fainted not twelve hours earlier.

The first arrivals were the brothers from Ohio. They brought as tribute two bolts of silk: aubergine and gold. The Duchess waved these offerings away, rudely, with an insouciance that made me smile. She then bade the brothers help themselves to drink at the bar, where the cut glass stood in Alpine array.

The brothers thusly dismissed, the Duchess said to me, "Choose one."

"I . . . I cannot," came my reply.

"Not one of the brothers," said the Duchess; and she snapped open a fan of Brussels lace, its fingers made of mother-of-pearl, to hide her smile. "The *silks,* sister. Choose one of the silks. There's a milliner not two blocks distant who will make for you . . . *comment dit-on? Une robe resplendissante.*"

I was firstly relieved, then flattered; though still I doubted I'd ever appear resplendent, no matter the color of silk, no matter the cut of dress. But I chose the gold, and thanked the Duchess. Adaline, I saw, awaited the gift of the aubergine silk; but it never came.

The next to arrive was Li'l Belt's Burtis, who had the busy, buzzing, and rounded aspect of a bee. He was ginger-haired, and plump, this Burtis; and when first he came into the parlor he acknowledged not the Duchess but the brothers, who now kept their own counsel in a corner. (They were, I saw, puzzling o'er a series of prints depicting Cimon and Pera: the former an aged and imprisoned Greek; the latter his daughter, who sneaks into prison to suckle him, to save him from starvation. I doubt the Ohioans understood the painted metaphors of the parlor; but still these had their effect: the brothers stood atremble in this women's world.)

Burtis had brought no gift, which I thought strange. "Burtis, dear boy," said the Duchess at his approach. "You come to renew your suit of our little Li'l Belt?"

"I . . . I am," said he, finally. "Rather, I do." And there he stood, staring down at the Duchess, who yet remained in full dress. The fabric at the fore of his slacks was stretched tight as drumskin. . . . I confess: I thought then of Li'l Belt, wondering how she'd tame the boy and his beast, and wondering, too, if I'd be let to watch.

Eli came to stand beside Burtis; and thusly did he appear all squares: square jaw, square shoulders, squared fists hanging beside his hips. All in black camblet, he was now: pants and a waistcoat covering that white blouse, rendering even more extreme its piratical sleeves. "Now?" asked Eli of his mistress.

"Now," sighed she.

And with this Eli pushed Burtis down onto one knee. He, too, went down; and with delicacy unpinned from o'er the Duchess's breast the pelerine, or capelet that topped her cream-and-blood-colored ensemble.The Duchess's breasts spilled forth. Burtis stared. As did I. And involuntary was my intake of breath when Eli set his hand upon the back of Burtis's head and pushed, pushed the boy forward. Onto the right breast of the Duchess. The left Eli took for himself. Together they teased each nipple to attention. As for the Duchess, she fell back, aswoon, upon the divan, raising her fan to cover her face; and only I saw why: her eyes had turned *crapaud.*

The brothers neared, moving from the contemplation of Pera's breasts to those of the Duchess, at which they stared wide-eyed, thirsty as old Cimon. The livid tips of her teats were kiss-slick, and gleamed in the gaslight.

Thusly was Burtis's first tribute made. Eli, I saw, was accustomed to the act; and evidently fond of it; for he had to set his length aright within his trousers when finally he rose and fell back from the Duchess along with the others.

. . . Stunned though I was, the night proceeded apace.

Sarah had opened the door to the boy whose birthday it was, come in the company of his father. The former was marked for Lydia Smash. The latter, when shown into the parlor, introduced his son to the Duchess and, kneeling, paid his tribute. The son was denied this right, as the brothers had been; and as Cinderella's men were when finally they arrived to complete the night's party.

In the witches came as the clock struck half seven.

It was a quite audible parade of silks and satin and beaded brocades as, unto the sparks, they showered themselves. Their own beauty they'd much accessorized: jewels abounded, and there were sashes, ribbons, and bows in abundance. Their sleeves showed all species of puff: some high, some low, others ballooning from shoulder to elbow. Waists were "natural," not high; and though the corsets and stays thought to show them to advantage were not at all natural, they were suffered.

The two, true sisters were dressed identically; save for Fanny's ensemble being dark blue and Jen's light. Li'l Belt's waist was further accentuated by a belt buckle of brass and tortoiseshell; a shield, rather gladiatorial in aspect. Lydia's auburn locks were up-pinned with combs of amber horn; her dress, too, was amber, with a ruffle colored to accent her emerald eyes. Cinderella had entered the parlor tossing off *"bonsoir"* and such in an English so heavily Frenchified that I had to think back: had I somehow failed to identify her as a countrywoman of mine? "No, no," said Adaline, when queried, "she has only the accent, not the French itself. She says"—and here Adaline paused to beg my pardon in advance—"that faking French lets her sell for five dollars what used to go for four." We laughed at this salesmanship—which showed the Duchess's imprimatur—and were laughing still when our mistress sent us forth from the divan with a fan-snap, a smile, and this well-known recitation from the Scottish play, wherein Hecate addresses her own "Wyrd Sisters":

"Black spirits and white, red spirits and gray;
Mingle, mingle, mingle, you that mingle may."

Parlor chat was free; but for all other liberties taken—few of which were truly proscribed—the Duchess levied fines. In this gamesmanship the witches were complicit, of course. And with the parlor full—and all pairings accomplished—the Duchess sidled up beside me to apprise me of the rules.

"Sarah will see to libations and such, and collect accordingly; for I'll not have such swine as Burtis swilling my rum, come all the way from Cuba. And she's tough as a nut, my Sarah." The Duchess leaned nearer, and spoke from behind her spread fan. Her left breast was flush against my bare arm. And she wore a delirium-inducing perfume. "You two are to mingle only. You do know how to mingle, Henriette?"

"Yes, of course," said I. Mingle, meander, maraud . . . what did I know but that I'd follow Adaline's lead.

"Yes, dear," said the Duchess, "a good idea, that. Follow Adaline's lead." And she winked, her eye showing a fast flash of Toad.

"Adaline, yes. So delicate, so . . . so very delectable. And of course, all the gents pine for her." Here the Duchess nudged the girl in question, whose gaze settled upon her own slippers: silver upon the plush purple of the rug. The Duchess addressed me now, though still she stared at Adaline. "We'll see a sweet return on her maidenhead if ever she opts to sell. Why, I've a spark—not a bad fellow, not at all—who's placed with me a . . . a standing order, let me say, for just such a one as our dear Adaline. Fifty dollars," said she, "*fifty* dollars he'll pay, for rights of defloration."

Adaline said nothing. The Duchess traced with her sapphired finger a split seam of Adaline's dress. I'd been blinded, earlier, by the girl's beauty; but now I saw that her habiliment would not stand close scrutiny. Fifty dollars was a great sum to Adaline; as it was, is, for any working woman—be she seamstress, servant, or chambermaid—more likely to reap fifty *cents* for a day's work.

"Now," directed the Duchess, "disperse. And levy your tolls as follows: twenty-five cents for any spark who kisses his witch, and fifty cents if she manages to get atop his lap. And coins of American mintage are *much* preferred. Whoosh now, and away! We've a half hour before they scatter roomward."

"What if . . ." I began, "what if they resist?"

"Dearest Henriette, of course they will resist. Therein lies their enjoyment. But they'll pay when plied. I see no fool among us tonight; but should any court trouble, or hold too tightly to his coin, call to me and I will—"

"Shout out, do you mean?"

The Duchess let fall her fan. "No, sweetest." A sigh. A smile. "You *do* have much to learn, don't you? . . . No need to shout; simply . . . simply *need* me, and look to see me at your side. Understood?"

No; but I nodded.

"Hush now," said the Duchess, though I'd not been speaking. "Coin is the second hardest thing in the parlor at present. Go gather it. . . . Whoosh! Whoosh, and away!"

I collected $1.75. A windfall, it had been, to find Fanny and Jen atop the laps of the brothers. Burtis, whom I fined for begging a kiss off Li'l Belt, tried to put me off with a fi'penny bit; but, yes, I turned from him to find the Duchess behind me. She took Burtis by the ear, somehow making the act seem . . . sensual. He all but defined apology, and paid up. Only then was he let to continue his clumsy courting.

I felt bad; for Burtis was but a printer's assistant, and had little more than ten tarry fingers to show for it. Already he was paying five dollars per visit for the favors of his beloved; and I doubt he made twice that in a week's time. So it was he could scarce afford a tariff on top of the love-fee; but it was requisite, expected, part of the show for which he'd have paid any price, unto his ruin.

As for Li'l Belt, she'd stash his five dollars away, adding it to . . .

Enfin, let me here calculate her take:

One, nay two visitors per day—for Li'l Belt liked wealth second only to sex—and let us say she saw sparks five days out of seven. Fifty dollars on a given week, then. From which we subtract the Duchess's take—twelve dollars, plain, for room and board, with no profit drawn from the acts themselves—and, well . . . suffice to say that a witch could do quite well within Cyprian House, if she were so inclined: $1,500, perhaps $2,000 per annum.

Now, for his five dollars, our Burtis might receive . . . Stay. Why not return to particulars, and let an account of my first night at Cyprian House stand for the many that followed?

36

Shooting Sparks

At the eight-stroke, all present shot to their rooms: billiards in search of pockets. Whereupon we—Adaline and I—followed.

Down to the kitchen we crept; and from the kitchen we climbed, up to the second floor. There we'd find four suites: two forward, giving onto Leonard Street, and two aft. A hallway running along the sides and back of Cyprian House connected the four. As this had no windows, gasoliers burned to leaven the dark. And Adaline led us to a lamp, which we lit and carried; but still I tripped upon an upholstered bench set below two eyeholes: a mask. On the interior wall there'd been painted an actual mask, grand in the Venetian style. Adaline gestured that I should sit. And I stared at my companion till finally she placed her hands aside my head and fixed, *fixed* my face to the mask. Whereupon I saw Li'l Belt's suite; and Burtis, naked as a jay.

"Look at the printer's little devil," whispered Adaline. Pulling back from the mask, I saw that she witnessed the same scene from eyes cut higher in the wall, eyes unadorned. To do so, she stood atop a tufted stool.

I returned to the tableau and, admittedly, gave no quarter to shame.

Burtis's "devil" had a carrotish aspect—a reddish thing springing from its patch of hair. And this hair was like shavings of ginger, allied by color to the hair showing elsewhere: his head, yes, but also the crooks of his arms, his legs, his chest and back, whereon it bristled like that of a boar.

And a bore this Burtis must have been; for, when he set upon Li'l Belt, she waved at the wall. At this I fell back. "She's seen us!" said I.

"Of course she has," said Adaline. "Now hush, or he'll hear us."

I retook my position.

As for Burtis's position, well. . . . He'd come about, as a boat does, and now there stood revealed his . . . his rudder; for he was in desperate search of port. My first thought was that I fared well by comparison; and indeed my own member was on the rise beneath my dress and silks.

Li'l Belt was now abed, and Burtis pushed her petticoats up to where they might have smothered her. But this she righted, taking charge—rather volubly—and speaking to Burtis as . . . well, *pardon,* but she spoke to the boy as one would to a pup that has shat the rug. Burtis reveled in being so debased. (It is evident, quite, when a naked man revels.) And when let to do so, he fell upon Li'l Belt. . . . And, to resume my maritime metaphor: Burtis ran his little boat aground, again and again.

Finally, he shuddered and was done.

A moment passed; and then there came such love talk as to defy belief. A conversation suspended since last Burtis had visited was resumed, seemingly midsentence; and Burtis spoke of his employer (whom he loathed) and his mother (whom he loved). Shocked I was to hear Burtis convey to Li'l Belt the best wishes of his mother. And shocked, too, to see Li'l Belt turn over to him a shirt he'd left for darning. What odd domesticity was this?

"He fancies himself all but betrothed," whispered Adaline. "In fact, he seeks her hand."

"And she?"

"She seeks his hand as well," said Adaline, ". . . leastways when it's full of coin. Now come! These sparks cool quickly."

Knowing Adaline and myself to be present at her mask, Lydia Smash showed more concern for our amusement than that of her virginal charge, who trembled before her naked length.

Kindly enough, she told the boy where to lay his every part: his lips, hands, and "prick," for so Lydia referred to his member even though, to my eye, it appeared not prickish in the least. Rather, it was stunted and blunt, big; and the boy fitted it only as a puppy fits its paws: he'd grow into it, in other words. Regardless, as the boy pounced upon Lydia, she turned his back to us, as Li'l Belt had turned Burtis. And she—a witch with powers I'd yet to hear or read of—caused to rise from beside her bed a heavy baton. A bat, in point of fact.

As the boy busied himself—with neither aptitude nor instinct—Lydia brought the bat just o'er his head. Once or twice she caused the bat to swing fast, just above the boy's ear; such that the displacement of air caught his attention. He turned this way and that, but never found the bat, the very wood of which seemed to want his skull. Adaline and I stifled our laughter. The boy returned to his work; for work he made it seem: his cheeks and chest flushed crimson, and he verily bathed poor Lydia in perspiration. Finally, at the climactic moment, Lydia let fall the bat upon the brass footboard of the bed; and though the sound distracted the boy, scared him, his body had set its course. Words and seed sputtered forth simultaneously. "What . . . what was that? That . . . that noise?" Finding the bat behind him, he leapt from the bed into a defensive stance. "Who . . . who's there?" We were, of course; but this he never knew.

Wordlessly, the boy dressed and departed the suite.

Lydia, having to rise, reset her room and ready herself for her second spark, waved us away. He was a regular, known as Hotheaded Frank, who paid for exclusivity, and thought Lydia his alone. It would not do—"No, indeed!" said Adaline—for him to discover that earlier in the evening Lydia had ushered a boy into manhood, albeit meanly.

Cinderella's show was of threefold interest: (1) She remained fully clothed throughout. (2) In her blue-green, sky- and sea-colored chamber she entertained two men; and both of these she would, (3) Bewitch.

This party she hosted in her third-floor suite, set at the back of Cyprian House, directly below my attic room. Within were the young men whom Cinderella thought enamored of each other. She was right: it was evident, even to my untrained eye. And the evidence increased as the witch poured once, twice, thrice from her decanter, and the boys—boys they seemed now; for they devolved as they drank—suffered well the effect of her wine, which was witch-fixed, and brought their truer selves to the fore.

The witch, for her part, remained fully clothed. Her blond hair was well-done, and her dress—of tomato red silk, with black appliqué—was sublime in its every detail. Still, it was hard to watch her work; for she insisted upon that false French and I, drunk on the night—not to mention the witch-wine of dinner, and the port I'd partaken of in the parlor—

had all I could do to stifle my laughter. O, but it would not do to be discovered, no. Innumerable sisters had watched from within this warren o'er the years, surely. I—H., Henri, Henry, Henriette—would not be the one to give the game away.

We arrived late in the game of Comparison. The contestants were nearly naked.

"Now, *assiet, asie*— . . ." tried Cindy; and when the French refused her, she said, simply, "Sit. Both of you. Let us proceed; as I'm *curieuse* as to which of you is best equipped to please. Take off your boots and stockings." The boys took to the carpeted floor, and began to do as told; but there came a clarifying command: *"Non,"* said Cindy, "each t'other. Remove each other's shoes and silks."

They hesitated. They drank. They shrugged and proceeded, shyly.

"Speed on!" said Cinderella. "Speed on, *mes guerres*." At which I nearly blew with laughter our cover; for, meaning to call the boys "boys"—or *garçons*—she'd erred and referred to them as "wars"; but neither knew it.

The game proceeded. This took drink, indeed. And the dimming of a gasolier that glared. But the witch's end was soon achieved: and there stood the boys, naked, face-to-face, a foot apart. Cinderella called them to the edge of her bed. "There's but one part left, gents."

Cinderella drew from her bedside drawer a white glove. Onto the middle finger of this she'd marked inches, in black thread; the thumb, too, showed marks I could not descry, though I assume those, too, were inches, and used to ascertain girth. She brought the boys near, nearer, so near she held their two members in her one hand; and she worked her gloved hand expertly.

"Oh my." She gushed, watching as the contestants—or rather, the contested parts—grew. "Oh my, what . . . what have we here?" . . . Of course, she declared a draw.

Was it a spell she spoke then? Perhaps it was but more bad

French. I cannot say; but its result was this: the boys stared at each other, fixedly.

"Kiss," commanded the witch; from whence the road down to pleasure proved a declivitous one. Cinderella fell back onto her pillows, satisfied, to watch. "Stride," said she, "stride like Spartans the back roads of love." This I thought *un peu excessif;* but then I realized she spoke not for the boys' benefit, but rather for ours.

Indeed, it was a carnal revel the like of which I'd never seen; for every act was mirrored. Yes: there was a complementary quality to the love I witnessed. And it was love, assuredly so; powerful, too, as a genie finally come from his bottle after long confinement.

Spent, love-tossed, and lost, the boys settled atop the carpet, smiling and calling for wine.

Cinderella came near the wall behind which we hid. She spoke, in a whisper—the boys, had they heard her, would have thought she spoke to a child's portrait hanging above the bureau before which she stood: the child whose eyes were actually mine—and said, "Blessed be the waters of Lethe." Whereupon, with a wink, she poured wine from the larger decanter into a second, smaller one; into this she stirred a powder like pink sand, which she'd spilled from a scarab ring worn on her thumb.

To Adaline, I explained the sister's reference to the legended river of Hell: Lethe; the crossing of which causes forgetfulness.

Minutes after their first sip the boys fell from consciousness. The one was midsentence when he did so. There they lay, atangle. Standing o'er them, Cinderella said with a sigh, "They've not the strength, yet, to meet tonight's joys on the morrow."

"They'll . . . they'll not remember?" Adaline pressed her mouth to the mask to ask the question.

"No," said Cinderella, coming nearer the wall, "they'll

not. My wine renders them bold, not brave. Their souls, I suppose, will know some measure of satisfaction. So, too, will their bodies; for, *mon Dieu,* look at that spill of seed!"

I watched, aghast, as Cinderella stooped to mop the seed from off their skin with a kerchief of black silk. Happily—for I wanted not to watch that harvesting—I set my mouth to the mask and asked, "Your wine . . . . It can effect such forgetfulness?"

"The wine and certain spell-work, yes."

"Can you show me? Will you, please?" Again I fixed my eyes to the mask, and saw Cinderella tuck the sodden kerchief up her sleeve.

"There's desperation in your tone, sister," said she, stepping quickly to the mask. From within the suite, she'd have appeared nose to nose with the painted child. "You've an interest, witch?"

Ridiculously, I nodded. My head knocked against the wall; this Cindy must have heard as affirmation; for, *"Très bien,"* said she. "I respect a curious sister." And only when her eyes retook their shape—black circles within the blue—did I see that she'd shown the Toad. I set my own eyes to the mask, and—with will—returned that strangest of salutations. "Tomorrow in the atelier," said Cindy. "You'll teach me the cant of your country"—by which she meant words otherwise known as "dirty"—"and I will teach you what it is I know of Lethean wine. *D'accord?"*

"Oui," said I. (Note: I knew not the slang of sex, yet Cinderella, on the morrow, honored our deal; for I traded my *thé de traduction* instead.)

"Go now," said Cindy. "I have to rouse my dandies and see them to the street." Only then did I realize I'd reached for Adaline's hand; to which I now held, tightly.

Down the vespertine hall we went, taking a corner so hurriedly we smacked into Eliphalet: a darkness within the greater dark. "The Duchess wants you," said he. "There"—he pointed into those shadows stretching away—"down where the sisters work."

The Duchess lay in the near dark, on a divan that may have been brown, black, or green; it was, I may report, soft as moss. Her pale skin glowed, as does the moon when the sky is hazy and hinting of snow. And something else shone besides: a brassy apparatus of the Duchess's own design. She had in hand a . . . a thing she'd commissioned from an oculist on Anthony Street. Imagine the spawn of a French horn and a lorgnette; for this thing—with its runnels and tubing and inlaid mirrors—seemed best suited to an orchestra pit or opera box. Its purpose, I saw, was to let the Duchess spy from a prone position; for she'd affixed its eyes to the mask, and her own eyes to it. "They've just begun," said she at our approach.

Eli directed us to two stools set very low to the floor, before masks that must have been hidden, on their other side, by the wallpaper's pattern. Eli sat at the Duchess's slippered feet; and they shared her odd glass, trading it off as pashas might pass the hose of a hookah pipe. "Jen," said the Duchess, bringing us up to speed, "has been rather hard to heat, I'm afraid."

The brothers had been slow to disrobe. I suppose there'd been some measure of courtship, which we'd missed. But it had devolved to this: they were three against one within the suite, with Fanny and the brothers trying to persuade Jen to participate in acts she saw fit to resist.

Fanny, despairing of words, finally led her sister with action: she stood to take the brothers' kisses; and then fell back abed, beside her sister, bidding the brothers "show yourselves." They'd have stripped themselves no faster if their clothes had been afire. Jen giggled behind her hand. Fanny laughed as well, but hers was hyena-like: harrowing, harsh. The effect of all this on me was bodily; for I thought the brothers beautiful, two variations on the themes of Paleness, Muscularity, and Boldness besides.

They—the silk men—had attributes which outdid mine. Horns, they seemed, sawn from off the brows of some African beasts. Fanny quite approved of the boys' show; and might well have applauded, had she not been so busy with the undoing of her laces and stays. Soon the whole of her dress was discarded; and she rose to stand between the brothers in naught but her shift. The three of them seemed a Grecian triad, statuary; and their common gaze was fixed—as though it, too, were marble-hewn—upon poor Jen.

"H.," whispered the Duchess. *"H.!"*

How long she'd been summoning me, I cannot say. *"Oui?"* said I, flustered, when finally I heard her.

"You'll have them both, I've decided."

"Both?" I was incredulous; for again I thought she'd referenced the—

"The *silks.* You'll have both the purple and gold. You'll want clothes, will you not? And a souvenir of this night."

I thanked her in whispers, though I spared a thought for Adaline. I then watched as the Duchess raised again that quizzing-glass. Eli sat staring at her, and raised a pale hand to set it atop her paler breast. From the Duchess there came a soft, soft sound: a half sigh, let me say. Then: "They've got her," said she, "finally!"

At which I retook to the mask.

Fanny had handed to one of the brothers—he whose hair was blacker, eyes bluer, shoulders stronger—a set of silver shears. This brother—the *more* brother, I will call him—set to cutting away Jen's dress; for she'd acquiesced to some act and neither he, nor his brother, nor Fanny cared to risk Jen's change of heart. A dealer in silks, he cut deftly, decisively.

Now the lesser brother—he who was but a fraction less fine, in every way—knelt before Jen, who'd lain back upon the daybed. Fanny sat beside her, cradling her sister's head in her lap and bending to bedew her brow with kisses. Both brothers set upon the shyer sister's petticoats. I could see only Jen's legs; down which the more brother rolled her pink stockings, revealing flesh only slightly less pink. At her ankles they were massed, till the lesser brother plucked them from her: ripened fruit from off the limb. Both brothers kissed Jen's bared legs, beginning at the high arch of her tiny foot.

Poor Jen, thought I; laid bare to so many hands, and so many eyes. But O, how I envied her, too.

There then commenced a lesson in sexual arithmetic, the like of which I shan't soon forget. For it was clear that the brothers—their engines athrum—were to take turns upon the girl, with Fanny granting better access to her sister by holding her legs asplay. O, but Jen, poor Jen, with both sets of coralline lips aquiver, seemed not . . . well, it appeared she simply was not divisible by the sum of the brothers' parts. Truly, I feared for her; and found my hands falling to my own sex, as if it were I about to suffer a like assault.

In they went as I watched. Both brothers: the more and the lesser. Inch by inch.

As the more brother took his third turn, I heard the Duchess sigh; no half sigh, this. Still I stared, rapt, and saw the more cede rights to the lesser; and this they repeated for well nigh a quarter hour, till Jen's mouths—the higher suffering kisses, the lower braving a battery the likes of which . . . —well, in time both mouths were *O*s, open, and showing lips rather more red than pink, rendered thus by hard usage.

As the ecstatic moment drew near, Fanny bade the brothers desist. This was not easily effected. In fact, she joked that two ewers of cold water stood just outside the door, that she'd fetch and cast them upon the brothers, if need be. All the while, Jen lay in a state of suspension; and I could not assess her level of pleasure. But pleasure there was; for something—her half smile, or her eyes—bespoke it.

Fanny asked after the boys' "*baudruches,*" and though I

heard the French word, I knew not its meaning. Neither did the boys. And so it was explained to all of us at once: "Your French protectors," said Fanny. "Don them now."

The two sheaths were drawn forth, and applied to the parties in question. This, of course, I'd never seen done; and the immediate impression was one of chimpanzees struggling to put skins back onto bananas.

Once all was in accord, Fanny again granted access to her sister. An end to the act came quickly. The more brother went, nay came first; with the lesser let to follow. Neither seemed in need of encouragement, yet each brother cheered the other with words seeming better suited to the racetrack or ring.

Done, the boys redressed with haste.

"Sarah will see you out," said Fanny. In her lap, still, lay Jen; who now covered her face (feigning shame), rather than bid the brothers adieu. Her shoulders heaved with her (false) sobs. Jen's seeming discomfiture at once pleased and gave pause to the brothers; and so it was they excused themselves before the majority of their buttons had been seen to. Once they'd stumbled from the room—boots in hand, red gallows hanging like slingshots from their hips—the sisters quite surprised me: they sat up, tidied themselves, and turned to the wall behind which we sat: the oddest of tribunals. Smiling, they held high the two skins, weighted now with the brothers' seed.

"Très bien," breathed the Duchess, rapping twice upon the wall to signal her approval.

37

En Ville

Up to the attic I climbed, by the proper stairs. The night was ended, and I needed no one to tell me so; for I was exhausted. Yet riled, too. As who would not have been by such a show? In truth, I was fair desperate to offer my double prayer to Onan; for, if I didn't do so, sleep would be a long time coming.

The attic, I saw, had known a night's usage: its screens had been shifted, some folded away entirely; candles had bled wax onto the tables; books lay hither and thither, on worktables and on stands of wrought iron; pestles of white marble showed fresh stains; vials of every size could be seen, the empty ones rolled to odd angles, the full ones set in stands; and, most disconcertingly, I discovered a table whereon there lay a dead cat. Not a simple cat, of the household sort; no. Its face was pinched, palsied. Only in time would I know it for a civet: a sort of spotted skunk.

Crates of the creatures came regularly to Cyprian House, shipped from the far Western woodlands. (By daylight I'd see them—stuffed, seeming too real, their marble eyes aglitter—a phalanx ranged upon the highest shelves of the attic.) The Duchess preferred her cats alive upon delivery; whereupon she'd pen them in the yard and, one by one, smoke them, smother them in the cellar. Thusly were they unsullied by blood and unmarked by bullet when stuffed. Bloody work it was, this taxidermy; but the Duchess had long ago deemed it wasteful to discard the creatures once she'd excised—from near their sex organs—those sacs from which she pressed her own perfume.

This discovery dulled the edge of my desire. Indeed. And well this was; for I found company in my dark corner of the attic.

Parting the drapes, I found Eugénie and Sarah seated upon the sill. Each was in undress: stay-less shifts of white cambric which caught the moonlight. They were listening to a song that rose to the window from elsewhere.

Eugénie raised a long finger to her lips, lest I speak. She pointed then to my cot, the linens of which had been turned down. I undressed, and slid into bed; from where I watched as the Creole sat stroking the hair of Sarah, who leaned upon her shoulder. The song we heard—and to which I'd become accustomed o'er the nights to come—rose from Palermo's, the Italian opera house sitting not a half block distant. This, of course, I did not know at the time. So it was I fell asleep that first night fancying this new world magical, full of moonsong and secrets told.

O, but far less magical was the morning after; for I was awoken by Eli, who said I was to dress and descend to help

Sarah at her chores. "Be the boy," said he; and upon my cot cast a bundle of clothes. His, I suppose: black worsted slacks, a shirt that was none too fresh, and that same waistcoat of camblet he'd worn the night prior.

At Sarah's side, I hauled water and wood, carted chamber pots to the privy in the yard, roused the witches, and helped them to dress. . . . By ten I was tired and hungry, too. I set upon my breakfast greedily, without grace, whilst into the dining room the witches traipsed, one by one, some sleepy and straggling, some chatty, and all raising an eyebrow at seeing me so attired. " 'Tis she," said Li'l Belt, with a nod toward Cinderella, bent o'er her berries and cream, "who is supposed to turn into a pumpkin come midnight."

I tried to explain, but stopped, as explanation was neither warranted nor wanted.

Within a week, I'd take to the morning routine and know no resentment of it. Sarah proved a most patient teacher, and in time opined that I was indeed a help. Adaline, who'd assisted prior to my arrival, had not been. "She's a bother," Sarah said, adding with disdain, "Ask to see the burns she got taking biscuits from the oven." Neither was Eli reliable; for he did the Duchess's bidding, and attended her all the day long.

Together they took to the streets each morning at seven; returning, yes, at the nine-stroke. Together they saw to the house's needs; or so I supposed. And no matter the hour or chore, the Duchess went about town in full dress. Often she passed in shadow; for Eli held o'er her head a parasol, no matter the strength of the sun. Thusly did the Duchess protect her hard-won pallor. Just how she won it . . . well, let me leave off that detail for now; for, it being rather . . . perverse, I fear I'll prejudice you against a woman and witch who was all goodness. To me, at least.

. . . Eli? His heart seemed on a swivel: he met me kindly when I was in skirts, but could be cutting, even cruel when I was in slacks. At Cyprian House, of course, I was a witch foremost; but I slipped between sexes at my convenience, and manifested my two sides by turns.

Chores were best seen to in boy-dress. Midday, when Cyprian House was "Witches Only"—by rede, or rule—I dressed as the others did: simple frocks free of corsets and stays, and studied in the attic. At five I put aside my studies, and whilst Sarah saw to supper and Eli wrote out the night's calendar for the Duchess, I built hickory fires in the suites—as the weather wanted; and indeed a cold, cold winter came that year—and, in general, did what needed doing; which included seeing to my sisters' dressing. All the doors on floors two and three stood open, and from one suite I'd rush to another when hearing my name called. ("H.! H., darling, *do* come. I need you.") Up the stairs and down. Bounding room to room like a kicked ball. Li'l Belt needed her laces pulled as tight as could be. Lydia Smash liked the way I set the combs in her hair. Cinderella was all thumbs where buttons and bows, false cuffs and collars were concerned. Fanny and Jen sought my approval of their dress; for I checked to see that they matched, and were identical in every detail save color. Eugénie and Adaline were self-sufficient, perhaps owing to the fact that they saw no sparks.

During the hours of dressing, I had conferred upon me sundry accessories. And any clothes that fit me—or might, if mended—I was let to take. Thusly did I augment my wardrobe, which already featured three dresses of purple and gold, sewn from the brothers' silks. Too, the Duchess had deemed me in need of some dandified clothes; and it was she, along with Eugénie—who offered to stand in for me beneath the tailor's dancing hands—who decided on the cloth and cut of an armoire's worth of frock coats, pants, ribbon ties, and such. I was grateful, of course; but finally I had to refuse a cane—topped with a tortoiseshell pommel—and a monocle. "They're all the rage," argued they;

but I could not sport the eyeglass without my cheeks flushing red.

So: by morning, whilst at chores, I was more often than not a boy. Midday, I was a witch, and learned by Book or practice. I showed the Eye with ease—as salutation, mostly—though still it left me a bit . . . *mal à la tête*. More: I could achieve things which would have been beyond me in the days prior to my meeting the Matanzan dead. For example: I heard from a much-amused Cindy that a batch of wine I'd mixed from her recipe was strong, quite so: said she, a constabulary "acquaintance" of hers had forgotten his address, and roamed in search of home all the night long. And when finally Lydia Smash tested my telekinetic powers, she was as surprised as I to see that corps of stuffed civets dance upon the shelf. . . . So it was I learned.

To the parlors? Well, sometimes I went as Henriette, and sometimes Henri. As a woman, I was well complimented. And once, when I descended *en masculin,* Burtis came to me, introduced himself, and asked had I seen . . . myself. Seemingly he'd taken a fancy to Henriette—though still his heart beat only for Li'l Belt—and wondered if I (Henri) had had occasion to appreciate myself (Henriette). A confusion of compliments, this was; and the tale much amused the sisters at supper.

When finally I ventured from Cyprian House, I dressed as logic dictated: I went to the post office as a man (for that place is infamously inhospitable to women), and visited the stalls of Fulton Street's fishmongers in slacks as well (for in skirts I'd once been cheated). Sometimes my mind and dress were decided by economy: as a man going to the Park or Bowery Theaters, I'd have to buy a box for a dollar; but as a woman I could access the third tier for a quarter. From on high I'd watch what play or review was set astage, though often the greater show surrounded me; for, the third tier was "whore-crowded," as Eli deemed it, and there the less fortunate of the frail sisterhood plied their trade in plain sight. Once, at the Bowery, I had to turn my back to the man beside me; for, from his far side, some *nymphe du pavé* worked his lap with her crusted glove; and never was butter more broadly churned from out its urn. I was present, too, when Hal Grandy—who'd given herself, wholly, to the sloe berry—raised high her skirts and let fall her water, hoping to hit a certain swell who sat below. O, what a row ensued! We Cyprians who were present—it was a Wednesday evening, and we'd voted for an evening "atown"—were spared the watch's hard questioning only by the quick-thinking Duchess, who gathered us all whilst still Hal pissed her gin and marched us home past the police, past the sportsmen and sharps, past the drummers and diners-out: the nighttime crowd, which rarely we saw; for always we were home, safe within Cyprian House.

O yes: Cyprian House came to seem a home. So at ease among the sisters was I that I well nigh forgot those who'd previously been *ma famille,* my world entire. I'd come as a coward, fleeing Celia. I'd come seeking Sebastiana, answers, and salvation. Soon I'd denied them both, found I could not accommodate them within, so crowded was I with shame and secrets, and a soul rendered bone-hard by lies. . . . O yes, much was denied; but still I could not shake the truth every sad traveler discovers: the self is a place one cannot quit.

Still I wrote Sebastiana; but she replied at a rate that merits not the term *correspondence.* One letter to my every five, perhaps. I sent but two or three letters to Celia. This shames me, terribly; but let me qualify the fact thusly: it was likely she'd not receive my letters; for she'd not brave the precincts of the post office. And when finally I got hold of a territorial newspaper—St. Augustine's *Gazette*—indeed I found listed within the name of Liddy Collier. In fact, I found my own name as well: Henry Collier; and knew that the letters awaiting me in St. Augustine could have come from no one but Rosalie Poe. Perhaps the letter in which I'd apprised her of my plans had been miscarried. Perhaps—and this seemed the more likely explanation—she'd misunderstood my meaning, though I'd made it plain, and had directed her, expressly, to write me in care of General Delivery, New York.

Upon this discovery, I wrote the postmaster of St. Augustine, enclosing five dollars for his troubles and asking that he forward to me, in New York, those letters attending my return as well as any others that might arrive. I dared not ask him to deliver "Liddy's" letters to her; for this would have upset her. Nor could I involve Erasmus Foot, whose curiosity sometimes bettered his sense. I resolved instead to write Celia again, and seek out a private carrier who'd convey my letter to her door, nay *our* door. This, though, I never did. O, how cowardly, how cruel! To leave Celia wondering where I was, and when I might return. To ignore the wrongs I'd done. Had she money enough? Was she well, or worse? And I'd no idea if I'd succeeded, those final days, in breaking the spell I'd set upon her. No idea at all. . . . Not only had I tended the seed of evil sown by Bedloe, I'd let it run wild: heart-weeds, those were; growth of the strangling sort.

In time, Eliphalet warmed to me, and I to the city. On his arm Adaline and I stepped out. Blessedly, I found I was unafraid. More often than not I stepped out as a woman. This I did for two reasons: it was my preference, then; and Eli preferred his people petticoated, rather than panted. Together, we three strolled the Third and Fifth Wards. We kept from passing the hospital; for on its far side sat Paradise Square, or Five Points, a morass of petty miscreants: landed pirates, women who'd fallen and were falling still, and pickpockets who'd take your life as they'd take your watch. Indeed, only once did I brave the area, having begged Eli to take me thither. As men we passed through it, and onto the riverside, where rats the size of cats scampered o'er the cobbles and women writhed as advertisements in the top-story windows of taverns. These brothels had their specialties—girls, Negresses, boys done-up or plain . . . —but when Eli asked if I wished to enter one such establishment, I declined. And from Paradise we hied, back toward the better wards, and home.

As dapper, if not dandified Henry—in suit-parts of navy serge; my preferred waistcoat the one sewn of black silk, set with toad-shaped closings down its front—I also saw to many errands at Eli's side. To the stationers we went, procuring for the witches all that was requisite to their vast correspondence: inks, nibs, Li'l Belt's paper of cornflower blue, Lydia's plain, Cindy's pink, Eugénie's cream, bordered in navy. (Only the sisters and Adaline wrote to no one.) Eugénie, too, insisted upon her bottles of Cardenio ink, ordered down from Boston. These bottles of blue, filigreed glass sprouted atop the scriptorium's tables like stemless tulips. All these supplies we charged to the Duchess's account.

From the stationers we'd cross to the post itself, which sat in what had formerly been the Dutch church, and wherein there remained a pulpit and other such churchly architecture. When first we went, I embarrassed myself terribly; for, dressed as Henry, I sidled up to the women's window. Luckily, those men present made a joke of my confusion, and I resorted to French, thus furthering my excuse. In fact, upon entering the place, I'd grown confused. It was warm: early springtime of '31, perhaps. Still, I doubted the sun was responsible for my fever. Only later would this episode be explained; for I'd learn that the Dutch were then engaged in carting their dug-up dead from the post office's yard and reinterring them in a more commodious place. It was the death-presence, thusly stirred, that had affected me and caused me to forget those habits—be they manly, womanly, or what—which, at all times, I took such care to maintain.

Understand: I'd not yet reconciled myself to the death-alliance that is my fate, and that I'd first known in the Richmond theater-cum-church; and later, in the territory. I knew the dead—when massed, and unquiet—affected me, yes; but still I denied it along with much else. And thusly did I leave myself open to it. As per:

That night when next I met them: the dead.

I'd been out (as Henriette) with Adaline and Eli. We'd seen a show at the Park Theater; with drink and oysters afterward at the Shakespeare Refectory, where the crowd was ever lively. It was late spring, or early summer, I recall; for talk had turned to fever and a certain cholera, said to be creeping westward from Asia. O, but why should I care? I was a witch, with naught but the Blood to worry me. All I wanted was idle time for idle talk; and champagne to chase my oysters.

Earlier that day, we three had had an hour of confession. Finding ourselves before a boardinghouse on Dey Street, the one in which Eli had stayed when first he'd come to the city—"We were five boys to the room," said he, disgustedly—he spoke of his mother. A Canadian maiden, unwed, who'd died of the Blood some years prior. Coming down from Amherstberg, Eli had clerked through his early teens; but when first he visited Cyprian House, and met the Duchess, he "knew" her—in ways witchly and biblical, both—and became, that very night, the first man—or boy, rather—to sleep the night in Cyprian House.

This prompted a sharing by Adaline, who had told little of her past; which was bad. Indeed, she spoke of Maine as Dante does the underworld. Seems she was witch-born beside a sister: twins; but their mother knew not her own nature, nor her daughters'. From Augusta the girls had run, living a year in Boston—with their Mystic Sister: a beldam by the name of Hannah Bliss—before Adaline's sister fell to the Blood; whereupon Adaline made her way to the Duchess's door.

I told my story in fits and starts, not wanting to relive it;

moreover, I was troubled, deeply, by Adaline's tale: I'd not known the Blood could come to one so young.

It was this saddening talk that led us to the enlivening revue and restaurant, where we partook of "bubbles" and oysters by the bucket. This, in turn, led to tomfoolery. So it was we found ourselves stumbling northward beneath a new moon. To Hudson Square; where we made fun of the lovely lives lived within the O-so-lovely homes.

But as we strolled, I felt again that certain . . . disquiet. It is, in fact, akin to that quaking and quelling that can be caused by a bad oyster; and to this I attributed it. But I knew better when we crossed the square and I saw we'd come to St. John's Burying Ground. Now, of course, I would simply turn back from such a place. Then—in denial of the dead, and spurred by my fellows—I walked the graves beside them. Eli saw that I grew unwell; but this he ascribed to our having overindulged and to certain "airs," which, said he, teasingly, I'd donned along with my dress. Thusly goaded, I kept on. I can recall the sexton's shed. And two rude and uncapped graves behind it, so new the soil had yet to settle. It was at this latter site that I fell to the hallowed ground; for the dead therein were innocent men, wrongly hanged, and such types are always strong.

The next morning I woke, unwell. My head hammered; from the yammering dead, yes; though there had been excess of champagne, too, it's true. Apparently, I'd fallen, and could not be revived. Adaline swore I'd shown no pulse. Eli went into action; and stole that corpse cart by which the two brought me back to Cyprian House.

Waking all of a sudden, I saw several sisters ranged around my cot. The Duchess had roused me with salts. Sarah was asked to warm a basin of water; for the aforementioned cart had rendered not only my dress but my very skin death-scented. To those assembled I told the tale entire—from the theater fire through to Matanzas, to the lesser facts of the

Dutch dead and St. John's—and it was decided: we'd convene the half hour prior to supper, and I'd tell the tale, again, in its every detail, for the edification of all. This I did, at a table well set and better suited to celebration than confession. Several of the sisters brought their Books to table, and wrote as I spoke. After supper, we disbanded; for the Duchess expected a "randy" house that night, owing to some astral misalliance.

I sat out the parlor games; and forwent the masks. Instead, I retired to the attic to read, to search out a Book by some other, death-allied sister. I searched to the sounds of Palermo's distant soprano; but did so in vain.

38

The Master-piece

THREE of us—Adaline, Eugénie, and myself—opted for bookish pursuits o'er the Duchess's sex-practicum. None of the others begrudged us our choice; for, indeed, every witch availed herself of the Duchess's library.

I often found Eugénie in the attic, seated before the Leonard Street windows at a long desk of dark woods into which visiting sisters had carved initials, short spells, and such: a sort of guest book. This precinct we referred to as the *scriptorium,* and there much copying from *Books of Shadows* was done by daylight. Other sisters studied in private, borrowing volumes and returning with them to the privacy of their suites.

On shelves hewn from hardwoods, and showing graven plates of brass—identifying the subjects by which the library was so carefully ordered—there stood books by the hundreds, nay thousands. Some large, some small; some newly covered in kid and pressed with the Duchess's mark, others seeming to sigh when touched, as if exhaling the breath of ages past. The subjects? Reform Physiology. Folklore. History. Novelists: *East,* and Novelists: *West;* by which ordering the Duchess kept Lady Murisaki safe from de Sade. There were books in languages I knew, and some I'd never seen, such as Sanskrit. There were books on the Yoruban traditions, and other religions. Books on the Craft, of course, by the score: Albertus Magnus, John Dee, and those bulls in which the Church refuted these and other rogue philosophers.

Of course, *Books of Shadows* composed the bulk of the library. They were ranged by geography and alphabet both: Books by witches of Africa (very interesting, these); Books by two sisters resident in the Apennines; Books by a dead sister who'd passed her days on the shores of Bantry Bay (this witch's four volumes stood alone, separate from those of the other Irish witches); and Books from sisters in Bulgaria, in Cairo, high in the Carpathians, in China (a much-referenced herbologist, this witch), in Cuba, in Damascus, on the Danish isles, in Edinburgh (with the Books of a Highlands witch grouped therein), and yes, in France. It was there I found, copied in full, the Book of Sebastiana d'Azur. Into it had gone several plates, by which some of Sebastiana's portraits had been reproduced; the dates of the reproductions were recent, and the work was attributed, of course, to Sebastiana's *nom de plume,* or more accurately, her *nom de . . . palette.* Above a plaque that read MISCELLANY: *THE COURTS OF EUROPE,* I found many Books by Sebastiana's contemporaries. I read with avidity those in which she figured, and I learned a thing or two about my Mystic Sister: most markedly, it was stated again and again, by witch upon witch, that Sebastiana had ought to "do away with" that consort of hers: Asmodei. A pity, thought I, that she'd not heeded such sound advice.

O'er these *Books of Shadows* I pored, yes, reading and

copying innumerable entries into my own Book. . . . But I confess: I leavened this study by turning to the eroticists (*EROS,* read the plaque that referenced a whole half-shelf of books), many of whom represented my home country, of course:

Venus en rût, L'École des filles, Latouche's *Histoire de Dom B.* Occasionally, I read aloud from these for Eugénie, and for Adaline (for whom the Creole and I translated in turn). Adaline we convinced to read from those in English. She blushed deeply, in so doing; still, she read from *The Lustful Turk, The Confessions of a Lady of High Rank, The Autobiography of a Footman,* et cetera. A particular favorite of all parties, present and past—to judge by the Duchess's well-thumbed volume—was *The Memoirs of a Woman of Pleasure;* wherein Miss Fanny Hill is bandied bed to bed, each time meeting her ruin anew. These books, written to give rise to men, gave rise in our case to questions; for Adaline knew less than I did when it came to . . . *les jeux d'amour*. Eugénie did sometimes explain; but more often than not we applied to Li'l Belt or Cindy, both of whom relished such salted talk. Thereby, we learned; and once or twice saw the explanations put into practice. Said Li'l Belt on one occasion, when neither Adaline nor I could grasp the acrobatics requisite to a position much lauded in *Venus,* "Come to my mask tonight and I'll show ye"; and show us she did, in the company of a man who paid again twice to have the feat repeated.

But lest it seem all our debts were payable to pleasure, we did sometimes try to extract from the texts commonsensical things. This was difficult. And one text with origins in the past century confused us terribly; such that we, nay I—for Adaline was all but silent on the subject—appealed to the whole sisterhood one night at supper. Thusly was Aristotle dismissed.

Not *that* Aristotle; no indeed. Another. From whose *Master-piece*—thusly did the brazen author entitle it—I'd culled all manner of confused and confusing things. "Is it true," I asked of the sorority, "that females are cooler than males?"

"But who'd know better than you?" asked Cinderella; to which I had to explain:

My "particulars," when put into practice—as they so rarely were—added up to a sum of pleasure, the components of which I could not, *cannot* subtract one from another. (*Enfin,* I am myself; and knew nothing else.) This intrigued the sisters, who begged further explication. I demurred. "Far be it for me," said I, "to explain the differences between the common sexes." And raising up the *Master-piece,* I read this puzzling passage:

"Says this secondary Aristotle, 'Men are the hotter, drier, lustier sex; women, the cooler and more moist.'"

"Ah," opined the Duchess from table's end, "that I may translate as follows: What a man wants done often, a woman wants done well. *C'est tout.*" To this all present—including a chagrined Eliphalet—assented.

The witches quite rebelled at this Aristotle's take on "the moon's effect on the machinery of menarche," which (and I quote) was this:

"Girls need blood for growth; yet at maturity the red humour sits in surplus. In accord with the moon's phases, and monthly, this is discharged." It was what followed that set the sisters to hissing, for Aristotle goes on: "A woman of sanguinary Complexion hath her terms in the moon's First Quarter, a cholerick in the Second, a melancholy in the Third, and so it follows."

"Aye?" asked Li'l Belt. "The man's a fool! He'd like to read our rags against the calendar and tell us our types? What more does he put forth, pray?"

I read what even I knew to be absurd; and the witches laughed in accord. "Says he," I began, "'Preparatory to the convulsive embrace, the love parties ought to look upon the Lovely Beauties, each of the other, careful to have first ingested those foods—shellfish, wine, and things both salty and spiced—that fill the body full of sap.'"

"Well," said Jen, all innocence, "he's in the right there, if oysters be shellfish."

"Better you'd be," said Li'l Belt, "ingestin' anything but that there book. . . . 'Lovely beauties'? says he. He ought to set down his foolish pen, and undo his buttons for a look-see. Pricks are fun, they are, and I'd miss them plenty; but 'lovely'? No."

"Frivolous, this," said the Duchess. All turned toward her, and were quiet. "H.," said she, "you have yet to shed your shyness here. I wish you to. Know that you'll find no harm, no hurt, no judgment here among us. Do you know this?"

I did, said I.

"Ask then the questions I hear—*hear,* say I—crowding the fore of your mind. On with it; for there are nine bawcocks in the city proper, stiffening as we speak, and each is destined for our door this night."

"Nine?" it was asked.

"Nine, yes," said the Duchess, "for Li'l Belt has her Burtis and two sparks besides."

The Irish sister dipped her pointed chin to her shoulder, coyly; but then spoke her true motive, saying, " 'Twill be a twenty-dollar night for me, miladies," which fact received its due appreciation in the form of applause; which the Duchess cut off by rapping a ring upon the table. Said she, "The parlor hour draws near. . . . H.?"

I'd more pressing questions, indeed. If love was not lust, when—if ever—did the two meet; and what then? Was each whole, or half the other? And if man and woman were two poles of a path, where on that path did I stand? O, but fearing I'd sound the fool, I asked no such questions; and instead took up my Book, into which I'd copied much strangeness, and much I'd not understood. I began by quoting what it was I'd found in Ashton's *Book of Nature.*

"'The Orgasm,'" I began, "'is, for men, so intense that all

consciousness ceases, and a perfect insensibility to one's surrounds is produced.'"

"Eli?" asked the Duchess.

"True enough," said he, with a wink to the witches, and a smile for his mistress.

"I find," offered Lydia Smash, "that men are insensible *most* of the time."

"Aye," said Li'l Belt, "and surely they ain't orgasmic all the while."

"*Aren't* orgasmic," corrected the Duchess.

"'As for women,'" I read, "'Women do not always experience orgasm—'"

" 'Tis sadly true, that," said the Irishwoman. "But I surely would—mark me—if 'twas I payin' for the pleasure."

Amidst all this, Sarah served: chicken with a cherry sauce, I recall.

Unable to eat, I read on, all the while wondering if the pleasure I knew in release was male, female, or both combined. "'And some females of cold temperament do not know what orgasm is at all, having never experienced it.'"

"True." This was a rare comment from Eugénie, who'd little interest in such.

"But none among us, I'll wager," said Fanny. "Sister and I have donned enough masks in this house to have seen each of you melt a time or two."

Laughter; upon which I approached my point, and read, "'When women do experience orgasm, it is often more intense than in the other sex, causing convulsions and involuntary cries and—'"

"Aye," said Li'l Belt, who raised high her glass for a sort of toast. "Sisters, hear this: I've a spark—whose name I'll share for a quarter eagle and no less—who, by prick, tongue, or fingertip, can set me to spurtin' till, I swears it, I can't feel a thing in me end parts—me hands and me feet, dead as doornails! Once the little death was *so* deep"—and here Li'l Belt paused, and looked to the Duchess for the censure she knew would come—"... once—and I could not control it, Duchess, I swear—once I was so swept up that I let the Eye come, and well nigh scared me spark away! Says he, 'What's come over ye, girl?' Says I, ' 'Tis *me* that's come over me, can ye not see as much, man?'"

"I know the man to whom you refer," said a smiling Duchess. "I've had the pleasure myself; though he is old, has grown rich, and reeks of the indoors. But still, you'd best take care; for if he—"

"Worry not, Duchess," said Li'l Belt, "I made sure he left out of here that night drunk on Cinderella's forgetful stuff."

"Well done," said the Duchess; and turning back to me, she said, "H., dear, won't you please—"

"I know not my nature," said I. And, thusly having interrupted the Duchess as I did, the flood began. Words I'd never dared speak; accompanied, of course, by a salt-torrent of tears. "I . . . I pleasure myself in both ways, in both places," rambled I, "but I read somewhere—*eh bien,* I read *everywhere* of the sins of Onan; and how I should stay my own hand lest I spoil my humoral balance and bring upon myself fevers that'll dry my brain and eyes, render me stupid and sightless, and—"

"Nonsense!"

"We'd all be so," said another, "if that were true. Stupid and sightless, I mean."

Still I stammered on: "I read of lust and love's satisfaction. I read the science and philosophy of the body, and of the heart. But still . . . still I know nothing." Here I cut to the quick: "And I left a woman I loved in ruins!"

"You refer to the spellbound one?" asked the Duchess.

I nodded, but did not add that it was not the spell alone that troubled me. I wondered why I'd done what I'd done. Had I loved, nay did I *still* love Celia? Or was it loneliness had driven me, that Platonic notion of the deep need to be with another? Or was I already two, a remnant of that ancient species described in *The Symposium* by Aristophanes, that split male from female such that each lived in search of the other? If so, had I no other to search out and secure, to love? Was I already whole, or fated to be forever halved? . . . None of these thoughts found expression. Instead—yes—I cried, and kerchiefs were proffered from the four corners of the table. "She trusted me," said I, shoulders heaving, "and I . . . I . . ."

"You'll take up the specifics of that with Eugénie, please. It's she among us all who's most efficacious when it comes to spells and such. Quite the Spellcaster, she." To this all the sisters assented. I looked to Eugénie and saw her lips upturn, just so: a smile?

"What's more," continued the Duchess, "as it pertains to love, beware your beloved Byron. He's muddied many an untried mind. As for the vagaries of love, they cannot be taught; one learns them, or one does not. It's a fiery trial, that. But lust? The practice of love, its near-infinite expression? That is my endeavor: to teach it to every witch sent to Cyprian House.

"A decree," said the Duchess then. We'd progressed to dessert; but now all the tiny, two-tined forks fell still. "When we meet on Wednesday next, on Witches' Night, we will do so in the attic, and our purpose will be this: to strip these two of their . . . innocence, shall I say?

"Adaline, dear," said the Duchess, "I'm afraid your hour has come; now so, too, will you." Laughter; and I wondered not for the first time if the Duchess disliked Adaline.

"As for you, H., you are book-sick, and only a dose of life, of lust will set you aright. Maybe then you'll see what love is, or is not, hmm?

"So then, sisters: prepare for Wednesday next." And with that the Duchess took her leave. Behind her trailed the witches of Cyprian House, till there remained we three: Adaline, Eugénie, and me.

None spoke. When I turned to Adaline, I saw tears. She showed me her back. Then she, too, rose, and ran to the foyer and the stairs beyond. I alone would attend the Duchess that night; for Adaline retreated to the private room of her suite, and answered not my most insistent knocking.

When but two of us remained, Eugénie—*la vaudouienne*—bade me come sit beside her and cry my heart dry.

39

Suitors Old and New

It was on the Saturday preceding Wednesday next that the Duchess declared the red parlor "in play"; thusly did she imply that the night would be special. Somehow.

Days previous, Adaline had run cold, cutting me when I dared to speak to her. She kept to her rooms, and deprived me of her company. I whiled away my time alongside Eugénie, who'd begun to direct my reading in the many Books present at Cyprian House; for she'd been resident well nigh a year, I believe, and had copied enough from the library to fill five volumes of her own. Too, affording myself some measure of leisure, I lost myself in Lady Blessington's recent *Life of Byron* (careful not to flaunt the title before the Duchess, who cautioned against its subject). Having exhausted the erotic store of books, I'd turned to the Blessington in hopes of finding romance. All the while, of course, I awaited the Wednesday ritual with great, great apprehension.

So intent was I on Wednesday next, so worried was I, that when Eli invited me to walk the wards, I declined. No doubt he told the Duchess this; for it seemed she meant to assuage me when next I was summoned to her side.

We were in the red parlor, that Saturday night. The Duchess was resplendent in coal-dark silks, which set off her pallor such that she appeared . . . violet, might I say? Yes: one saw the systems beneath the skin by which her blood coursed; and a web of palest blue spread out from the ruddy center of her breasts, rather like the cracks in ice. All color was contained in her lips, and on the tips of her fingers and breasts; all of which showed shades of red. Summoned, I left off chatting with Burtis and Li'l Belt—having already fined him double for a lingering kiss—and crossed to where the Duchess sat upon the bench of a pianoforte; which—with its lid open—resembled a great bat, alight upon the parlor floor. Eli stood beside the instrument, behind the Duchess. I think that he'd not yet unveiled her, as each night he did; no, indeed: he would not have; for still she awaited her special guest.

The Duchess slid to one side of the bench. Behind us the piano played of its own accord, the keys pressed as if by phantom fingers. It was a mere mechanism did this; no ghosts were in attendance. I'd have known, if so.

We sat upon the bench, taking in the parlor. The girls had been introduced a quarter hour earlier. There they were—all but Eugénie and Adaline, of course—at work, at play in the blood-hued room. Center all, from a pendant of sculpted plaster—in which a careful eye would have discerned the Duchess's "crowned cunny"—there depended a great chandelier. It could be lowered to lighting height by a gibbet-like apparatus worked from the corner; and, in fact, it was I who'd lit the candles that night, and raised the whole to watch them gleam, glisten, and give light to the rubicund crystals adorning the silver mass. Red tears, they seemed. No: stay: let me better that and say the thing seemed to cry blood; and one watched the chandelier to see if such tears would drip. Had they, the stains would have gone unseen: red carpets, red divans, red detailing throughout this rarely used parlor. It was by this light that the Duchess and I sat, taking in each spark and witch in turn. Finally, she leaned toward me to say, "I've a notion . . . yes: a notion and nothing more, that soon a sister will take her leave."

"No," said I; for I thought the house well balanced, and no witch had come or gone during my residency. "Who? Which . . . which witch is it?"

The Duchess dismissed my concern, met my clumsy question with a light laugh. With a fan snap, she added, "Nothing extraordinary in it, dear. The sisters—dare I call them daughters?—they . . . they come and they go." She turned to me, and shot me the Eye; so quickly I only saw it fade. Again, that laugh, so wonderfully delicate yet tough: like iron wrought to a filigree. "And that, dearest, is just as I would have it. . . . Which leads me to wonder, H.: have you any interest in the soon-to-be-free suite?"

I stammered the truth, which was this: I hadn't a plan; I didn't know how long I'd stay; I didn't know if or when. . . . *Enfin,* where was it I belonged? With these maenads, amidst these lusting men? What was it Sebastiana had meant for me to learn at Cyprian House? So many questions, and—

"I know, dear," said the Duchess, adding with a sympathetic *tsk-tsk,* "I hear your countless questions." Of course she did. I had better take care. "It is an offer I make," said she, "and nothing more. You'll think about it, won't you?"

"Yes. Yes, of course," said I; and then I asked, "But, Duchess . . . if I were to stay, in a suite, would I be expected to . . . to . . . ."

"If you wanted to, yes, of course. But dearest H., may I say it outright?"

"Please," said I.

"I fear your . . . your particulars are such that profit would elude us."

We turned to each other. We stared. And we laughed, embracing so suddenly, so deeply, that sisters and sparks alike all stopped to take the scene in. "There are those, surely," said the Duchess, "who'd revel in your many pleasures; but I'm not at all sure we'd want such men within . . . within our respective parlors, *tu comprends*?"

Indeed I did. Moreover: I was not inclined—neither by nature nor greed, nor need—to take up the trade. And my sigh of deep relief would have made this plain, had not the Duchess already known as much.

I thanked the Duchess, and told her I would consider her kind offer; and then I sat beside her in silence, looking o'er my sisters and wondering which would leave us, and when. I hadn't gotten far in my assessment of the situation—Li'l Belt, I thought it might be, or Lydia, if either had saved money enough—when suddenly the pocket doors of the red parlor were slid away by Sarah to disclose our guest, he who merited the red parlor when so very few did.

Propriety precludes my naming the man: he who'd adhered, in his youth, to the *code duello;* he whose bullet had deprived the young republic of a certain Federalist of renown; he who'd stood trial for high treason in Richmond, only to have that same John Marshall who'd stared me from Monumental Church acquit him. There the man stood, white-haired and wiry in his seventy-fifth or eightieth year, smiling at the Duchess. All the sparks were cooled, and silent. On tinkled the piano; and to its tune there came into the parlor—his step light: a canter, it seemed—he whose name I'll mark thusly: with initials and stars: A**** B***.

I knew him not by sight, but rather by title; for, "Welcome,

Mr. Vice President," said the Duchess, raising high her ring-heavy hand. Only then did I know myself in the company of Mr. Aaron Burr and—

O, *merde*! I've slipped and written it; and I so hate to sully my Books with obliterating spills of ink. So be it, then. Yes: it was Aaron Burr who came that night to Cyprian House, and not for the first time; this I knew from his deep bow, and salutation:

"My Aspasia," said he, "my Sappho, my Phryne, it has been far too long since I've been let to grace your most hallowed hall."

"Aaron, darling," said the Duchess whilst digging an elbow into my side, unseen, "you've no idea just how hallowed my hall has become. . . . Your bride: where is she this night?"

Burr slipped the question as though it were scandal. "It's you, Lenore, whom I bow to tonight." And yes: down onto one knee he went as Eli stepped forward. The Duchess's fichu was unpinned, and tribute was paid. The Duchess swayed toward me—such that I had to raise a hand to brace her—as I watched the old man kiss, nay suckle at her breast. His lips were sere, his tongue so long, pointed, and pink I thought, *He's a dog's prick for a tongue;* and at this I smiled so broadly the vice-president-that-was sneered. Too, the Duchess shushed me; though of course I'd only thought the insult.

Tribute paid, Burr offered more. From his brocaded waistcoat he drew a tiny sac of red velvet; and from this, in turn, he drew a ring. A ring, said he, "composed of carats numerous enough for a whole hutch of rabbits." It was large, quite; and onto the Duchess's left forefinger it went, where it sat above a band ringed in freshwater pearls. "It's but a bauble," said Burr, "for my Lenore of old." And paid for, I'd learn, by his wife "of new": the infamous Widow Jumel, who'd once plied the Duchess's profession but had since risen to uncommon wealth and repute. An unhappy alliance it would prove to be, too; for Madame Jumel had made a trade with Burr—her money for his fame (or infamy)—but would divorce him, some few years hence, as he lay upon his deathbed.

"I am much obliged, Aaron," said the Duchess, "truly I am." Just how obliging she was, well . . . I cannot report. In advance of the hour, the Duchess sent everyone from the red parlor, including Eli; who, I thought, closed the pocket doors with a protesting *clap.* As for me, I was happy to retire to the atelier, wanting not to watch—by mask or other means—any further tribute paid the Duchess by ancient Aaron Burr.

The Sunday, Monday, and Tuesday *suivants,* I alone attended the Duchess in the purple parlor; for Adaline stayed from common sight, and even took her meals in her suite. Those nights leading up to our Wednesday, the Duchess bade me use every mask to find a man whom I admired. A man was needed, said she. A man whom we'd use, and then render dumb with Cinderella's wine.

As directed, I kept watch for just such a one; but liked not what I saw.

Burtis. Burtis, four nights of every six. Burtis, drained of his inheritance by Li'l Belt, who nearly convinced *me* of her love for the boy. One night, I watched as he read his love to Li'l Belt; that is: he'd organized his thoughts, and encased them (sausage-like) in some lines of metered poetry. Too, he gifted Li'l Belt with his miniature, commissioned from Mr. Peale—Rembrandt Peale—whose studio sat not two blocks distant from Cyprian House. With this gift the show of courtship turned bathetic. Indeed, the charade saddened me; and I declined Li'l Belt's mask if Burtis were within her suite. Too, I came to like Li'l Belt less for her part in plying Burtis; for he'd no defenses. Said the Duchess of the dim-witted boy, "He has but two ideas, I fear; and they appear disinclined to breed."

So: in searching out another "manly machine," I took to

masks other than Li'l Belt's. I watched as La Rousse entertained a mature man with a certain appeal; but he was more word than deed, and needful of a certain white feather if he were to let go his seed. This plume—and spare a thought for the poor egret who'd surrendered it to such purpose—Lydia grudgingly applied to the man's reservoir, as well as that orifice that sits due southward of it. Fanny and Jen, too, had recourse to props on a night precedent to our rite. Props of a darker sort, which surely had been forged for use by stable boys. These they applied to a portly Italian who spoke his own tongue so loudly, so insistently he caused Jen to cry; whereupon Fanny alone had to . . . ride the Italian home, as it were. (Upon squaring with the Duchess, the Italian—a tenor in the employ of Mr. Palermo—was handed back his *carte de visite,* and thusly were his rights of visitation rescinded. He cursed the Duchess in Italian, and she returned his insults with interest—and in Italian—before allowing Eli to intercede; which he did, clamping his hand to the rolled fat aback the Italian's neck and hurling him to the curb.)

There were others I watched who showed attributes, of a kind: ardor, or eyes of a sympathetic hue, well-turned limbs, or clothes of a complimentary cut; but there was no one whose name I'd carry to the Duchess.

And so we'd no spark in our sights as Wednesday dawned. I'd drafted a short list of candidates; but finally I had to own the following: My true list was short indeed, and bore but one name: Eliphalet Rynders.

Early that Wednesday morning, I made my appeal.

At some point, we'd established this habit, the Duchess and I: on Wednesdays—when the Duchess forswore her town-walking and chores—I would sit beside her bed whilst she worked her ledgers, tallying profit from the previous week; for, though she did not profit directly from the acts for which the sisters charged, she did collect and dispense all payment, taking for herself an executor's fee of unknown (and unquestioned) percentage. From the Duchess I learned much about the means of doing business, be they above- or belowboard. She was honest; and I mean not to imply otherwise. But she did seem to find a third side upon every coin, and this she turned to her advantage.

While we worked at her figures Eli slept on beside the Duchess, propped upon an Olympus of black pillows. With difficulty, I kept my eyes on the columns of numbers—for the Duchess did sometimes quiz me—and off the sleeping form at her side. . . . Did the Duchess know who it was I wanted in attendance that night? I imagine she did; but, too, I'd been a while in admitting it to myself, so perhaps all she could cull from my mind was confusion.

Finally, I had out with it; and quickly, too; for Eli slept restlessly atop sheets of black silk—the Duchess's suite, adjoining the red parlor, was all black, with gold chinoiserie on various surfaces: the drapes, the rugs, the sheets . . . —tossing and turning, showing every angle of his self and . . .

"Duchess?" said I.

"Yes?" She did not look up from her ledger.

"I wonder . . ." And on I blathered, saying I'd a request that she might see fit to deny, et cetera. "I wonder . . ."

"Eliphalet?" asked the Duchess, suddenly. "My Eliphalet?"

"Yes," said I. "I was wondering . . ."

"Yes, dear, I hear what you're wondering. It is deafening, in fact." She thought a moment. As she trailed her pencil o'er the sleeping boy's shoulder, it was her turn to wonder; and she did so aloud: "What harm could come of it? . . . Very well, then."

To thank her I said I'd found no man I liked half as well, said I'd prefer to partake of what pleasure would come alongside a man I knew, and liked, and—

"H., hush!" said she. "There's only so much permission I can give."

"Will I need permission from Eli?"

At this the Duchess laid her ledger aside. She looked to the boy, and set her hand upon his brow. (Only then did I remark that the Duchess slept without rings. And—hideously—there they were: on splayed fingers reaching up from her bureau top: real hands, human hands, thick with shellac.) "Permission? No, you needn't seek that. His will is mine. But you'd do well to secure his . . . cooperation," at which she smiled a long while.

Quitting the Duchess's suite that morning, I was startled to see Adaline—in rude dress—descending the central stairs with two chamber pots in hand. Who'd charged her with this lowly chore? She, whom I'd long ago relieved as the least senior of the sorority.

I stared at her; for suddenly it was plain: it was Adaline who'd leave us. And indeed she did, that very afternoon, with nary a word of farewell. The Duchess announced her departure—on the very day of our initiation, mind—to those sisters who'd joined her for an early supper. Said she, "Cyprian House suits not every witch who passes through it." *Poor Adaline,* thought I; for, literally, she was poor and hadn't the means to depart. (That last day's slop work earned her fare from the city, I suppose, and little else.) Later, I'd burn at not having offered her some money from the store Sebastiana had sent. Simply, by the time I thought of this, it was too late; and already she'd left. All I could do was worry and wonder: would Adaline make her way northward, to Boston or beyond?

The clocks of Cyprian House ticked double-quick that Wednesday; and next I knew, we'd all of us assembled in the attic. Where the ritual played out apace, on naught but me.

40

I Am Initiated

THE consummation was sweet, and followed upon rites of undress, ablutions, invocations, et cetera; in which all of the sisters partook. They'd come *en déshabille:* shifts of lawn or cambric, pure white; coiffures were down, accessories were few.

Cinderella had decanted wine, and saw to its pouring. This was not the Lethean mix, but another that rendered all the senses one: the witch's sensorium. Exquisite, it was. Li'l Belt had carried up from her suite a music box, the key to which she conferred upon Eugénie. The latter would wind it throughout what followed; for Eugénie remained apart, and dressed, seated in the shadows alongside the Duchess. Neither of them would stray from their *sièges,* though the Duchess . . .

The Duchess—her black hair flowing to waist length; her

breasts bared, as ever; her robe black, and of a finely worked silk that shimmered in the candlelight— . . . the Duchess did most certainly move atop her couch, if not from it. Seeing her Eliphalet in action quite thrilled her. To this the movements of her unringed fingers were testament; for she worked them o'er her breasts, yes, but also upon, and into, her nether mouth, replacing them there, finally, with a faux member, a wand tipped with an egg-shaped head of hammered gold.

O, but I'll not detail the evening, lest I render this pen a sex-prop, akin to the Duchess's apparatus of pleasure.

. . . But I suppose I should, by way of particulars, say this much at least:

That night in the atelier I was well sexed, and suffered none of love's confusion. Pure, it was. Indeed, I partook of sex in all its purity. And therefore knew the act a lesser thing.

O, mark me well: I took my joy. And greedily, too. . . . But love? No. Love was the one spice absent from the stew; and so all seemed bland. If not in the act, then in the aftermath, till now the memory—the aftertaste, if you will—is redolent of regret.

True, Eli—who'd come up the stairs last, already "in readiness"—was kind. His member, even at half-mast, cast an arcing shadow all the length of his thigh; at which sight I quickened, to be sure. The more so when he let it be known by deeds—such as a rough kiss that left my lips tingling—that he did me no favor. No: he'd take what pleasures he could, and offer no apology after.

And thusly did it begin. Eli arrived and stripped, showing no shyness; and bestowed that kiss. His eyes met mine and the Duchess's, alternately. From the half circle surrounding the raised bed—a stage, it was, set with a feathered mattress laid in white linens, and tilted at the head, to tip us toward our audience—there stepped forward, then, Fanny and Jen. The sisters took my shift from me. There I stood, revealed. And—

as a lifetime's secrets are less readily shed than a simple shift—I recall trying to cover myself *here, there, everywhere* with only my two hands. The Duchess denied me this: "Stop it," said she.

I let fall my hands. I raised high my chin. I'd brook what would come.

With balms applied by every hand, I was calmed. Each sister rose in turn to circle Eli and myself—there we stood upon our platform, still as idols—and blessed us in her way, applying a salve, or casting a benison o'er some part of our persons. Li'l Belt's lubricity bested her, and the Duchess—with a click of her tongue—called the Irish witch off Eli; for she'd begun to fist his length, and had bent to swallow him down. I'd been shivering prior to this, though the attic was not cold; but in time I warmed, owing to the balms and the bodies that came in procession; and to the many candles ranged around the mattress, upon which we were finally let to lie down.

Prone, I was examined; and what followed spoke not of sex but of education. The sisters took in my surfeit of attributes—lifting, poking, prodding . . . and, I suppose, found edification of a sort. None had seen such a one as I, surely. This was said time and again, but with words that did not offend. I was less a curiosity than a challenge, the sisters seeming to ask themselves, *How might I best avail myself of . . . of these?* Some made suggestions to Eli. Others asked me questions, which I answered as best I could; but more often I demurred, and told the truth: I didn't know. And they were sympathetic, greatly so; and redoubled their efforts to help me know myself.

Soon I was beset; for they'd done with questions and comments. Mouths went to work, though none spoke. Fingers, too; though none pointed, accusingly, as others had in the past. I responded well: as a woman, as a man, and as a witch.

Li'l Belt, Fanny, Cindy, and Lydia prepared me for Eli; for, though the priest had taken my maidenhead, still I'd an orifice unaccustomed to entry. Or, as Li'l Belt put it, with typical indelicacy, I'd a cunny "tight as a frog's ass, and that's watertight." And it was she who was first to apply her fingers to same, lubricating them in a font set bedside: a brassy basin Eugénie had filled with sweetened rainwater and a greasy, gluey resin the origins of which I will not wonder at. As for Eliphalet, there he knelt, upon a crimson pillow, tipped back onto his haunches and showing himself very much ready: his testes had already risen into recess, and his sex was hard as horn.

In time, yes, I grew accommodating. No figurative speech, that: well nigh an hour passed—blessings being cast o'er the show, and with the wine aflow—in the course of which I was rendered accommodating by the use of props of progressive girth. Some were of slickened wood, others of rubber. Some engraved, others plain. Some bent, others straight. Some pleasurable, others painful. Against the stretching pain, the rending pain, the near-ripping pain, Eugénie brought me a briquette of brazil wood; and this I bit down upon, hard. Still, I was not let to shy from any of the false phalli; nor from Eli.

. . . Eli. Who came to take me. Repeatedly. Whilst all withdrew to watch.

The sisters urged variety. In this Eli complied.

O'er the trill of the music box, I heard the Duchess moaning. I saw her, there, her head at rest upon Eugénie's chest, the Creole comforting her, stroking her pale brow. From the floor before them Sarah rose, on occasion, to indulge the Duchess in her snack of preference. I saw Eugénie raise a delicate teacup to the Duchess's painted lip; for our hostess opted for her "pleasure tea," as she called it—steeped in cantharides (Spanish fly, I suppose), and flavored by the zest of citrus—rather than our wine. The tea had a second purpose, too: with it she washed down those cakes made for her—and her alone—by Sarah; cakes baked with . . . O still I hesitate to cite their chief ingredient, so long I've delayed doing so. Alas, into these cakes Sarah baked the seed harvested from the suites. It was to this the Duchess owed her strength, said she. Too, into this batter went arsenic: the preservative of her pallor. These cakes were kept in the larder, under lock and key; though—an understatement, this—no witch at Cyprian House would have deemed herself covetous of the Duchess's cakes.

I'd been lifted and lain atop the feather bed hours earlier; and had enjoyed that prone, passive position. "To facilitate," said Fanny as she held my legs high, and asplay, offering me to Eliphalet as she'd offered her sister to the dealers in silk. Minute by minute, inch by inch, the pain had dissolved in the pleasure, as salt will in wine; till Eli came to seem a beast in rut—save he smiled all the while—battering at my woman's part. Jen and Cinderella sat on either side of me, and it was they who traded off my man's parts, the one stroking me stiff and the other holding high my scrotal sac; for this—O, the bald and brazen facts of the act!—overhung my cunny (*pardon;* for I take up the Cyprians' slang, the better to speed this recollection), and would have been in Eliphalet's way. Too, when let to hang in the place nature had put it, the sac covered my clitoris; and this Cinderella could not, would not suffer, for she'd a deep interest in seeing me spill, doubly. Li'l Belt abetted her in effecting this: she set a finger upon the lesser erection whilst Cindy worked the larger.

The two fell into conference, the particulars of which escaped me; for I was . . . otherwise occupied. But soon their plan was plain: Li'l Belt, tiny as she was, verily leapt upon my prick. The aftereffect of which was so uncommon as to draw applause from all present; for: Eliphalet was in me, and I was in Li'l Belt.

Soon we three arrived at the melting point. Concomitantly came the quaking, the quivering, the shiver and spill of release.

Previously, I'd not known my good fortune in suffering that simultaneous "double spill"—which term was coined by Cinderella—that is particular to my nature. But that night it was made evident to me; for all present were let to compare my ecstasy to those of my mates, Eliphalet and Li'l Belt. In short: it was adjudged that I was twice blessed. Further, it was observed that since I'd traveled twice as far and twice as fast as they toward Ecstasy, it was but commonsensical that I'd be twice as long returning. And indeed, there I lay, spent and seeming far away, and hearing not half of what was said.

Wine was offered, cakes passed. (Not the Duchess's, no.) Washing was seen to. Some of the sisters robed themselves; but Eli kept himself on show. Amidst all this I was called back to my senses by a question I heard asked: Could I conceive? Surely none could answer but I. All waited; but of course I'd no idea, and shrugged to say so. O, but next I suffered a sudden-coming chill occasioned by that secondary question which needed no voicing: What if I had just conceived by Eli, who'd upshot his seed within me?

I begged Li'l Belt to prepare a second batch of what it was she'd already flushed herself with; for she, in turn, had taken my seed. Mother and father . . . both would I be? Both *could* I be? . . . Regardless, thusly was Eros banished; for, knowing no shame, I douched before the assembly. A wash, it was, of sulfate of zinc, alum, pearlash, and semen-ruining salts, applied by syringe.

Relief. And exhaustion, soul-deep and true; for which there is no remedy save sleep, restorative sleep.

But we were not dismissed. Instead, the evening devolved into recitation, with the Duchess coming to the fore. Windows were opened, and night breezes were let to pass through the attic; for it had become close, and was rank with love's aroma. Incense was lit; the scent rose visibly, in swirls of grayish red. A question was asked; and its answering launched a discussion of things Eastern. The Duchess bade Eugénie take down a tome from a high shelf whose plate read *ARABIA;* and from this she read with all the avidity of a connoisseur. She told of sex practices, the likes of which . . . Alas, this was of interest; and I revived. Others among us were roused to action by the recitation. A second round of sex-acrobatics ensued; and in the course of this, we aped those acts that have so pleased our Eastern sisters down through the centuries, from Scheherazade on. No practicum, this. None of us pretended it was more than pleasure.

And pleasure it was, yes. But again it suffered the want of something; which I supposed to be love. And though I supposed, too, that I'd come to love Eli, Li'l Belt, the Duchess, and the others, what I'd felt that night had been but an approximation of what I'd felt for Celia and those few who'd preceded her to my heart's core. Only with Celia had my heart hammered, my palms slickened, and my soul, my very self, gone aloft: a thing akin to a kite, risen on her winds. *That,* I further supposed, must be the love worth longing for, worth searching for; and—if one had found and befouled it, as I had—worth fixing.

The sisters had set the attic aright before retiring to their suites. Now—having stood a long while in receipt of kisses and hugs which still I savor—I slipped to the attic's end, and there took to the sill. A light fall of rain corded down and quieted the city entire.

I was sated—physically so, yes—but deep within myself I discerned a hollowness, a hole hanging at the height of my heart.

I knew it that night: I would not move into Adaline's suite.

And on the morrow, when I rose in advance of the dawn

and descended to tell the Duchess of my decision, she woke saying, "I know, dear. I know." And, whilst Eli slept on in her arms, she sent me back to bed with a kiss; and thusly did we begin our good-byes.

41

Good-bye to Gotham

DETERMINED though I was to return to the territory, and to Celia, still I did not hurry; for cowardice proved a strong deterrent.

Already I'd lingered overlong at Cyprian House, passing more than a full cycle of seasons. Now the late-summer nights were whispering of autumn. I had not missed the territorial summer, no; but neither was I eager to suffer a second New York winter. The winter just passed—in which 1830 had ceded to '31—had been dire, as cold as any in living memory. I reasoned that finally the time had come: I would return to the territory in September.

I wrote Celia of my plans, though I knew she'd not get my letter. And indeed, her name was listed again when next I got hold of a *Gazette*.

I'd packed in haste; but there the trunk had sat a long

while. I lived from it as earlier I'd lived from the bureau. Days, nay weeks passed before I—as Henry—went with Eli to the island's southern tip, where we questioned shippers and stevedores. All talk was of steamers, but these were not yet common. Schooners, though, sat offshore by the score. It was not hard to find a southbound one. The *Majesty* had only recently come in. She'd lie at anchor a while, and sail for Savannah in early September. I secured passage. From Savannah I'd travel southward by what means availed themselves (suffering a stage, if need be); and in time I'd return to St. Augustine.

As some weeks remained before the *Majesty* would sail, I determined to make the most of my time left at Cyprian House, and in the Empire City. This I did, largely, at the side of Eliphalet Rynders, whom intimacy had made an even better friend. Ours was a relationship the Duchess very much condoned.

Too, hours of each day were passed with Eugénie; or with those Books she'd all but assigned me; for she'd become a tutor of sorts. Indeed, not long before my departure, she informed me that she thought, nay hoped she'd discovered a way to free Celia from the spell I'd cast. She'd written to her own Soror Mystica in New Orleans—Sanité Dédé; who'd been deposed by Marie Laveau—and had received in return a detailed rite calling for cat's blood, mulled urine, salt stolen from off the beloved's skin, the yolk of a lapwing's egg, and sundry other items I'd have been hard-pressed to gather on Canal Street, or any street sitting east, west, north, or south of it. Still, I copied the spell into my Book; and memorized it, too. Would it work? The answer would come only with my return to the territory.

I knew the best of town life that late summer of '31. And to strangers Eliphalet and I must have appeared either the perfect couple, or the best of buddies. Sometimes we went about arm in arm, I the prettified miss and he the dandy. Other times we were Henry and Eli, sporting types eager for a show of any sort.

We verily gorged on theatrics, and knew the best boxes of every venue. I kept from the third tier; for there I was either known (as Henriette) or accosted (as Henry). Once, most confusingly, Eli and I (in skirts) were approached by a drunken bawd, who proceeded from warning us of the Duchess's wrath—for she'd discover, surely, that her Eli was stepping out on her—to telling us what form said wrath might take. Such invective she spewed! And she confronted me a second time that night whilst I waited to avail myself of the women's privies set out on Elizabeth Street. Again she lashed me with that stippled tongue of hers. Surely my cheeks rouged themselves. Surely my fists clenched, gloved though they were in pearlescent kid. Perhaps I showed the Eye. Regardless, I had my revenge; for, when the whore cut me and stepped into that loo of which I had urgent need, I worked a bit of the Craft, as taught me by Lydia Smash. And the fireboys were well nigh an hour in extricating this tart—name of Helen—from that privy whose latch I cracked simply by strength of mind. I imagine there are still some cheeries thereabouts where one might hear told the story of Shithouse Nell; for so she came to be called.

Other locales were, of course, avoided: Five Points, parts of the Bowery, Rotten Row, where the brothels were private but of another type entirely. Too, we steered clear of St. John's and its burying ground. I'd heard enough from the dead, said I. . . . O but I'd hear more; for once, whilst passing a stable that sat on Park Street, behind the College of Physicians and Surgeons, I suffered again from that death-alliance, from corpses I could not counter.

I heard them. They were few. Wordlessly, they made themselves known. Their voices were weak; and I thought perhaps I heard not the dead, but the dying. No: I'd know in time: this was the dead. And what I heard were the soul songs of those—hardly stiff—being snatched by the college's chief ghoul, Dr. Valentine Mott, a man whom the Duchess had barred from her door. Through this stable the dead would pass en route to the anatomical theaters of the college; there, in secret, they'd be dissected. Dr. Mott knew profit, I suppose; for tuition must have far exceeded the sexton's fee: he turned his head to the snatchers' depredations, and they in turn paid him three dollars per corpse. All this Eli knew. Once told, he and I toyed with intervention: what a fright I, we, might arrange for Dr. Mott! I'd have only to summon the more active dead; and I supposed I was strong enough to do it, if only I could retain consciousness. But as none of the snatched spoke to me in specifics, the plan was abandoned. Moreover: time was fleeting, and we'd better things to do.

On occasion we'd sit in City Hall Park and let town life pass us by; for sometimes we tired of chasing it. On the day in question, I—Henriette—had raised a parasol against the sun, and sat sharing the shade with Eli as his talk turned to a show that had come to Mr. Barnum's American Museum, but a half block south of our location. This was called "a cultural center," one chock-full of curios. I'd been before, of course; both in skirts and slacks; for some things were off-limits to women: such whatnot as heads, shrunken and pickled, and like attractions, nay atrocities. I'd found the place tawdry, and told Eli so; still, he pressed the merits of a new waxworks show therein, which he was keen to see. So: we went; most regrettably.

I had to return to Cyprian House in order to trade female attire for male, lest we find our access to the show proscribed. I recall carrying a coat too heavy for the heat, and worrying because I had not bothered to bind my breasts. I worried less after we'd downed several beers; after which we proceeded to Mr. Barnum's door.

We paid our twenty-five cents and slipped into the dark, cool hallways, crowded with waxen pirates, murderers, dwarfs, African "negritoes" and conjoined twins said to be indigenous to Siam. Not once did it occur to me that . . .

Alas, and onward:

That precinct of the show which treated of sexual matters was disguised as a cautionary tale, and bore the imprimatur of certain reformers and moralists. Alcott's *Young Man's Guide* was handed out free of charge. For coin, one could avail oneself of Woodward's capsules—equal parts iron and tree bark—to blight the masturbatory impulse. Too, there were present several adherents of Sylvester Graham, propounding the benefits of vegetarianism, cold baths, mattresses of straw (never feather), and, of course, Graham's own crackers, said to set your every system aright. (Bite your shoe, should you wish to taste their like.) All this we ignored as civilly as we could, pressing on; for Eli was eager to gain the core of the show, where he'd heard waxen figures were fixed into sexual poses.

Of course, dear Eliphalet had not heard, did not know, that a centerpiece of Barnum's show was a . . . . *Enfin,* I was the first to find it standing—a butter-colored grotesquerie—in its sarcophagus of glass. A gasolier shadowed its placard, but still I could read it: THE FREAK HERMAPHRODITE.

Mustachioed, it was, with a brow modeled on that of our earliest ancestors. The hair on half its head had been shorn; beside this, long hair had been upswept into a ridiculous coiffure. The half face below this was made up to rival that of the lowest of ladies. Too, there was this egregious touch, alluding to man's greater intellect: the manly half of the creature sported a monocle. Both eyes were glassy, as eerily vacant as those of the Duchess's stuffed civets.

The body? One large dug depended, its areola covered o'er in moss; or what appeared to be moss. This same "hair" was tufted all up and down the man half, from shoulder to ankle. Even the feet were—preposterously—of two sizes; with a boot set beside one, and a high-heeled shoe the other. As for the genitalia . . . . Would that I could spare myself the telling of this. But no:

A member of monstrous proportion hung beside—beside!—a vaginal mouth the livid lips of which were parted, puckered as if readying for a kiss; and around the orifice red paint had been daubed, thus adding to its wound-like aspect.

Beside me where I stood, staring, two boys began to jeer. At the specimen, of course; but they might as well have turned on me; for I imagined they did—along with everyone else present in that shadowed place—and so from the hall I ran. *Ran!* From Barnum's onto Broadway and all the way home. To Cyprian House; where I was known, and not for a freak.

In the days following, Eliphalet sought to make amends. I told him, time and again, there was no need. He hadn't known. Still, he insisted on apologies of every sort.

And so it was he came from the post office quite happy, one afternoon. He'd retrieved a bundle of mail forwarded to me, finally, by the postmaster of St. Augustine.

Cutting the twine that bound it all—magazines and newspapers in which I'd little interest—I found several letters from Rosalie and none, of course, from Celia. I set the whole stack aside. I cared not to read the *Courier* or the *Visitor,* sent by Rosalie and containing some effort of Edgar's, some critical epistle, some prose or poetical effluvia. Neither did I take up Rosalie's letters, of which there were four. I was busy; for in the days since the debacle at Barnum's, I'd tasked myself with the business of good-bye: packing for true, passing afternoons with the witches, et cetera. In days I'd set off for the territory, wherein I'd deal with the dregs of my dream. I'd free Celia. I'd tell all my truths and let the consequences come.

Therefore I let the letters lie. Till one afternoon in early September I took them up. I'd been tidying my trunk for the twentieth, the thirtieth time, and had deemed it silly to carry Rosalie's letters southward, unread. So, I took to the sill. Birdsong could be heard. Horse hooves, too. The sounds of the town . . . far away, faint. I took up the most recent letter, dated not two weeks prior; and, slitting the seal and unfolding it, I saw that the parchment was black-bordered. Far worse were the words upon it: a scrawl: hysteria, in written form. And the heart-darkening gist of Rosalie's letter was this:

Mammy Venus had been murdered.

Part Three

42

A Change of Plan

THAT last morning in Cyprian House, Sarah ascended to the attic to help me with my trunk; into which had gone the two wardrobes I'd acquired—petticoats and pants, shawls and suspenders—as well as the many *Books of Shadows* I was taking, some of them original, others copied out whole at Eugénie's insistence. The night prior, I'd stopped my preparations only to bid farewell to the sisters as they came, singly or coupled, between sparks or at night's end. No eye was dry.

Gifts had been given. Two bottles of Cardenio ink, tightly stoppered, now sat within my trunk. Eugénie had handed them over more as admonition than gift: *I had better write.* To her, yes; but to myself as well. I was to sift my experience, distill it down, and stow it in the Books I'd keep. And indeed I'd much to sift and stow: I'd come to Cyprian House confused, more so than I'd known. The lessons Sebastiana and the Duchess had intended I learn, what were they? They concerned the Craft, certainly; but life, too, was at issue . . . life and love and lust. Leaving, I knew not, or could not have articulated . . . nay, rather let me say that already I felt the *effect* of what lessons I'd learned. Arriving, I'd been as water in a bottle, my self taking its shape from without. And it was the Duchess, Eliphalet, the Cyprians, and even their sparks who changed me, as surely as if they'd each in turn dropped ink into that water. And then Mr. Barnum's waxen man-woman and news of Mammy's murder came to further stir and trouble those waters of self, so blue they'd have appeared black. *Were* blue, *were* black. Still, what could I do but wade on, ever on?

Finally, that night, sleep settled o'er the house, and all the sisters save one: me.

Not long after dawn, Sarah and I descended to find the Duchess in the foyer. She stood resplendent, in full dress. It seemed my departure would not disturb her routine: a morning round of the city—done no matter the weather, on six days out of seven—with Eliphalet at her side. At this I took no offense; for I knew the Duchess wished I'd not go.

"H.," said she; and smiling, she tilted her head, opened her arms, and was, in a word, sympathy. I stepped into her embrace, steeling myself against tears.

Through the open doors of Cyprian House—to which I finally removed; for in the Duchess's embrace my resolve was weakening—I saw at curbside a horse cab. Atop the box sat a black boy. To me he tipped his tattersall cap, a twin of which crowned his nag. Just then, as I was turning back to the Duchess and Sarah, ready to make my final good-byes, I saw . . . someone. Yes: someone sat within the cab, half hidden, showing only a trousered leg.

Odd. Had I to share a cab to water's edge, and at so early an hour? I'd no wish to do so.

O, but then the figure leaned forward; and up the stoop of Cyprian House there flew—as if it were winged—the smile of Eliphalet Rynders.

"Duchess!" said I, turning on the heels of my new button boots. But the Duchess only smiled; whereupon my stanched tears fell; for only then did I understand how fearful I'd been of traveling alone. And on so dark a mission. To a place from which I'd long been fugitive.

"But," I began, "will he . . . ?"

"To Baltimore," said she, "and not beyond." She wagged a red-tipped finger in warning. Again she opened her arms; and again I fell onto the perfumed plush of her embrace. *"Bon,"* said she, "on to Richmond then; but *no* further."

"Ah," said I, "now I understand"; and with a broad gesture of my gloved hand I referenced my dress. Early the night before, the Duchess had sent word with Eugénie: I was to travel as Henriette. She'd send me off as a woman, as Sebastiana had. *Why?* I wondered. Women's dress had oft been my choice whilst at Cyprian House; but for travel? Surely the simpler dress of men was the wiser choice. An increase of comfort, yes; but also, in slacks, I'd more easily earn that quiet solitude that was my want. As a woman traveling alone, I'd know not a moment's peace, suffering solicitation from some and pity from others. But the Duchess had insisted, and now explained:

"Wiser to return to Richmond as Henriette, don't you think? And coupled. As for my Eliphalet, well . . . he has a few rough edges in need of honing; and for that, such adventures as this are prescriptive."

"Oh, but, Duchess," I rejoined, "pray that our adventures are few, and fast-ending."

I'd spoken figuratively, and meant not to solicit a prayer from the Duchess. Still, wont to advise me a final time, she said, "Never ask a witch to pray, my H. Many are the things we might do to affect the days as they lie, but common prayer is not among the lot. . . . Go now. And mind my boy. Send him safely home, *d'accord*?"

"*Oui*," said I, "*d'accord*."

A final hug of the Duchess, and Sarah, too; and then I stepped from the witchery, wondering would I ever return.

Towed by steamer or shoved by tug . . . I cannot recall which it was; but in any event we'd put to sea by midmorning aboard the *Bhalin'dio;* for alternate plans had been made upon receipt of Rosalie's letter. Our progress was slow, despite a great show of sail. "We haven't the eye of Aeolus, yet," said our captain. Thusly did our destination—Baltimore—seem to sit quite distant. But that was just as well: the day was fine, if still; and I was not at all eager to reach that city wherein I knew Edgar Poe was resident.

There'd been letters from Rosalie prior to the black-banded one, yes; and in these she'd alternately crowed and cried o'er Edgar's exploits. It seemed that he, having enlisted in the maritime services, had acceded to West Point; from whence he was soon expelled. Still, he was soldiering on with his pen at least: poems and stories were appearing in print.

I'd lost track of Edgar whilst living city life; but now I knew he was in Baltimore, living with an aunt Clemm, which surname I committed to memory, the better to avoid any who bore it. Rosalie wrote of a girl-child of eight, a cousin Clemm. And a grandmother, still gathering that pension of General Poe's on which they all subsisted. Too, there'd returned to the fold the peripatetic older brother, Henry, whom Edgar worshiped as Rosalie did her Poet. . . . Stay: Henry may have died by then. Yes: he would have been dead when we passed fast through Baltimore; for hadn't Rosalie written a cold half sentence informing me of same? Indeed she had; and that letter—written weeks earlier—had come among the bundled four that brought the news of Mammy Venus's murder. I'd not read it directly; though typically all such news of the Poes was read upon receipt and promptly forgotten; for all I wanted to know was that Edgar was far from John Allan. All the better if the two were incommunicado, and writing no letters to needle each other. But when I knew I'd sail to, nay *through* Baltimore, I reread the letters, tracking Edgar by Rosalie's words and wondering where his mother might be. If able, Eliza Arnold would surely have abandoned her grave to sidle down the James and hover o'er Baltimore-town. If so, I could only hope she'd be too busy with her boys—the one dead, the other drawn that way—to bother with me.

Odd it was, to be under sail again. I felt at home, in fact; and knew a great deal more comfort at sea than did Eliphalet; who posed as one Mr. Ryan, to whom I was newly allied by rite and ring. Poor Eli's skin shone greenly—like flame from a greasy candle—as we rode swells which hardly merited the term. And when offshore we found the winds, well . . . Suffice to say that my friend kept his own counsel, and said not a word, seeming to fear that if he opened his mouth to speak, something decidedly . . . *other* might slip from his lips as well. I half wished it would. Mean of me, yes; but I enjoyed my sea supremacy and told Eli so. When he countered with curses, I asked if I might count the shades of green he showed. He smiled, despite his discomfort. I laughed—as I hadn't in a long while—and thanked him for his company.

In time a cry of *"Land ho!"* was heard. I knew the herald for a novice; for we'd hardly been out of sight of land. Still, here we were: arrived; Baltimore sitting off to starboard.

I had a purse strapped to my wrist; and into this had gone what Sebastiana had sent as well as what the Duchess had contributed. Indeed, this was a hand-sewn purse from the Duchess's own collection; and into its roseate silk she'd stuffed notes and specie gathered up from the girls, blessed be that sweet sorority. In short, we'd more than money enough to spend the night in Baltimore, making for Richmond at first light. To this Eli readily assented; for he was done with motion that day, and sought only land, stillness, and a place to lie.

Questions were asked by my Mr. Ryan, and soon a room was secured at a most ornamental pile at the crossing of Calvert and Lafayette Streets, near to which there beat—well nigh audibly—the very heart of the city, its businesses and other such bustle. When first I heard the hotel referenced, my heart seized. Later, I'd read its sign as a curse writ large: BARNUM'S HOTEL. What a plague the man was! Yes: our hotelier was that same damnable showman whose hermaphroditic display I'd fled. O, but I was too tired to fuss; and so at Barnum's we bedded down. Singly; or rather, alone together. That is: we carried the ruse of our marriage no further than the room's threshold. Travel dulls desire, it's true; and what's more, I was on a mission with the murder of a loved one at its core. What blood ran, ran cold.

Too, let this be said: Eliphalet loved another. One whom the wise—witch or otherwise—would not betray. She'd loaned him to me once, the night of my initiation, but thereafter there'd been no reprise. Now we'd come to seem siblings. So I fancied us, even though I'd known no siblings save Edgar and Rosalie Poe, who were models for naught but bizarrerie.

That night at Barnum's Hotel we undressed without shyness, and fell onto our common bed. We napped, and supper woke us when finally—with a rap upon the oaken door—it arrived. We dined à deux upon the bed. There was bread, freshly baked, and a most restorative beef broth. After this we set upon a stuffed pheasant, which Eli carved so expertly I wondered what role he'd played in the preservation of the Duchess's civets. I refrained from asking; and when dinner was done, I turned our talk to the days to come. More accurately, I spoke of the present and future by way of the past;

and, reading Eli—how much could I tell him, truly?—I fed out my story as a fisherman does line.

How much witchly discourse was Eliphalet accustomed to? Though he was the son of one witch and consort to another, still I wondered. Would talk of revenants send him hurrying home, with me left at heel? He knew I'd not weathered well our nocturnal trip into St. John's Yard; but if he knew of my death-alliance in terms certain, well, he'd not heard it from me. And so I told the story selectively: the Poe siblings, yes, but not their mother; and Mammy Venus's sad fate, including the fire, but not her first death and the Faustian deal she'd struck with Eliza Arnold, by which she returned from same. Of Celia I said little; for all at Cyprian House had heard that confession in full.

"This Edwin . . . ." began Eli.

"Edgar," said I.

"This Edgar . . . we're in Baltimore to seek him out?"

"No, no," said I. "Happenstance has us here. I want no sight of Edgar Poe."

"You fear him?"

"'Fear' him? No. But his is boggy company, into which I'd rather not step. And Edgar Poe knows of our running: Celia's and mine."

"He alone knows of it?"

"No: his sister and Mammy Venus know it, too; or knew it, rather. . . . But only Edgar would turn the knowledge to his advantage; for he loathes his father, and would shame his house at any cost."

"I see," said Eliphalet; but I told more; and spoke of the men and their step-relation, of Frances Allan, of infidelity, of Edgar's bastard brother whose name I share, of John Allan's deeming Edgar a mere poetaster. . . . "And money," said I, "further spices the mix; for John Allan is rich. He sits atop a hill of money, and he'll roll not a nickel down to Edgar."

"And so the poet is—"

"Is poor, yes. But these are two men long divided by taste and temperament; and much else besides money."

I spoke on: "Mammy Venus knew the plan in full; Rosalie knew less; and Edgar some. But the aiding and abetting of an absconding slave is a crime, of course, in these parts and—"

"And so, too, is murder," said Eli.

"I . . . it was not I who . . ."

"As I heard tell," said Eliphalet, "the man merited murder; and whatever came after," by which he referred to Bedloe's eternal and perhaps infernal reward; and lest I wonder at his meaning, Eli cast his gaze—eyes of smoldering jade, lashed with sable—downward, hellward. "Let him roast, I say; and good riddance. . . . But enough of him. What about this bothersome poet?"

"The point is this. There are laws, be they right or wrong; and Edgar knows I stand in violation of several. He cares not a whit for the law, mind. No: he fancies himself above the laws of men. But still he'd use them, would in fact use any- and everything to cut John Allan. Even if that meant implicating himself in our crimes."

"Or his sister?"

"No," said I, "not her. . . . That's rather complicated. See: Rosalie is but his half sister; and a wedge John Allan has driven down, again and again, between Edgar and the memory of his mother; for there are questions of . . . legitimacy. Let this suffice: Eliza Arnold was not the angel Edgar holds to. . . . Nor is she now."

"Pardon?"

"Never mind. . . . Allan implies that he has knowledge of Rosalie's paternity. And he prods Edgar with same, as if it were a hot poker."

"He's the bastard, that Allan," said Eli, "not the poor girl."

"And so by protecting his sister, Edgar, in a way, guards his mother's honor. And at the same time atones for his own genius."

"Plainer, now," cautioned Eli.

"She is . . . daft, this Rosalie."

Eli tapped his forehead twice; and I nodded. "Yes," said I, "daft; though some would apply a sharper epithet."

"Do I follow? . . . This Edgar, you think, might involve himself, even criminally, if, in so doing, he could bring low the older man, or sully the name they share."

"I fear he might, yes."

"Even with the years having run on, and no one seeking to avenge this Bedloe?"

"We don't know that no one works for Bedloe's heirs. We don't know if Celia is being tracked, or if she's been sold as she runs."

"All right; but to stir the pot of this cold crime, wouldn't this Edgar need a body, and criminals besides?"

"Bedloe must have been found fast."

"You, then? Or Celia? He'd need one or the other."

"And he'll have neither. I'll not chance it. We'll hie from here at first light, and set any chance of bad luck behind us. We'll take to a Chesapeake packet; and from the bay's far shore we'll go overland to Richmond." This suited my traveling companion well; for he'd no interest in finding himself afloat on the morrow. As for me, the James would cost me a half day or more; and so—though I am no advocate of stage travel—a road running to mimic the river's course seemed the sounder, speedier plan.

Eli was undressing, his large hands at work upon the bone buttons of his shirt. "It seems you overworry, H.," said he. "Even if Edgar should chance upon you in the street—on this one day that you're in Baltimore, a city of how many thousands?—he'd not know you as . . . you are." He looked me o'er, from my hair ribbons to my hem. "You'd fool him, Henriette, were he standing here in my shoes." Here was logic, and a compliment besides; neither of which I'd refute.

Eliphalet announced with a yawn that sleep was wanted.

"I'm hardly right yet from the sea," said he, patting his stone-hard yet upset stomach. He proceeded to clear the bed of the meal's detritus. Plates, bones, silverware . . . all of it clattered onto the carpet. I heard again the Duchess, saying he'd edges in need of honing; here then was one. Followed hard by another; for Eli stripped and stretched himself atop the cloud-like coverlet. "Do you mind?" he asked.

"Not at all," said I. "Sleep. . . . I think I'll worry over another glass of wine."

My own sleep was hard won that night. Though my mind was troubled, my body was tired, and sleep might well have come had it not been for the sawyer beside me taking tree upon tree, felling whole forests. The deeper Eli's sleep, the steadier his snore; but in truth, I minded not at all.

I lay under the sheets. Not naked, but nearly so; for I'd no secrets Eliphalet hadn't seen. I edged nearer, so near I felt the warmth of his skin, smelled his fruited breath. (Cherries, there'd been, with cream: to cap the meal.) O yes: the musk of him, too, rose to my nose. For he lay aback, atop all the linens, legs splayed and arms raised o'er his head. I'd lowered the lamp; but I'd gone to the window to set back its drape, the better to let moonlight through, till now Eliphalet verily glowed and . . .

His curls spread: an inky spill atop the pillow. So thick was his hair it seemed to sway, as if the moonlight were water and his hair eelgrass. The green eyes I could not see in sleep, of course; but I saw by their motion—the skitter beneath the lids—that Eliphalet dreamed. And as he sank deeper into sleep, I worried less that I'd rouse him; but stock-still I lay. I wanted him to sleep, yes; for I wanted to watch.

Shadows pooled at the base of his neck, where a pulse kept his heart's time. Striate shadow spread down his chest and stomach, to a deeper pool near the navel. There the taut stomach slipped to concavity before rising, rising so slightly to fall again at that tufted hair—blacker than black—on which his sex lay. His sex: stiffening, twitching. Surely I smiled, thinking I'd tease Eli on the morrow, ask after the content of his dream.

I cannot now say when it all went sad. Can say only that, as I lay on my side, watching Eliphalet—and yes, lightly trailing a finger here, there—a single tear coursed sideways o'er my cheek, fell fast to the pillow, as if weighted. Why? Was I sad that I was not so whole a man as he? Did I want to be him, or have him? Once he'd been inside me. Did I want the same again? Or was it a turn-of-the-tables that fired my desire? A possessing of him? . . . Was it envy of the Duchess, or wonder at how she'd found and bound the boy to her? Was it by her witch's will? Or love alone? . . . Had the sleeping Eli been but a brief distraction, from whence I now returned to mourning Mammy Venus? To thoughts of the morrow's sad mission? To ash-cold memories of Richmond? . . . And Celia, still in the territory? . . . O, too many questions. Too many truths. And all of them echoing off this page these long years later; till now I want no more; and so here close.

43

Eclipse

"There shall be signs in the sun."
—Luke 21:25

THEY killed her in the yard. Cracked with bats the veiled head. Left her to die beneath a tree, to rot amidst the fallen fruit. Two days she lay there; till Rosalie found her; whereupon that poor girl's dissolution began.

. . . Who are "they"? To tell it I must first return to a winter's day, some months prior: the twelfth of February, 1831.

A terrible, terrible winter it had been. Those of no means—and a multitude they were—froze where they lay, huddled in the streets. Those of means marked the worst days of winter for recreation; and took to the frozen rivers, skating bank to bank to find booths thereon, hastily built to serve a warming punch or roasted sausages or cigars, selling ten for a cent. Down south snow may not have fallen, and still the rivers ran; but crops had failed, and it seemed doom depended; for when the eclipse came, many folk—city and country alike—saw it as heralding the prophesied End of Days. So cold a winter, so ruinous a season; and now the sun would shy from the sky, would meet the moon and render it to ash.

People in the path of the eclipse took to their darkened yards, raising shards of smoked glass to the sky so as not to blind the naked eye. Fowls, confused, retired to roost. Prayers were widely cast. And then . . . and then it was done; and the world seemed none the worse. The sun had seemed but sickly; and shadows had been perceptible all the while. Any who'd witnessed a summer's thunder gust had seen the like. Life went on, with the moon and sun returned to their rightful turn-taking.

That day, we—the witches of Cyprian House—came in from off the roof, and consigned our wraps and furs to Sarah's care. Some of us had greatly anticipated the event. Lydia Smash and the Duchess had set out vials of I know not what, wondering if the odd darkening would strengthen their contents. Eugénie, I recall, wanted no part of what she deemed "the sun's denial," and slept the day away. None of us had been scared, certainly; save for Jen, who fell prey to Li'l Belt's apocalyptic play. All in all, it had been naught but a midday show: shadow theater on a grander scale.

In time, though, we'd learn that a Virginia slave had read the darkened sky differently.

Nat Turner, this was. A slave well more than literate. A prophet, some said; a villain, a drunk, a false messiah and murderer, said others.

Turner would tell the bonded that the occluded sun had come as a sign from on high. Said, too, that voices bade him rise. To wait, and then to rise in summertime of that most ill-remembered year. August, to be exact.

Later I'd read of the rebellion in the newspapers, of course; but I confess it: Cyprian House and its surrounds were too great a distraction, and I gave the news short shrift.

At that time I was readying to leave the city, and my soul could accommodate no sadness but its own. Moreover: the accounts were contradictory. In one I read that a hundred whites had had their heads dissevered, whilst the next edition of that same paper lowered the toll to eighty-odd. Still, there'd been bloodshed; that was certain. Whole families—from fathers down to babes-at-suck—had been slaughtered. A schoolmarm and her ten charges (twenty, some said) had been butchered, their bodies cut to parts and piled center all upon the schoolroom floor. The Southern papers implied that "outrages" had been done unto white women and girls; and this seemed a crime worse than murder.

As I say, soon I forgot the rising; for it seemed of no moment to Richmond proper, Turner's Jerusalem sitting well southeast of that city. I retook to the affairs of Self, and not once did I fear for Mammy Venus; who—when first I read of Turner's rebellion—was already dead, drowned on the blood-tide that rose behind it.

Rosalie was in the hospital when we arrived in Richmond. I learned she'd been there some weeks, too disordered to return to Duncan Lodge and the care of the Misses Mackenzie.

I went to see her; but wanting not to be seen myself—neither by Rosalie nor by any other visitor, spectral or otherwise—we, Eli and myself, held to our ruse: Mr. and Mrs. Ryan we were, down from Canada via the seaboard. Further, if pressed, we'd say we were church-allied, and visiting the sick with charitable intent.

"Quakers?" suggested Eli. "I like the Quakers."

"All right, then," said I as we approached the hospital, "Quakers." But I made fast amends: "No! Not Quakers." Into the gloom we stepped, amidst the sick. "They'll take us for abolitionists; and that won't do, not at all, not here."

"No," said Eli, "I suppose not."

On went this conversation; for we were nervous, and inclined to overspeak. Meanwhile, there appeared before us a woman, well kept and crying, and ramping fast toward middle age. She is forever fixed in my memory as a Mackenzie—the adoptive mother of Rosalie, or an aunt perhaps—though this I cannot confirm. She came to where the late sun shafted into the shuttered ward, and in the shadows sought to hide her tears. This we saw too late; for already we'd approached her, Eli bowing and asking after a patient, "name of Mackenzie."

The woman looked at us queerly. "But who are . . . ?"

"Friends of good faith," said I, wringing the epistle I held as though I might get from it a few drops more of that good faith. This was, in fact, a copy of *Niles's Weekly Register,* procured for its listing of the mail coaches; for, our business seen to—and still I was not entirely sure what our business was—we'd follow the mails, fast, from Richmond. And eager I'd be to see that city recede.

From the supposed Miss Mackenzie, whose spirits brightened at our enquiry, we learned that Rosalie was resident four doors down. From Rosalie herself we learned less; for a soporific of sorts had been administered: poor Rosalie seemed but a corpse, insensate and cold.

I could not leave my name. Neither did I dare to leave a note, or anything else to token my having come. Edgar would take too great an interest in the former, should he find it; and the latter—some trinket, or a bunch of blooms—would only further addle Rosalie, if she knew not from whence it had come. And so, with Eli at my side, I walked from the ward, and from that hospital reeking of sickness and its supposed cures.

Turner's vision, they say, had recurred; but always it featured spirits white and black, locked in battle. Blood colored his dreams: droplets of it, rolling down the leaves of tobacco and stalked corn, seeping deep into cotton; pressing from the pores of drovers; causing the streams to run red. O'er this theater, thunder rolled; and always the sky went dark at the height of day. So it was that Turner saw February's benighted sun as a sign: to actuate his plan. Of slaughter.

Well known he was in the southeastern corner of Virginia; for he'd been hired out here and there, and let to preach. Thusly, he'd primed the minds of many; and by late August a band of bonded men had sworn to rise at his side. Newspapers would tell of rebel black men roaming Virginia in hundred-packs, pikes and rifles shouldered. In truth, it seems the rebels numbered less than ten, though some half-million slaves crowd the state.

That late August, they slew some sixty-odd Virginians o'er the course of several days. By month's end, the rebellion was done; and Turner himself lay hidden away in a forest cave. I'd come and gone from Richmond by the time he was found in late October; on or very near All Hallows' Eve, I think. In time, Turner was convicted, tried, condemned, hanged, and dissected; with legend coming to hold that he'd been flayed, his flesh fried to grease and his bones ground to powder, sewn into sacs and sold for souvenirs.

For months to come, every eye was set upon his *Confession,* taken down at a rush and sold by a man name of Gray, Thomas Gray. It sold swiftly, yes; for white men wondered what it held. Therein, they read that the rebels had not been runaways, as supposed. Neither were they agitators, spurred to bloodshed by abolitionists doing the Devil's work. No: they were slaves, "ingrate" slaves. And this boded ill indeed; for it told that the sandy underpinnings of slavery were shifting. Virginians feared they'd come to a red end if something weren't done. Thus: retribution.

Mobs, deeming themselves militia, mounted up and rode. Volunteers, these were; low white men, who exacted rather more than an eye for an eye. In Norfolk they harvested the very head of General Nelson, which title had been conferred to convince society that a true shadow army had been defeated. Others allied to Turner—by ties both true and loose—were tried and hanged all that September. As the number of executions grew, some right-thinking whites sought to slow the hangman. Whereupon things worsened; for, thinking they'd soon be deprived their rough justice, the vigilantes sped.

More heads were had. Piked, these were, roadside; to warn any blacks who might wonder what it meant to rise. Such heads as these I saw. As I made my way overland to Richmond, to see for myself the who, what, where, and how of Mammy Venus's murder. Already I knew the why.

We'd come to Richmond from Norfolk by coach, arriving nigh three.

Six silent heads we'd seen roadside, their skin sun-cured and taut. Crow-covered, they were; though the birds rose at the coming of our coach. Four were near Norfolk; two we saw nearer Petersburg. These latter a coach mate of ours applauded. He was a man of equine features, his face of a length that begged a bridle. His wife wore an ensemble of spotted black and white; and her sitting in dumb silence as her husband held forth only added to her bovine aspect. I wondered if the two hadn't met when put to pasture.

Of course, the man's speech broke upon Eliphalet and not myself. I was let to sit in silent contemplation of some aspect of the Craft; and soon I determined I'd try to break by force of will that suction that held the man's plate in place, reasoning he'd talk less with his foreteeth in his lap. But Eliphalet spared me this; for finally he responded to the man in true American fashion: he spat. A gob of spittle—half eagle size—settled quite near the woman's hoof; and Eli, feigning the worst of country ways, excused himself by touching two fingers to his brow, as if he'd a hat to tip, and muttering, "Ma'am." Further protestation was put off by Eli's setting his squared fists atop his knees. Finally, the woman smoothed her shoe o'er the expectorate, thusly denying it.

We rode on in rocking silence, the river rolling at our side.

I'd tried for newspapers in Baltimore and Norfolk, too; but I'd only been able to procure a single one: the *Army and Navy Chronicle.* From this I'd quarried little news of Turner. He was thought, then, to be hiding in the Dismal Swamp, wherein runaways had been known to hide for weeks, months, even years, subsisting on frog, snake, terrapin, and whatnot. I read nothing of any riot in Richmond. Nothing of the militias.

Disinclined to stroll the streets of Richmond, I struck upon a plan by which we'd be able to both hide and learn.

From Rosalie's bedside we proceeded to the Market Square—where I saw with satisfaction the charred outline of Celia's pen, which Fortune or Fate had burned to the ground—and onto a reading room I'd once seen near Bowler's Tavern. There, for a quarter, Eli and I accessed a collection of newspapers, arrayed by state and date. Savannah's *Georgian.* The *New Orleans Bee.* Key West's *Enquirer.* Nary a one offered news of the Virginia militias. Locally, we fared better: it was in Richmond's own *Constitutional Whig* that Eli read of a free black woman—"a fell Negress, friend to the Insurrectionists"—who'd been "put down." The piece—an odd sort of advert, really, ringed by rewards for Turner's capture—went on to report that there'd been resistance, that said Negress had fought Justice when it sought her.

At dusk, this Justice had come. In the person of five white men and a boy, each brandishing bat or blade.

I saw their coming. Conjured it when later I could by casting a sighting spell widdershins, to show the past. For no newspaper told the truth of Mammy's end, this I knew; and so I'd no recourse but to induce the dream and witness it myself.

They came through the bushes banking the property, led

by the boy. Perhaps he'd seen Rosalie (or Edgar, or me) step similarly through the scratching privet. Too, this boy had once seen a ghost at the Van Eyn mansion; for, yes, in the dream I saw and knew the fire-haired child: he who'd looked up to see me standing at a second-story window that long-ago morning.

Slight fortune it was, I suppose, that the posse found Mammy Venus in the dining room of the manse and not the cellar, wherein they would have found more to incite them. I dreamed this setting as I'd seen it in life, save all was a watery blue. The dreamscape wavered, but all stayed true to its shape. Movement was slowed, terribly so; such that it seemed Mammy Venus sat an eternity at that long, long table, the scar-tight pads of her palms upon it, her tipless fingers tapping out a most impatient tattoo. I heard too clearly the stutter of the clocks. And the slap of the screen door. The scratch and shuffle of the booted men and boy. Their coming on, room to room. There she sat, so impassively. I wanted to call to her, warn her. But of course I could not. More: I saw that she needed no warning; for she'd known they'd come, had seen it.

It was that devil-child found her. Backing from the dining room, into which he'd bounded doe-like and dumb, he called down the center hall to the others, his voice girlish, shrill. Two men answered and came. One was his red father. Neither dared step into the room. They waited, whilst the others took the house's inventory with rising wrath: *Who is this wench to live amidst such splendor? How came she to be both free and propertied?* None of them knew the truth, of course; they'd heard lie, lore, and legend, but all that mattered was that Mammy Venus sat too well provisioned.

They called her Conspirator. They killed her because they could.

. . . O, that dream of long duration! It comes again and again, unbidden, to blacken my deepest sleep, to deprive me of peace; for a dream thus conjured owns the dreamer.

. . . See it, as I do:

There they all stand, in the door of the Van Eyn dining room. Were they hounds, they'd bay; for their prey is treed. There is speech, words I cannot discern. A square bottle is passed. One man stamps his foot upon the threshold, and the sound drums through the dream.

Into the room they come. And Mammy Venus resists, yes; as she is able.

. . . "Resistance," read the account in the *Whig*. What, screams from a shapeless mouth? Screams born in lungs well smoked? Screams rising up a throat so raw she must let soup cool to gelatin, and then suffer it to slide down the scarred channel, the walls of which are too thick for swallowing? Screams appealing to what savior? Or punches, perhaps; from arms that do not shift, arms capped by fists formed by default? Or did she run; on feet that are but bunched muscle, supported by bone in which the marrow has boiled?

No: she has but fear to fight with. Their fear. And so I see her raise her skin-winged arms to lift high her veil.

Some circle behind her, whilst others—seeing the ruin of her—backstep to the door.

Silence. Stillness. The blue of the dream turns ice-like.

Something spurs the pack. They spring, they pounce upon her. And she is up. Raised up.

From the dining room they drag her. The tips of her slippers trip o'er the rugs, and the wood of the hallway; down they bounce upon the back stoop. Three men handle her. Two and the boy come behind. So roughly do they hold her that the caul of fabric and skin soldering shoulder to neck rips. Drily. Bloodlessly.

The veil falls to hide her face. Relief: to not see her in the dream. To not see that face that is to me sweet.

They choose a peach tree, but its branches are too brittle, too low to the ground. The men are bothered, but search out a suitable gallows.

... Bothered? O, where was Eliza Arnold, when the bothering of the living was wanted? Asleep in her hillside grave? Hovering o'er the corpse of Henry in Baltimore? Had she settled beneath Edgar's bedstead, having already brought his older brother home, to her, to death? . . . But the poet, he will resist. I'm sure of it; though sure I am, too, that he hears her constant call coming from without the dark, yet knows it not for mother-cry.

Bothered, the men are; but soon they choose a noose-sturdy branch upon a second tree. To its base there come the hens, rising fatly to fly at the men. One gets high enough to task its talons to the boy's eye: a blinding scratch. Other birds now. I see, I hear the cacophony of their coming: jays and ravens, gulls up from the riverside; two hawks wheel before the risen moon, then swoop upon the posse.

The beating begins. And ends whilst I watch, unable to wake.

Finally, blessedly, the blue of the dream goes black, and two hearts fall still: Mammy Venus's and mine.

The swing of bats brought death fast; but in that I find no comfort.

Yes: a single swing: the crack and shatter of skull. And Mother-of-Venus died a second, final time. This death she'd long attended. I wonder: but for the means, was it welcome? I know she doubted it would come: a death from which she'd not return. "The going," she'd once called it. But I never knew how long, how deeply she'd pondered her mortality—would it come, or had Eliza fixed her to the earth forevermore?—until the discoveries of later that night; for, slipping into the Van Eyn cellar, Eli and I would find much that would later prove of interest to a witch such as myself.

44

The Risen

NIGHT was long in falling. When finally it came Eli and I quit the reading room and took again to the streets, which lay now in shadow; for a slivered moon had risen only to clothe itself in cloud.

The back door of the Van Eyn manse stood open—like a mouth set to speak. No one was within—the coldness, the quiet, and the dark told it—but someone had come of late; and it seemed they'd left in haste. Crates sat half packed, spilling straw. The dining-room table was crowded with plate, piled to be counted and carted off. To where? What heir had descended? And what had Jacob Van Eyn to say in the matter? Did he live still? Or had Eliza lured him to his end?

Eliza. . . . I had no sense of her being near; but still I sniffed the air, ready to run if it fell foul.

The cellar door was closed. I sprang it on its hidden hinges; and down we went by the light of a single candle.

Cold rose from off the earthen floor, and caused the candle flame to gutter. When its twisting light steadied, we took in the cellar.

Scattered about was much *materia* common to the Craft. Mammy Venus had experimented with witchery in the long years of my absence. I saw that now. Firestands of iron sat near the fire; and from them hung kettles of various size. Glass vials, stained, sat in racks upon the table; others crunched underfoot. A beeswax candle had burned atop a skull, till now it sat as but a stub. The dank air stank of herbs—the kind few cooks are familiar with. I knew what it was Eli was thinking; but I was even more surprised than he to see the cellar so fitted out for Craft-work. "The woman who lives . . . who lived here," said I, "she was no witch. She had gifts, yes, and knew of witches and much else besides; but she was no sister herself."

Brackets of wrought iron had been driven into the whitewashed walls; and pinewood planks set upon them had served as shelves. These were bowed by the weight of what once they'd held; but now the shelves sat empty. Books, surely.

I saw Mammy Venus's chair, there, in the chimney corner. I stepped to it, and with my fingertips set a kiss upon its slatted back. And there I stood, wondering how Mammy had bade good-bye to the girl she'd known from infancy.

I heard a dull thud: a kick. And from a darkened corner Eliphalet asked:

"What's this?"

I knew before I saw it: my *nécessaire.* And the tone of that thud told me more: within it Mammy Venus had set the books and much else besides. She'd readied the trunk for me. Set within it our secrets, hers and mine. A tag affixed to it showed my false name; and—in red letters too rude to be Rosalie's—this: *Sainte Augusteen.*

No time to tackle its lock. I'd take it away intact.

It was heavy, yes; but not overly so, not for Eliphalet and myself. We carried it up the cellar steps and away; and with it we left the Van Eyn house.

No one was about, yet we were glad for the moon-occluding clouds. The night was close, and the trunk kept slipping from my sweaty grip. But I'd have let no gallant relieve me of its weight: I'd carry it: it seemed a duty. . . . Thankfully, though, Eliphalet had other and better plans.

Spotting a driver and coal cart two streets away, he whistled. Next I knew I stood watching the trunk roll away. Eli sat beside it, waving that I ought not to worry. He'd see to things; as planned. Then he raised high his other hand and crossed two fingers: middle and fore. To wish me well; for he knew it:

I had unfinished business in the boneyard, the potter's field; wherein the poor are left to fester.

I found it easily enough; by scent, if I must say so. I could smell their presence. (Not their rot, no; though there is that, too.) The air takes on something ferrous, as of iron newly wrought, and wet. And I smell it as some say they smell oncoming rain. . . . Rain, yes; rain fell that night: lightly, incessantly; and strengthening along with the dead.

I heard that murmur familiar to me now. The sound of residual life. The sound of life slowly diffusing from the dead, running first to the ground, then the air, then Away. Imagine iron, again: two bars of it, struck together; the resultant vibration would be akin to the death-sound. Sometimes it bears speech, or a thing similar. But only the most disquieted seek to speak. Few hear them; yet still they try, hoping, waiting for the advent of one such as I.

That night none of the dead spoke too distinctly; and I ignored the hum and thrum of those who did as I stepped grave to grave. The moon had let fall her mantle of cloud, and shone now o'er the potter's field; by its light I searched out Mammy's grave.

Soon I found it: a hole, not even dug to decent dimensions. So shallow and squared that a corpse must, perforce, lay curled within: fetally; or with its broken limbs folded beneath the body. Dirt—soft and unsettled still—had been mounded above. Easily I dug it away to a depth of three, four feet.

Surely it was my digging disturbed the debtors, the dissolute, the nameless dead whom the Richmonders had discarded down through the years; for they grew ever louder. Within that sound I discerned the occasional appeal. This disquietude gave strength to the rain, so that soon I stood knee-deep in mud. But on I dug; till finally my fingers found it: texture: burlap? cerecloth? Yes: they'd sewn Mammy Venus into a winding-sheet; and had lain her down—crookedly—without benefit of coffin.

Light as a kite, she was. The worms had had but weeks to work, so still I felt her flesh. I could not see her, well sewn as her shroud was.

I had her, held her in the manner of myriad pietàs. Rising, I made for the boneyard gate, deaf to the suits of the dead. Though I was resolute, still the dead confused my every sense, even that sixth which is the witch's own: strength, say. Indeed, it was my increased strength that let me defy the dead that night.

The dead who sought—as ever they do—one of two things: a return to loved ones, or the redress of wrongs. Their complaint is that of convicts: their confinement is unjust. But what could I do? Nothing. Not that night. O, I suppose I might have tried this or that, might have stayed to hear their appeals, might have done the bidding of some. But no: instead, I all but skipped o'er their souls, casting apology as if it were seed. I told them I hadn't time. They'd worlds of it, yes; but I was sorely pressed; for Eli awaited me. Us, rather. In the rounded shadows of Monumental Church.

As I carried Mammy Venus from her grave, I grew conscious of . . . of something coursing within the cerecloth. No wriggling, no writhing: it was not that. And if it was not life, per se, neither was it death. Suffice to deem it: disquiet.

With words I soothed her, stilled her. Said good-bye and spoke my intent; which I'd formed not a half day before.

Rather bold of me, it was. And bold, too, commandeering the sexton's cart and tools, setting Mammy within and wheeling her o'er the streets of Richmond. Bold: bringing the body to where it had first fallen, years ago.

The rain fell heavily, sluiced through the streets. It washed the grave's dirt from me; but now my cold clothes clung like a second skin. Shivering, on I went with my odd barrow. And as we neared the church, I felt . . . I felt it, yes, but also I saw it: the sack began to shift. Now this *was* a wriggling and a writhing; and it heartened me; for it seemed the Seeress knew, knew and approved of my plan.

And so I was able to see it through. . . . Boldly.

There stood Eliphalet. Years at the Duchess's heel had taught him to hold his questions; and never was I more happy for the boy's training. Had I been asked to state my plan in full, the absurdity of it would have stilled me, and all would have been lost.

Of course, on the seacraft and coaches that had carried us southward, I'd told dear Eli about Mammy Venus: most if not all about her. And I must have spoken well of the woman; for that night Eliphalet Rynders lifted her from the death-cart with a deference she'd rarely been shown in life.

To the side of the church we crept.

The moon drew back, and left us unseen. The rain came in cords: silver through the black night. And just as I picked up a paver—with it I'd knock away the lock—the sky showed a seam of whitest lightning. We hunched our shoulders against the thunder to come. Of course, the weather was worsening. . . . A strange welcome, this, from the dead resident in the cellar, all of them disquieted by so brutal a death, so binding a grave.

"Eli," said I as we stood within the church, "I know not what this night will hold. Should I fall—for an hour; or longer; or forevermore—I entrust myself to you."

"You'll not fall," said he. "The Duchess says you are stronger than you know. Now go. Go!" And he came behind, both of us keeping close to the curved wall. Darkness; save for the lightning that lit windows stained blue, red, gold, and green. Those windows . . . I feared the wind might render them to multihued shrapnel; for the panes seemed to pulse in place. Best to descend; and fast. I turned back to Eli, who carried the corpse as if it were no weight at all. Looking at me by that jagged light, he said, "You are not the witch you were an hour past. Your eyes . . . they hold to the Toad. I know what that means. . . . No, you'll not fall this night."

We'd crossed the church to a narrow, winding stair. Down we went, with the loss of all light. Into the cellar. The dark was abject, and the cold—out of keeping with the season—came in waves from off the crypt.

At the bottom of the stair I sat. Eliphalet lay Mammy Venus in my arms; for he had to quit the cellar: I'd left the tools in the sexton's cart. Yes: there I sat, whispering to soothe my charge; for she was unsettled. Upon my lap I felt the slow grinding of bone on bone; which caused her flesh to fall away. My only thought was this: sing, *sing*! And as no lullaby came, I took up that song Celia had once sung:

"Over my head, I hear music in the air;
There must be a god, somewhere."

But o'er my own head I heard naught but that whipping wind; and, finally, the tread of Eliphalet upon the stair.

He returned with the tools; but also he'd found a lamp. By its light we three went further into the cellar, crouching beneath the low, low ceiling, letting the cold lead us nearer the crypt. The floor was uneven, its dirt set with rocks large enough to trip a witch whose step was uncertain; for now I held Mammy Venus, lest she unsettle Eliphalet with her . . . what? Her yearning?

Eliphalet knew what, or rather whom the tomb held. Did he feel them, as I did? That is to be doubted, greatly. Still, he sensed something: rarely had I seen him so stilled. By the light of the lamp he held, I saw his eyes were wide, were white.

As for me, the chill coming from the crypt set my teeth to chattering. My knees creaked, so deeply did the cold seep. Bone-deep, it was. And the death-scent came: iron rusted by a hard, hard rain.

The resident dead were riled, indeed. The storm raging o'er the church told it. So, too, did the shattering of an upstairs window, blown from its frame. I'd need to work fast; and so I set to it:

I lay Mammy Venus against the crypt wall, upon the consecrated ground.

I took the chisel from Eliphalet. Already I had in hand a flat rock. I felt for and found a seam in the crypt's side. With each successive chip the cold broke upon my body, bored deeper into my bones. My eyes were wide, and no doubt held tightly to the Toad. My unbound hair blew back. Soon the cold came audibly; or was it the death-sound I heard, words on a risen wind?

My fifth or sixth blow breached the tomb; and there came a whistling from within that was, I suppose, the siphoning off of that life force long trapped. . . . Wetness. Much wetness, there was. Coming from within the crypt. The whistling rose;

was shrill; was so . . . constrained that I knew what next to do: I drove the chisel deeper to widen the breach. The whistling and the wet redoubled. I was blown back from the crypt; for the force that freed the dead came not from without, not from me and my gravekeeper's tools, but from within.

The cement facing fell from off the rude tomb. Onto Mammy where she lay, seeming to writhe in the deep shadows. And just as the bricks themselves began to fall from off the wall, I took up Mother-of-Venus and . . .

And as we jiggered and juddered back from the tomb, and as I called o'er the death-storm to Eliphalet—meaning to tell him to retreat—the wall gave. Cracked. Delicately, at first. Seams came: siblings to the one I'd made. From these there issued the wind and the wet, like steam from off a kettle. The cracks ran one to another: streams to rivers to a final sea. It was this sea—the breach complete, it came flooding forth—that tipped me onto my back. I lost hold of Mammy Venus and . . .

Alone I rode that cold till it smacked me flat against the cellar's far wall. O, no ordinary wind, this. No: I speak of a blasting cold, rivaling fire from off a furnace. It blew me some ten, twelve feet from the crypt. Horrid: the taste on my tongue of that indrawn cold. It froze my nose as it rose to chill my eyes and fill my skull. My brain felt snapped from off its stem; for my sensorium was unsettled: sight was sound and touch was taste. O, but then I saw the light. No, no, no: I speak not of life's light, or Heaven's, or any such triteness: this was the lamp, flying at me end over end to smash beside my head. Darkness then. Within the whistling—so shrill I pressed my muddied palms to my ears, yet failed to stifle the sound—I heard Eliphalet calling. He'd been buffeted, too: this I knew.

. . . Witch, doubt not the urgency of the departing dead. The whistle of their fast passing was a supernal sound, one I will never forget. . . . But where was Eliphalet? I feared for him; for that death-stream was tanged, too, with anger, a menace no mortal could mistake.

And where was Mammy Venus?

I called to Eliphalet. I called to Mother-of-Venus. No answers came.

Silence. Stillness, too; for the dead did not linger, but rode their wind Away.

"Eli?" I cried a second time, a third, a fourth and final time.

"Here," said he, tremulously.

"Eli," said I, "speak!" I meant to make my way to him, tracking his voice through the dark of the cellar. But he said nothing more. Still, I crawled, calling for him. And for her. Back toward the crypt. Back to where I'd last seen him. Back to where I'd lost hold of her when . . .

Fabric. I felt fabric. Dry; though the earth on which I found it was muddy. Fibrous, it was; and slick:

The cerecloth of her shroud.

Both hands now, flat upon the cellar floor. Patting, patting. It was the shroud, entire; but there was nothing left within it. No flesh, no skin, no skeleton.

Feeling a warm hand lain atop mine, I started.

"Eli?" asked I, of the dark. He drew me close. He was wet, and shivered from more than mere cold.

"What . . . what did this?" he asked.

"The dead did this," said I. "Just as I'd hoped they would."

We left Monumental Church and hurried, hurried down a hillside to the shore.

The storms had broken, within and without. The moon shone as if she were proud. Stars sparkled. And the James seemed to steam. Beside it we sat, our souls as turbid as the rapids upriver.

Eliphalet had questions, surely; but again he let them go. Just as well; for my answers would have been few. I'd known the Monumental dead had sought release. I'd known it since first I'd felt them. But I'd not known if they'd take . . . well, it was a witch's gamble: Would they, would *he* reclaim Mother-of-Venus?

It seemed he had.

I held Eliphalet's trembling hand. Or was it mine trembled? Regardless, both fell still as we sat riverside that night; till, well . . .

In time there came a sky-show: an arc of light. I knew it for a shooting star; but my heart insisted it was they:

Mammy Venus and her Mason; dancing Away.

45

Adieu

THE day prior, Eli—not knowing what was to come, but presuming, rightly, that it would be strange—had taken it upon himself to procure a room in a tavern near Shockoe Slip; a place so like the Bowler's of my first visit—in its aspect, if not its every attribute—that I shan't describe it here, save to say it provided a doubly wide bedstead and an ample *table d'hôte*. And glad I was for Eli's prescience when, sitting shoreside beneath the stars, spent utterly, I learned we'd a place to sleep. Glad, too, to follow him there and find the *nécessaire*.

Next morning, I slept whilst Eli saw to our plans; for there was a buzzing in my blood, and I suffered a lassitude the likes of which. . . . *Enfin,* I slept. And dreamed so vengefully I'd wake with a blood-taste upon my tongue.

In my dreams I met the militiamen who'd come to the Van

Eyn house; and I drew a bat upon them. As for the red boy, well, I meted out a more witch-worthy punishment. Into my dreams there came a Belgian sister—I'd read ghastly things in the Books of old Europe—telling how once she'd sewn to the face of a sneaking neighbor the snout of a red fox. Too, a tall and sharp-angled Scotsman ambled o'er that dreamscape with talons for feet, pecking for flesh and coin. I could find John Allan at Moldavia, or at Ellis & Allan, and I could, would . . . smite him. I'd smite him, yes, strike him down Old Testament–style. Such was the heady strength, the silly strength I felt in sleep; though even as I woke, even as my senses settled somewhat, still I saw John Allan through a blood-lens; for if he were dead, Edgar Poe would worry me no more. O, but I turned my thoughts from the Scot, lest somehow I will him ill, or worse: I'd revel in the fact of his demise, yes, but I'd *not* partake of the act itself. . . . Wakeful, still I wondered: hadn't I loosed a host of ghosts upon Richmond? Some would linger, surely. And who knew what they might do, as regarded Vengeance.

. . . Rosalie. Would I try again to parley with her in what hours remained to me? I decided not. She was in no state to see me, to hear my half-truths. I'd write from the territory, hinting of our old friend's release, and happiness. It was best: that I leave without seeing Rosalie. . . . I'd leave. Only when I thought that—*I'll leave*—only then was I blindsided by the baldest of truths: so, too, would Eli. We were set to part.

Sadly, I rose, dressed (as Henry), and waited.

Good Eli, capable and handsome and kindly Eli, returned having seen to all requisite things. He had in tow two porters. Off went the *nécessaire,* addressed to one *H. Collier, St. Augustine, the Florida Territory*. The trunk would go to Norfolk via coach, and from thence to Florida by sea. For me Eli had arranged a faster passage: a mail stage—*merde!*—was to depart Richmond at noon, headed southeasterly through Turner territory, and on to Charleston skirting Elliot's Cut. From

Charleston I'd proceed by sea. As for Eli, well, I'd learn he'd an errand to attend to in the capital city; where there sat King Jackson upon his throne.

The Duchess, in the days prior to my departure, had been a veritable font of advice. Among the things she offered were the names of two witches. The one I should seek out, if ever I were able; for she was "fun." The second I should avoid at all costs. The former was, nay *is* well known; infamous, rather; and history will tell of her worldly effect. The latter is a legend of another stripe, altogether. I would come to know her as few have; indeed, her history is mine to write, and mine alone.

O, but for now, let a fast accounting of the "fun" witch suffice.

She was a friend to the Duchess, a Sabbat sister from days past; and so it was the Duchess charged Eli with the delivery of a note, nay quite a long letter, the content of which I cannot here record. I imagine it was somewhat . . . incendiary, in nature; for the Duchess deemed her letter too precious for the post. Eli would deliver it, set it himself into the hands of Peggy Eaton, wife to the minister of war.

"Pompadour Peg," she is called now; for she and John Eaton have recently decamped to Spain on some mission of diplomacy. And O, spare a thought for poor Spain! Split as she is by her wars of succession, well . . . surely Peggy Eaton will play some part therein; for she's shown herself quite adept in affairs of state.

Indeed, not more than a half year before my return to Richmond, Peggy Eaton had brought about a thing without precedent: Jackson, that April of '31, demanded the resignations of his entire cabinet. This was the culmination of a scandal that began with the snubbing of Mrs. Eaton by Floride Calhoun, wife to the vice president. As Peggy's past was rife with rumor and disrepute, the old hen Calhoun refused to associate with her; and showed her disdain rather broadly at some levee or another. See, Peggy Eaton—the young Miss O'Neale, that was—had resided on the top floor of her parents' boardinghouse in the capital, the lower floors of which were crowded with the country's legislators. Widely was it whispered that she'd entertained said men . . . deeply. And later, as Mrs. Timberlake, it was said she'd induced with infidelity the suicide at sea of her young husband. Society—shocked, appalled!—saw the widow fast-allied to John Eaton, courtier to the future King; who was yet staking his claim as a Tennessee Elite; and destined soon to mourn his own wife, Rachel, who'd outlived her reputation by some years. (Duels, there'd been; coming hard on the heels of bigamous charges.)

Un vrai scandale! Camps were claimed. In Peggy's there stood but two men: her husband and Jackson. O, but they knew how to wage and win a war. This triad triumphed; and all the men (and wives) of the cabinet fell to the Eaton Malaria, as it is referenced.

Yes, indeed, pity the poor Spaniards; for this Mrs. Eaton is a witch of scant scruple. . . . But I am glad she's gone; not only from this country, but from Florida in particular. For the Eatons made their way from Washington to the territory not two years past. John Eaton sat as governor in Tallahassee; but Peggy, deeming the capital a backwater, installed herself in Pensacola, much preferring its Spanish laxity, its Creole ways. There she reigned o'er the Patgoe pageants and Carnivale, and sowed scandal as ever she has: tanning herself to Spanish tones; and holding her salon at the racetrack, where she was known to sit amidst the men, her headdress high with ostrich feathers. Our paths might well have crossed; but I saw to it they did not. For, in those years following my return to the territory, I was . . . distracted.

Which leads me to speak of the second witch, the one I'd been warned against: Sweet Marie: legendary, yes; to all but luckless me.

O, but stay. I won't do it. . . . My pen wants not to spill its ink o'er Sweet Marie. Not yet. It wants more of Eliphalet Rynders; and I'll indulge it, though the tale ends in tears; for:

Eli would die within a year of our good-bye.

I had the news in a letter from Eugénie, dated 26 September, 1832.

That very morning, whilst descending the stairs in the course of a common chore, Eliphalet—with Sarah at his side—had been seized by a spasm, a sudden cramping of his innards so severe as to cause him to clutch at the banister, to settle himself in a crouch upon a carpeted stair. There he remained a long while; for—despite the ministrations of those sisters roused from sleep by Sarah's cries—Eli hadn't the strength to remove himself to the black suite he'd long shared with the Duchess. Doubtless, too, my dear Eli suffered a slackening of his will; for surely he knew it: the plague was upon him.

. . . The *cholera morbus*. Which had crept to the West: from India to China, from Siberia to St. Petersburg, and on to Liverpool. I'd heard tell of it. We all had. But I'd believed those who'd said America was safe, that the plague would not, could not, cross the ocean. But of course it did; and quarantining came too late. The summer after I left New York—'32—thousands fell there; as they did in Baltimore, Cincinnati, New Orleans . . . One among them was Eliphalet Rynders.

Its progress upon my friend was fast. ("Though in that we found little solace," wrote Eugénie.) After the cramping there came the revolt of his every system, with vomitus and viler discharges the result. Eugénie wrote of seeing Eli's beauty fail: his cold skin darkened to a purplish blue, and his tongue went white. "White as maggoty meat," it was written. It protruded stiffly from between lips no longer livid. And his eyes of smoking jade burned down to ash. They shrank in their sockets, shriveled and dwindled till it seemed naught but the fluttering lids held them in his skull.

The Duchess summoned two of the ward's three surgeons; and both came, of course. The one, looking around the house of which he'd heard so much, "dared to disdain the Duchess," and was dismissed when he opined in passing that the plague was "God, coming forth." That the surgeon made it away from Cyprian House seems testament enough to the Duchess's state. "Desperate, she was," wrote Eugénie, "such that our hearts were doubly rent to see it." The second physic dispensed peppermint water into which the sisters were to drop, alternately, thirty drops of ether and laudanum. Of course, the atelier was busy with activity, as the witches took down Book upon Book, searching out cures of another kind. So it was they wore sachets of scarlet silk; for Eugénie herself had led them in the decoction of a healing incense: busy they'd been, I'm sure, gathering the eucalyptus, thyme, and winter's bark, grinding these and adding cinnamon and powders of myrrh, frankincense, orris root, violets, saltpeter, and sage, the lot of which Sarah then sewed into the sachets. This had seemed to strengthen Eli's pulse, and his senses sharpened; such that he and the Duchess spoke, for some while, behind closed doors. I cry to wonder at the nature of their good-bye.

The voodoo's effect was short-lived; and when Eli refused the surgeon's lancets and cups ("wanting to die with blood in his veins"), the sisters could only see to his comfort. At this they'd grown adept; for none who stayed in the stricken city would nurse, no matter the money on offer; none save the Cyprians, who of course knew themselves immune. All the sisters turned from care of the carnal sort to nursing. Some did so in the wards at Greenwich Hospital, and down at Corlear's Hook. Lydia ladled soup at Hubert Street. Eugénie did the same at the North Battery; and also invoked the loa Zacamica, albeit too late to aid the stricken. Soon Cyprian House itself stood as a lesser ward; and so it was that Burtis died in the lap of his Li'l Belt. Others came, too. They'd pay to die amidst the memory of pleasure. But of course these men died none the poorer; for my sisters gave their embraces away.

On the first of her letter's three pages, Eugénie suggested I hie to New York; for, apparently, upon his return from Richmond, Eli had told of my emptying the crypt beneath Monumental Church. Did Eugénie think I might summon spirits to ease Eli's passing, or to accompany him? Did she think I'd the power to stay Death's hand? No matter; for she signed her letter by moonlight, adding the saddest of postscripts: Eliphalet was already dead.

The Duchess sat a day or more with the corpse. The sisters wondered what she'd do; for she was despondent. She let settle o'er her bare shoulders the full weight of the blame. Which I thought absurd; till a subsequent letter from Sarah explained:

Those mornings when the Duchess and Eli had strolled the city, they'd had business, yes; but it was business of a saintly, not sisterly sort. It seemed the Duchess, never forgetting the gutters from whence she'd risen, went among the poor to better their lot. She shied not from squalor—pigs penned in foreyards; immigrant families living twelve to a cellar, the walls of which trickled filth . . . —and did what good she could. She gave them money. (And O, how her strict yet sly accounting struck me differently upon reading this.) She converted favors-owed into jobs and food; and she sought no reward. Indeed, Sarah herself—a "wild-eyed" orphan of African Grove—had been a beneficiary of the Duchess's largesse. But others knew not their benefactress; for she kept to the shadows as best she could. And woe, woe betide any who dared venture to her door, be it to thank or to seek. . . . All the while Eli had stood at her side. Now she was left to mourn him, to chide herself and wonder how, how had she forgotten that he was a man, merely, and would know no immunity?

When next the cholera came to New York—in '34—Cyprian House was no more. The Duchess had dissolved it, and the sisters scattered on the four winds. Some write, or have written; but most devolved to colored pins upon a map I've long since abandoned.

Eugénie returned to New Orleans despite the disfavor of that city's queen, Marie Laveau. There she lives at a safe remove, far down an alley off the rue Dauphine. It seems she is the keeper of a onetime Priestess (and true witch) whom the Widow Paris has all but exiled: Marie Salope, who once was allied to Sanité Dédé, Eugénie's own Soror Mystica. But now this witch Salope insists on street-living and answers only to Zozo LaBrique; for she sells brick dust by the bucket, at a nickel per, and will use it to scrub spirits off your stoop for a nickel more. We write, Eugénie and I; and someday I hope to see the good *vaudouienne* again.

As for the Duchess, she gave much away—first staking Fanny and Jen to a town home of their own—and quit the city. Among we Cyprians who write, our letters all end the same: "What news of the Duchess?" But none has come. Yet.

The news of Eli's death and the subsequent dissolution of Cyprian House, all this ought to have laid me low. And it would have; had there been a lower place to go.

But by that summer of '34 the larger world had devolved to a distraction; for, though I was three years back in the territory, still I struggled to reaccustom myself to solitude; for yes: I'd returned from Richmond to find Celia gone.

Onto my knees I fell before the locked door of a house,

our house, showing signs of desuetude: on its walls—from within cracks and crevices—there sprouted airborne ferns; and the roof of Spanish tile shone with silver moss, tufted here and there. Shells and stones bit into my knees, split the fabric of my slacks as I knelt. How, *how* had I not considered this? That Celia in her turn might abandon me? Simply, I had not; and so it was that the solitude to come, the shame and lovelessness that was my lot, flooded me then, finding form in tears I could not stanch.

I knelt a long while in the silence of the yard, in shade cast by red bay, swamp magnolia, and a single live oak, the branches of which dipped so low they seemed to rest upon the lawn of risen weeds, and I sobbed till it seemed the birds began to mock me. So still was I—the saddest of hours passed—that squirrels worked the weeds around me, querying the ground for things fallen from on high: acorns and nuts and such, I suppose. . . . O how I envied them the simplicity of their search.

46

A Sister in Solitude

It was a close September day when I returned to St. Augustine and to that house sitting shuttered, north of the Parade, in the customs house ward on a street named for a saint. The sun sat high o'er streets still steaming from a fast rainfall. Waiting till no one was near, I'd slipped through my own rusted gate, down a bricked path, and into the backyard. The rain fell a second time—slowly: like tears, or sweat—as it sieved through the trees.

I saw, nay I stared at the lock: an iron eye that had cried its rust down the door's cypress planks. It was then I knew Celia was gone. It was then I sank to my knees.

When finally I stood to search out the key . . . yes: it was where I'd hoped it would be: tucked in a queen conch, set beside the door. There Celia and I would leave it on the rare,

rare occasions when we'd been apart. It was a habit we'd established whilst living on Hospital Street.

The dark, undusted interior told it true: Celia had been gone a long while. And leaving, she'd not set the house to rights: her own bed was unmade and cold, and had surrendered her scent; a bottle of wine sat uncorked upon the pianoforte; and nature had had its way with a bowl of fruit upon the sideboard, such that it was acrawl with ants, aswarm with flies well nigh too tiny to see, and the whole still life was rank with rot. Beside this I found those blue spectacles we'd made her, when first we'd run.

Upon my return to the territory, I went to see the postmaster. He returned to me those letters I'd posted to Celia. Had he tried to deliver them? I asked. Once, said he, twice perhaps; but the door of the addressee never opened. He shrugged. He smiled. He fingered the coin I'd lain upon his counter.

I gave him letters for Sebastiana, the Cyprians, and Rosalie Poe; all of which informed my correspondents that I'd arrived in St. Augustine, and ought to be written to at my address of old. I told the postman that I'd returned to stay, and that I had living with me a sister—Henriette—who was shy but would show herself from time to time.

"Women," said he with fraternal sympathy, "they are wanton as the winds."

"I suppose they are," said I. And then I pressed for news of Celia. He had none. Only when I said, "Liddy; some call her Liddy."

"Oh yes," said he, "the slave. Pretty; yes, yes, *yes*. I see why you wonder so. . . . Tell me, has she run?" Something in the prospect appealed to him; and I hated him for it.

"She has *not* run," said I, knowing I'd misspoken. "Being free, she has no reason to run . . . Good day to you." And I stepped to the door of his store, leaving naught but my coins, my letters, and my lies behind.

* * *

I asked after Celia again when I went dockside to recover my trunk. If she'd sailed, perhaps someone had seen her. But no: nothing; and I dared not overask, fearing I'd peg her as fugitive.

Better luck I had finding the *nécessaire;* for dear Eli—whom I'd mourn within the year—had seen well to its transport. Two boys carted the trunk to my door. I had them set it in a pantry next to the kitchen. And its contents—a great weight of books lay within—would occasion my sole visitor: a shipwright met in my days as translator, who owed me a favor; which chit I cashed in for the building of bookcases. These stood tall—sentinels of riven cypress—against the coquina walls. Around the shelves I ranged all my accoutrements of old. Here was quite the witch's den. Any who saw it would deem it queer indeed; but of course none would see it. Only Erasmus Foote threatened; and when first he came around I put him off with rudeness.

On the shelves I ordered by subject those volumes Mammy Venus and Rosalie had acquired. Conspicuously absent from said collection was my first *Book of Shadows;* and often I've wondered where that volume has gone to. I suspect Edgar found and took it. I've no proof, of course; but so strong a suspicion, when born of a witch's intuition, well. . . .

The books:

Several bore on Floridiana; that is: those tracts published in years past and meant to lure people onto the peninsula. This touched me; for what possible interest could Mammy Venus have had in Florida save one: the imagining of that place to which she had freed Celia. O yes: doubtless Rosalie read to Mammy from such tomes as Forbes's *Sketches of the Floridas,* Vignoles's *Observations,* and Simmons's *Notices of East Florida;* all of which proclaimed the place Paradise, and made it seem that one need only drop a seed, wait a season, and return to claim one's orchard. The crops—from cotton to cane, from silk to sea cotton—verily begged cultivation. And though the salt air was salubrious, the authors did concede that there came each summer "a sickly season." I read the propagandists' every word; and thusly did I travel the territory from the safer side of my vine-laden gate. When on occasion I did venture forth, I did so by the cool of the moon. By day my house sat shuttered; for the sunlight seemed to accuse. And I needed no reminding of the world beyond my walls, nor of the wrongs I'd done within them. . . . I saw to necessities, and little else. And I shan't detail the disarray that overcame my home, my person, my soul other than to quote Augustine himself and say, "I became to myself a barren land."

O, but as a witch I was well. Stronger; owing to the strength I'd siphoned off the dead.

How did I learn this? Simply: returning to the Craft, I found success where earlier there'd been its opposite; and things far worse than failure.

At first I'd been reluctant to work the Craft. But one night, sitting before those portraits of ancestors not my own, unwitched wine in hand, I turned a random thought to action: I closed my eyes, muttered Words of Will learned from Lydia Smash, and caused to slam, in succession, each interior door of my home. This amused me; for I was drunk. From across the parlor I played the piano. Mere dissonance; yet still a feat, no? This success I celebrated with, yes, more wine.

As for all I'd learned from Eugénie, well, I let it lie; for voodoo wants an object, a person on which to play. I, of course, had no one. Not even a too-near, annoying neighbor on whom I might loose Agarou-Tonnerre, Simi, or some other loa of malevolent intent. Indeed, the residents of St. Augustine would've sworn my house uninhabited.

And so, with neither kinetics nor voodoo holding any interest—though I did sew a doll of Barnum, sticking red pins in its secret places—I took up certain books found within my trunk, the better to stave off boredom. Only then did I understand the nature of Mammy Venus's collection.

Suffice to say: the Seeress, it seemed, had long wondered was she living or dead. Where would she stand on a line stretched taut between those states? O, how I pitied and missed her; and hoped she was at peace. . . . There were books in French, and I wondered if she'd awaited my return to Richmond to read them to her? Or had Rosalie done this? She may have, albeit with the deep and frequent aid of dictionaries? Or perhaps . . . perhaps Edgar had been lured into this odd study? Regardless, I found Bruhier's *Dissertation sur l'incertitude des signes de la mort,* and Thierry's *La Vie de l'homme respecté et défendu dans ses derniers moments.* And I recut my Latin teeth on Winslow's *Morte incertae signa.* These and other works spoke of the "apparently dead"; that is: they questioned the signifiers of death, commonly used, and accepted only putrefaction as proof positive of death.

Poor Mammy. . . . But I confess it: soon my thoughts turned from the Seeress; for these works were of great relation to me, and what I'd undergone. Hufeland, in his *Der Scheintod, or The Death Trance*—which, blessedly, had been procured in an English translation; thusly was the Teuton's body of work shorn of its original but gangrenous German—wherein he, too, puts forth putrefaction as the sole signifier of death. O, but Hufeland goes on to speak of a state all but indistinguishable from "real death," one which might last days or weeks, wherein a human—like a hibernating bear—is found to be devoid of all arterial pulsations, all muscular reflexes, all respiratory movements, and yet, *and yet he recovers. . . .* The same had happened to me at Matanzas.

Other books and lesser pamphlets came from the anti-premature-burial camp; and chief among these was one signed with a name I knew from Sebastiana's Book: Madame Necker: wife to Louis XVI's minister of finance and mother to the writer and *salonnarde,* Madame de Staël. It seems the great lady had once visited the Salpétrière prison, its hospital or charnel house—one and the same, I suppose, in those red days of Revolution—and there had seen porters placing the dying in their coffins; not the dead, mind, but the dying. Thereafter, Madame—fearing she'd find herself sentient in the grave—stumped for burial reform. She advocated the building of waiting mortuaries—so plentiful now in Germany—wherein the "apparently dead" lay in wait for a prescribed period, bells or flags attached to their fingers by means of a ring. Napoleon deemed this too costly, thusly depriving the French of death's surety. As for Madame, she was buried with a hammer in her hand and naught but a pane of glass sealing her grave. Of greater interest was this: in her pamphlet she referenced one La Jumelière, a woman of Angers who'd once been prosecuted for delivering the dead too precipitously to their graves. La Jumelière. I knew the name. . . . Yes: a witch: I'd seen her Book at Cyprian House, had copied from it in fact.

I searched out the relevant pages—certain I'd happened upon a death-allied sister—and . . . and I was disappointed. Still all was not lost; for La Jumelière's writings led me to three thin Books I'd borrowed from the Duchess's collection. These were the work of a Tuscan witch who—rather grandly—signed herself Umbrea, after the goddess of shadows and secrets, and wife to Dis, god of Death. I quite took to these *stregharia,* and soon I was practicing olden witchery in the Italian style. I even dared to dabble in divination, which long I'd avoided; for:

Most means of divination scared me, and scare me still; for unlike that of the Italian *streghe,* they do not claim to be able to affect the future. (And why would anyone—witch or otherwise—want to foresee things both dire *and* ordained?) The Italian sisters, though, state the aims of sight differently.

They hold that the sighted thing is *not* inevitable; it is merely what will come to pass if the patterns forming in the present remain undisturbed. That is: they look to the future in order to alter it, presently.

O, but how, by what means of sight?

I pored o'er the three Books. My atelier—too fancy a name for that pantry wherein I'd long been pent, and which I'd rendered a sty—spilled out into my courtyard and garden, and there I practiced the Craft by candle- and moonlight.

First I made and cast runes of the Tuscan type, on a glyph sketched in whitest chalk. Thirty-three stones I searched out myself; and twenty-seven I inscribed in *strega* script. Six stones—in shades of black, white, and gray—bore no rune. All went into a bag, were drawn from it and cast as directed. And . . . I saw nothing, read nothing in their fall. All seemed without sense, inscrutable. Why? Well, eventually I learned that certain runes are considered feminine, others masculine. Doubtlessly, I—the thrower—had confused them. To be sure, I prepared a second set of runes: on shells I drew the marks in berry juice. These I cast upon a glyph of sand. Again: nothing. I despaired. It seemed I'd little talent for such sight.

But then, in the third of her Books, Umbrea wrote of divination by fire:

> Carve a goodly-sized puppet of wood (any sort) to represent the witch Befana, the gift-giver, the Ancestress binding generations past and present. Within the hollowed belly of the effigy set grapes, dried figs, chestnuts, pears, apples, carob, with sapa and cotnognata. Build then a fire in conical shape, stacking straw on horse chestnuts on brambles on wood. Set it to burning brightly. Eat from the belly of Befana; then cast the effigy into the fire. And chant:

Fire, blessed fire,
Burn as I desire!
Fire, blessed fire,
The future, sire!

Ask Yes and No questions of the flames.

Steady flames signal *no,* or so it was written. Affirmation would come as exploding chestnuts; and the resultant sparks would show patterns a witch could easily read, thusly:

Upwelling sparks indicate Abundance and Good. Downward sparks: Decline.

A fire sparking off to the witch's right: Someone Comes.

To the witch's left: Loss.

Sparks coming straight-on, at the reading witch: Danger.

The night I burned Befana on the beach by moonlight, sparks rose on the salted breeze. To the right and to the left they blew, in a perfect split; but then the fire set to swirling, and rounded upon me, touching its red fingers to my bare knees.

It seemed I had my answer:

She'd come. She'd go. And danger would befall me.

And so I waited. For weeks. For months. For a season or more.

Scared, wanting not to face the foreseen danger alone, I tried to summon friends—some dead, some alive but distant—in the only way I knew: I strung brass bells through my garden, tying them tree to tree. Perhaps I'd draw down Father Louis, last seen in Marseilles. Or Madeleine, if still she hovered to sex-haunt humanity. (This I doubted.) Or maybe even Mammy Venus. These three I called by name; but none came. And soon I abandoned all Books, all hope; and told myself I'd seen naught but flame in the fire of Befana. By day I slept; and the long, long hours of the night I drank away—dissolute, I was—till dawn brought again that dreamless sleep.

Then, on an autumn day—as I lay abed, sweltering, watching a rainstorm prove the inefficacy of my roof: *drip, drip, drip*—there came a sound I'd not heard in years: the light grinding of my backdoor bell.

At first I thought I'd misheard it. Surely this was some thunder-trick, or cracking branch. But then it came again; and I leapt from the soured bed, knowing, *knowing* it was she.

Down the worn steps I went, taking them by twos. But when I opened the door, there stood . . . not Celia; rather it was Yahalla. The ruined Seminole, vending who knew what. He was sodden, but sober; his skin the color of cooling ash. His attire was neither tribal nor white. (Surely I appeared no prize myself.)

"Ha!" said I. "What have you now? Firewood for these hot nights, I suppose."

Waiting not for the Indian to answer, I stepped back to slam my door. But then I saw he'd no firewood upon his back; neither did he have his barrow of oranges, outfitted with the brazier on which he roasted them, selling them slathered with honey. "What then?" I asked. "Speak!" My long solitude had left me impatient. My sudden disappointment had brought me to the brink of tears.

Yahalla craned his neck this way and that, and cast his dark gaze past me, into the house. He looked at me. Deeply. His eyes now held a question; which he mimed:

He raised his crooked forefingers to his face, to his eyes. When I failed to understand, he stepped to snap two faded morning glories from off a heart-leafed vine woven through my fence. These he raised to his face, to his eyes.

"She is gone," said I. "Lost."

"No," said he, with emphasis. "Found."

47

Wanderers All

THE Indian Yahalla had long been subject to the Whiskey Gentry: low whites of ill repute who traded in too-ardent spirits. The day he showed at my door, he stank. I brought him inside, to the parlor. He was wet, and shivering; for though the day was hot, the rain had fallen cold. I lit a fire, only to see the logs smoke and hiss, and never catch.

I sat staring at Yahalla. Here was neither the warrior nor the noble Indian I knew from Mr. Fenimore Cooper. This was a saddening ruin of a man, who looked with reddened eyes at my sideboard, whereon he'd espied a decanter of port. From this I poured, finally, and Yahalla spoke: Muskogee, but also Spanish and a smattering of English, which he showed strategically. But soon I drew forth his best English; for, cruelly, I stoppered the port and would pour no more until . . .

"They know of the Flower'd-Face," said he. "They search."

"Who knows of her?"

"Indians," said he, "and trading men." Whereupon he mimed certain acts of capture. Accoutrements, too: rifles, shackles, and such.

"They search for Celia, for Liddy in particular?" Were these slave catchers in the employ of Bedloe's heirs? After all these years? Or perhaps he referred to mere traders, the rogues who range through the territory taking what is not theirs—horses, cattle, slaves; and who prize their two-legged quarry above all else.

"Where is she?" I asked. "Is she nearby?"

Yahalla sat shaking his head; regretfully, mournfully so. When he took to passing his forefinger eye to eye, and pointing down at the parlor floor, I lost patience.

"What? What is it? Is she . . . buried, do you mean to say?"

"No buried, no. . . . Runs. She runs upon the land." Subtly, he indicated that he'd earned his reward.

"Listen to me," said I, brandishing two bottles drawn from out the sideboard. "Tell me where she is, and these are yours." The bribe shames me now; but I was no less desperate than my interlocutor.

"I have no seen her. Yahalla *hears*. Only hears."

"Hears what? What have you heard?"

"She, the Flower'd-Face, she runs, runs from San Agustin into the Nation."

Many blacks—be they freeborn or runaways—were living with the Seminole in camps scattered throughout the territory. The Seminole owned them, I suppose; but it was, is, a relationship more feudal than brutal. Sometimes the black men live apart, farming and tithing to the Seminole in tenant fashion; more often, they are incorporated into Indian life. This—and little more—I knew.

"But where is she? Yours is a mighty Nation, and big."

"No big. No mighty." And when Yahalla snatched the decanter, I did not resist. I let him pour. I watched him drink. Now he was dry, his skin held no sheen at all; it was slack upon his bones, papery and sere.

I left Yahalla in the parlor and searched amidst my papers for a map of the territory. This I opened and spread upon the long-undusted table. I asked Yahalla to show me what it was he'd "heard"; and before doing so he tucked the two bottles away, one under each arm.

He'd heard talk of one who had to be Celia when he'd traded for glass beads at Fernandina. And, recently, much further south, at the Volusia settlement, he'd heard things similar.

"Now," I said, "where is she *now*?"

But already the Seminole was backing toward the door.

Owing to Befana or no, now I had hope; and decisions to make.

Celia was near, perhaps very near; still in the territory, at least. And so it stood to reason: she might return. But what if she were unable? If she'd gone among the Seminole herself, fine; but what if she hadn't? What if she was there against her will? What if she had no will at all, what if I'd so debased her by those spells I'd so stupidly cast? . . . O, how I tried to convince myself that she'd run, that she'd wanted out of St. Augustine; for it was true: she'd never felt safe within the city.

But no: what if, what if, what if . . . ?

Finally, I knew my options to be two:

I could leave her be, hope she was well, and attend her uncertain return. Or I could search her out, and render her well if I found her otherwise.

I was some days in deciding what to do; for yet again cowardice played its part. So, too, did denial: denial of all I'd done. I turned not to any *Books of Shadows* or other sisterly resources, no spells or sight: perhaps I feared what I might find there. And so it was I found that thing which decided my course in a most unlikely place: the *Collected Works* of the city's namesake and patron saint, wherein I read Saint Augustine's definition of the Evil-doer:

He who chooses the lesser of two goods.

I knew then that I'd not leave Celia. I'd search her out. Find her. Help her, if need be.

Dawn of the next day saw my haversack packed, and the house key secreted within the pink of the queen conch sitting doorside. By noon I sat astride a horse, a bay gelding who knew well the King's Road (so said its seller). Slowly, O so slowly, I rode from the city, and toward absolution. Or so I hoped.

I was not the sole wanderer that fall and winter; but much would pass before I heard tell of the seven Seminole chiefs.

Seven chiefs there were, yes, then wandering the West; for they'd been told to go. And if the land they looked upon suited them—as it did no white men—they and their tribesmen would remove to it, to the banks of the river Arkansas. They would surrender their lands and march en masse to live amidst the Creek, a People of No Peace with whom they'd once warred. Too, they'd leave behind their black allies: a bequeathal, as it were. So said good King Jackson.

He—Jackson—had come to Florida in 1819, sent by Monroe to suppress the Seminoles and roust out those runaways to whom they'd long offered refuge. This Jackson did; no matter that Florida belonged to Spain. O, but Spain faced war on other fronts, and hadn't the resources to resist.

See it thusly: the land is but a ball, bandied about, batted this way and that by war and treaty. The Spanish seize it from sundry tribesmen, but later pass it to Britain, via the Treaty of Paris, in 1763; which document ends a conflict known on *that* side of the sea as the Seven Years' War, and on *this,* the Franco-Indian. Thereafter, the territory is British; and split into the fourteenth and fifteenth colonies: East and West Florida; which never will rebel.

As the Revolutionary dust settles o'er the eastern seaboard—1780 or so—the conquered British retrocede the territory to Spain; and so back from Havana come the former Floridians. Twenty-odd years they rule this time, with a laxity most decidedly un-British. It is this same indolence—by which both black and red men benefit—that allows Jackson to invade. . . . And so it is that the territory is tallied to the American score.

But what to do with Florida's natives, now the game is won?

Remove them, of course.

Attempts at treaties are made:

At Moultrie Creek, near St. Augustine, in 1823, thirty-odd chiefs cede thirty-odd million acres of Indian land to the Americans. In return they receive four million acres sitting well inland, lest allies or arms come to them by sea. And they agree to desist in their trading with the Cubans who ply the coast. More: they must surrender all slaves living among them.

Resistance to these terms comes; but so, too, does removal. Into Middle Florida the Seminole go, onto the sand hills where deluge and drought will play upon them. Only when it seems they will starve does the Great Father in Washington open his hand, offering one thousand rations of beef and salt pork to the two thousand Indians who have removed.

Starving, the Seminole roam off-reserve, killing cattle and so disquieting the inflowing settlers that eventually it is decreed: An Indian found beyond bounds is subject to thirty-nine whip strokes upon his bare back.

The Nation will starve; or rise against the white men.

And so: removal, again. But further this time. To the unwanted West.

By late '32, early '33, I'd long been mourning Eliphalet. And all I lost, I longed for. As the Seminole longed for their fathers' land; but I thought not of the Indians' plight, which I suppose was well covered in those newspapers I no longer read. The Treaty of Payne's Landing, which had sent the seven westward? I once heard it referenced through my streetside shutters: hardly a source for the historian; whose pen I take up again:

. . . The seven chiefs report back to the Nation; and the Nation says no, they'll not go to the cold, to the Creeks. But this is unacceptable to Jackson, who's acceded to the presidency. Moreover (says he): the chiefs have signed a treaty of intent at Fort Gibson, in Arkansas; to this they must abide. Yes, say the seven: they touched pen to paper; but they had not signed their approval of any treaty or terms. They'd but agreed to carry their recommendation back to the Nation. This they'd done, and the Nation spoke. *No* is relayed to the white men by Chief Micanopy. There it ends, by the red men's reckoning. But no:

More talk. More treaties. More trickery. Till finally one man rises. This half-breed arrives at a council whereat the whites push the treaties of both Payne's Landing and Fort Gibson, spread upon a table and showing the seven disputed signatures. This warrior rises, yes, walks to the room's fore, lets go a war cry, and signs the treaties with a slashing knife. This is Osceola.

Who now rules the warring Seminole.

So, as I took to the King's Road that winter, I was not the world's only wanderer, no. Seven chiefs there were, far away and wandering. And if I sought a lost love, they sought a lost world.

They'd not find one.

Nor will they now; given what's come.

48

Southward

BEFORE leaving St. Augustine, I'd made due preparations.

Into my haversack went some foodstuffs, lesser (and lighter) tools of the Craft, a second shirt, and little else. And though I'd not heard from those whom I'd tried to summon with my brass bells—shining in my trees like golden apples—still I practiced a rite sent me by Eugénie, whereby one solicits the Aid of the Dead; thusly:

Into a hardwood bowl, mix this:
1/2 ounce of Frankincense incense
3/4 cup of Sandalwood incense
1/2 cup of Musk Powder
1/4 cup of Wormwood (crushed)
2 cups of Wood Betony (crushed)
1/4 cup of Allspice

1/2 cup of Vetivert Powder
1 teaspoon of Tobacco
1/2 teaspoon of Saltpeter
1 teaspoon of Verbena leaves (crushed)
2 teaspoons of Solomon's Seal (powdered)

Cover and set aside. When next night falls, mound 13 teaspoons of this mixture upon a black dish bearing no marks. Light each mound, starting furthest from you and proceeding widdershins around the dish. As the smoke rises, set a black candle upon the dish and entreat the Dead (by name, if known) to play well upon your Fate. This done, set a pinch of Solomon's Seal in each corner of each room in your house, and with a rag of black cloth rub grease onto every doorknob. On the midnights following, burn the mixture in mounds of nine till it is gone.

Of course (as sisters will) I'd had to improvise: Eugénie's spell called for treating the doorknobs with grease gotten from the boiling down of a dog, cat, or rooster ("black, perforce"), or a cow's hoof. Disinclined to such foul work as that, I opted not for grease but for oil, pressed from olives. So: perhaps I perverted the spell; for I cannot say I saw its effect. . . . Silence; all was silence. Again I'd been forsaken. O but the dead, seeming deaf, do sometimes intercede unseen, slyly, quietly; of this I reminded myself.

Further, I tied onto my left wrist a kerchief of yellow satin on which I'd sewn concentric circles in brown threads, filling the center circle solidly with cross-stitching. Thusly I asked the aid of Salango, loa to those in danger; and this I sought to ensure by leaving an offering: an earthen pot of cooked beans set upon my kitchen sill.

Rather more practically, I stuffed in my pocket a piece of

paper on which I'd written several declarations and questions in those languages I was like to encounter: Muskogee, Hitchiti, Spanish, Italian, Greek . . . for en route I'd have no recourse to my translational *tisane* of old.

I am no slaver. I search for a free woman who has run from St. Augustine.
Have you seen a woman with skin like creamed coffee and violet eyes?
Flower'd-Face, she is called. Liddy, also.

Such were my preparations, both Crafty and practical. All that remained was the hiring of a horse, and the strapping of my wary self to its saddle.

The roads were of ever lessening width beyond St. Augustine. Finally I found myself on paths unpassable to carts; and then narrower trails nearly ovegrown with greenery. I'd set out southerly; for Yahalla had most recently heard talk of Celia at Volusia; from which trading spot several roads ran, like spokes in a wheel.

I skirted Matanzas at a trot; though in fact I sensed no deathly disquietude there.

Down the coast I went, upon my nameless horse. I grew used to the mount, and even spurred it to speed as the byways allowed. We kept to the deep shade of hammocks when we could. Save for the slow clopping of hooves, we were silent as a blown leaf. I listened to insect-song, and the fronds whispered on what wind there was. Snakes I heard slithering o'er the scrub; and I was ever watchful for those known to stream from the trees. There were deer, of course. And wolves I heard. Once or twice I sensed a heavier tramping, too near; and listened with relief as the threat trailed off.

Often we rode near enough the beach to hear the surf; and our first night out we, rather I, slept upon the white sands, tucked in the lee of a dune whose grasses sang me to sleep. My horse I'd tethered to a gumbo-limbo. At dawn, I rose; and on we rode.

My map led us to the Bleach-yard; and from thence it was onto the Money-Bank, where the surf is legended to have once combed coin from off a Spanish wreck. Far less poetic was Mosquito, named for that area's too populous pest. Soon time was of no consequence; which is to say, I forgot what day it was. The land showed a sameness; and had it not been for my map, a compass, and the plainspoken straightness of the road, I'd have sworn we rode in circles. . . . Perhaps we did.

I had as my loose goal the headwaters of the river St. John's; for I'd read with interest the annals of the Messieurs Bartram—John and Billy, father and son—and learned that the great river starts in the south and flows northward, toward the sea. This very few rivers do. . . . Odd: I found I was developing a great sympathy for that lost and shambling river.

I saw springs of pure blue and lakes of brown, and rode with saw grass and sedge slashing at my legs. Cypress climbed skyward, and water oaks showed banana-leafed barbs of cat brier, winding high into the canopy. I spied limpkins as well as ibises, snakebirds and species I cannot catalogue. Herons I knew—shaded white and blue—as they poked in tannic streams. Where it seemed the river ought to begin, I saw nothing to mark said fact upon the floodplain. By then I'd slipped far far south; and when finally it seemed naught lay ahead but the Never-Glade, I altered our course: northward, and west toward a setting sun. . . . In time we gained Volusia proper.

There I was able to reprovision myself—I'd a store of pickled fruits and hardtack—for a journey further west; for, though none whom I encountered had heard tell of Celia, I was directed toward a maroon encampment—said to be friendly—on the shores of Charlotte Harbor: southwest, this was.

The trail—easily found, and easily followed—is now but a blur of browns and greens. Indeed, it was so numbing a slog that often I resorted to my liquor skin, desperate for daylit dreams to hurry the days. Blessedly, before suffering hardship of any sort, we'd well nigh crossed the territory.

I'd been well directed to the camp; and there I was welcomed, if not roundly so. Perhaps I was too travel-worn to seem a threat; and surely my appearance told I was no agent of the government, come in search of illicit trade. From the Indians, black men, and Cubans I encountered I had food for free, but paid well for wine and stronger spirits to fill my skin. And O, how happy I was to sleep upon a chickee that night: a thatched platform set three, perhaps four feet above the hammock.

There was the Seminole-style chickee, yes, but also two broad log houses built to sturdier, nay whiter specifications; for only white men presume permanence upon the land. At the settlement there were many women, working here and there; and at the camp's edge I came upon children at play in a ditch dug for the purpose. I understood they'd been hidden; for when they resumed their play—casting a wary eye my way—they spoke in signs, were silent lest they draw attention. For yes: there were runaways here; and—at this camp sitting so near the travelers' and traders' routes—all were watchful of slavers.

Tired of travel, I stayed at this camp three days; for the sleeping was safe, the food good. I'd assumed the fare would be plain, but it was not. Corn, beans, squash, et cetera: the staples; but also there were nuts and berries I'd never tasted. There I first met that odd, globular fruit the Spaniards call *toronja*. (Grapefruit, white men call it; owing to the clustered way it grows upon its tree.) Hearts of palm, too, hewn from the core of the cabbage tree. And I suppose it was owing to the Cubans then resident that I had plums and maguey on which to feast, as well as coffee and cane; which latter product they brought in their canoes, the stalks stretching bow to stern. Too, we had meat; including that of the gopher, or terrapin; turtles fished from under palmettos. O yes, a feast this was. And there I ate as I hadn't in a long, long while, knowing not that well north of where we sat the reserve Seminole were starving.

Sated, well victualed, I nearly forgot my hurry. Too, I'd asked tens of people, and had gotten no news of Celia. But then, my second night at camp, there came to sit beside me a white man, a trader whose route mirrored mine: down from Tampa he'd come, out of Espíritu Santo bay and along the coast, onto Charlotte. Mosquito was his goal. By the light of a late-night fire we spoke.

"A runner, you say? A nigrah? Black, but not overly so? Well, many there are out there, many. You couldn't count all them outliers if'n you had a hundred hands, five fingers per. But you talkin' now of one with . . . with partic'lar looks, eh? Hmm," said he, "yes'r, it seems—"

"You've seen her?"

"Seen her? No. I ain't seen her. . . . But I have heard tell of one such. Might she have run from the North, not more'n a year past?"

"No," said I, crestfallen, "the woman I'm looking for ran from—"

"North Florida, I mean to say. Up St. Augustine way, wasn't it?"

"Yes, yes; she ran from St. Augustine."

"Hmm," said the trader. "Hmm," and I thought he'd wait out my best offer. But I had too little on me; nothing, really, save . . . save for some notes drawn on the Planters' Bank. But just as I made to draw forth my money, resigned to counting each note onto the trader's hardened palm, he said:

"The Cove. Yes'r, that's it. Up Fort Brooke way, I heard tell of a nigrah woman with bright eyes—white eyes—who came one day to a camp lyin' well outside the Cowford; or what's to be called Jacksonville now, I s'pose, in honor of—"

"Yes, yes," I said, "but what of the woman?"

"Well now," said he, picking at his teeth with the tine of his fork, "them red folk up that way, they runnin' this way and that nowadays, and draggin' their black folk with 'em, too. Skittering like lice off'n a scalp, they all is."

"The Cove?" I led.

"Yes'r. As I heard it told by one, this nigrah—who'd fetch a price, certain; if y'all speak true of the figure she's cuttin'—she be lyin' out with others in the Cove of the Withlacoochee."

Out came my map, so fast the trader thought it funny.

I, however, found nothing funny in what followed; for he set his thick and nail-less forefinger upon my map and said, "You're sittin' here, as we speak. And the Cove, well, it sits between the two Withlacoochees—the Big and the Little—and that's . . . way . . . up . . . here."

His finger traced a route, finally falling still upon a spot far north. I read the rivers' names. I could reach it, said he, in ten days of hard riding. "Maybe less," I was told, "if the rains fall light, and don't set them damned trails to sucking at your horse's shoes. I *hates* that slowin'-down sound." He made a sucking, slurping sound, by which he meant to mimic mud; or so I supposed. But already I'd risen, nodded my thanks, and turned away, lest the firelight find my welling tears.

Had I ridden this far to fail, to surrender? Or would I hie northward, toward the Cove, sitting due west of where I'd set out from?

That night I decided I'd retrace my route, and return home to St. Augustine. Yes: I'd let it all devolve to failure. I'd leave Celia to the fate she'd found. And what then seemed sensible, I will here call cowardly. . . . O, but this confession is for naught; for I changed my mind the next day.

I woke to find the camp quite active; and soon I knew it: traders had come in the night. Skins were spread o'er low branches. Bottles of this and that were being passed. Beadwork was being torn at with teeth, to test its strength. Beneath the cover of this rude commerce I'd slip from camp.

I packed saddlebags and my haversack. I thanked the black woman whose chickee I'd shared, and bought her a fistful of beads. She'd a daughter, perhaps ten, whom I'd let braid my hair—for long it was, and wild—and this girl, name of Pau-kée, I hugged. Too long it'd been since I'd touched another: this was the saddening thought I held to as I quit the camp, walking my horse past that fire pit where now there sat men I'd not met: the newly arrived traders. Cubans, these were. Young and rough; such that I was hastening past them, eyes lowered, when I heard one of them speak a name. It settled like a shroud o'er that assembly; but I heard it as hope. Silence. He spoke it a second time. At first I thought I'd misheard him. But this second time the name came plainly, such that I, too, fell still and silent.

For he'd spoken the name of Sweet Marie: the witch of whom I'd been warned.

Riojo, they called him. And his regret at having spoken the name came in time with my resolve. "Can you take me to this Sweet Marie?" I asked, once I'd lured him from his fellows. . . . Surely the legended sister could, *would* lead me to Celia; and directly so.

The trader proceeded to deny all knowledge of Sweet Marie, and smarted each time I spoke the name. I repeated my question; and earned as response a flat and most definitive no; but he did not walk away. His chin he let fall to his chest. His eyes uprolled toward mine. And I understood: he had his price.

"How much? How much to lead me to this wi . . . this woman?"

I was glad I'd not doled out my store of notes to last night's trader; for now nearly all of them would go to Riojo; who spoke this caveat even as he counted: "I will not lead you to her."

"Then you will tell me where to look?"

"No," said he. "I cannot tell you where to look. None can. But I can set you ashore where you will not need to look."

I asked what he meant; and he said it a second time:

"No need to look"; to which words he appended these: "She will find you."

Not far west of the camp, we launched Riojo's skiff into a slow-flowing stream; from whence we fast achieved the harbor, and open water beyond. The sun had not yet reached its height by the time we betook the Gulf, sailing its shoals, keeping close to the coast.

I sat at the fore of the dugout, watching for snags and such. Riojo poled and paddled us through the shallows, and spoke not at all. When finally I turned to warn him of something—a shadow in the water—I saw what it was quieted him: fear. Fear absolute.

I turned back to the bow, and my watch. The shadow had passed. So it was we broke o'er naught but the tea-colored sea; and sailed on, ever on.

Finally, Riojo set me ashore. Rather, he poled inland to where the waters were shallow enough for me to step from the dugout and walk ashore. When I turned to wave, to signal that I was safe, I saw that the Cuban—silent whilst we sailed, and refusing to speak on the subject of Sweet Marie—had already turned. Surely he sailed back to the encampment, where he'd add my horse to his reward. Having swapped pole for paddle, he did so hastily; and not once did he look back, no doubt deeming it bad luck to look upon the dead.

He was forsaking me; selling me to my death for a fistful

of notes and a horse I'd not bothered to name. Only then did I regret the risk I'd taken. There I stood on a white sand beach bounded by mangrove and sea grape, without a mount on which to make my way. I had my haversack and nothing else. I was barefoot, my boots tied astride my shoulder, my stockings wadded and stuffed in their maws. My pants I'd rolled to the knee. Beneath my swaddling, salt—from the sea, from sweat?—was but one of many irritants. O, but I'd little choice now; and so, with the sun high, and no clouds to occlude it, I set to walking the strand, following the line of detritus drawn by the tide: shells, sea grass, piscine skeletons, et cetera.

On I walked. No boats could I see upon the green; and a vasty green it was, speaking too eloquently of my solitude. No sound but the surf, and the rustle of palms. A far wall of sea grape defined the dune.

Finally the sea grape showed a break: a path, leading inland. I determined to take it; and so sat upon higher, deeper, drier sand to don again my stockings and boots, and to take a fortifying draft from the skin slung o'er my shoulder. A second drink washed back a corner of the corn bread I carried, wrapped in sea-moistened moss. It was then I wondered if my heart was refusing my plan, the leaving behind of sun and sand for inland shade; for it beat a new tattoo: deep-spaced and timed to a count of four. But no: this pulse came not from me, but from the sand itself. It wended its way up my very spine. Ever steadier, ever louder it grew; till finally, looking down the beach to my left, or southerly, I saw it:

A single unit: horse and rider; coming on too fast to be friendly.

I ran, ran for that shaded opening leading off the strand.

True: I'd wanted discovery; for I hadn't the means to wander till I found Sweet Marie. As Riojo had said: she'd find me; and I needed her to. But here was a rider high upon a horse of too many hands. Bare-chested he was, with black hair twisting on a wind of his own devising; for he came on fast, indeed: the surf foamed o'er the horse's forelegs.

. . . The path, yes. O, but that designation is perhaps too kind; for the way was overgrown with roots and boles below, and vine-tied above. I had to writhe along in snaking fashion, knowing true snakes mocked my every step. On I went, as quickly and quietly as I could, turning time and again to see if horse and rider came behind. Surely this scrub was too dense, surely I'd evaded whoever had come riding, had come pounding down the sands to . . .

From such self-delusion, from such reverie I was rudely drawn; for, turning back to the darkling forest before me, I saw it snap to life:

The trees. Something moved amidst the pine and palmetto. It set the shaded green to swaying at some midstory level; and so it was too tall for a panther, lest said cat were stalking me by slinking tree to tree, limb to limb. A bear? No: too fast. A stag? Yes. I'd startled some grazing deer, surely, and now they were scampering off. I was relieved; and wrong:

For down onto the path before me there dropped a man of indeterminate color. And dress. And intent.

I'd have screamed, had I not been stunned.

Turning to run back in the direction of the open beach (despite the horseman thereon), I found my way blocked by a second man of similar description. I was stilled. And heard the first man let go a cry, one that chilled my fast-coursing blood. Thusly were two more men summoned, coming from without the green so that now I stood penned.

In the sweltering dark, reeking of rot, redolent, too, of sap-trickling pines, I knew fear as never before. As the men closed from all four sides, I saw them more clearly. First this one, then that. I spun, looking to each.

Hewn from hardwoods, they seemed: well squared and strong; and dark. In the deep shade I could not descry their races: red, black, or brown. And as they neared, what first I took for masks of a sort became faces. Faces too stiff, too stolid. Faces showing a deep impassivity. Faces like stopped clocks. Faces of an age out of keeping with the suppleness of their limbs; which now they displayed, leaping o'er logs and looped vines to close upon me.

Odd as those faces were, it was the clothing of the four that frightened me more; for I recognized it:

One wore a crown, the silver plate, nay silver paint of which had worn away. Its gemcrack gleamed 'neath what sun sifted down. Another wore a robe of regal purple, sewn with silver stars and symbols seeming those of an old-world wizard. The other two were plainly dressed, albeit in the fashion of a day long passed. By these clothes, by these costumes I identifed this band; for, some months prior, all the territory had been afire with news of the Shakespearean troupe that had been waylaid and slain on the plains well north of Tampa. One of the actors had lived to tell of the massacre, to speak of his own scalping. . . . Yes: here were murderers. Prince Hal, Prospero, Horatio, and Falstaff, I will call them; but I mean no mirth, and name them only for narrative expedience. And fast I'll write of what came to pass, the worst of which began as the Prince approached from the forestage, as it were, to stand before me. His eyes were drawn, shrunken, and desiccate. His face was well lined yet still taut; and called to mind a streambed run dry. O, but his chest was broad and unmarked save by muscle and a necklace of hammered silver disks, strung to hang like smiles, smiles that mocked his stone-set face.

Spurred by the Prince—who must have muttered something direct, though the words of the four were but a mess of Muskogee and Spanish, and an English sounding equally foreign—the three closed upon me: their quarry. And as they shoved, as they pushed and pulled at me, I saw they were each . . . incomplete. They'd been marred, maimed in too exact a way:

Prince Hal hadn't any ears; rather, they'd been cropped, their squared tops showing against his faux-silver crown. The deposed duke, Prospero, hadn't a full complement of fingers. Horatio limped terribly, foot-flappingly, such that I imagine one or both of his heel strings had been cut. And Falstaff had had his tongue shorn. This, though, did not stop the maroon—now I saw his skin showed both red and black blood—from speaking, or trying to: his stub of tongue shivered like a snake's rattle.

Imagine their demoniacal delight. Further: imagine it showing on their faces not at all. . . . Doubled was my dread.

Prospero danced his six digits upon me, seeking knife or gun. Falstaff brought his wooden visage so near I saw his skin: the brown of sun-cured steak; with bands of berry juice streaked upon it: war paint. Too, I saw now the scarred, flesh-soldered tip of his rattler's tongue. Horatio had my arms pinioned behind me, such that it seemed my shoulders would pop from their sockets.

We stood in deep shade, yes, and still I was clothed; but these scarified savages seemed to be urging one another on, toward the doing of misdeeds I need not describe. So fearful was I of what would come should they strip me, should they discover me in full and find . . .

Enfin, fearing I was to die either this way or that, I determined to fight, and upon the hip of Prince Hal I saw what I sought: a knife in its buckskin sheath. As I sprang for it . . . No. Stay; and rather let me say that just as I *determined* to spring for the knife, there occurred things so numerous and sudden that this listing must suffice:

Horatio tightened his hold upon me.

Unseen birds fled their roosts; and all the forest came suddenly, loudly alive.

Falstaff fell back from me to join Prospero and Prince Hal; and the lot of them seemed to cry, nay chant, nonsensically.

I heard again that drumming that told it plain: though the way had seemed too close, too overgrown for speed, here came that horseman from off the beach.

Horatio shoved me, such that I fell to the ground. And there I lay, amidst the stirred muck and the stink of things in decay. On came the rider; till finally the forelegs of a horse some fifteen hands high stopped so near me I might have reached to touch them. . . . Of course, I did not. I did nothing; for I was . . . in a state. A state whose nature I knew only when the rider leapt from his mount, lifted me to my feet, looked upon me—long and hard—and spun me, spun me to face my four attackers. Who—to a one—drew back. They stood shoulder to shoulder, stilled into silence; for there was light enough in those piney surrounds to show that my eyes had turned.

The time-set faces of those miscreants showed what they could of awe; but their bodies bespoke it the better as they turned their backs to me, dropped to a knee, and bowed their heads. Yes: at the sign of the Toad they all four fell. And whereas earlier they'd chanted, now a lowing rose from them; and the supplication within it only stirred me the more. O, but thankfully I've no need to confess that I took red retribution upon the four; for the fifth stilled me.

He, too, had ancient eyes, but his shone as those of the Shakespeareans did not: a fire still burned within the horseman, whose face showed its Indian contours despite being death-set, decayed, crisped, and sere. Those kindly eyes were set off by that long black hair, banded at the brow and bedecked with cock feathers fanning out to show their russet tones. He wore only a breechcloth, well beaded; and his body bore little relation to his face: the former was somehow . . . beautiful, the latter moribund.

This fifth set his hand upon me; but not as the others had.

Still I showed the witch's eye. I could feel it, and held it by dint of a risen, riled will. O, I was angry indeed; yet I held the horseman's eye. And his steely gaze upon my witch-turned one told me he'd seen the Eye before, yes.

I watched as the Indian stepped to the kneeling four. He tore the purple robe from off Prospero's shoulders and set his moccasined foot upon that man's back, shoving him down, into the dirt. I heard a crack that was either spine or foreteeth, finding rock or risen root. It seemed the fifth man would grind this duke—now deposed, truly—to dust. Indeed, the fallen man's hands—deficient of finger—clawed at the forest floor.

Rough words and actions, both, had he for the other three.

When finally he spoke it was to command the four; who rose and fell into single file, faces downturned. There they stood in the humid dark, ready to run behind us as we rode from the smothering green to retake the beach, so blindingly white.

Fivekiller, this was: he who hauled me up behind him, set me upon his steed, and delivered me to Sweet Marie.

49

Glass Lake

GAINING the beach again, we turned southward; and we rode a long while before cutting inland, o'er grass-grown dunes and into deepest shade. Before that eastward turn, Fivekiller stopped. So, too, did the four, standing well back, behind us in the surf. They turned from us; from me, specifically. They took to their knees. Heads bowed, it seemed they watched the sea suck at their footprints, at any sign of our having come this way.

Fivekiller did not dismount; rather he half turned in the saddle, so that for the first time I saw his face by the bright light of day. His skin was the ruddy red of fresh-baked brick, as smooth on his prominent cheeks as on his back. O, but that face! The eyes were well-deep and dark. The features fine, and regular; but their fixedness was eerie. What handsomeness he showed was that of a thing . . . preserved; as when once I'd found a dragonfly upon my sill, death-still, dry, and admired its armor, the fine webbing of its wings and its high color, which yet it held. His body, though, was supple, strong; for as we rode I'd no choice but to hold fast to my captor.

When Fivekiller turned, I saw he meant to address the kneeling four. Evidently, he'd intended to requisition one of their kerchiefs, or a length of something with which to bind my eyes; but instead he saw the yellow fabric I wore around my wrist: talisman to the loa Salango. He untied and took it; and though it seemed he knew it for witchery, still he tied it so as to blind me. And blind me he did: the yellow of the silk stifled the yellow of the sun. Only then did we make our inland cut.

After riding a while more, we stopped to drink from an upwelling spring, the trill of which told me I was thirsty, very much so. Fivekiller untied my blind, and I saw the Shakespeareans sitting at a distance, forgoing water in favor of a skin they passed in silence. Their backs were toward me. Some great tide had turned; this was plain: I'd a power now, born of the witch's eye. Though their fear was extreme, I did not attribute this to Sweet Marie, which now seems foolish; but I understood that ragged, denatured band knew of witchery. As did their leader, certainly; for:

Fivekiller took my haversack from me and dumped its contents onto the ground, where first he'd laid a tray of sorts: sea-grape leaves snipped from off a rambling stand. He was not curious, not idly so; rather, he was taking stock of what I carried, as if readying to report on same. So it was he untied pied scraps of fabric, and found within them such items as I'd thought to pack: the ingredients of spells I'd cast on Celia, if ever I found her. Some of these bespoke Western witchery, and the *stregharia* I'd come to favor. Others bespoke voodoo: *cascara sagrada*, Gilead buds, wood betony, quince seed, meadow queen, et cetera; all of it crushed, of course, for easier carriage, and tied into the scraps or set in tiny vials of sundry sort. Of course, I carried a complement to the Book I then kept. This was a hidebound journal of handy size into which I'd press biota for later discovery—leaves, skins, and such—and onto the pages of which I'd copied certain spells that might prove useful: to break the love-bound, to lessen or transfer their allegiance, et cetera. Too, as ever, the Book held my innermost thoughts. These Fivekiller perused. Whether he could read the words or not, I did not know; but by the time we remounted, it seemed he knew me for what I was: I'd shown the Eye earlier, yes; but also—being fearful, clinging to his back as we rode—I suppose I'd pressed my bound breasts to his back, and further betrayed myself.

We'd come to a clearing. I'd no idea where we were, save southeasterly from where I'd been taken. And I knew it for a clearing only when I felt the sun shining without filter, directly down. The air, too, was lighter than it had been within the wood. Finally my blindfold was taken from me: a clearing, yes; but not of the ordinary sort.

There spread before us a savannah freshly mown; but when my eyes adjusted to the sun, and to sight, I saw the ground was black: burned, not a season past. Somehow the fire had been confined to a perfect circle: the bordering slash pine, bay, and bastard ash showed no blaze marks. The hearty palmetto had returned, of course; and fiddleback ferns, maidenhair, lesser grasses, and saplings were asprout. Upon this charred land there grazed long-horned cattle: a herd of ten, twelve head. But these I soon discounted; for this odd meadowland bounded a spring, or limestone sink, full of water so blindingly blue I was transfixed.

Blue and still. Perfectly still. Center all in this clearing, spreading like a flat-cut sapphire. And within the sink there sat an island, dense with growth, and dark. Perfect circles, they seemed—savannah, sink, and island—set concentrically.

Across the clearing, just inside the forest wall, there stood a second, smaller clearing; and here Fivekiller picketed his horse, alongside four more. Coming out again onto the burned land, I understood our destination to be that island sitting in the too-pellucid pool; for there lay a raft of lathed cypress. On this we poled o'er that jeweled lake; and never, never had I seen its like.

It was still, as said; and I could see to its depths. There, on a bed of white sand, sat shells and stones and . . . things less suited to the scene: a rifle, I saw, and pale branches—broken and lying massed—which now I wager were bones. A shadow flitted across the sandy bottom; and I looked up to see a vulture circling. I watched for fish, but saw nary a one. How deep this water went, I cannot say: fifteen feet or fifty? Neither do I know from whence it sprang.

Soon my regard shifted; for things far stranger awaited us upon the island's shore, clotted with cypress and live oak maned in Spanish moss. I refer to things living, things unseen but heard; which hearing was accompanied by my blood going as still as the water we'd traversed. A breathing, this was; and as we neared I mistook a concomitant sound for oncoming thunder. But no thunder, this. And indeed those sounds married to a roar as our raft slipped under an oaken arm to tap the shore. There I saw eight bamboo cages of unsturdy construction, stacked two high. In these there glittered the sixteen eyes of eight panthers, turning tight circles.

Each cat wore a collar braided of palm; and beside the cages—themselves set upon a raft—there hung withes, or long leads braided of hemp, horsehair, and husks. From another tree there depended the haunch of an animal—a deer, I suppose—aswarm with flies, half of its flesh already cut away and fed to these felines, who yet yearned for more. Flesh, that is: deer or otherwise.

"Come," said Fivekiller to me. "No reason to fear the cats.

Not yet." And then he released the Shakespeareans: "Go," said he; and they ran as if the cats came behind.

I walked as directed, with Fivekiller following. Glad I was to put the cats behind me; but for all I knew I walked toward worse. As these:

Trees; death-adorned.

Yes: three skeletons: human: hanging from the high branch of an oak, and decomposed to disparate stages. On one I saw the scraps of a soldier's uniform. The second had hung the longest in its noose of slip-knotted vine; for bones had begun to fall from their place to the ground below. The third was naked, its stomach distended; and—heinously—the soft flesh of the cheeks, the chest and buttocks had been beset. By whom? By what? I hadn't long to wonder; for the higher branches of this very tree were thick with carrion fowl: grizzled, fat-bellied buzzards, brown and black blots upon the branches. Fish crows, too, had come in for their share; for one of these now let go its cry, as if to warn me away from the meat of the hanged man. At this cry the tree was vacated, the birds rising in black waves and twisting away. Only the dead men remained.

How long I stood, staring up, I cannot say; but there came a gentle shove from Fivekiller, saying, "She waits."

I kept my eyes upon the ground, and followed a path worn through the muck and mire; thusly I saw but a few feet ahead. So it was another clearing came upon me suddenly.

A fourth circle set within the larger three. This was sunlit; such that in stepping from the shade, I blinked back the sight of . . . another corpse? This one slung o'er a saddle tied between the thick, down-dropping roots of a strangler fig. This saddle swung two, perhaps three feet above the ground. O, but stay: this withered, withering thing was no corpse.

Here was she: Sweet Marie; and never was a witch worse named.

* * *

When first I saw her she was slung o'er that saddle, in a posture of half sleep: arms hanging down to the dirt of the ground. And between her spindly arms there ran—as a filthy river, flanked by chalky banks—a flipped-over length of hair, the likes of which . . .

O, hideous this was! It was a burnished gray, veined in silver and black. From its widest point—at her nape—it tapered five, six feet to a point, like the scaled tail of a crocodilian. Here was hair that had never been cut. Too, the braid of many strands had been woven long ago, and rarely if ever washed; for it stank. As to the action within it, well, it was a veritable hive. All down its length winged things were aswarm, bright-bodied flies and white ants. Like a ladder it was; and multilegged, carapaced creatures scuttled up and down its length. I saw two translucent scorpions scurry to its frayed end, bristly as sawn rope; from whence they gained the ground.

I stood, sickening, in observation of this sister. Profoundly did I wish I'd never sought her. Far better to have left her legended.

Fivekiller let fly a whistle, and soon there came through the trees courtiers of a sort. Maroons: men of mixed, indeterminate race. They were naked, or nearly so. Blessedly, I saw none of the Shakespeareans; but this lot was worse.

One hobbled into the clearing on a leg of wood; rather, a limb had been whittled to match his own, and was harnessed to his thigh stump. The others showed lesser losses: half arms, fingers, a nose shorn from its place. It was this noseless one—again, supremely fit, yet with a face as fixed as every other I'd seen, save for holes where his nose had been—whom Fivekiller sent to assist Sweet Marie. The rest knelt at the clearing's edge, their backs turned to their mistress; and to me, I suppose.

No Nose approached Sweet Marie, bent, and took up her

length of hair. He passed it o'er her back, between the vines of her sleep-saddle, and there held it draped across both his arms, moving in accord with the crone's rising up.

O yes, she rose up and stepped from behind her saddle. Slowly, slowly, to show:

Bare feet rising to coltish legs, banded and bony; and knees like knots. The sun-dark flesh of her thighs—which showed; for she wore a skirt of sackcloth tied at her crotch—was slack. She was emaciated, slight, standing not five feet in height. The plane of her stomach was concave. And too near her waist there hung her teats, within a halter of that same soiled sackcloth. Her ribs showed, clearly enough to count. The skin of her chest was thin, and seemed shriveled to crepe. Elsewhere, her skin was scrofulous. It hung in sags and folds, and showed nodes of no color. Patches of pink, too, where it was raw from blisters, burns, and sores. And then there was her face:

Which bespoke beauty gone bad:

Set between high cheekbones were sloe-shaped eyes. The irises were gray, as spittle may be described; and their surrounds—which ought to have been white—were rheumy, and corn-colored. The lids were lashless and darkly wet. These she blinked inconstantly: now fast, five times; now slowly, or not at all. The nose was snub, and oddly delicate. The mouth severe, as though it had been honed on steely words such as those she then spoke, in a voice hoarse from infrequent use:

"Set her there," said she, with a directional nod. "Upon the speakers' spot."

I was led to where the ground was worn away, before an aged oak. And there I waited, my eyes upon the creature who slowly approached, the death's-head Indian tending her train of hair. This he set upon a hook; for there, into the tree before which I stood, there'd been driven—long ago; for it was rusted—a curl, iron-wrought. Other trees showed the same: hooks, hammered into the wood at the height of her head.

Relieved of the braid's weight, Sweet Marie stood to her full height and yet stared up at me as Fivekiller approached her and spoke into her ear words I did not need to hear; for it was then I knew for certain he'd discovered me, both as witch and man-woman. And surely, as now I knew she must, the hag bade me come nearer to where she stood, the better for her to . . .

"Both," said she. "Both?" And up shot her horn-hard hand, to prod, to knead . . . to *know* me.

When I withdrew from her touch, her hair had surrendered its slack to the hook, and her scalp shifted back to show a forehead too broad, too rounded and high. I saw she wore chandeliered earrings in the Seminole style: beaded and long. As she came on, still, still I withdrew; till finally I was beyond her reach. Surely the skin at her hairline would tear. "No, no, dear," said she. "Struggle not from Sweet Marie." Whereupon I willed the Eye; but so, too, did she.

"A strong one. And showing both sexes. . . . You are a thing entirely new to Sweet Marie." She drew out the word *new,* insultingly so, and spoke it as if it she'd spell it with a *G: gnew;* as if I were of some pestilential species midway between gnat and gnome. Too, she hummed as she took me in with unwitched eyes. That is: she'd blinked away the witch's eye faster than I'd ever seen a sister do. My Eye held, I knew. And through it I saw Sweet Marie in greater detail:

She was far older than I. Telltales, there were: the long lobes from which those earrings depended; teeth bearing a blueish sheen; and the ridge which descended from her nose to her upper lip was creviced, and showed a silvered mustache. Her breasts were pendulous within the worn sackcloth of her halter. Around her neck she wore the calcified skull of a snake, well fanged; but what else I'd mistaken for necklaces I now saw as dirt: dirt ringing her neck, as if in tree-like testament to her great age.

"Why," she asked, of a sudden, "why have you sought Glass Lake?" She swept her stick-thin arms, swept them to indicate the whole of her realm. Doing so, she loosed a musk I shan't describe. "Why have you sought Sweet Marie?"

Before I could answer, Fivekiller whistled again; and at this the courtiers dispersed like shot, all save the carrier of her hair, who knelt now in her shadow, his ruined face turned to the dirt.

"Why?" asked the witch, when only we four remained in the clearing.

"I come seeking help," said I. "I search—"

"Help? Help, do you say?" And she laughed a laugh as shrill as the limpkin's cry. "Succor and such—'help,' as you'd have it—these things are not the forte of Sweet Marie. Nor does she speechify for free, but only as it pertains to trade. . . . Do you understand Sweet Marie as she speaks?"

I nodded only; for now she'd come so near I held my breath against her stench.

"Trade," said she. "I speak of trade. What is this . . . this help you seek, this thing you search?"

"I am searching for a woman," said I. "A friend. Name of Celia."

"Are you?" She seemed amused, and drew back to ask, "A witch, is this?"

"No. A friend, as I say. She's run—"

"'Run'? You brave *this,*" and she rapped at her chest, hard, sounding out its hollow, "you brave Sweet Marie to search out an absconder? Fool!"

"She is no slave," said I. "Not anymore. She is a friend."

In rapping at her chest she'd nicked a finger upon her fanged necklace. It bled. Bothered, she hissed: a summons of a sort; and the noseless Indian spun upon his knee to lick, to suck the witch's blood from off her filthy finger.

"Come," said she to the slavering man; who understood her meaning as I did not. He unhooked her hair and led Sweet Marie back to her saddle, where he staked the braid again and lifted the witch up to sit upon the worn leather. She swung, childlike, as she spoke. "So then," said she, "the Witch of Two Sexes seeks information from Sweet Marie. Is this so? . . . Celia, you say?"

"Yes."

"No!" shouted Sweet Marie, such that unseen birds bounded from branches, which bobbed now, freed of their weight. "That name she has shed. As a snake will its skin." She spoke not at all for some while: . . . two, three, four arcs of the swing; and then: "The one you seek, white men call her Liddy; and the outliers call her Flower'd-Face. . . . Sweet Marie knows this."

"You . . . you know her?" I'd not quake before this sinister sister; but O, my legs were loose, my knees aknock: Celia was near.

But the witch would not answer; instead, she swung. Violently now, rising higher, describing as broad an arc as her staked braid allowed.

Finally: "So it is this Liddy you seek?"

"Yes. Is she . . . here?" I wanted to find Celia, desperately so; but far more did I hope to hear that she'd never graced so plutonian a place as Glass Lake.

This question Sweet Marie thought rich; and again her laughter resounded through the green and gold, and through the deep shadows of her domain. "No," said she. "What use has Sweet Marie for a Negress, no matter how prettily made? None. None! Sweet Marie wants no tarry wench." And she pumped her legs, swinging so high her hair threatened to tug her down onto the ground. No Nose saw none of this; for he had turned toward the trees, and stood as still as they. It was Fivekiller approached, lest this fall come to pass; but Sweet Marie stayed him thusly: "Sweet Marie wants no help." She freed a hand from the vine, from the swing's support, to point at me. "*That* witch does."

"Yes, I do."

"Say then the word *trade*. Say it!"

"Trade," said I.

"And if Sweet Marie gives, will Sweet Marie get?"

"Yes," said I.

"And if Sweet Marie gives, and if Sweet Marie gets, and if Sweet Marie lets the Cocked Witch live, what will the traded thing be?"

"Whatever you want." I'd let her insult me, threaten me, as long as she told what she knew of Celia. "Whatever Sweet Marie wants," said I.

Raking her toes through the dirt, the witch slowed her swing, leapt from the saddle, fast took her hair from off its hook, and crossed the clearing in a near crouch. Now she stood not a foot from me, cradling her hair as if it were a babe at suck. Said she, "Trade, yes. Sweet Marie will trade. Sweet Marie will give you the Flower'd-Face, yes. But in return Sweet Marie wants from you . . . something." She rose onto her toes so that verily I smelled the next word she spoke:

"War," said she. "Sweet Marie wants war."

50

The Secreted Sister

"SPEAK a sister's name." This command came from Sweet Marie.

We'd followed her from the clearing, Fivekiller and I, with No Nose holding her hair. Through the virid growth we went. Ever darker it grew, ever more shadowed as the sun went west. The island had not appeared so large as this, yet it took well nigh a quarter hour to reach the witch's encampment.

Smudge pots set upon bamboo sticks defined it, and burned to smoke mosquitoes away. Not quite a clearing, this; but trees had been felled to make way for two buildings. Nay three there were: two longhouses of notched pine and thatch ran parallel to each other, ending at a third, much smaller building. The logs were bowed and bent, such that one might easily have passed a hand within; water, too, would pass in and out of such a structure, leaving it to stand. But did the waters of Glass Lake—so lifeless, so eerily still—ever rise? The third structure was a square, its logs tightly sealed with tabby: that admixture of lime and sand and silt. At first I took it for a smokehouse. Within the courtyard formed of these three buildings, I saw more misshapen men at work. No women; only men. And as we came from without the forest, all fell still. The tanning of hides stopped, the grinding of grain stopped, the mending of seines stopped, the stoking of fires stopped as all fell to genuflection; backs were shown, stony faces turned to the ground.

No Nose was dispatched. Handing Sweet Marie her hair, he raised not his ruined face to hers; and left her thusly: by taking two backward steps, turning on a heel, and sprinting off. This spurred the witch: I heard her hiss after him; or perhaps she spat.

Into the right-side building we went. It was raised up, and reached by stepping onto flat-cut boles of increasing height. Four, five feet above the forest floor it sat; with the four sides of its understory penned in bamboo. I thought I heard a rustling below-foot as I stepped onto the gallery, which ran the length of this longhouse and looked out o'er the yard. I remained beneath its overhang of thatch as Sweet Marie entered through a door of deerhide, hanging in strips. I saw the men resume their work, now their mistress was out of sight.

The inside of the longhouse was plain, and sparsely furnished. Windows had been cut into every wall, but still it was dark. In the shadows, I discerned more stumps set about as chairs, topped with canvas cushions oozing moss. Two plank tables had been laid end to end; and a third spread across the narrow room, before its far wall. No one was within, save Sweet Marie, Fivekiller, and myself.

Following Sweet Marie to the room's end, I heard a sort of snuffle, a snorting, and the plank floor bucked beneath me. I stopped. Silence. A few steps more and, well . . . had it not been for Fivekiller setting his hand to my elbow, I'd have stepped onto if not through a grate, a grid of bloodied bamboo set into the floor; and no doubt I'd have lost a heel to . . . Stay. I'll get to the telling of that grotesquerie.

For now let me say I was directed to a dark corner, where—folded upon the floor—I found a change of clothes: buckskin slacks and a full blouse that tied at the wrists and neck, the better to keep stinging things from off the flesh. This blouse was not black, as first I thought, but rather its color had been set by a boiling in indigo: it was the blue of a half-mooned midnight; and I'd wear it long and well.

We three sat on the stumps, ranged triangularly. Sweet Marie had her back to the wall upon which she'd hung her own hair. Soon others entered from off the gallery, backward, bowing to the dark wherein we sat. Tallow candles were lit to little effect. And two men—whose deformities I was spared by the dimness within—set about preparing a meal.

It was as we sat in attendance of same that Sweet Marie spoke, saying:

"Speak a sister's name."

"Sebastiana d'Azur," said I.

"No. Sweet Marie does not know her. Another."

"She lives in France," said I, "and knew its queen before—"

"Another!" She drove her horned heel down upon the pinewood floor. Yes: there was something beneath us; for now it stirred and knocked with its . . . what? Paw, claw, snout? Or perhaps it was a hand I heard, rapping.

"Lenore," said I, seeking distraction from such thoughts. "They call her the Duchess and—"

"Ah, yes," said this hideous sister, "Sweet Marie has heard tell of the New York whore. And the cats knew well a witch of her late acquaintance, yes, yes. A witch who sought Sweet

Marie, like you. A witch who tried to . . . to take from Sweet Marie. A witch whom the cats tracked and tore and—"

"*Whist,*" or a sound similar came then from Fivekiller; and stunned I was to see the crone thusly stifled. Too soon she resumed, asking of no one in particular:

"Is Sweet Marie forbidden to speak of the tracking cats in company?" Verily she mewled the question; but then she screamed, screamed so that I saw—with my own wide-open eyes—the two cooks start, terribly, and fall still. Their knives trembled in their hands. The blades shone slickly, darkly, catching what light there was. Fivekiller whistled, lightly, and the men retook to their work as the witch ranted on. "Sweet Marie wants no word of Frenchwomen and whores. Another!"

"Eugénie," I offered, "who hails from New Orleans. She was priestess to the queen, Sanité Dédé, but is not allied to Marie Laveau, the Widow Paris, who now—"

"No witch! No witch, this Widow Paris. A base conjurer, a broker of bone dust and song. A dealer in fear. Sweet Marie would strip the hide from off this *fausse* Marie, would flay her should . . . should *she* ever seek Glass Lake. . . . More. Sweet Marie wants more."

Doubtful it was that Sweet Marie would have heard of any other Cyprian; and no names came to me from out of the Books. . . . O but then there came one name, and quickly I spoke it; for Sweet Marie showed impatience with my silence:

"Peggy Eaton," said I. That most infamous of sisters, who then was resident in Pensacola.

Sweet Marie rose fast. She leaned near me, as near as her hooked hair allowed, and taking my chin in hand, turning my face full to hers, she showed the Eye and asked, "You know this witch? You know Sweet Marie's mistress of war?"

When I said I did not, Sweet Marie unhanded me, and sat. Was it relief at hearing that I did not know Peggy Eaton, that I was ignorant of what collusion there'd been between them, if any? Was it. . . . Alas, words are wasted in wondering as to Sweet Marie's ways, her whims, her wishes, and whatnot. Let this suffice: She sat, seeming satisfied. And soon our attention turned to supper.

I'd not had a meal of note since leaving camp in the company of Riojo; but what preparations I witnessd put my hunger off; for:

The cooks were tasking themselves with two terrapin then acrawl upon the table: flipping them, rending flesh from off the soft underbelly. Beyond the door, somewhere in the courtyard—from whence its smoke came—a fire had been set; to this the second cook went, presumably, turtle steaks in hand. He was replaced at the cooks' table by a third man, who came carrying two large redfish. These were fast filleted; which action I watched, thinking, *We are close to the shore. Good.* O, but my next thought was this: *There can be no escape. Already the cats have my scent.*

The cooks came and went in silence, showing that odd deference to the dark wherein we sat. Finally the third man—whose fault I could not find—approached, tin plates in hand. On these were turtle steaks and redfish, as well as a dollop of some well-spiced jelly. I followed the lead of Fivekiller and ate with my fingers. As for Sweet Marie, she looked at her plate, and though she seemed not to disapprove of its show, she handed it back to the man who'd brought it. She said nothing, but he fetched for her a pipe, already lit; and whilst we ate—Fivekiller and I—Sweet Marie puffed an acrid-smelling, green-smoking weed. That is, until a certain . . . *bonne bouche* was served:

Into the longhouse one of the cooks had carried, slung o'er his shoulder, what first I'd taken for a rug. A red rug, sewn of rags. But when he set it upon the gut-strewn table, I discerned legs and a longish neck. And wings. The candle flame shifting just so, there came a flash of shadowed scarlet and. . . . A flamingo. . . . Such birds were to me well nigh mythical; though in fact I had seen one before: the ubiquitous Mr. Barnum had shown one in New York, stuffed of course.

Yes: here was a full-grown flamingo; which then had its tongue wrested from it by that cook-chirurgeon via a process from which I could not turn away, though I had upon my own tongue a rubbery cut of terrapin, fast falling cold. The lower mandible of the bird he broke away by hand; whereupon he took up a knife to slit the long and slender neck, from the root of the bill to the pinfeathers. Out came the tongue, trailing its secondary parts. I swallowed the turtle away. And retched at so cruel a culinary act. Too, I knew the tongue would make its way to my plate.

Only for the flamingo tongue—cubed, uncooked, and served in a citrusy wash—did Sweet Marie set aside her pipe.

I hadn't a choice: that much was made plain. And so down I swallowed one, two, three pieces of the dense, oily, and too-rich organ. Of course, Horace writes of the Romans deeming the flamingo delectable, a delicacy; but that same populace fed Christians to cats. Risky, the adoption of Roman tastes. . . . And by way of Horace and sundry Roman horrors, I return to the understory of that strange Colosseum in which I sat, and to the grotesquerie referenced above.

For, as we ate—Fivekiller and I partaking whilst Sweet Marie piped and picked with filthy fingers at her flamingo—the three cooks set to ranging their station; cleaning up, as it were. The cracked shells of the terrapin, their feet and fins, the fish heads, Sweet Marie's declined portion, et cetera, all was swept onto the floor by the broad swipe of knives, hands and blood-dark brushes; and there it fell. A broom of reeds was brought, and this mass was swept toward that hole which earlier I'd stepped o'er; whereupon there began a violent knocking about below, and a rooting sound which bespoke boars, or some such carnivora.

Bristled snouts poked up through the bamboo grate. This

was latched shut, if loosely so; and I told myself no boar could launch itself up through the opening. Or could it? For it seemed they climbed aback of one another, desperately so. . . . A most disquieting scene, this; and one which worsened when Sweet Marie rose, took up her hair, and stole onto the pinewood stage. There, she brought her heel down upon the grate, occasioning the sound of tooth-crack. Yelping ensued. Finally, the boars receded. Through the floorboards I saw shadows pass. Again: silence; silence more eerie than any sound.

Sweet Marie took from off the table the flamingo carcass; and, shuffling with it slung o'er her shoulder, hung it upon a gallows of sorts: a hair-hook upon the wall; beside which there hung two others, their heads lolled to death-angles, their plumage blood-sullied and dull.

As Sweet Marie had moved, so, too, had two of the cooks slipped from the longhouse, leaving the third man, he who'd served us, he who seemed . . . complete. He: whom she attacked.

He did not hear her coming up behind him; and before he saw her, before he begged her indulgence with words belying his mask of placidity, she'd taken up a cleaver. To its blade there clung bone shards, shimmering scales, and blood; such that it seemed a jeweled thing. Was she unhappy with the man, with something he had or had not done? Again: Sweet Marie hadn't faculties of the regular sort, and reason bore not on her behavior. How could it, when what next she did was this:

Falling to her knees—with a knocking that brought again the boars—she hacked, hacked at the foot of the man around whose other leg she'd wound herself in the constricting style of a pythoness.

I stood, horrified. Fivekiller looked away, closing his eyes in as great a show of upset as he could evince.

The first three toes fell away of a piece, but the second two she dissevered separately. Another downswipe of the cleaver and a squared portion of the forefoot fell. The foot and toes Sweet Marie snatched up; laughingly, lightly, she tossed the flesh to the boars beneath the grate. The maroon bit back his pain as best he could, and badly bloodied his own lip in the essay; but it was Sweet Marie who screamed. She called toward the courtyard a command. Soon there came into the longhouse a man clutching to his chest—albeit with his one arm—what evidently the witch had called for: a basket.

From this basket, Sweet Marie drew a necklace of bloodroot, casting it o'er the crying man to stanch the life flow; but this styptic was slow to take effect, and the boars' tongues rose between the floorboards to taste, to take the running blood. She then cauterized the wound with seared punkwood. At this the man did finally scream, such that I set my hands to my ears. Between his teeth, the basket bearer set a silencing stick. From within her halter, Sweet Marie drew a greenish root; which she chewed to a certain consistency and spat upon the ruined foot. Finally, she bound the whole with green leaves and bandages of pine bark. And the Indian left the longhouse hobbled, leaning heavily upon his one-armed mate. Sweet Marie taunted him till he was gone from sight; whereupon she returned to the table, slowly, her braid dragging o'er the bloodied floor.

. . . From whence it came I cannot say, but I found strength enough to say, "Celia. . . . What of Celia? What of . . . Flower'd-Face?"

Nothing.

"Sweet Marie," said I, pleadingly, "where is she?"

"Far from here," said she, so offhandedly I rose fast, and set my stump to rocking. I stared down at the smiling sister. "Sit, witch," said she. Fivekiller's eyes—cold as stones in a stream—echoed the order; and so I sat. And waited what slight concession came:

"Far away, yes; but Sweet Marie will find her for you. . . . Time. It may take time. But Sweet Marie trades fairly, and will find your . . . your lost love." At this last, she laughed; and I knew it for true: here was cruelty incarnate.

51

The Spanish Waters

SWEET Marie kept to no calendar, heard not the tick of any clock; yet she was the Mistress of Time. To explain . . .

I cannot reckon too accurately my own time at Glass Lake; for days spent in servitude are best denied: one counts them at too great a cost. (Never was I told I could not leave Glass Lake; but I knew it.) Hours passed unto days, days unto weeks, weeks unto months. We sat southerly: the sun held sway: it was ever warm; and so the seasons passed too subtly, with scant distinction. Thusly did time accrete. Thusly was it confused.

The communal silence of Glass Lake I attributed to Sweet Marie's butchery, the misdeeds done upon the men; none of whom dared speak to me, or even meet my gaze. If I spoke to any man, he stilled himself and stared o'er my shoulder till I desisted. Some even fell with a tremble into their accustomed stance, rising to run once I'd released them. Fivekiller spoke, yes; but sparingly; and primarily when I was let to leave the island in his company. I ventured into the swamplands alongside my silent guide and guard, helping the husbandmen to hay the horses, or bring in beans or coontie for bread, but never could I gain a sense of where Glass Lake sits; for always I left the island blindfolded, and returned the same way. On this Sweet Marie insisted.

At first I kept from the witch, as best I could; but there was nothing, nothing with which to occupy myself. And so, in time, I turned to her. She made a great show of suffering me. On occasion I walked at her side—never was I asked to carry her hair; and so never did I have to refuse to do so—and she'd toss off this or that, opining that the purple fruits of the prickly pear were "delectable," or pointing her staff at some poisonous weed, pronouncing, "Leaves of three, let it be." If I asked her a question, directly, she'd huff or bluff, she'd go silent or lie. Rarely did she deign to answer. And the question she liked least was the one I most often asked: Had the letters she'd cast out with her runners and traders netted any news certain of Celia?

The witch later made me watch her at work, the nature of which . . . nay, there was nothing *natural* about her work, though she fancied herself a healer, of sorts. And in the longhouse opposite our odd refectory, Sweet Marie stored her "healing" wares. On the floor there lay a maze of multicolored vials, set in low stands of split and twined bamboo. There were knives and stiles and syringes; and tools of scarification. Among these the witch would walk, holding high her hair, lest she sweep anything from its place; for all was carefully ordered. When first she left me alone in this dispensary, I took an inventory that showed: guaiacum, sarsaparilla, lobelia, puccoon, cohosh, coca, jalap, cinchona, as well as balsams and herbs both indigenous and otherwise, had via her gardens or the mails, in which she so actively engaged. The garden sat beside the longhouse, and soon I was charged with its care and tending. Here was a poisonous plot, indeed. Vines of velvetleaf crept up and o'er the longhouse walls. Beneath a tree of angel's trumpet—its scent divine, its stamen deadly—there grew its lesser sibling: the coarse and sturdy devil's trumpet. Too, I tended pokeweed, bloodberry and sundry poppies. In my gardening I was guided not by Sweet Marie, but rather by Mead's *Mechanical Aspects of Poisons* (to which the interested witch is referred; as was I). This and other volumes I found within the library at Glass Lake, such as it was.

One, perhaps two seasons had passed before the witch showed me her store of books, which were few and far too specific. The *Pharmacopoeia Londinensis,* dated to 1618, set forth the attributes of many simples, listing such ingredients as mummy-dust, stag's penis, and the excrement of sundry creatures (Homo sapiens not least among these). Too, at Glass Lake I first read Boerhaave, whose last-century miscellany touts the effects of dragon's blood, oil of scorpion, troches of ground viper, crab's eyes, and chalk. Gratefully I found the tamer prescriptions of Esculapius. In addition to these and other tomes—from the *Materia Medica Americana* to its most current incarnation, the *United States Pharmacopoei*—there were tracts in the Indian languages, including a Seminole syllabary, written in the witch's own hand. Oddly, Sweet Marie kept no Book of her own; nor did she have any other witch's. That is: I found no *Books of Shadows*, though I pried away floorboards, felt in the crotches of the trees from which her saddles depended, et cetera. It seemed the sister preferred letter writing, sending her epistles off to secret correspondents via a runner. (Surely a post road ran near Glass Lake: rarely were the runners gone longer than two days. . . . Unfortunately, I cannot situate the sister's refuge, even now.)

Once, when it seemed summer had descended, Sweet Marie summoned me to the courtyard. There I found that despised Prospero of old. Now he proffered a gift, which I snatched from his fingerless hands: a *Complete Shakespeare* bound in kid; and no doubt had off the murdered mummers. Each day, at the break of day, I'd turn to the Bard—his was the sole book that mattered to me—and I'd read and read and read whilst waiting for Sweet Marie to use or free me.

One evening of that same summer I saw the men line up behind and beside the third of the camp's three buildings: the squared and sealed cottage, wherein Sweet Marie lived alone and unvisited by all but Fivekiller. They'd been summoned by the blowing of a conch shell, the same sound which drew me up from deep within *Macbeth*.

I came from without the longhouse. Torches had been lit and staked about the camp. By their light I saw the twenty-two men of Glass Lake; and counted them, as they stood in silent array. I saw that Sweet Marie had been busy of late: many of the men showed wounds still suppurating, yet to scar, and quite troublesome to see. Slowly, slowly, they filed past a smallish window cut into its side. There stood Fivekiller—the twenty-third man—handing amber vials to the brethren. These they threw back fast, as drunkards do. What elixir was this, which—like the waters of that river of the Cicones, of which we read in Ovid—turned to stone all those who drank it?

As I approached, no man did that shunning dance to which I was accustomed; so intent were they on their drink. It was dark before the last of them received it; whereupon they retired to their trees—those bridges of rope, platforms of pinewood, and hammocks woven of hemp which constituted their homes—and slept the sleep of the drugged. Meanwhile, o'er the island the animals roamed. Yes: on these Days of Dosage the panthers came from out their cages, the boars saw their penning bamboo lifted, and other animals arrived as well: black bears, wolves, foxes, and myriad birds . . . among which there was an odd harmony, a peace unknown to Noah.

All this I witnessed from a blind set high in the branches of a live oak, to which Fivekiller had led me. From that safe vantage—the tree was spiked, against any cat or bear seeking to climb it—we watched the witch walk her torchlit camp; for she alone dared the setting free of her menagerie. A ninth cat kept at her side. A panther seven, eight feet in length. Her pet: her familiar: Coacoochee, she called it.

I knew not what had transpired; but the indolence that overcame the men of Glass Lake lingered. When finally they woke and resumed their work—trading parties departed, cattle were rafted to the island for slaughter . . . —I understood: they were healing. Limbs I'd seen dissevered had grown in length, though their scars were freshly rent, red. Fingers sprouted—in knuckled increments—on hands from which they'd been hewn. Cut tongues regenerated such that men spoke, spoke to learn what could be said with an inch more tissue. Still others—pardon the indelicacy—sat stroking their sexes openly; and it was then I saw the particular suffering of those who appeared intact. Their members were uncommonly long, and wrist-thick; but they lacked scrotal sacks. Sickeningly, I knew then that reticule, that drawn thing that Sweet Marie sometimes wore around her neck, puckered and empurpled and filled not with gonads but with what the voodooists call gris-gris: powders, charms, witch-work of a sort; for every part of the men at Glass Lake grew back—the fingers fastest, in perhaps a month; legs and arms a half year or more—but the testes, no. And these eunuchs seemed the particular favorites of Sweet Marie. Foremost among them was Fivekiller.

O, but regeneration was the least of it. For a man could live without fingers, without a tongue, lacking this or that limb, but no man could live without the dispensed drink; for it was death's antidote the witch doled out.

* * *

How so? From whence had Sweet Marie come? . . . *Enfin,* know this about the Witch of Glass Lake:

Long about 1760 or so, when the Spanish were losing the peninsula for the first time, a Britisher—name of Rolle: Denys Rolle—had conferred upon him by the crown a settlement of some fifty thousand acres on the east-central plains of the peninsula. Thereon he meant to raise indigo on Oglethorpe's model—that of the Georgian plantation—save Rolle would use not slaves but white men and women willing to trade a seven-year indenture for overseas passage. In a word: he sought the destitute. Specifically, he'd reform a certain class of unhappy females, culled from the slums of London: whores, drawn from the Drury Lane district.

Rollestown failed, falling to disease and dissent. Few indentures saw their contracts through; instead, they fled. Some shipped back to Britain. Some went north, into colonies on the cusp of rebellion. Others stayed in Florida. One such was known as Mean Marie. This whore was a witch, and knew it; and when later she'd give birth to a baby girl they'd call the child Sweet Marie, to both distinguish it from its mother and (no doubt) will upon it a sweeter disposition.

As Fivekiller told it one night o'er a mandatory supper—we three sat upon our stumps with the boars snuffling and snorting below, and Sweet Marie silent—this Mean Marie still bore some semblance of the beauty with which she'd been born; and by virtue of this—and her witchly wiles besides—she allied herself to King Payne, a Seminole chief much older than she. He—it is supposed—fathered Sweet Marie.

The three decamped from Cuscowilla, in the Alachua, to what would become known as Payne's Town; and there they lived well, in the European style, their home well stocked by traders and tended by some twenty-odd slaves.

King Payne soon died, to be succeeded, as customary, by

his sister's son. This nephew died, too; whereupon there rose his brother—Micanopy—who rules now, as I write. Payne's Town was burned by the Seminoles in that death-rite accorded their chiefs, and Mean Marie was cut loose from the tribe, left to cull what she could from the short-lived alliance. Where the two witches went, I cannot say; for Fivekiller did not know, and Sweet Marie did not say.

In time, the Blood came to Mean Marie, and her daughter was left alone with naught but the knowledge of her witchery, and—it is safely supposed—disdain for, hatred of, all men, no matter their skin shade. Where she came of age within the Florida she covets so, only Sweet Marie knows. But when the Spanish returned for their second tenure, she was deemed marriageable, quite; and strung for herself a rosary of rich men; upon whom she preyed, indeed. All of them died. Propitiously. (At the telling of this, Sweet Marie smiled.) And all of them left the widowed witch land; including a certain tract no settler vied for, as it was scrubland, featureless save for its deep spring and its limestone sink. Few had ever seen this place, and no map knew it well. O, but Sweet Marie wanted that land on which Glass Lake sits. Wanted it badly. Would have it. Sought and secured the deed to it; for upon it there sat a spring and . . .

Stay: not so much a spring as a fountain.

The fountain.

The same Ponce de Leon had sought.

. . . Now whether Sweet Marie learned of the fountain by means of her alliances—Indian, Spanish, or otherwise—or by Craft-work, I cannot say; but by the time I was brought to Glass Lake, it had been hers for forty-odd years. During which time no word of its existence had passed off-island; for those few who learned of the Spanish waters faced a simple choice: live long by its grace, or die speaking of same.

52

I Sue for Freedom

NOT long after that first Day of Dosage, yet before I knew of the drink's provenance, I determined to petition Sweet Marie for my freedom. I was spurred to action by a maddening solitude; for only Fivekiller spoke to me, as said, and he'd been away from Glass Lake for days, tracking or trading. Indeed, I determined to speak to Sweet Marie before he'd return to dissuade me, as already he had, often. On the subject of that strange sister, Fivekiller was characteristically silent until the one day we sat in contemplation of Shakespeare. *Richard II,* it was. Yes: Fivekiller and I had begun to sit with the Bard—me reading, he listening and learning a language he'd long disdained. And well I recall a certain line I read aloud that day:

King Richard, deposed and detained at Pomfret Castle,

says: "I have been studying how I may compare this prison where I live unto the world."

O, how it resonated with us both, that line. There passed between us . . . something, a charge well nigh electrical; for hadn't we both prisons aplenty to study?

From that day forward I wondered would Fivekiller and I break from Glass Lake? Could we? But I said nothing; and Fivekiller, knowing what it was I wondered, what it was I wanted, counseled patience. Still, we were silently allied: we two against Sweet Marie, our jailer, our mutual Machiavellian.

Patience? Perhaps Fivekiller had patience to spare, but I'd exhausted my supply. Sweet Marie had learned nothing of Celia. Or if she had, she'd not told me. Nor would she. So it was I woke one storm-dark dawn, dressed in my buckskin slacks and that blue blouse which already was threadbare, and set off for the witch's door.

My courage had been a long time coming, yes; but now I summoned it with this tacit refrain, *How* dare *she, How* dare *she, How* dare *she detain me?* I went so far as to wonder how my witch's will would fare against hers, should it devolve to that. I'd grown strong on death, yes; but strong enough? O, I was ready to risk it. . . . Rather, I would have been, or might have been, had it not been for those tracking cats, which posed another problem entirely.

Still, I hied to her door; which had always shown a padlock (if Sweet Marie were without), or was fastened by unseen means (if she were within). This day—to my great regret—the door stood ajar; and I had only to push upon it to . . .

Stay: let me first say that though Sweet Marie often chose one of her several saddles for sleep—a sleep which was not sleep, but rather a trance she'd induce; whereupon she'd hang for half days at a time, neither fully awake nor fully asleep, yet ever watchful. . . . And though she preferred her saddles to a bed or pallet, and showed innumerable other eccentricities, still I'd assumed her cottage contained that same odd mix of European and frontier wares I discovered within the "healer's" longhouse, at one end of which I slept beneath bug-bedecked nets of tulle. I refer to such dainties as a box of burled elm, replete with a set of filigreed silverware—ignored; for still we ate with our fingers. Or the portable toilette set, which I did put to use: I passed countless candlelit hours combing out my hair—trying it this way or that, full or fixed into a bun set with ivory sticks—before retiring to my horsehair pallet; which, alongside a chair with no cushion, a lamed table, and a tiny mirror, constituted my suite entire. . . . Yes: I'd assumed Sweet Marie's abode would be similar. O, but within that square of sawn logs, so tightly sealed, I'd find a single saddle and no other adornment; for it wasn't so much a cottage as a safe.

. . . That morning the padlock was off and hanging on a peg. The door itself showed a wedge of shadow, and creaked on its iron hinges; for there'd come a breeze, betokening rain. The palms were asway, whistling and chuffing as though the wind were an engine steaming through the canopy. I'd heard the first of the raindrops fall as I reached her house; which sat flat to the forest floor, in defiance of flood. Raising my shaking hand to rap at the door, I saw it swing inward, slightly, as if the abode had drawn back its breath. I did not knock; but rather set the flat of my hand against that plank and pushed . . . nay, I did not push. And from out of the strengthening rain I stepped into deep shadow and still, still air. There I stood; and before I could see I heard, heard a breathing too heavy to be that of Sweet Marie. Too heavy to be human. This neared, neared till I felt the warm, wet exhalation and smelled the beast's blood-breath.

Coacoochee: of course.

As I fell back the cat sprang, slamming me against the door. Thusly was a saddle-hung Sweet Marie roused.

She called off her cat; but none too quickly.

Its forepaws pricked my shoulders. (I've scars to show for it.) And as it brought its head, its face, its mouth so near mine I turned away as best I could; but that was a mistake: so said Sweet Marie:

"Never, never bare your neck to a big cat, sister," said she. "The plane of it, the smooth, sweaty, blood-pulsing plane of it . . . to resist *that* . . . well, I'm afraid that is asking too much of my Coacoochee." And just then the cat spread its jaws, tilted its squared head to the angle of attack—one knows it when one sees it, assuredly—and . . .

And with words of Muskogee Sweet Marie backed the cat down.

Never have I known a like fear.

What happened next, well . . . this requires the setting aside of pride and all delicacy. Yet I'll do it; to say:

I'd shat myself. And the cat wanted at it.

Its claws came like tenterhooks, silver in the shadows. And I heard within its drumming purr a most dire, a most dread desire.

"Satisfy her," said Sweet Marie; as if I knew how to.

What panicked words I spouted, I cannot say; but far worse was what I heard: the witch's directive:

"Take them off. Or she'll shred them, along with your skin."

I was to strip, yes; and bare myself to the beast.

"Do it now," said Sweet Marie. "Now!" Still she hung o'er that saddle, her hair coiled on the packed dirt floor before her. Her face she'd upturned, so as to witness this oddest of shows: there I stood, naked from the waist down, the buckskin pants bunched to my boots. The cat set to with her hot and roughened tongue. Cleaning me of excrement. Laving my . . . my *self* till I could suffer no more and . . .

And the last I recall is Sweet Marie saying, cooing to her cat, "Sweet Marie ought to have stooled for her Coacoochee, eh? Cat-cat misses its witch-shit? . . . Cat-cat forgives Sweet

Marie?" At the cat's answering roar I fell, nay fainted; and can recall no more.

I woke not wanting to. I woke wishing I'd died.

There sat Sweet Marie at work in the candlelit dark, humming. Though it was warm, quite, Sweet Marie wore her coat of sailcloth, onto which she'd sewn the feathers of her well-delected flamingos. Into the dirt beside her there'd been driven a length of cane, which had a hook and was bowed now beneath the weight of her hung hair. Outside the rain drove down. Thunder drummed. Where was the cat? *Where is the cat?*

The panther lay behind me, too close, its body contoured to mine. I scurried from it—from its heat, from its hammering heart, from its fecal breath—to a far wall, drawing up my pants as I did so. I was sticky from the cat's tongue, and slick with sweat. Confusion honed the sharper angles of my shame, but still I'd have shed that skin, were there a way.

"Coacoochee will sleep now," said Sweet Marie. "She has fed, and is fatly complacent. *Shh!* Listen. . . . Hear her happiness." The sister smiled, bemusedly. All I heard was the cat's snoring.

"Sweet Marie wonders: are you not familiar with the ways of familiars?" Laughter, as she pleasured in her pun and made another: "The cats prefer catamenia, of course; but Sweet Marie's monthly flow ceased long, long ago. So Coacoochee settles for whatever is witch-made."

I said nothing.

"Sometimes Sweet Marie must cut herself for Coacoochee." And with this she took up the snake-skull necklace and drove, drove its fangs into the flesh of her forearm, upon which scars were writ. O, to see her revel in that pain; and to see it devolve to pleasure as she crawled o'er the dirt floor and set her bloodied flesh to the smacking lips of the half sleeping cat, whose whiskers still were shit-flecked. "A relief it is, having a second sister about," said Sweet Marie. "After all, Sweet Marie can produce only so much; but still they *purr* so plaintively for it, and lap at what effluent they get. Sweet Marie has waited, yes, and Sweet Marie has watched, but you do not bleed as . . . as a *whole* woman would. Still, you stool, and there has been witch-waste aplenty; such that the panthers have been pleased." Whereupon I knew what became of my bucket when each morning an earless maroon backed into the longhouse to take it away.

Never had I hated Sweet Marie more.

Stay: that is untrue; for my hatred increased when I appealed for my freedom, only to hear the witch laugh as she retook to her work; as follows:

She sat before an earthenware jug fixed to the floor. Colorless, and perhaps a foot high, it was encircled by a stony basin some two feet in circumference. O'er the lip of the jug some substance bubbled, audibly so. I'd have thought it water but for the weight of it, and the slowness of its flow as it fell down into the basin. Into this basin Sweet Marie was dipping those amber vials, the same in which she dispensed the drink: the elixir: *this.*

Here sat the Spanish font, though I knew it not. . . . Not then. Not yet.

The cottage was close, damp, and deeply redolent of . . . of blood. Was it mine? The cat had cut me, yes; but it was not my blood I smelled, no. It came from the upwelling water, such that I wondered: *Is it the earth herself who bleeds?*

"Sweet Marie takes care," said the witch, as still I wondered from whence the blood-scent came. And indeed she did take care; for each vial was labeled, and each label had lines marked upon it in lead. "Sweet Marie has made mistakes, yes; and then the men, they suffer, grotesquely so." She showed the Eye, which belied her seeming sympathy. "In one drop there is a week; in a quarter vial, perhaps a year entire. . . . For the uninitiated, that is. Sweet Marie's men need more."

I'd known the men of Glass Lake bewitched, or worse. But when I asked, Sweet Marie told me more. And when Fivekiller returned, I'd have it all confirmed o'er supper. . . . The Mistress of Time, indeed.

"What is it you dole out?" I asked from the shadowed corner, where still I cowered, careful to keep from the cat.

"Sweet Marie keeps a key of life," said she. Her pipe was in its place, and away she puffed. "There are few such keys. From this fountain flows one: Sweet Marie's."

"I don't understand," said I; though in truth—for I'd read the histories, the legends, the lore—I suspected she spoke of Ponce's fabled fountain. What was this but proof positive of what already I knew: Sweet Marie was insane? Still, I played my part, and asked, "These waters heal? The men, I mean?"

She nodded. Ranged before the witch were twenty-three bottles, to which she now fitted twenty-three corks drawn from a coconut half. On these were written tiny numbers in white.

"The drink is . . . regenerative?" I thought of the maimed men, and wondered what deals they'd made. I confess it, too: instantly I knew the appeal of such an elixer. . . . Illusory, of course; for surely we spoke now of myth, not magic or witch-work.

Sweet Marie looked at me as if I'd spoken my suspicions, or pressed for proof. Turning from me to the lazing cat, she called it to her. It fitted itself to her side and, at an Indian-sounding command, it set its paw—the size of a saucer—upon Sweet Marie's knee. Whereupon the witch again took up that fanged necklace, to pierce the paw. Deep, deep the fangs sank into the fawn-colored fur. Coacoochee drew back with a hiss and unsheathed her claws, but reacted no more than that; for soon Sweet Marie took up a sprinkling of the Spanish waters and cast it onto the cut. Which healed. As I watched. The cat's blood flowed to—not from—the wound. Dried from off the darkly matted fur.

What clock-stopping Craft was this?

Stunned, I was. Yet when Sweet Marie said, "Come," I scurried to her side. At her order I let fall my blouse, to show my freshly furrowed shoulders. I leaned across the cat, and gave it no thought at all. Mindlessness, this was; madness. O, but I was fast brought back to my senses; for all six rose in revolt as Sweet Marie drizzled water o'er my wounds and . . . and they burned as if the flow were salt.

Falling back, faint from the pain, I came too near the waters' font; such that Sweet Marie sprang onto her haunches and—nearly tearing the scalp from off her head—shoved me from it. "Fool!" spat she. "Keep from the spring! Sweet Marie will not have a blunderer blast the Spanish waters with a drop of witch-blood."

"Do you mean my blood . . . *our* blood could . . . ?" Loath was I to admit I'd anything in common with this crone; but here it seemed I'd discovered something.

Sweet Marie shrank from the truth she'd spoken, a secret she'd not meant to share. I thought little of this, then; for I was in pain, and had my cuts and the cat to consider. Still, I may have cursed the sister, may have hissed as Coacoochee had. O, but unlike the cat, I did not heal. Instead, I scarred. Instantly. Permanently. Hideous, they are: thickly raised and purple-red, seeming to writhe as worms would; but, strange though it sounds, soon I came to prize those scars. Yes, precious they were; for they came to manifest the *why,* the *wherefore,* of my existence—Celia, herself scarred—and often I'd find myself fingering them, much as a Christian might tell their beads or contemplate the cross. . . . Celia? Would I ever find and save her? If so, would I find and save myself?

I crawled to my corner and cried. So debased, I'd been; so embarrassed. Yet the witch, caring not, spoke on:

"The Spanish waters work not on sisters. To her tongue it is bitter. To her nose it comes as blood. But her soul it affects worst of all; for it shaves not a day off the life she's lived, nor adds an hour to her allotment." She showed the Eye and said, "It is as naught against the coming of the Blood."

"You might simply have told me so," said I; for still my shoulders stung.

This she ignored, returning to her work. "Care, yes; Sweet Marie takes care. Too much or too little and the systems come undone. Understand?"

I did not, and said so, hating her but covetous of what she knew.

"Too much or too little of the Spanish waters and the healing turns hurtful. Drops, at first. And over time—time, time, *time*!—they want it, they need it. Want it, yes. Need it, yes. Would steal it from Sweet Marie. Why?"

"Tell me," said I. "Tease me not."

"It is simple, witch: without it they die. And with it . . . with it, they never will."

It was then I knew, knew she'd not let me go; for I'd learned the secret of Glass Lake. And what had I to balance the scales of trade, to offer in exchange and thusly secure my freedom? Nothing, thought I. . . . Nothing.

53

Fivekiller

AMIDST the irreality of Glass Lake, I thought less of Celia. Rather, I tried to. Less of finding her, of freeing her, of gaining her forgiveness. Staving off thoughts of Celia let me survive my island internment—for such it was—through several seasons more; until:

"The time is now," said the warder-witch one night at supper, puffing, puffing upon that meerschaum pipe of hers. "Sweet Marie has had word . . ."

"Word of what? Herculine wishes to hear it." My sarcasm was lost upon the witch; but Fivekiller heard and—it seemed—pleasured in same. I expected her to speak more of war; for this she'd begun to do, increasingly. It seemed she sought to protect the peninsula itself, and her secreted stake upon it. Still, I paid her little heed; for I'd come to believe the true war lay within her: insanity.

"Sweet Marie has had word of your wench." I fell still; for I'd stopped expecting same. "She camps in the Cove of the Withlacoochee."

This I'd heard from Yahalla, and from traders at Volusia. Months prior. I'd needed, attended more from Sweet Marie: specifics. And when I said as much—in a tone rather heated—Sweet Marie smiled as she asked, "Why, then, didn't you go to her? . . . Go to her now," said she, finally. "Sweet Marie is ready for you to go. . . . The time is now. Go. Go!"

And I did. Two days later—with Celia returned to my dreams, both daylit and dark—I left Glass Lake, bidding good-bye to no one.

The men of Glass Lake . . . well, I knew none of them; and can record here no proper names. Locked in a bargain, they were; locked and lost; and I suppose I've a measure of pity to spare them, all save the four Shakespeareans, seeing as how I'd . . . Stay; and let me first speak of Sweet Marie.

The witch had locked herself away, and I dared not go to her door for fear of Coacoochee. What's more: she'd nothing I wanted, nothing I needed; and no politesse interposed. Let her keep her font. Let her have her secreted island, her coterie of time-stopped men. All I wanted was to be rid of the witch. And happy I'd be to set her stink behind me. Still, I suppose her indifference to my departure rankled; and to my anger I can attribute that act by which I'd soon surprise myself.

As for Fivekiller, I'd no reason to bid him adieu; for—blessedly—he was to lead me from the island, northward to Fort Brooke. Sweet Marie had decreed it. Too, as she'd stood in the sunlit courtyard the morning prior to our departure, dressed in her frock of flamingo feathers, she'd let fall her hair—like an anchor it sank, onto the sea of sand—and stepped to me; *at* me. "Sweet Marie trades fairly," said she, showing an Eye wild yet tight. "So, too, will you." She offered no specifics, and I solicited none. Trade? I gave the transaction little thought, so relieved was I to go from Glass

Lake. And go I did, yes; knowing not that Sweet Marie freed me as one frees fire unto kindling.

Two maroons—the one without ears, the second lipless and sporting an eye patch which seemed somehow to pulse—poled us ashore, o'er the springwaters to the once-blackened bank. Onto the raft in our stead went two beeves set for slaughter. O but first I bled.

Yes: I bled. What was it seized me? Surely there was no forethought, nothing but the surrendering to instinct. . . . Simply: I saw Fivekiller's knife strapped to his hip; for he stood before me on our crossing, with the maroons at the raft's fore. The blade was exposed, and so, too, was the steely tip. And as I turned from its glinting edge to look down through Glass Lake itself, suddenly—as though I saw the scene played out there upon its white sand bottom—I knew what I would do to defy and deny the witch I was leaving behind.

I opened wide my right hand and fast, *fast* I slid it the length of Fivekiller's knife. Opening a gash three, four inches in length. At first it did not show, and I wondered how could I have failed? O, but then the pain and the blood came in sickening unison.

The raftmen knew not what I'd done. Fivekiller, of course, did; but he turned back to me slowly, so slowly I'd already knelt to set my bleeding hand in Glass Lake.

Red trailed the raft, red diffused down. I wondered were these the same waters that fed Sweet Marie's font? Did these waters rise from a common spring? The answer was readily had: pain; and sudden scarring. This was not the same pain I'd known in Sweet Marie's hut, no. Rather, it was alike in kind, but lesser in degree. And so: yes, this too was springwater. . . . I'd succeeded. At what, exactly? I'd not know for some months more.

Upon the lake's far shore we were traded for the ill-fated

cattle. The maroons knew not what had happened; for I hid my ruined hand and the blood that might have betrayed me had dried on Fivekiller's blade, where it would arouse little suspicion if seen.

Fivekiller blindfolded me, using a colorless length of muslin that reeked of rotten fruit. "They watch," whispered he, as apology. So it was I'd leave that clearing as I'd come: sightless. "She watches," added the Indian. "Somehow she sees."

Fivekiller led me into the woodland on foot; for we were not granted a mount. But as soon as we put the maroons behind us, my guide relieved me of the blind and asked, "What have you done? We must now run. Run to the sea. By sunset."

Could Sweet Marie already know what I'd done? I cannot say, even now; but neither Fivekiller nor I wanted to wait for an affirmative answer to come in the form of her cats.

The sun was setting, bending to the Gulf, when finally we broke cover of the green. Of the scratching, clawing, smothering green. Onto open beach.

I suppose I'd anticipated a canoe or simple dugout; for otherwise I cannot account for my joy upon seeing Fivekiller drag from the thicket a fishing smack rigged with sail. Now we'd the wind to assist us in our escape; for so it had come to seem: an escape.

Sweet Marie had said I'd find Celia at Okahumpky—Micanopy's town—one hundred-odd miles northeast of Fort Brooke; which information was grudgingly gotten from her. To Tampa we'd sail, Fivekiller and I; and at Fort Brooke—situated where the Hillsborough River debouches into a bay of the same name—we'd marshal our needments, hire horses, and proceed overland, into the Nation proper. Or so I supposed. And not even the distance ahead daunted me; for I knew, knew Sweet Marie had spoken truly of Celia—the cruel are oddly attuned to the truth, and wield it well—and that finally I'd find her. Simple, it seemed; to one as naive as I was.

Northward, the territory showed signs of autumn or earliest winter as the days drew in; but still there came the occasional heat-breaking, summerish storm, when late in the day the sky putrefies—the clouds necrotizing from white to gray to a gangrenous green—and seems to die, with thunder its throes and lightning its last will and testament, scribed into the sky. Rain cords down, coldly; and the stricken earth steams. Then come the frogs, nonplussed, seeming to call for sustenance: *fried bac-on, fried bac-on. . . .* Or so it sounded to me.

"*Skin-co-chaw,*" said Fivekiller, one such rain-sodden dusk. We'd found dry land on which to bivouac, and sat listening to the inland chorines thusly identified. Frogs less hearty let go whistles and trills; one sounded like a fingernail run the length of a fine-tooth comb.

Thereafter, I asked questions; for I saw that Fivekiller could not help but teach, taking for his text the green and gold and blue book of the world. In so doing his eyes nearly shone, but I cannot aver they *did* shine: for fixed was his face, no matter his heart-state.

He'd offer identifying words and such, yes; but conversation this was not. Fivekiller was proficient in Spanish and English, which latter he refused and would not willingly speak, not at first, seeming to fear it would sully his tongue. Me? I struggled with the Indian language, so unlike any I'd learned; but some words he taught me I retain; such as:

"*Hey-a-ma,*" said my companion. It was deepest night, our second day out. We sat shoulder to shoulder upon the sand, gazing seaward, skyward. "*Kot-zesumpa eparken.*" I understood when Fivekiller unfurled six fingers, and pointed with a forefinger: *up*. The Pleiades, *there,* with six of the seven-sister stars visible. Too, there was Aldebaron and the scintilla of Orion's belt, to both of which the Indian introduced me.

We sat stargazing a long while; till finally:

"Nochebuschee," said Fivekiller; and he rose, ascended to the dunes, and stood amidst the tall grasses. He set his gaze southward. He'd keep first watch. And I'd sleep in the firmer sand just above the tide line; for he'd told me to: *Nochebuschee.*

The sidereal show faded, and the sea's song proved a lullaby: sleep came.

It was the risen sun woke me, warmly. Of course, I'd kept no watch. And now I wondered how long Fivekiller had been standing there in the surf, gazing southward, waiting, ready to sail.

Fivekiller had made the trip to Fort Brooke before. He knew the sinuations of the shore—such as no map can show—and sailed us with cunning. He knew where to put ashore, where to pile palmetto and moss for a shade-blessed respite. I needed the shade; for the sun, the constant sun, stunned me: sunstruck, I was. Indeed, I burned as the sun struck me twice: once as it fell, a second time as it glanced off the glass of the Gulf.

It seemed the shoreline had been gnawed by the sea's offset teeth: there were coves and swamps and piney islets. Mangroves hugged the coast. . . . O mangroves: which ought not, *cannot* grow as they do, thriving in that brine that smothers aught else; which have only the land they make as they float freely, searching out their like and letting fall their common roots; till, in time, an island rises. (When solitude descends, and loneliness seems my lot, I think of the persisting mangrove.) . . . Too, pinewoods rose amidst the palms, all of them leaning this way and that, as the wind led them. Shorebirds cried and rode the air currents as best they could. Upon the ivoried strand, heron pecked fiddler crabs from their pinhole caves. In the surf, they guzzled guppies and such. To this sea-show I succeeded in surrendering my fears; until our fourth day out.

With the main of our journey behind us—now we'd only to cross the bay of Espíritu Santo to Fort Brooke: a sail of some duration, still—we went ashore, onto a key; for the bay showed itself tufted in white, and our sail was too full for safe passage. It was on Mullet Key—so called—that I found fears anew; for:

Inland we came upon a hammock grown o'er with fern and scrub. And a charred circle of earth, none too cold. It seems to me now that the fire was smoking still; for I'm inclined to fancy that the pirates who'd laid the blaze had sailed not an hour before we'd come. O yes: pirates, brigands, bad men . . . call them what you will.

They ply the western shore from Cape Sable northward, loosely allied to the Indians or to the Cuban fishermen with whom they sometimes trade, from whom they sometimes steal. But far greater is the loot to be had off those hapless craft that run aground on reef or shoal, the crews of which willingly trade their wares for their lives. These pirates are Bahamian, by tradition, though truer it is to say the lot of them are landless, and lawless. And so: bad enough it would have been, this coming upon a pirates' camp; but Fivekiller—was that a layer of fear I saw, rising to his too-stolid face?—explored a bit more; and what he found only disquieted me further:

A bottle palm had been blazed up its seaward side: burned, yes; but only to the height of a man's hips. Behind it, on the ground, we found rope: evidence enough for Fivekiller to pronounce that "bad work" had been done upon the site.

"Burned, do you mean? A man was . . . burned?"

The Indian made no answer, and instead searched to find:

. . . a silver fork, hinged for folding away; iron shot, such as is fired from the swivel guns of the lesser (and faster) vessels the pirates prefer; feces—clumped quite near the fire—which he identified as human by means which I shan't describe here. . . . O but nothing was as bad as that act testified to by the ropes and the blazed tree; at the base of which Fivekiller found no bones but plenty of blood, dried to black and beset by ants. Ants which I trailed to behind the bole, where not far from the rope I found a large land crab, rather peaked in aspect and seeming frozen in its crawl; and which, as I approached, fast assumed its true and rightful shape: a human hand, this was.

I reeled back from the thing, which Fivekiller prodded with first a reed, then a finger. I begged him not to take the relic up. Falling into a crouch, I sought some means of defense; for I knew, knew we were ringed by wreckers, pirates, or whatnot: trapped. Ambush was imminent. . . . It was not; and so I set down the coconut I'd taken up. O, but still Fivekiller failed to persuade me we were safe. Said he, no pirates would return to a campsite so recently the site of such summary, sea-born justice. This was no permanent base of operations we'd found; but rather a place some piratical types had come to impart a lesson—as concerned thievery, I supposed—to one of their own. Regardless, I insisted we sail off at once.

"No," said Fivekiller, flatly; and his only concession was this: we'd encamp far across the key. Still I protested. Finally Fivekiller spoke his detested English, saying:

"No pirate is more powerful than you." This he followed with words of Muskogee. Something rhetorical seeming; for he shook his head, and *tsked* his tongue. Were I to venture a guess as to what he said, it would be this: *How does this witch not know her worth, not see her strength?*

Owing to dreams of piracy, I slept not well upon the key.

Waking at dawn of our fifth day away—grateful I'd not been desexed, spitted like a sow, or otherwise used by men rum-drunk and depraved—I cast a fast eye for Fivekiller, who I hoped had readied our boat for the bay crossing. But no:

There he sat in the shade of a pine some ten, fifteen feet distant. From a haversack of his own he'd taken provender—my breakfast of bread heel and salt beef, beside which he'd set a treat: a coconut, its side stove in to access its meat and milk—as well as a thing I'd seen before, but knew only as some tool of his simple toilette: a bundle of deerhide; which now he untied and unfurled, as though it were a pennant. There, by first light, I saw aglint that amber glass I knew too well. Into this pouch there'd been sewn many pockets, each of which fit one vial. Within it were ten bottles, sitting five to a side in finger-like array. Fivekiller uncorked a full one. I watched as he threw back all, *all* of the elixir within. Time served at Glass Lake had shown me that such a dosage was extreme. Even the worst-mangled men had had their medicine doled out by the drop, not the bottle; and certainly none had drunk from the Spanish well daily. I counted five vials of the elixir left. Feigning sleep, I calculated thusly:

We were five days from Glass Lake. We'd gain Fort Brooke by nightfall, if the winds were kind; but there he'd leave me. Fivekiller could go no further: he'd have to depart immediately in order to make his way back to Sweet Marie by the eleventh day. Otherwise he'd exhaust his supply and . . .

What? Begin to die?

Only then—with a sickening twist within—did I begin to wonder what fate I'd loosed upon the men of Glass Lake.

54

Arrival at Fort Brooke

AFTER an eastward sail of some twenty-odd miles, we'd passed o'er Espíritu Santo and into its lesser sister, the bay of Hillsborough. Some ways northward we found the fort; and a welcome sight it was.

It was midafternoon; or leastways it was bright and hot. We sailed with land not far off to port. Before we gained sight of the fort, there'd been but blueness; for the sky was devoid of cloud, and all about us there spread the great bay. I sat aft, watching sea creatures breach the bay wholly or in part: mullet skimmed the surface as skimmed stones will, once, twice, three times before sinking; and there came the wing tips of rays, the fins and blue backs of dolphins, the muzzles of manatees . . .

The coast wore its mangrove fringe; and the sun played off the mollusks trapped therein: they glinted and shone amidst the trapping roots, and called to mind men I'd seen with droplets of beer adorning their beards. In New York, that must have been. At some portside sink. Such thoughts recalled the Duchess, dead and oft-mourned Eliphalet, Adaline, and all the scattered sisters. O, but here I was, sailing to Celia; so I cast off the past, and grew heart-strong.

. . . And finally: Fort Brooke:

Which is young enough to bear the name of a man still living. Built not a decade past, it sits well acred amidst live oak and hickory. Its walls of tall timber triangulate toward the northeast, toward the Seminole Nation, the boundary of which sits some eight miles distant; its third wall is shoreline. Within there sit pine-hewn barracks, storehouses, stables, smiths . . . : things needful to a hundred-odd men living far from any brethren.

The fort was then an open place. Settlers hadn't moved within it: still they manned their riverside shanties and stores. Slatterns, some of them were, in service to the soldiers; but others—the foreign-born, men on the lam, young families: frontier types—had come to begin anew. Only later would they abandon their stakes to camp in the fort's shadow; and eventually seek the safety of its interior. But fear was unfounded when we arrived that winter of '33–'34; for war—yes: war—had not yet come.

Arriving at the wharf, we were met by an indolent-seeming corps of soldiers whose rifles were employed as walking sticks. From far away I saw their sky blue slacks; nearer, I noticed their uniforms were lax, in concession to the sun and heat of their posting: shirtsleeves rolled or ripped away, kerchiefs tied at the neck and wetted with water or sweat. Their welcome was a mixture of curiosity, civility, greed, and mistrust.

Curiosity: who were we, sailing up the river to their cantonment?

Civility: such as Americans observe.

Greed: what had we on hand?

And mistrust: the peaceable years of coexistence with the Seminole were passing; and we were welcomed as we'd not have been months later. . . . We: a willowy white man with a blond braid hanging down his back, fashioned to appear part pirate, part Seminole; and in his company a stoical red man standing to an equal height but seeming much, much stronger. In response to the soldiers' queries, I told a story the details of which I cannot recall; but it had its effect: we were let onto land. And when I remarked the way these men looked at Fivekiller—taking him in fearfully: his body, yes, but more so his face—I heard myself say, "He is sick." And only then did I know he was.

The second day at the fort—after having met the striped-shouldered men in charge, who kindly granted us board and beds, albeit in the hospital ward—Fivekiller and I set out alone in a canoe to see what we could, and find food of our own; for thusly had we been advised, strongly so. Fivekiller had not been out of my sight all that morning; and so it was I turned to him as he sat behind me in the dugout. "Your morning drink," said I. "What of it?" He'd not had his water. Had he forgotten? No: I knew he hadn't; so doubtless my question came well freighted.

"No more," said he, turning to show a profile hard and sharp as honed steel.

Nothing more was said of the matter. Instead, we took to the bay, seined for redfish, and returned with a surplus catch that earned both our keep and the approbation of the soldiers. The next day Fivekiller pegged a turtle, which yielded steaks for ten. Thereafter, his skills—at sea and on land—were sought.

I sat out such excursions, keeping to the fort's hospital and doing what I could therein whilst planning—with lessening patience—the search for Celia. I assisted the fort's surgeon: a melancholic—name of Gatlin—who was unpopular among the men (as the Keepers of Leeches so often are). Far from overworked was this Dr. Gatlin; still he gave o'er to me what work there was. And I earned my keep by swabbing brows, salving scars, rewrapping wounds . . . : none of which I much minded. (Hadn't I seen much worse?)

Whilst I nursed what few patients there were, and whilst the hundred-odd soldiers of Fort Brooke saw to duties of the fatigue sort—repairs requisite to keeping the several outbuildings standing in so corrosive a climate—Fivekiller was asked to join a party setting sail for Anclote Key. They'd hunt, fish, and frolic; though, officially, I suppose, they were on the watch for pirates. I was unhappy when he nodded his assent; for now we, or I, would have to delay our setting out until his return, some ten days hence. But if I was angry and confused when he left—for still I knew not if he planned on accompanying me; or what toll his sudden disdain of the Spanish waters would take; or if Sweet Marie's coprophagous cats could track us as far as Fort Brooke; or . . . —stay, and let this suffice: I was naught but sympathy upon Fivekiller's return; for it was irrefutable: he'd begun to die.

Fivekiller returned from Anclote Key with the fleet of low-drawing craft—smacks laden with venison and fish already salted; but in the catching of same, he'd assumed the first signs of aging. His black hair now showed gray; and an excess of new growth—whole inches—had come in coarse, so brittle it broke beneath the brush. Patches of scalp shone through. Still his eyes were stony cold, his face set; but his body had begun to change at a rate all out of keeping with any natural process. Rather, this *was* the natural process of aging—was it not?—which the Spanish waters had retarded.

On that excursion, Fivekiller suffered the first of many broken bones. He'd been drawing in fish by main force, alongside three soldiers, when suddenly there was heard a snap, akin to the clap of a gator's jaw (or so I had it from a witness). Fivekiller had not felt it at first; and only knew he'd broken the bone of his forearm when another of the men pointed to it, breaking the skin like a just-cut tooth. Thusly did he return to Fort Brooke with his arm splinted; but never to heal. In time other bones broke. The smaller ones of his hands and feet snapped like matchsticks. His hands swelled terribly, seemed bags of splintered and splintering bone. The feet were worse still; they, too, surrendered their shape as the nails grew too thick for tending. Within six, seven weeks of our arrival, Fivekiller's hands were inutile and he could not stand.

Thereafter, we kept to ourselves. In truth, I hid the Indian away; for I'd no choice. The soldiers and Dr. Gatlin were held at bay by my talk of contagion. Soon Fivekiller and I had a ward within the ward: our two bunks, set behind a scrim. There it was that his end began in earnest with the breaking of larger bones. Nothing caused this, per se; for Fivekiller lay still all through those long days and nights. But dully, horridly, the sounds were heard: the hollow-sounding bones went off like wet shot, with a smothered, skin- and sinew-muffled *pop*.

His skin fell slack as age ate the muscle away. Indeed, it seemed to liquefy and sip it, suck at it as once I'd seen a giant, poison-spitting water bug do to a bullfrog; whereupon the frog sat upon its bank, emptied, slowly surrendering its shape, deflating unto death. Soon Fivekiller's body was rumpled and rucked, pale and psoriatic. Folds hung where formerly the skin had been firm, as still his face was. Bespeckled, he seemed; for livid, coin-size age spots had come: yes: the very currency of age, so long hoarded. Bespeckled and dry, such that a struck match might send him skyward as smoke. And though he ate not at all—nothing—fat pooled beneath his skin, and made of the lightest touch a bruise; till violets bloomed in profusion.

He'd not let me work any Craft upon him. Neither would

he sip what water remained in his possession, not even to allay his pain. . . . O the pain. No vocabulary exists for its articulation; and blessedly so: surely such words would wound anew.

As for me, I found suffering of another sort. I had not meant to . . . to do whatever it was I'd done to the men of Glass Lake. I'd only meant to deny Sweet Marie her hold o'er them all. Now, unless she knew some spell-work by which to undo the ruin of the Spanish waters, it must be supposed she ruled o'er naught but a corps of corpses! And to those dying men, well, I doubt the witch showed much kindness. . . . Yes, the night-mare brought to me such dreadful dreams. And waking from them, I found I'd no facts with which to counter all that I supposed: suppose the men suffered as Fivekiller did; suppose Sweet Marie had begun to experiment, or sickly play upon them; suppose her cats were coming. . . . These suppositions, these fears I sought to still by caring for Fivekiller. What more could I do?

When on occasion Fivekiller spoke it was with age fast progressing; such that it seemed he sought to testify, and resisted no enquiries; one of which was, of course, "How old are you?"

This he answered in riddling fashion, speaking of an event long past: the loss of the Negro Fort on the Appalachicola. It was reputed to be full of fugitive slaves—seen as gold in a vault—and an artilleryman under Jackson's command launched a lucky hot shot o'er the walls, into an open powder magazine. . . . Fivekiller muttered names.

"What year was this?" I asked. "I've heard tell of such a fight, and an imploding fort; but could it be I'm in mind of another, similar incident?"

"Summer," said he, with lucidity, "Eighteen-sixteen. People blown to pieces. Three hundred people." Among the lives lost were those of Fivekiller's helpmate: the mother of his two children, who'd had children of their own, also lost. Thereafter, the Indian had wandered; and somehow made his way to Sweet Marie, and back to a youth that preceded all loss.

Not being of an arithmetical bent, I struggled with the calculation. "Nearly twenty years ago, then? But . . . but if you—I am sorry, Fivekiller—but if you lost *grand*children on the Appalachicola, then . . ."

"I was born long ago," said he. "I am old, and ought to die."

How old he was, exactly, I cannot say; but several-score years broke now upon his body. He aged decades in the span of some months: well nigh a year, it was. And whilst I tended him my life was equal parts secrecy and sly Craft-work, and saddening thoughts of Celia: I'd come so close to her, but had lost her, surely. I despaired. I'd only death to anchor me now: Fivekiller's, which ever impended. O, but his dissolution slowed as death approached; till finally I worried that he'd devolve to some cruel stasis the like of which Mammy Venus had suffered: a dying that did not eventuate in death.

I'd have asked more of Fivekiller; but by the spring his faculties had fled. And there was naught to do but wait out the cachexia, let time render its cruel accounts; as indeed it did:

One morning I woke knowing Fivekiller had gone. And upon his face I found a smile, disclosed by death.

I sewed Fivekiller into the winding-sheet on which he died; for when I'd tried to move his body, in the hopes of burying him befittingly, well . . . the skin split, and there seeped forth a life-sap I'd not tap further.

Two soldiers from the Anclote excursion helped me load the shrouded body into a barrow. This I pushed shoreside, to a great hickory sixty, seventy feet tall. Into the tree there'd been set a platform. Well high it was, above the canopy; and from it a soldier with a glass could spy ships approaching o'er the bay.

In the generous shade of the hickory I buried Fivekiller.

The grave was perforce shallow; but somehow the very roots that blunted my shovel seemed to welcome him, even as I bade him good-bye. *"Nochebuschee,"* said I. Sleep.

Tired, sweaty, and dark with dirt, having conferred a friend unto the earth, I climbed that hickory. On the ledge I sat a long, long while, wondering would I surrender to the Blood as peaceably, as nobly as Fivekiller had suffered the sudden-coming years. Looking southward o'er the bay, toward Long Point, I saw five sandhill cranes upon the tide-bared shore. Further south, somewhere, lay Glass Lake; and then, again, I saw its men—the same who haunted my dreams—given over, returned to Time; and I feared the rage, the retribution of Sweet Marie, mistress now of naught but bones. All around me osprey circled on currents that riffled the treetops. Westward went the sun. In the east there rose stars; and these I saluted by their Seminole names, which now I knew. When finally I turned northward it was dark. So dark I saw nothing, least of all the path I'd take.

55

Soldiery

WITH Fivekiller gone, I might have left the fort for the Nation; for Big Swamp specifically: the Cove, wherein Celia was, or had been resident. Sweet Marie had said as much; but I was heartened to hear a sutler met riverside say the same: recently he'd seen a woman meeting my description of Celia at Okahumpky. Two other men—one black, one red—swore they'd seen a violet-eyed runner at Peliklakaha. *Enfin,* it seemed Celia was out there still; and I might have gone to her then save for cowardice, cowardice and fear, cowardice and fear and circumstance.

. . . No, I did not go when I could have, with Fivekiller interred and peace yet upon us; and soon it was too late to leave.

That early winter of '35, civilians were recruited to aid the soldiers in their mounted patrols. I'd declined such active duty before, during my tenancy at the fort; but now the situation beyond our walls had worsened, and it was made clear to me that I'd two choices: help—actively—or leave. The latter—to leave; go overland into the Nation—was tantamount to suicide. So said a kindly General Belton. To sail off, well . . . failure; and the loss of all I sought: Celia, absolution. . . . Too, was I not the sole guarantor of Mammy Venus's great wish: to see Celia free? I was. And when one knows the will, the wishes of the dead, well . . . it's best to see such things through.

So: I'd stay till tensions eased; and I'd help, as already I had: I was the fort's infirmarian, doing all Dr. Gatlin deemed beneath him. Blessedly, Fort Brooke had been free of fever, and I encountered no more than could be cured by stitches, splints, poultices, and such. No soldier slipped from my care; though one, approaching death, I recalled with two drops of the Spanish waters, which yet I retained, and which proved salutary in the smallest of doses. Other soldiers benefited from sister-work as well: herbcraft, mostly, alongside a few simples I'd learned at Glass Lake. Thusly was I left alone, drawing scant notice and holding to a single goal: to go northward into the Nation when I could. But tensions did not ease, not for many months. And then things worsened, as in November the weather went red: a hurricane scythed up through the Gulf, foundering ships as it blew northward to spill our bays. More: this hurricane was followed hard by the coming of Halley's Comet and—just as comets and quaking earth had presaged the theater fire; just as ice and eclipse had told of Turner's rising—again I heard it said that the End of Days was upon us. Idiocy. Idolatry. . . . Although, I did wonder if somewhere in the world a witch had done dark work; for too well I recalled Sebastiana's esbat and all that followed from it. And I'd reason to wonder; for within a year or so hundreds of buildings burned to the ground in Gotham, men of the Alamo were mown down by Santa Ana, Zulus rose in far Africa, and soldiers at Fort Brooke told of insurrectionists in Mexico, Ecuador, Central America, Peru, and Bolivia besides. . . . O, but we'd worries of our own: the fort needed fixing.

The hurricane brought no loss of life, only property; such that all within its walls were enlisted in repairs. Surprised, I was, to hear it commanded that the fort be reset in a state of defense. The oaks we left alone; but much of the surrounding pine was hewn into planking, and with this the fort's walls were made whole. Too, we fenced the perimeter in pine, and dug ditches wherein we set sharpened stakes covered in straw. The palmetto and scrub were razed, lest the Indians approach under cover of same. Asking the *why* of what we were about, I had it explained to me that the Seminoles had split into factions, friendly and hostile. Now what little news I'd heard of the Nation, I hadn't much heeded; and shamed I am to say it. Only then did I learn of the seven chiefs; who now had returned from the Arkansas territory to dispute what it was they had or had not signed, and what the Seminole would or would not do.

Some among them agreed to remove, westward. Charley Emathla led this lot—the friendlies; and they worked with the Indian agent, Wiley Thompson, to plan their long trek. Others—Micanopy, Jumper, Holata Mico, Arpeika, Coa Hadjo—determined to fight; and to their fore came Osceola. He it was who met Charley Emathla that November as the chief traveled back from Fort King, where he'd sold his cattle preparatory to removal. Osceola slew him, and scattered o'er the savannah what specie the chief had received; for he'd let no man say he'd coveted that Iscariot silver.

Thereafter, those willing to remove decamped quickly to Fort Brooke. Some four hundred Seminole—led by Holata Emathla, brother to the slain chief—settled on the shore opposite us, giving themselves o'er to the protection of a government that already had set a date for removal: one January of the coming year: 1836: this year.

With the hurricane come and gone, it was noticed that some months had passed with no communication from General Clinch, installed at Fort King, sitting northeasterly across the Nation. It was feared the fort was under siege, or had fallen. The last expressman bearing a letter addressed to Clinch had ridden out in August, only to fall not far from Fort Brooke: shot, scalped, and disemboweled, he was. The hostiles had even shot his mount, lest any misread the red message writ upon the rider.

So it was that in early December the command of Fort Brooke came to debate a march to the relief of General Clinch. Before doing so, they'd make a final attempt at correspondence. Lest the post rider fall and the letter come into enemy hands, it was decided to write in French; for it was known Clinch could read the language, and assumed no Seminole could. And so I was sent for, though I'd told no one I'd served the territory as translator, nor had I spoken of my patrimony. Someone, I suppose, had discerned the French that girds my English, still.

I agreed to write the letter, of course. I less readily agreed to my recruitment, which was requisite (I was told) and followed fast, so fast I was a soldier in Jackson's service before I knew it. Me, a soldier! Of brevet, or honorary rank, and earning three dollars a day. Now I'd no choice but to live among the men. Thusly did I lose that privacy I'd established. Worse: the fort soon grew crowded; for red men and black men, both, had begun to attack. It was said no settlers remained on the eastern coast, south of St. Augustine. And the western settlers—white men, their allies and property, human and otherwise—crowded into Fort Brooke. No longer were its environs enough, no: *within* the fortified walls they came.

Not since my convent-school youth had I known so little privacy. Bad enough I'd had to surrender my bunk in the hospital and move into the barracks house, but now I woke to reveille, and rose alongside tens of men. I kept to myself as best I could; but this had been easier among schoolgirls than among callous men living en masse. One morning, when a too-familiar man of County Armagh, Ireland—thusly did he describe himself, in full, whenever asked—made enquiry regarding my swaddling, I said it was owing to a rib I'd cracked in the company of Fivekiller; one which hadn't properly healed. Thusly did I remind him of the mysterious Indian—whose odd mortality had been remarked by several soldiers and whispered into legend—and achieve my goal: the setting of some distance between us.

Of course, all things witch-related I had to stow. And still I carried all I'd brought from St. Augustine, most of it bearing on spells and such. To my great regret, I had nothing—no Books, none of the monographs taken from the Van Eyn cellar—pertaining to prevision, or sight; and never, never had I so wished to see the future.

How high would these flames of war rise? Was this the war Sweet Marie had wanted? If so, I was relieved, thinking I'd played no part in its advent. Would soldiers come by sea to stop it? (All that winter the bay waters were watched; for relief was rumored to be en route: four companies aboard schooner and brig, sailing from New Orleans and Pensacola to accompany us to Fort King.) As ever, I wondered would I find Celia. Panicked, I worried she'd remove with the friendlies; and so:

I searched the Seminoles across the water for violet eyes, for word of the Flower'd-Face'd one; but nothing: few of the Indians would speak to a white man in soldier-dress. If Celia was not removing—and I doubted she would; for in so doing she'd risk being discovered as a runner, and murderess besides—then surely she'd go deeper into the Big Swamp.

There one could outlie forever, unfound. Worrying so—with no recourse to the Craft; and no choice but to wait out a fate I could not control—I wondered, *What am I doing?* It had been years now since I'd skulked from our house in the night, a witch of the worst sort; one who—like Sweet Marie—served only herself. Was it love drove me still? I'd have said so, yes; but I've since come to see it was absolution I sought. And only Celia could grant me that.

O, but first I'd have to find her. How, when, where . . . ? So many questions. And finally, an answer I'd not anticipated:

Late in December—with no response come from General Clinch, and the bays showing no signs of our reinforcements—it was decided we'd march to the supposed relief of Fort King. We: all of us soldiers. Including me.

Yes: I'd been recruited and outfitted, and paid; but never had I bethought myself a soldier. Indeed not; but here I was, readying to march alongside a hundred-odd men into a Nation of some three thousand war-sharp Seminole awaiting the white man's first move; which now we were to make.

Who was it made the decision to march? I cannot say. Much blustering there was among the Striped Shoulders, the West Pointers. O, but I will not defame the men of Dade's command; neither will I name the lot of them, instead letting scribed stone speak of them to the ages.

. . . Major F. Langhorne Dade was a tall man of middling age; one whose body sat atop his legs as powder kegs sat atop stilts within the magazine. He sported a great black beard; and when he was seated it was hard to distinguish this from his high boots, which rose to meet the beard amidst his middle. In his hat was a cock feather, always. And never did I see him—whilst living—without his sword at his side, rattling and smacking the jamb of every door through which he passed.

As for my own sword, well . . . I hadn't one. Neither had I been commissioned one of the .69-caliber smoothbore flintlock muskets that the soldiers tended with care, now it seemed they might need them. No: no weapon had I—save for my witchly ones—and that suited me, until our marching orders came down.

O, but I did have my stripeless slacks of powder blue kerseymere; and a cape with standing collar and forage cap to match: both a steely gray. White straps and belting accessorized all this, and had, too, some utility, I suppose; but when first I dressed in full, I appeared . . . bandaged. In time I got it right. And in time, too, my boots took the imprint of my own feet, and surrendered those of the soldier who'd last worn them, and whose fate I cared not to consider.

Provisions? I ate better than the citizenry within our walls; for the freeze of February last had blasted citrus and other crops; and the warring state of things had kept all parties from both the harvest and the hunt. Yes: foodstuffs were few; but along with every other member of Companies B and C, Second Regiment Artillery, I received my stale bread and my one and a quarter pounds of salt beef; all of which went into my haversack. I had no cartridge box to carry; yet still my sack was heavy, owing to Fivekiller's few effects and the witch-things I carried. (With due ceremony I buried the Shakespeare: a most befitting fate, given that of its owners; whose murder Sweet Marie had happily seen attributed to some rogue Seminoles, as per her plan. . . . I'm sure of it.) Thusly did assembly and inspection prove most tense: would I have my haversack spilled, its sisterly contents shown? O, but even if I'd been discovered, doubtful I'd have been furloughed: such were the odds against us: all bodies were wanted. For word had come to our commanders from Holata Emathla that his opposites—the hostiles—had sworn to attack the Big Knives if they marched.

Which now we did.

56

En Militaire

Adieu the supercilious air
Of all that strut *en militaire.*
—*Byron*

THE morning we set out was clear, and suitably cool. A Wednesday, this was: the twenty-second of December.

The government road runs northeast from Fort Brooke, rising to a low ridge. We marched past groves which had been burned by frost—most ominous, this: Florida bare of fruit—and some eight miles from the fort proper we came upon the boundary of the Nation: a strip of land sixty miles wide and twice as long, sitting well inland.

Two bands we were, stepping o'er the sandy soil, still wet from a recent rainfall: rather a slog, it was, in fact; and I was glad to be let to walk as I willed, on what dry land I could find. See: little was expected of me; for I'd no stripes, no soldierly training. I'd been brought along to swell the ranks, see to any stricken soldiers, and—officially—to translate: so read the enlistment papers I'd signed *H. Collier*. Now my sole order was to stay within a shout of Major Dade, who rode at the van with a guard of seven men. Behind them came the corps, followed by four oxen dragging the six-pounder, a horse-drawn wagon, and the rear guard. I kept midway down the line, as did Dr. Gatlin.

Though the sun was high, it fell upon us with no consistency; for the road was overgrown, its canopy thick, and its clearings few. The piney woods pressed upon us, rendering the roadway—which was, perhaps, twenty feet in width—darkly green, and shadowy. All the marching men knew it: we'd be seen before we could see; and so we marched in quietude.

And so what sounds we made seemed loud; and well I recall each one. The drum with its muffled tattoo, to which the men marched. The suck of the cannon's wheels, which sank spoke-deep into the road. The breath of every beast: oxen, horse, and hound; the last of which ran this way and that in raggedy packs, rousing every roosting thing, baying at snakes and who knew what else. Too, I recall the creak of leather and the symphonics of kettle and canteen, clanging where they hung from harness or belt.

The oxen slowed us terribly; such that I wondered: Wouldn't we do better to hurry, forgoing the cannon and its carriage even though it could clear any theater, leveling trees (and enemies) with its six-pound balls of shot, both canister and grape? With four rivers to cross—by bridges (if unburned), or by fording—we'd be in the Nation an eternity with this wheeled beast lumbering behind. I said nothing, of course; but I held fast to good sense, worked my will, and may claim a witch's part in what orders came to pass. Finally, Major Dade ordered the cannon stripped of its utility and left; it could be recovered later. The horses were freed of the wagon, and replaced with the oxen; whereupon we verily sped; and none more so than I, who most benefited from this switch of beasts: I was granted a mount. Four had been unburdened. Three went to men of the highest rank; and as there was no order by which to confer the fourth, Major Dade gave it to me; for I'd been standing at his side whilst the surgeon—whose suit would have been superior to mine—had stepped off the road to loose his water.

She was a roan; and I rode her well, and with relief.

We reached the banks of the Little Hillsborough at dusk. Its bridge was intact. We crossed it, and on the far bank fast established camp. Trees were felled, notched, and set end to end to form a breastwork, three logs high. Beyond this pickets were sunk, and to these the horses and oxen were tethered. Pine knots were burned as flambeaux, and lesser wood was thrown upon the fire. The cooks were seeing to their chores; the results of which we all attended, most eagerly, when there was heard the approach of a single horseman.

All took heart to hear horse and rider come from behind us; from Fort Brooke, presumably. Further presumption had the rider—as yet unseen—bearing news of our reinforcements: those companies that had been all but lost at sea.

But no: up the darkened pike there came, at a sloppy trot, a horse well-worn. Upon which there sat a man who appeared neither young nor old, neither black nor white, neither . . . Stay: let me say that all his attributes were of the middling sort, blunted hooks upon which I can hang no description. That said, I well recall the man's first words:

Having ridden into camp, he clambered from off his horse to speak two names. By his tone I knew he relayed orders; and presumed to do nothing more.

Name the first was Major Dade's.

Name the second? Mine.

As for the order he carried, it was this: he was to replace me as translator; for:

I knew French, English, a smattering of Spanish, and had let it be supposed that I knew the Indian tongues, too; but here came one—a slave; Luis Pacheco, by name—whose French was worse (*bien sûr*), whose English was equal, and whose Spanish was better than mine. As to his Muskogee, his Hitchiti, and such, well . . . this Pacheco had learned from a brother who'd been twenty-odd years among the Indians. He could write the Indian languages and speak them as well. This latter I'd never been able to do, not even with the help of my *tisane*.

Moreover: there was the matter of cost. On a month's journey, I'd cost the government some ninety-odd dollars—a goodly sum; though of course I cared not at all for the money: I sought only safe transport nearer to Celia. Contrast this with the deal struck between Major Dade and Señora Quintana Pacheco—a Spanish widow, and the keeper of a trading post at Sarasota Bay—by which she hired out her bondman at the rate of twenty-five dollars for the month. It seemed this Luis had been requisitioned in advance of our march, but had been delayed. And though a slave, he'd a measure of renown; which of course I could have trumped with my own sundry truths, had I wanted to.

The sense of all this was put to me plainly by a lieutenant; the same who then summarized thusly, "And so, you are free to go."

"Am I, then?"

The lieutenant said I might sleep that night at camp, and make my way back to Fort Brooke at dawn. It was I who would tell of the abandoned cannon and urge its due recovery. Further, said he, I could keep my rations; which I suppose was a greater kindness than it seemed at the time. And I'd be let to return upon the roan; but upon reaching Fort Brooke I was to give it o'er—"Hay it first," said he—and swap for pay a promissory note bearing the signature of Major Dade.

None of which I did.

O yes, stay: I did sleep among the men that night. Rather,

I remained at camp but found no rest. No one did; for the woodland was alive with whippoorwill (crying) and Seminole (calling). There came rifle shot, too; and war whoops.

Well before reveille, with the moon yet high, I rose to ride. And ride I did.

Any who heard my leaving must have told the tale often: of how the strange, solitary, short-term soldier had ridden off fast, and in the wrong direction.

For I was too near Celia to retreat now; come what may.

With white men behind me, there'd be red men ahead: this I knew.

Somehow I'd procured a rude map. (Truth: I stole it.) And this showed what I'd hoped it would: Forts Brooke and King, and all points between; including the known encampments of reds, blacks, and maroons. Northward, to the nearest of these I rode.

At first light, I surrendered to the trees my coat. I kept the cape, thinking it might prove a most handy bedroll. My hat, too, I tossed away; and I undid my plait. From my haversack I drew Fivekiller's triangular loincloth. It was buckskin, with glass beads depending from its fringe; these clicked and clacked as I rode; for yes, I tied this too-skimpy suit o'er my slacks of blue army issue. This I paired with a white blouse milled from refuse cotton, showing a full and concealing cut. Thusly outfitted, I hoped to identify myself as neither soldier nor Indian, but a hybrid of both.

The day grew hot; and when the road delivered me down to the banks of the Withlacoochee (where indeed the bridge had been burned), I was not unhappy to have to ford its cold water. I led the roan across, through black water that rose as high as her belly; till finally we scrambled up the slope of the far, friable shore. I emerged mud-covered; and had an idea: I rolled higher my soaked pants and caked my legs in loam. I was tanned already, yes; but wouldn't a good mudding down make me seem less . . . less suspect to any I came across? I thought so; though now I will not vouch for what logic led me thither. Onto my cheeks, into my hair I worked the earth.

With the day declining fast, I rode hard; and what wind we made—the roan and I—turned the mud to cake; such that I must have been quite a sight as I rode into Peliklakaha, which sits well east of the soldiers' road.

They'd known I was coming. I'd been watched a long while, I suppose. And so it was I rode a gauntlet, proceeding into town down a pike formed of red men and runaways, and leading straight to the chief, Micanopy.

Here was the descendant of King Payne, sire of Sweet Marie. As chief, he sits fatly o'er the tribe entire; just as he sat fatly at his feast that night.

A long table had been laid with viands and vegetables; and Micanopy showed what fierceness remained to him as he set about victualing himself, both hands shimmering with grease. At his side sat Abraham, his Sense-Bearer. This latter seemed to me well made, save for an eye—the right one—wont to roll in its socket. It was to these two that I made my appeal:

I'd come in search of a woman. Beautiful. Black. Free. Who'd been a friend. Perhaps she'd run; but in any event she'd come from St. Augustine a long while prior. "She has," I began, "eyes—"

"Most do," said Abraham; whose English testified that he knew white men well. He'd meant no joke; yet those in attendance smiled to see me handled so.

"I mean to say that her eyes . . . You would know her by her eyes. Flower'd-Face, I've heard her called; by some who've seen her hereabouts."

Micanopy shook his head no; and this simple negation caused his jowls to quake. Tremors proceeded down his neck, onto his breasted chest. All the while he sucked a bone thick as his braceleted wrist. *No.*

Silence ensued. I feared for my safety; which fears were somewhat assuaged when Abraham, opening a hand, invited me to sit. I did; and well was I hosted that night: food was slid o'er the table to me, and spirits rather too ardent were poured, and poured again.

A black woman—with a sleeping child tied to her hip by a parti-colored sling—came late to our assembly to say she knew of whom I spoke. My heart skipped at hearing spoken the name Liddy. This woman had not seen Celia at Okahumpky, no; but she had heard she'd been there of late. In her telling I heard the name Osceola, but it came braced by words of Muskogee; the which I could not have comprehended even if I'd abstained from the spirits, as I most certainly had not.

. . . Celia: so near now.

I'd sleep that night in the Seminole town and ride to Okahumpky on the morrow.

O, but when later I lay peering o'er the verge of sleep, readying to descend, I sat bolt upright on my bed of skins. All about me lay my maroon guard: a family of five; several of whom I disturbed as I sat cursing myself.

What had I done?

Lulled into it by liquor, I'd spoken without censor. I'd answered every question put to me by sly Abraham and a second red man, Jumper. And yes: by night's end I had word of Celia; but unwittingly I'd traded away all I knew of Dade's command.

. . . From soldier to traitor in the span of a day.

57

Outlier

I'D not been lied to; but neither did I find Celia at Okahumpky. She'd recently left that place. Still, some there knew her whereabouts; and doubtful they'd have told me, but they did confide in the brave who rode there at my side, sent by Micanopy—or, more likely, Abraham—to ensure that I'd not retrace my route and return to Dade's men; whom I'd fated. . . . I knew not to what degree.

I stayed a day and night at Okahumpky. I'd wanted to ride on at once, now I had news certain of Celia; but I was . . . dissuaded by both the red rider and those maroons with whom he conversed in the click-and-whistle of a tongue unknown to me.

The next day was Christmas. I woke to rainfall, and found my guard had returned to Peliklakaha. Others gave me battercakes and coffee-water; and told me to ride. I was told what way-marks to watch for. I rode for some hours—watched, surely, by scouts unseen—and finally came upon a camp cut into the peat-stinking swamp.

No maps could have known it; for it had been recently staked, and hadn't the permanence of other settlements I'd seen. Its buildings of thatch and swampwood were unsturdy. I saw no horses. The few head of cattle were scrawny and—to judge by their mixed brands—stolen. If the camp had a name, I never heard it spoken by its tenants, who numbered twenty, thirty: the majority men, young and maroon. Several Seminole there were as well, wearing red paint upon their faces. Women? Arriving, I saw none; but soon I'd find there were three:

One of whom was Celia.

A knife set coldly to the throat . . . Suffice to say that to suffer that fate is to know, of an instant, what has happened.

I'd just dismounted and stood attending some measure of welcome when suddenly my loose hair was taken hold of. Tugged back; such that I found myself staring wide-eyed at the low and leaden sky. It was then I felt the blade laid to my neck, aligned to the right side of my jaw. It bit. It stung. I felt not the cut, but the trickle of blood.

Words of English came hotly to my ear; but I cannot here record them. I was too fearful to hear, to speak, to act. Then there came a second voice:

"Leave him."

I felt the knife withdrawn. I fell to the dirt, and wheeling to see my attacker, I found Celia instead. Behind her—sheathing his knife as he walked away—there strode the maroon who'd drawn upon me. But him I fast forgot; for here Celia stood.

. . . O, but she, too, walked away; wordlessly.

I scrambled to my feet and followed.

She traced the camp's border: a bank of tall palms, the

dead fronds of which hung as skeletal hands, scratching at the trunks. It seemed a sound I'd never heard. Celia was clad in a Seminole skirt: a wrap sewn of brightly striped cloth, its edges frayed from sweeping the ground. Her chemise of purest white showed billowing sleeves; and these she'd rolled to the elbows, for she'd been busy with that work to which she now returned:

Another woman stood before a cooking platform. She was dressed similarly, save she sported bracelets and beadwork necklaces. Rings, too; though her hands were bloodied from working a knife upon the haunch that hung before her. She stripped sinew from bone. She hacked strips into cubes, and dropped them into a kettle that overhung a failing fire. This I watched in silence till Celia turned to look at me. Those eyes: just as I'd seen them in my dreams. She was unadorned, but her beauty was undiminished. Still she said nothing; only sat upon a low stump, and hiked her skirt to settle a mortar and pestle between her knees. When finally Celia spoke, it was Muskogee, surprising me; and the second woman—she was Seminole, purely—took her leave.

Celia ground corn. The kernels seemed teeth, loose in the mouth of the mortar. They cracked as she ground the pestle down. This she did a long, long while; till finally . . .

Her eyes. They shone the brighter for the tears that had come. Said she, "What . . . what did you do to me?"

My answer was a spill of shame: hot tears from my own eyes.

What spell I'd cast was broken; that much was plain. But had I effected this with some clumsy Craft-work, done in the days before I'd abandoned her? Or had the spell held a while, lessening o'er time? I cannot say; for I could not ask.

Understand: Celia knew me not as a witch. To her I'd been but Henri; later, the false American: Henry: another white man full of wrongs. And what but further harm could come of my confessing? More: there'd come no occasion to tempt me to it.

Celia waved away three Seminole who stared as she led me to an ill-made chickee. (Their discontent was evident; but to Celia they deferred.) And upon the piney floor of same we sat. And spoke. She first, saying:

That she'd long wished me dead for what I'd done. Not for leaving; but for having stayed so long, for using her as I had. As she'd wanted me to. O, even the memory of our life together confused her. I saw this; for she held her hands to her head, as if the very recollecting hurt her. And though I hated her confusion, her show of pain, I was glad for these. Yes: the more confused she was the better; for perhaps then she'd take on less of the blame. I did not want her to think she'd elicited my . . . my low ways, my lechery; for I knew she'd think back to Bedloe, and deem herself responsible for his ways as well. Complicit, somehow; if only due to a beauty she must surely have disdained.

Blessedly, she did not press for a close accounting of what had passed between us. Best to let rest the inexplicable, thought I. For what might I have said? I could not have spoken of spell-work or witchery. And I'd no wish to speak of the baser things that had driven me: loneliness, lovelessness, lust; for those things were upon me again—mightily—as I sat beside a woman I'd loved; and lost, irretrievably so. I saw that now, bright as light.

Celia said again that she'd wished me dead, and it was most disquieting to hear. But she lightened, visibly so, as she said, "Seeing you, there, beneath Arpeika's knife . . . I knew it: my hatred was gone. I did not, do not wish you dead." For which I was glad, yes; but far less gladdening were the words which followed: Celia said the red man, this Arpeika, would have slain and scalped me, nay scalped and *then* slain me, had she not intervened.

If she'd let go her hatred, so, too, had I let go my love. What was it—guilt, shame, the passage of time . . . —that had trimmed my heart's wick till now it held no flame?

There was naught between us now but lost time; for which I began to account. I told her of Mammy Venus, saying she'd passed in her sleep. I lied a second time to say Rosalie was well, and Edgar no longer a worry. She asked if still I saw adverts for her capture, and I told her no. When I spoke passingly of the places I'd been, I saw her interest was feigned. And indeed, why should she have wished to hear where I'd gone, whom I'd met, and what I'd seen—truths twined in lies—when I'd left her alone in St. Augustine, spellbound, her every sense confused?

As for Celia, and what had passed since last I'd seen her, left her, abandoned her, well . . . she did not speak of this; and I knew not to ask. Still, a sort of answer came that afternoon when a scouting party returned to camp.

He walked toward us; and I felt, verily *felt* his force of will, as I had but once or twice before: in the company of certain witches whose ire was up, whose Eye showed strongly.

He was tall. And though he was not handsomely made, still he stirred me deeply.

His face showed that whiteness he abhorred: his skin and eyes were light. Into his black hair there'd been set a band of buckskin; and dark feathers fanned out from this to frame his face. O'er his broad chest he wore a necklace: three half plates of hammered silver, each seemingly modeled upon a sliver of moon. A gaudy shift fell to his knees. From his belt there hung two knives; and an odd thing that I fear may have been a scalp, long-withered and sere, its hair hanging in wisps. High boots of hide rose nearly to his knees; and I remarked—incongruously, it may seem—that his feet were small; so, too, were the hands in which he held a blue rifle.

Here was Osceola. I knew it, and needed not to hear his name spoken.

Nor did I need to hear why he'd come to us; for, approaching, he looked from Celia to me, and back again. Turning, I saw her smile. Saw, too, that her smile sparked the warrior's eye.

The two spoke English only when Celia's Muskogee failed them. And when Osceola spoke—in a voice ranging from jagged to shrill—it was not to me. Instead, Celia parleyed between us in two languages; and thusly was it established that:

No: I was not a slaver. Rather more the opposite, in fact. In English she told of our absconding. In lesser detail—the which I was thankful for—she spoke of our life in St. Augustine.

Yes: I'd come from Fort Brooke. And yes: it was I who'd had council with Micanopy. Hearing the latter confirmed, I tried to untell what I'd told; but was left sputtering my story to the warrior's back.

Celia and I followed him to a meal of venison hash and sofkee. There was whiskey, too; but this time I took care to pass. Words were few. And it was with relief I saw our small party disbanded.

In truth, I was sent away. Alone. To sleep at the fire's far reaches, beneath a badly lathed tent of stripped pine. I woke later that Christmas night when again the rains came. . . . Damp, dark, and cold, indeed; for now no fires burned, neither without nor within.

58

The Ensilvering

I WAS still at the camp three mornings hence: the twenty-eighth of December.

It was cold and dark when I was woken. I lay bundled in skins; for I'd slept beneath stars which yet were bright: the day would be clear, and for that I was glad. It was then I felt the nudging foot, saw the shadow standing o'er me.

It was the camp's third woman, a lithe and mean mulatta who'd thrown me work the day prior: moccasins to mend: woman's work, given to humble or shame me, I suppose. But I didn't mind. I was grateful for the occupation, as two days had passed with Celia paying me scant attention. A stranger, I seemed; set apart. And all about the camp there'd been comings and goings, plans being laid—that was plain; yet a sort of pall descended as well. I don't know how better to describe it. Meanwhile, I'd not been let to leave: the roan had been secreted somewhere, and I feared what I might hear if I asked after her.

"What is it?" I asked of the woman, whom now I recognized. "What do you want?" I was annoyed; for her nudging had progressed to a kick. So sudden, so rude an awakening had brought on the Eye; which came concomitant with a headache. Blessedly, and owing to the dark, the Toad went unseen.

"He wants you," I heard. "Says you are to ride out with him."

"Who? . . . Who says this?" But I knew: Osceola.

He'd returned to camp late the night prior. There'd been a council beyond the camp, and all during it I'd not seen Celia. Whether she was in attendance, whether she was privy to all that came to pass, I cannot say.

But what did the warrior want with me? I asked, and in response was nudged, nay kicked again. Surely my Eye twisted like flame on the wind. "Thanks to Liddy, you're alive. Others gonna have less luck today. . . . Now get ready to ride."

I hate the hunt; always have. And never had I set a sight upon a living thing. Until that day. And only later would I learn who it was I'd watched die:

Wiley Thompson. The Indian agent. A white man at the fore of removal.

Thompson it was who'd clapped irons on Osceola, bound and jailed him when the warrior had slashed the Payne's Landing treaty. And now the hour of vengeance tolled, I was to witness it.

We—Osceola, whose saddle I was made to share, lest I try to ride off alone; and some dozen warriors—rode hard to Fort King. Of course, I'd no idea why; nor did I ask, or wonder overlong; for upon arrival I saw with surprise that Fort King had not fallen. Nor was it under attack. Its soldiers came and went at their leisure, few of them shouldering arms. The garrison had been war-fortified, yes, but otherwise appeared normal. . . . Could I break from the Indians to stop Dade's men, marching through a rising Nation to save soldiers who needed no saving? Could I? . . . Would I? Should I? . . . A torment, this wondering was as we lay unseen in the scrub, not a hundred yards from the fort itself, all through the long hours of that forenoon.

I knew we'd come not to trade, not to negotiate. The stealth of our approach, the silent watching, the warriors' readiness with rifle and knife . . . I knew it, I saw and slowly came to admit it: we'd come to kill.

Osceola stayed at my side all the while. The others fanned out through the hammock, seeking angles of advantage. Some steadied their rifles on tree limbs. Others lay flat upon their stomachs. All barrels were set on the sutler's house, beside the fort; so it was that place I watched, too, seeing:

Men at their midday meal. Readily I identified our target by his grander uniform and the deference paid him: he was served first, ate first, spoke first. Other men sat at the round table; some uniformed, others not. Busied by service were two white boys, both answering to a barrel-ish black woman. The boys set heaped plates before the men, and saw to what was wanted. Through an open window banked in calico, I watched.

As the men—done with luncheon—sat back fatly to sip from snifters, Osceola passed me a rifle. I declined it. *No,* said he, wordlessly. And so I took the rifle from him, arranging it as I knew I must. Thereafter, I saw Thompson clearly, too clearly: through crosshairs, living the last hour of his life.

My hands slickened upon the smooth steel of the gun. I could smell the powder, could feel the chambered ball. All the feculence of the forest rose to my nose: the rot and rankness of it. We'd lain still so long crawling things returned to us, and I suffered some multilegged critter upon my back; for though we lay still in the committing of murder, to move was to invite it.

Suddenly, the trees were busy with birds; . . . but no: not birds: these were the war party's whistles. They set themselves to action by means of bird-sound now; for the white men were readying to rise from table.

At first I thought we'd been foiled, and hoped we had; for Thompson stepped out of sight. But no: suddenly he appeared upon the porch. To stretch. To digest. To light cigars alongside his men. And to die.

I fell chill as I heard the readying of one rifle, and a second, sounding like snapping twigs. The first shot—Osceola's—tore through the stillness. Deafened by same, still I held to my rifle, steadied the sight to my eye. Thusly did I see that first ball burst the blue of Thompson's chest whilst a second clove his head in two, sundering skull, spattering brain onto the sutler beside him. Osceola rose to let go a war cry so sudden, so shrill, that I rolled from him, onto my side. Again he fired. I saw with my naked eye men running to and from the fort. Others appeared o'er its topside, pointing at the brush, at us, at me! I pressed my belly flat to the ground, shouldered the rifle, and saw through the sight the boys and woman inside the house. She hurried them into what must have been the kitchen, and I thought all three safe. O, but then into the sight there came those with whom I'd ridden: maroons and Seminole both, bounding onto the porch and into the house. What fate befell the woman and boys, I cannot here record. I searched for them, but instead I saw a soldier shot. Framed in that window, he was, and raising high his hands. Surrender? No: fast, fast he dove for the open window. There came shot and smoke from an unseen gun; and, too, the ball that made meat of his face.

Osceola, too, I saw through the sight: doing knife-work upon the fallen Thompson; the which eventuated in the warrior rising from his crouch, crying shrilly, and seeming to offer to some Watcher in the sky the white man's scalp.

Two men—one old, one young; one uniformed, one not—found themselves face-to-face with Osceola upon the porch. They were unarmed. I saw the Seminole motion them toward the fort: *Run!* And run they did, slipping down the blood-slick steps; but fifteen, twenty steps from the fort's closing doors they fell, shot by another.

Others of the men who'd been with Thompson fell as well; and dark work was done unto them. The shot were stabbed; the stabbed, shot. The scalped skulls of the dying were stove in by rifle butt. Through that same window I saw shelves being tipped, fires being set. Out came the warriors, back to the hammock. Some had bloodied hands. Others carried spoils: one red man bore two bottles of wine.

I kept to the hammock, hoping I was hidden, wanting to run but stilled by all I saw. O, but now the trees were taking shot, splintering as finally fire came from the fort.

I had to be lifted, bodily, and set upon a horse behind a rider. Bullets whistled through the brush, finding trees with one sound and flesh with another. I was roused from my stupor when I saw my horsemate struck. Blood burst onto my belly from his blown-open back. As he fell his face told it plainly: he'd been heart-struck, and was dead. Only the angle of entry had spared me. I turned from his wide-open eyes, the blood abubble upon his lips. Reddened reins in hand, I set my heels to the horse and rode as I'd never ridden before. The bullets, the blood drumming in my head . . . I was deafened, dumb; but somehow I knew, knew my choice was no choice at all: ride or die.

We rode fast; and were not followed. And though now I had a horse to myself, I gave no thought to striking out alone. . . . O, would that I had ridden and made it away; for then I'd have been spared what news the night brought.

Though the forest was but a blur of greens and browns, I saw we were not returning to camp the way we'd come. And right I was; for finally we slowed into a second camp. This was empty of all men; and none of the many women were Celia. Only later would this strike me as strange. Then, what sense I could master fell to fear, and to a trembling I could not still. Finally I did still myself, aided in the effort by that wine stolen from the sutler's house.

I had been sitting for a long while with my back to a trickling pine when there came from behind me a man. I saw his moccasins, grass-green and wet. I could smell his sweat, and the ferric scent of the blood he'd spilled and wore still: Thompson's blood. I looked up to see Osceola hand down to me a bottle of the wine, labelless and blue. Its cork had been drawn. I took it, saying nothing; and when the warrior walked away, I drank.

What a sink, what a morass my mind was as those late-day hours fell away. In a state of suspension, of stupefaction, I sat drinking. With drink I'd blind myself to all I'd seen. O, but no: the show came steadily on.

Understand: though I'd met the dead, yes, before that day I'd seen no man die by violence. . . . Death; it had shown itself a silvery thing. . . . Thompson and the others? I'd seen their twins—their spirits, say—stepping from their bodies as if rising from tubs of molten silver. From its hosts life had verily stepped, and seeped; for the ensilvered twins did not rise away but rather stayed to diffuse, confusedly, o'er their bodies. . . . And when I'd risen from off the forest floor to run, to ride, it seemed those spirits sought and knew me.

Now, returned to camp, I sat unsought, unknown. No one had approached me save Osceola. Lone riders came fast into camp, only to ride out again. All else was eerily quiet as the women prepared for . . . what? A feast?

Yes; for finally all the ridden-out men returned in triumph.

At first I was fearful; for I heard, felt the earth beaten by a hundred, nay a thousand hooves. Were the soldiers of Fort King come? No: here came celebration. Triumph, yes.

And odd though it may sound, by evenfall I'd be thankful I'd been made to ride with Osceola; for thusly I'd seen but the slaughter of several soldiers, not the one hundred and eight of Dade's command.

59

Penance

To a one, they fell: those men I'd marked for death.

Later that night a fire was set at the center of the camp. Beside this there rose a pole of pine, so fresh its sap yet ran to marry the red of blood; for upon this, as though they were pennants, there were hung the harvested scalps.

Micanopy I saw. Also Abraham and Cudjo and Jumper. They sat fireside, not in council but in celebration, passing pipes and liquor skins. Around them warriors danced, some wearing scalps; such that blood dripped down to sting and unsight the wearers. One maroon aped the white man whose scalp he sported; and when he squared his body and stroked an imagined beard, I knew it was Major Dade he charaded.

Elsewhere Seminole mourned. One of their own had fallen at Fort King, yes, but several more had not returned from the raid on Dade's command. Still, the scene that unfolded before me, by moon- and firelight, was naught but celebratory. A feast. A fandango.

And as I watched this, watched the men, women, and children of sundry color—red, black, and white, and showing every shade thereof—I knew I was no longer being watched. I knew I'd be let to leave. I'd been useful, yes. I'd been . . . used.

Used, indeed. . . . I thought then of Sweet Marie. Had I not traded fairly, as she'd said I would? Here I was at the heel of the hunt, having found Celia; and now it seems Sweet Marie will have her war; for I need no Craft, no sisterly means of sight to see that there will be retribution. Swiftly it will come, ordered down from Washington. War. . . . More blood; and all the spillers of it will be wrong: white men, red men, black men all wrong in their way, none of them noble. Slavers and slaughterers. Liars and thieves. O, but this I know, too: white men bear the greater shame, and ought to own the greater blame; for they have taken by might what is not theirs by right: freedom from the black men, land from the red. . . . War, yes: it will come. With me its lesser cause. . . . What now, but to recess myself into shadow?

The details I had from Celia, who came to me where I sat. She told it as kindly as she could. Did she have her account firsthand? Might she have been at the massacre? Could her blood have boiled so? Could the sum of her hatred have tallied so darkly to that? This last is a question I do not care to consider; for if Celia so hated, so hates the white man, well . . . haven't I to count myself among the reasons why?

. . . Micanopy (said Celia) was supposed to have waited for Osceola. The latter, warriors in tow, was to have hied from Fort King—Thompson seen to—to join in the ambush of Dade's men. This we'd not done, of course; for the taking of Thompson had drawn itself out. And so it was Micanopy who fired first from deep within the forest; for such was his right by custom, I suppose.

O, the details . . . Having the first of them, I wanted no more. Could abide no more.

Celia was sympathetic, and pleasured not in seeing me stricken, sick with remorse. Nor did Osceola. Who joined us at our remove; for the celebration had by then devolved to devilry, with children snatching down scalps and scuffles erupting among the drunken.

I remember the dregs of that wine upon my tongue. I remember saying I wanted sleep. Saying I would leave at dawn. Osceola assented to both—a nod; no words—and I stole off somewhere beyond the camp. At a far away tree I fell to my knees. I'd push together a mat of pine needles, fallen moss, and such; but soon my despair stopped me. I set my back to the tree. I closed my crying eyes. I prayed, yes prayed that I'd sleep and never wake. . . . O, but I woke before dawn to find a bearskin had been set o'er my shoulders. Too, leaning against my leg was the second bottle of the sutler's wine.

Celia? Osceola? One or both of them, I suppose.

It was then, of a sudden, I struck upon a plan of penance.

. . . As the sun rose, I spilled the contents of my haversack; and when the simple work was done, I went in search of Celia and Osceola.

I roused a boy who'd enough English to understand my order. I gave him a fip; and for it he found whom it was I sought.

They came to me beyond the camp. Celia led the roan. Osceola was clean of what blood he'd shed. There we stood, silence presiding; for what speech could suffice? Indeed, I was dumb with desperation, and knew worse lay ahead that day. More: here was good-bye. To Celia, so long sought.

From the haversack I took that square of red satin onto

which Eugénie had sewn—in threads silver and gold—Loco Attiso: loa of luck and good fortune. Celia, perhaps, took the gift for a mere kerchief. I can only hope she'll hold to it, and feel its effect.

Celia had a hug for me: much more than was my due, surely.

I mounted the roan. As I looked down, it was pity I saw in Celia's eyes; but pity was preferable to hatred. O, she'd a right to hate me as she had, yes; mistake me not. But so heartened was I to see she'd set her hatred aside that I gave my second gift; thusly:

Down from the horse I made to pass the second bottle of the sutler's stolen wine. Celia declined. She looked up at me, questioningly. I raised the bottle to my own lips—a penance, yes—and tasted that elixir, too bitter for any witch to want. It was all I could do not to spit the wine away. I tried to make of my face a lie: hide my distaste of the doctored drink. O, but perhaps this showed; for Celia smiled, and beneath the rising sun she shone, verily shone. Glad I was to watch her drink; even if only to indulge me in that strangest of toasts.

For into the wine I'd cut Fivekiller's last two bottles of time.

Celia passed the bottle up to me. Again, I drank. (My tongue revolted, seemed to shrink and shrivel as will a salted slug!) Again, I bid Celia do the same. She did. Deeply. And with that second, deeper draft she lengthened her life.

From Celia I'd taken much; now I gave back what I could: time. . . . And—blessed be—may she live it happily, and free.

I offered drink to Osceola. He declined.

I rode from camp upon the roan.

To the roots of a great magnolia I conferred the rest of the wine; and in its shade I stood watching as white blooms came full and fast to loose their scent upon the last days of the year.

From thence I went in search of the government road. I had my map. I knew where the ambush had passed. To that place I'd ride; for yet I was penitent, and had more amends to make.

60

Jubilee

THE dead drew me on; but the horse I had to spur: she sniffed the wind and knew it for foul.

The swamplands were still, and showing wintry shades. The sky was low, weighted with rain. As I'd ridden southward, down the government road, the weather had worsened; as I knew it must. Clouds came on, mounding to mountains. When finally I found the dead, the saw grass was whistling, the palms bent forward and back, and the live oaks groaned. Lesser limbs cracked and crashed to the ground, off which rose a silvery mist. On the nearby pond the water was white-capped; for the wind . . . Stay: I'll not yet speak of the wind.

A pond: yes: there was a pond.

Dade's men had marched well north of where I'd left them, just past where a pond opened on the eastern verge. Amidst pineland and palmetto scrub, they'd been beset. And what I found testified plainly: they'd not seen their attackers; for they'd fallen as they marched; and many had died in formation.

I came at the vanguard; and there found the bodies of Dade and seven others. Their weapons were unpowdered, unloaded: their ammunition was still boxed, and bulging within their haversacks and jackets. Some of it had been stolen; some of it spilled as insult. I knew Major Dade by his boots and the sword he'd not drawn. His black beard seemed a stream of ants, trailing from his face onto his bloodied chest. He'd been shot through the heart. His skull lay open to the air; and I knew where it was his scalp hung.

. . . The wind, yes. The wind was awhistle; and would rise to a howl, such that I'd wonder if wolves had come.

Further down the lines, the men lay in deathly array; for they'd seen the vanguard fall, and some had stooped to shoot. Others showed faces oddly passive: they'd died dumb, not knowing what had come. Now they knew, in death; but such knowledge as that partakes of the soul, the spirit only. And all the spirits had slipped their hosts: no one lay dying: all were dead.

I saw that the attackers had come twice; for the men who survived the ambush had had time to build a breastwork. A triangle of felled pine sat facing that direction in which the attackers had retreated; the same (presumably) from whence they'd returned. The soldiers had had an hour, perhaps, to build this bunker. Already their force had been much reduced; and no doubt they'd had to abandon the dead to fight further. O, but their efforts had been for naught: dismounting, tying the skittish roan to a tree, I stepped to the breastwork and peered o'er its low walls to see the men within. Some held the stance in which they'd fought. One lay on his stomach, rifle leveled into a warp in the breastwork wall; but he'd taken shot to the forehead, was wide-eyed and staring though his brain had spilled down his back. Another had spun, in spidery fashion, a blue web of guts. Others had been dispatched by a foe that had come much closer; for knife-work had been done, such that I hoped, hoped the victims had been dead, and did not see those blades drawn.

O, what a litter of life this was: bodies blue-clad and strewn about, set to the odd angles of death's geometry. Here were more bones I'd sown upon the land: first Glass Lake, and now this.

On the cold and puckered flesh fish crows had feasted, wrenching from faces their softer parts: eyes, lips, and oyster-like cheeks. Mind: I knew these men; some by their ruined faces, some by name. I shooed away the carrion fowl; and they retook to the trees, where they waited, sawing the silence with their *caw, caw, caw*.

O, but soon that sound ceded to another; and the birds took wing. For yes, the wind had risen to wolvery and beyond, till within it I discerned something . . . else:

I'd heard the massed dead before; but never had I heard those so recently slain, so newly disquieted by death's sudden coming. O yes: I knew the buzz and hum of the long dead, who did sometimes speak; but this was new, this . . . howling; so new it carried words quite distinct. Names, in fact.

The dead were rousing themselves, their souls massing; and as they did so, they each of them uttered, murmured the names of those they'd leave behind. O a true, true sadness this was, let it be said: their tone was desultory, the name-calling incantatory. Mothers and sisters, I suppose. Sons and lovers. Fathers. Friends. How long before that listing would cede to the inchoate song I'd heard before, and would have preferred to suffer then?

I steadied myself against this litany of loss. This proved easier; for soon my coming had drawn all the dead (as I'd supposed it would). And so the storm worsened: the wind whipped, stripping fronds from off the trees; the clouds seemed suddenly to skid, as if the sky were ice; the canopy came alive as birds drew off; and a cold, cold rain fell, such that the resurrection fern—those slimy sleeves of green drawn o'er the arms of oaks—revivified. Then: commune:

I gave myself to the dead for judgment; and cared not what might come.

It was as if the wind had hands; for I felt myself moved. Raised up where I stood. And thrown some feet back against an oak, to land trippingly o'er a branch reaching near the ground. On my back I lay, looking to the roiling green of the trees. I cried. And cried aloud into the silvering mist:

"Come. . . . Come!"

Raising my arms I felt my hands taken; and again I rose, was risen up. I was naught but fear, and will; and what I willed was for the dead to work upon me. That was what I feared as well.

I *wanted* punishment, wanted to suffer something . . . penitential, yes.

O but the dead . . . the dead men of Dade's command . . . somehow they knew that what I'd done I'd done innocently. This they conveyed to me, wordlessly.

The weather lessened. The wind fell still. That litany of loss could again be discerned.

And that is all I remember. That; and the fast-drop down into darkness.

When next I woke, I lay agrave: buried.

It seems I fell, that again the dead dragged me down to a state akin to theirs. Nothing new, this; but never had I descended so deeply into the death-state, not even at Matanzas. Indeed, so dead did I seem, I'd been buried. . . . How long had I lain amidst the massacred? How long had it been before word of the ambush made it back to Fort Brooke? I cannot say; but when finally the fate of Dade's men was learned, when finally soldiers marched into the Nation to bury their brethren, they'd numbered me among them; for there I lay, insensate. And none had lived to tell of my having ridden off in advance of the attack. Thusly was I accorded the burial of an enlisted man; such as it was:

Owing to the exigencies of death in a climate that will fast rot a body, the men of Dade's command were interred in pits dug upon the site: officers in one, lesser men in a second. It was within the latter pit I awoke.

At first I could not move, so densely did the earth lie upon me, upon us. My eyes and mouth were open, clotted and unsighted by dirt. My face was flush to the cold, cold and corroded back of him on whom I'd lain. I could not see, of course; and knew, somehow, that I had no need of breath, not yet. All my muscles lay slack; and only by will, by a great effort of will, was I able to move them, digging first with my fingers, flexing my hands, feeling the dead men beneath and beside me, above me. Their buttons, their hair, their bones, their worm-busy flesh. It may have been hours, it may have been days before I made my way up and out of that grave. . . . O but with the return of my sensorium there came that ineffable relief born of scratching, scratching, scratching at the dirt and the flesh set all about me to find that yes, O, blessedly yes, I'd not been encoffined. Well might it have happened: an interment of long duration, ended only by the coming of the Blood.

But yes I scratched, I pressed, I dug, I humped my back and pushed my way from the grave; which was shallow, for having had to be dug so wide. I broke the turf to find it sparsely grassed. How long had I lain among the dead? Long enough for grass to overgrow our grave. Too long; let it be said. Blinded, I was, by a low sun. And weak. Weak; and yet stronger. Of course. Ever stronger. . . . Blessed be the dead.

And here I must posit what first I learned at Glass Lake, when Fivekiller—or was it Sweet Marie herself?—spoke of the men who feared us so. Among certain red men there and elsewhere, it was held, has long been held, that the soul is tripartite, as Aristotle said it was; but the Indians see the three souls thusly: the first is the shadow the body casts, the second the image it reflects upon water, and the third, the primary soul, is that which resides in the eye. . . . The Eye.

Rising from among Dade's men, I knew I'd drawn upon the dead again; for I felt the Eye strongly, yes. Therein their soul-strength was resident. And indeed, from that day to this my Eye has been fixed, and holds the Toad no matter my will. How other sisters strengthen, I cannot say; but *my* Eye, well . . . Again I'd traded: the silvery strength of the dead for that quietus only I could confer.

Silence now. No sounds save those of the natural world: the weather was down, the dead were still. And in time my sight adjusted to the sunlight. My muscles learned their use. I could hear; and heard my heart restart. But it was a long while before I drew breath. I was caked with death and dirt, and maggots turned vainly o'er my skin; but they sup not upon the living: tasting my witch's blood, they dried to flake and fell.

I wanted to wash, badly so. Having reset the earth atop the grave, I walked from it to the pond. I stripped: I'd been interred with my haversack still astrap my chest, and my clothing intact. Naked, I stepped through reeds, into the cold, cold water. I walked out, then waded out further; and let myself sink to the pond's grassy bottom.

It was then I felt something; and had the sky not been clear, I'd have thought lightning had come. So alive was the air, the water; so charged.

I bounded up; and before I broke the scummed surface of the pond I heard a most preternatural song. *There . . .*

There along the bankside lay alligators. Ten, fifteen. Ranging in size from five feet to ten, at least. And all of them bellowing, bellowing and slamming their tails to create a chorus the likes of which, well . . . Was it still winter? I thought so; but to judge the season I had only the decomposition of the men among whom I'd lain. But yes: winter it was, surely. And so the alligators ought to have been winter-quiet, hibernating; but here was a show that quite outdid the courtship rituals of spring. The gators kept from the water's edge—oddly I had no fear of their sliding into the pond, and approaching—and their bellows progressed to a hiss, till each gator sounded like a gaggle of geese. O, the din!

To this there was added frog-sound. I saw great bulls sitting bronzed upon the banks. And fish flocked to the pond's sides as well, turning turbid the tea-dark waters. Its edges were alive; the reeds all arustle. Salamander and newt and black eel, these I saw slither and slide on the loam, seek purchase where they could, though soon the banks were crowded with crane and heron: enemies. The trees, too, were alive with birds. And a pack's worth of common foxes slunk from the tall grasses. Panthers? No. There were none. . . . At so uncanny and peaceable a show I could only laugh.

Laugh; and wonder what it was I'd drawn from the dead. What was this strength that every animal saw, and acknowledged by joining in this jubilee? O, how strange this was! . . . Surely no witch has ever received like tribute; surely.

In time, I waded from the water; and as I did so, all life retook its place. The gators fell silent and slunk into the water, up to their eyes. The fish quit the surface. Amphibious creatures hid from the pecking herons. Foxes stole back to the forest.

The sun was shying westward. Its dying fired the sky to violet: the very shade of Celia's eyes. I stood in the rushes, watching, listening as the chorus of tribute fell quiet, and the natural sound of the pond resumed. I was forgotten. It was as if I'd not risen, not come. . . . O but I had, and what had I learned? I cannot yet say.

What clothing I wore had been rendered to cerement; still

I'd no choice but to don it again. And the dirt that had worked its way into my mouth had given me a terrible thirst, which now I slaked on water tapped from the heart of a traveler's palm. Hunger? No; none. The only other need I had was for home. The roan? Long gone, of course. But still, I would head homeward. To St. Augustine.

I broke ten twigs into equal lengths, and—in Indian fashion—threw one away each day at dawn; thusly do I know I was six days in the brush, surviving on the land and the largesse of the dead. For yes, I set out for St. Augustine that very day, having thanked the dead of Dade's command for their forgiveness, for their indulgence, for whatever it was they'd conferred upon so unworthy a witch as I.

Epilogue

THREE letters of import attend my return to St. Augustine.

Letter the first, from Rosalie, lets it be known she is well enough to hold a post teaching penmanship at a school founded by the Misses Mackenzie. Bundled with this letter are torn pages printed with her brother's poems; which, though they are . . . striking, I scan only for references to the people and places of my recent past. Finding few, I am relieved; the more so when I read in Rosalie's letter that John Allan has died. And so: from the threat of Edgar Poe I may suppose myself freed.

Letter the second comes from New Orleans. Eugénie wonders: Might I come thither to help her depose the Widow Paris? She is summoning sisters. "We witches can do this work," writes she *en français,* the better to tempt me.

Letter the third is in cipher, and bears that *S* I'd once so longed to see. Sebastiana writes that she has strength enough to sail, "to see to promises made." Moreover: she's a surprise for me. I am to apprise a Cuban monk—whom she names but with a single letter: *Q*—of my plans. Why so? Has Sebastiana already sailed? Is she alone? Is she, are *they* en route? If so, will I be sought here, or am I to sail to Havana in search of a nameless monk? And what of this "surprise" to which she alludes?

. . . What will I do?

Well, some lines hence I will sign and shut this Book, as tomorrow I will shutter and seal this house. And I will hie inland from off this coast with naught but a new *Book of Shadows*—its blank pages awaiting my fate—and Celia's old spectacles hiding my Eye. It's that odd riverine route I'll take: the St. John's. Upon its confused current I'll sail northward, consoling myself with proof that even a wrong-flowing river can achieve the sea.

Thereafter, where? I know only this: I will let the sea decide.

H.

Acknowledgments

Thank you to the following at William Morrow for their expertise and enthusiasm: Michael Morrison, Lisa Gallagher, Sharyn Rosenblum, Juliette Shapland, Jeremy Cesarec, and, especially, my editor, Sarah Durand. And thanks once again to my agent, Suzanne Gluck, and her staff at the William Morris Agency.

Also, I am indebted to Sarah Cooleen at the Historic Richmond Foundation. While wandering that city one day, I stopped into Sarah's office to ask for directions, and within half an hour I found myself being led to, through and *beneath* Monumental Church. Some weeks later, a boxful of information arrived at my door—pages detailing the church's history—and *The Book of Spirits* was born. Of Sarah and the many other historians who have contributed to this work, I ask indulgence. Of those who lived the history with which I have taken license, I ask forgiveness.

If you enjoyed the wonderfully complex world of THE BOOK OF SPIRITS, turn the page for a glimpse at the next book in James Reese's epic Herculine adventure,

THE WITCHERY,

available soon in hardcover from William Morrow.

1

"It is a melancholy of mine own, compounded by many simples, extracted from many objects, and indeed the sundry contemplation of my travels, in which my often rumination wraps me in a most humorous sadness."
Shakespeare, "As You Like It"

WHAT a sight: Havana harbor seen by late daylight.

I remember it well; for indeed we arrived at sunset, and sadly heard it told that we hadn't time to enter the harbor before dark. This the firing cannons of the Morro Castle made clear: the harbor, indeed the city itself was closed till next the sun rose. It was slight consolation hearing our captain opine that it was just as well, that the harbor would be too crowded to navigate at night. And so we found a good offing within sight of the Morro's walls, near enough to hear the bells of the city count out the quarter-hours; and there we lay off and on all night, tacking in accord with the winds and the water.

For hours I'd watched the silver-green isle of Cuba rising from the blue, ever more anxious yet knowing not that the *Athée*—aboard which we'd sailed from Savannah—was racing the setting sun. Had I known this, had I known that each night the Morro's cannons announced that crepuscular closing of the harbor and city, I'd have been sick from nervous upset; for though I'd been sent to Havana, I had only the vaguest notion of what, *of who* I'd find there.

Would Sebastiana d'Azur—my discoverer, my Soror Mystica, who'd absented herself for so long, who'd cast away her courtly renown after the Revolution and retired to her crumbling chateau upon the Breton shore— . . . would Sebastiana herself be there? Who was the "we" of whom the aged witch had written so cryptically? *We have a surprise for you*, said the letter sent to me in St. Augustine. Would I have to face again Sebastiana's consort: the man, the menace, the faux demon Asmodei? He who'd hated me from first sight. He who'd sought to harm me. Oh but Sebastiana's absence had surprised me once before, had it not? In New York. In years past. When I—so deeply needful, so lost—had gone thither, as again she'd directed, by post, only to find yet another epistle apologizing for her absence and consigning me to the care of a houseful of whoring witches. (Mistake me not, sister: I loved the Cyprians, and still mourn their loss and the dissolution of the Duchess's House of Delights.) More likely I, nay *we*—yes: I had a companion aboard the *Athée*— . . . more likely we would walk alone among the Havanans with no clue but one: Somewhere in the city there lived a monk whom Sebastiana, in her directing letter, had identified by the single initial Q.

And so, though I knew not what, or who I would find in Havana, still I hoped to find such things fast. Thus, each wave separating the schooner *Athée* from its mooring in Havana harbor was a hated thing . . . But mark, for so it was the case: the waves had been few as we approached over the Straits, and our six-day sail from Savannah had been smooth, too smooth and slow: often we'd been becalmed, and had lain in want of wind.

Finally, *finally* all aboard knew the sight of the Pan de

Matanzas—that Cuban mountain molded by a great hand in mimicry of a loaf of bread—and nearer, nearer there could be seen sown fields of cane and coffee bordered by tall, wind-waltzing palms. Nearer still, and the lighthouse could be discerned in detail, so too the forts of the Morro and Punta flanking the harbor's entrance: like fists of stone they were, wrapped round the harbor's narrow neck and seeming to strangle the inlet. And beyond, faint as my fate, the city itself climbed the hillsides: buildings in pastel shades, showing roofs of reddish tile.

The *Athée*'s sails had been unfurled to steal from those swaying palms what winds there were; and we beat toward the harbor as best we could, forsaking the changeable hues of the Gulf Stream for the sapphirine seas nearer the island. I imagine now that we truly hurried; for our captain must have known that the harbor would close come dark. By the light of a low, westering sun, flying fish rose beside us: silvery knives they seemed, hurled shoreward by the hand of Neptune. Seabirds were ten times more numerous, now we were nearer land. Gulls cried, and signed their chalky Xs on the slate of the sky . . . so near, yes; but it was then, with the gulls wheeling overhead, that we aboard the *Athée* saw a schooner on the opposite tack make for the harbor even as the signals were dropped and the first cannon fired. Of course, I concluded the worst: here were pirates, espied by the Cuban guard and now taking shot. But no: my companion—even more anxious than I to debark, surely—passed to me the dire news had from the captain just as the lighthouse spun to cast its first beam upon the sea: the city was closing.

And so it was that, our suit for entry refused, the *Athée* bobbed another night at sea. Suddenly I found myself in possession of the thing I wanted least of all: long starlit hours to worry about what was to come, and to worry about what we'd done; for yes, a crime had been committed, such that we—the crew and cast of the *Athée*—were now one fewer than we'd been when setting sail from Savannah. Of course, none but Calixto and I knew the why, the when, the how of the crime that had been committed: murder.

Indeed, we two wanted off the *Athée* come dawn; and all that starry, windless night I sat wondering how best to achieve this? How best to avoid the captain, and Cuban customs, and the inquisition sure to come?

I'd locked and left my house on St. George Street, in St. Augustine, not two weeks prior, my departure prompted by two facts:

Fact the first: As said, Sebastiana had written directing me toward Havana; and promising the disclosure of certain "secrets" in that city; and:

Fact the second: I knew I'd die a wasting death, or lead a lifeless life in anticipation of the Coming of the Blood, that sickening spill that comes—sometimes suddenly, burstingly; sometimes slowly, as a malaise that can have no other cause—to claim every witch on the last of her days, regardless of whether she loves life or has suffered a surfeit of it . . . yes, I'd do naught but long for my own red-end if I were to stay in that house all alone, hearing its walls echoing, echoing the stories of all I'd lost. Through said loses, and the survival of same, I'd grown stronger, much, but only as a witch. As a man, as a woman, *enfin* as me *I was weak*, and hadn't the will to welcome or use said powers, powers that somehow I'd siphoned from off the dead, as we few witches who are death-allied must perforce do whenever we encounter massed souls still clinging to life . . . *Ego sum te peto et videre queto*. Which is to say, *The dead rise and come to me* . . . What these powers were, specifically, I could not have said, and cannot say now: The Mystery of Mysteries.

And once I returned home from deep in the Florida scrub, I returned to the shelter, the safety of St. George Street: a ship returned to port; but soon enough—in the accusatory quiet, in the stillness of an unhappy house—I came to understand that though ships may be sheltered and safe in port, they are built to sail. And so I set off upon receipt of Sebastiana's letter.

Set off for Havana, I supposed; though in truth, I might have ended up elsewhere. Indeed, I'd have gone as happily—that is to say, *un*happily—to Havana as to another place unknown; for I sought only motion, any sensation that yet proved I was alive. And all I knew as I rode inland from St. Augustine, seeking again the river St. John, was that I would ride its odd, northward flow to the sea, and let the sea decide my fate. This I did, hurrying not; for I no longer held to much hope—of salvation, of happiness—and only hope could have hurried me.

Hélas, I set out over rutted roads and long, long stretches of scratching scrub. Had I been in a hurry, I'd have hired a horse. Or taken directly to the sea at St. Augustine. Instead, caving to a nature too melancholic, and being ever mindful of the river's living metaphor, I sought the confused flow of the St. John's. I'd first sailed that river a decade prior, when first I'd come to Florida; and when finally I achieved the St. John's again and saw again its oaks overhanging the slow flow, their Spanish moss dripping down as a living filigree, I may even have been happy; for a spell.

I secured passage aboard a sloop of slight burden already laden with lumber, named the *Esperance*. I had money enough to ensure that I'd not be expected to earn my keep, neither upon the St. John's nor in the sloop's home port of Savannah. Mind: I am not lazy, or rather was not lazy then—admittedly, we dead might sometimes be said to laze—but rather, I feared that work of any sort would result in my weaving myself into the ship's web of ropes, or worse: falling overboard into that river crowded with crocodilians. . . . No: I told the captain *in terms certain* that it was not a working passage I sought. I had not come to "hire on," but rather would pay handsomely—and *handsome* is aptly chosen, as I traveled, then, in manly guise—to be let aboard, whereupon I'd secrete myself all the way to Savannah so as not to be any bother at all.

As said, the *Esperance* sailed low in the river, its shallow belly full of pine planks. Too, more boards had been laid upon the deck and fastened with strapping. Though space had been left abaft the mainmast for the pumps, sitting close unto the bulkhead, the rest of the sloop was crowded, quite. Pine was profit, and no shipboard space was spared: so very redolent it all was of pitch and planed wood. Neither was there a bunk to spare belowdecks. These—hammocks, in fact, in which the sleeping crew swung—were claimed by those who, to judge from their limbs, tarry to the elbow and knee, had felled, hewn and stacked the sawn pine. So it was I was told to bed down as best I could. Such an arrangement might have put off another gent—so I hoped to appear: a youngish gent of some means and strange ways: in other words: *a man best left alone*—but of course my relief was great at not having to share great quarters with six well-salted types. No: I'd have bared my breasts and strapped myself to the bowsprit, sailing as the *Esperance*'s figurehead, if it had meant securing that solitude that had long been requisite to the keeping of my doubly-sexed secrets.

The first day of the sloop's homeward passage ended without event; but not so night number one.

I'd been sitting amidships, well free of all stays and sails and such troublesome stuff, and had scribbled away the late hours of the afternoon. It's likely I dared not write in the *Book of Shadows* I then kept—too dangerous, this—but yet I recall having in hand a stub of pencil and some pages now lost, bound in a book of blackest kid (a hide nearly as dark as my disposition). All was well, with the salts too tired to trouble themselves with me. But then the sun set, and we—nay *I alone*; for no man of the *Esperance* seemed equally troubled . . . I was beset by so many millions of mosquitoes it seemed the swarm, with some coordination, could have lifted me bodily from off the deck and dropped me down in Savannah, sparing me the sail. But rather than carrying me hence, those pests determined to sup upon me, to stick deep their syringes and *draw, draw, draw*.

Others of the men seemed immune to the bother and bite, and took no action but to concede as little skin as possible to "the skeeters," rolling down their sleeves and slacks. A few lit smudge pots and carried them about like lanterns. The reflected lantern light threw ghostly swimmers in the drink. Later, the salts retired to their swinging hammocks to drink and sleep away what stings they suffered. Me? I had no refuge but the night, and the darkness which—fortunately—hid what happened to those stinging things once they'd supped too much of my witch's blood.

Yes: soon the chore, the challenge lay not in fending off the skeeters' bite but rather in concealing the myriad specks upon my skin; for the pests, witch-fed, fell dead with their stingers still sunken into my skin. No doubt by daylight I'd have seemed some species of Dalmatian dog, bedotted by the dead creatures. Indeed, even by moonlight I could see my exposed skin darkening to black: looking down at my hands, I saw what seemed the black lace gloves of a lady of Spain.

The two men of the watch I heard snigger. One of them winked at me with an ivoried eye, evincing delight that this *fancy-man* come amongst the crew suffered so. I thought to refute the sniggering, to say that in fact I was not suffering the skeeters but rather was . . . *bothered* by them, merely. Instead, I said nothing. Which is not to say that I did not act in my own defense; for—and now it seems I may have willed this—he of the ivoried eye soon was struck by a thunderous fit of coughing, one which caused him to gulp greatly at the black, buzzing air and swallow down skeeters by the battalion. Had I brought his barking on? I did not know for certain;

but yes, there came a *soupçon* of guilt, such that I rose and betook myself nearer the bow and further from the men of the watch. But when behind me it seemed I heard more sniggering, the guilt soon was gone and I fell to wondering, pointedly, what I could conjure to stifle the men. Were there catbirds in the shoreside trees who might be willed to dive, to dart about the men's heads? Or perhaps a snake might be induced to drop down from the branches overhead, branches that looked sulfurous now, well nigh infernal in that light coming from the braziers bolted onto the bow and crowded with tarry knots of pine? Such were my thoughts—I do confess it—when I turned to see not the sniggering men of the watch, but another of the crew: the cabin boy, name of Calixto.

Cal—as he was called—had brought me a bit of luncheon earlier on. Whether he'd done so of his own accord, or had been directed to action by the captain, I cannot say. Regardless, I'd been grateful for the fare, though it was but a bit of lobscouse—beef and bread, this is, cooked together without benefit of spice—along with a skin of switchel to wash it back. Now here came the boy again, burdened by a smudge pot and a mass of netting; which latter I supposed he'd cast over the river, for certain species of fish—like certain species of men—surface only after dark; the difference being: Such fish one might sometimes seek, whilst such men are best left alone.

But no: on came Cal, toward where I sat . . . And if earlier the sun had seemed to gild the boy—as indeed it had—now he was ensilvered by the moon sieving down through the trees.

As before, he said not a word, this blond, sea-bred boy of some sixteen, seventeen years of age. Rather he set straight to work; and by the scant light of the moon, and the flickering flames of the smudge pot and braziers, I watched in wonder—wonder that soon ceded to delight; and delight that ceded to gratitude in its turn, gratitude deep as the surrounding dark.

He had not come to fish. It was no seine he had in hand. It was netting of a much, much tighter weave: muslin, I suppose. It was a square, one side of which was weighted by a piece of driftwood stitched into its hem. Strings depended from the remaining three sides; and these—in an athletic show, done so fast I knew not what I watched—Cal tied fast to the boom, and to the shrouds, and to a davit, till finally the net hung upon the deck as a tent, a triangulate refuge from the swarming skeeters.

Quickly as he'd come, Calixto disappeared. I stood in wonder. A moment more and he returned, this time burdened by bedding. Crude bedding, yes; true, but bedding nonetheless. This he proceeded to set upon the deck. And then, carefully, he tucked the edges of the net beneath the palette, all save one side, which now he raised up. With the smile of a gallant, he motioned me into this odd construction. I knew not what to say, knew not what to do. Words of thanks stalled in my throat. But then the cabin boy nodded me on with a measure of urgency, and—as he scratched at his own welts, and I'd not be the one to cause him a moment's more suffering—I verily dove past him, ducking beneath his arm as if the boom were a sort of fallen maypole and he a suitor. Suffice to say: I may have let slip my masculine mask; but if so, I took it up forthwith. From within my shelter I thanked him. I sought some pocketed coin (thinking this was owed to—and sought by—all who did me a courtesy). All the while, the boy spoke not a word.

Having tucked me tightly in, he stood. I looked up at him. Stay: no doubt *I stared* as if I'd never see him again. He'd not have seen me staring, of course; for I'd long since had to sport, *at all times*, those blue-lensed spectacles that hid my eyes, eyes which—in time with my increasing strength—had grown fixed, and now, no matter my mood, showed constantly *l'oeil de crapaud*, the Eye of the Toad, or the true witch's mark, the sister-sign (so called because the circle of the pupil cedes to the shape of a toad's splayed-toed foot) . . . Yes, doubtless I stared. What? Did I think he'd swim from the *Athée*? That I'd wake to learn he'd ascended somehow, that indeed he'd been the angel he'd seemed? . . . Sadly, soon I saw naught but his back; for he turned on his heel and headed off, dissolving into the dark.

I may have sputtered a second thank-you. I may have bade him good-bye or good night. Regardless, my words broke not upon the boy. He was gone, and I might have spoken with equal effect to the trees or the stars and moon beyond; for now I lay upon my back, staring up. And it was in that same pose that I'd eventually fall asleep, knowing not that age-old superstition of sailors: To sleep topside, with one's face full to the moon, is to invite ill fortune.

. . . Indeed.